P9-DGB-801

I'LL BE WATCHING YOU

Also by Victoria Gotti

The Senator's Daughter

Women and Mitral Valve Prolapse
(nonfiction)

I'LL BE WATCHING YOU

A NOVEL

VICTORIA GOTTI

Crown Publishers, Inc. New York

Published by Crown Publishers, Inc.,
201 East 50th Street, New York, New York 10022.
Member of the Crown Publishing Group.

Random House, Inc. New York, Toronto, London, Sydney, Auckland
www.randomhouse.com

Printed in the United States of America

Design by Karen Minster

Library of Congress Cataloging-in-Publication Data
Gotti, Victoria.
I'll be watching you / by Victoria Gotti.—1st ed.
I. Title. PS3557.O82I45 1998
T 813'.54—dc21
98–22249
CIP

ISBN 0-609-60240-3

10 9 8 7 6 5 4 3 2 1

First Edition

This book is dedicated to my family,
with love and admiration for their relentless
support, encouragement, and devotion.
To my three precious gifts,
Carmine, John, and Frank—
there is no greater love.

ACKNOWLEDGMENTS

To my husband, Carmine, and our children, thank you for your unrelenting patience, support, and love despite the grueling hours of work that sometimes pulled me far from your grasp. The past was invaluable, the present is priceless, and the future is even greater.

For the angels in my life, Frank and Justine, you will always have a special place in my heart.

I extend my deepest gratitude to my mother and best friend, Victoria, for her constant love and nurturing, and I thank my father, John, for his words of encouragement and immeasurable strength, which continue to teach me that all dreams are within reach.

My sister, Angel, and brother Peter have an incredible sense of humor that keeps me sane and relaxed, and my brother John never fails to rush to my rescue at a moment's notice. Family is truly the key to my well-being and I cannot thank them enough. My love to all of you.

I especially thank my agent, Frank Weimann, for his dedication and persistence as I continue on this wonderful journey of storytelling. I also am in debt to Marvyn Kornberg and Nicholas Kass for sharing their courtroom experiences and legal expertise, and to Dr. Frances Colon for her keen insights into mental illness and teaching me about the "broken brain."

Kudos to all of those at Crown Publishers and especially Chip Gibson, Andrew Martin, Steve Ross, Hilary Bass (publicist extraordinaire), Amy Boorstein, Laurie Stark, Whitney Cookman, Anthony Loew, Karen Minster, Jane Searle, Sona Vogel, Jo Fagan, and Rebecca Strong.

A special thank you to Rachel Kahan, an invaluable source of trivia, humor, and precise vocabulary.

Finally, I extend a thousand thanks to my editor and friend, Sue Carswell, who was a magnificent advisor to me as I wove this tale.

Victoria Gotti
Old Westbury, Long Island

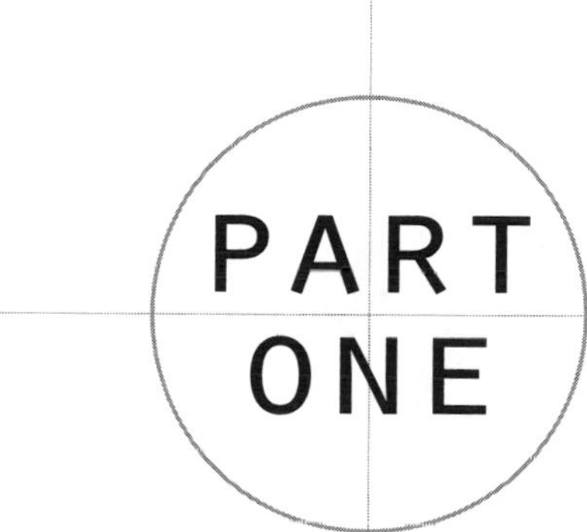
PART
ONE

PROLOGUE

There are many people who have walked this earth before me. I don't think of them now, for all belongs to yesterday. The gates to St. Charles Cemetery in Farmingdale, Long Island, are tall, obtrusive, and intimidating. On the right, hidden behind a long row of meticulously manicured pine trees, is the caretaker's cottage, from which a small old man with enormous deep-set brown eyes and a wiry gray beard hurries forward to greet one of my mourners, the one most important to my story. The mourner says something to the caretaker. While fishing for a cigarette in his shirt pocket, the caretaker smiles and points to the crowd already assembled, for they have come in the traditional way, a caravan of mourners.

The others gathered around the grave are all familiar to my favorite mourner, though they do not acknowledge each other. It is, after all, a solemn occasion, calling for decorous rules among the upper class, even if some of those here could not be found in any social register.

The priest begins the eulogy.

None of my mourners is listening. My senses, heightened from passing out of this life, pick up the thoughts of the individuals standing around my coffin; each is tuned in to his or her own private memories. The person over there remembers my bad deeds, my lack of remorse; another, with tears and grief, thinks of loving me—the things we once shared. Only my special mourner's thoughts are indecipherable to me.

Dozens of red roses lie neatly beside my grave, where the priest is now silent. Each person steps forward, picks up a rose, and tosses it on my coffin. It is horribly cold. Snow lies scattered in patches on the ground. Beneath, the dirt is half-frozen. Soon my body will lie there for eternity.

The priest waves a hand over my coffin in the traditional Catholic gesture, and my family and friends, my enemies, my child, all bid me farewell one last time.

My daughter goes through the motions of the ceremony because it is what is expected of her, but she never knew the person I really was. If she could hear my thoughts, I would beseech her not to be harsh to my memory. I was weak, fallible, therefore human. Life, my beautiful child, brings so many surprises and bends in the road, some of them unpleasant. Wait, my little one, until you've lived out yours before you condemn me.

The service is over. The gravediggers are left to lower my coffin. I notice my most significant mourner exiting first, probably not wanting to engage in niceties. The rest of the crowd drifts away, and I want to yell after them, "Hold your tears, for I feel no pain." My body, wrapped in its wooden cocoon, is no longer a part of me. My soul has separated and risen above it, probably to someplace easier and better. I float higher and higher.

"Bless me, Father, for I have sinned . . ."

1

The appearance of imminent death always exhilarated him. Billy moved from the bed, pulled up his trousers, and took a step backward to better view the scene. He stared at the inert form lying with arms and legs gracefully stretched on the mound of cheap velour blankets and threadbare sheets. She looked perfect, serene. Her eyes were closed as though in sleep; long blond curls like expensive lambswool delicately embroidered the edge of the pillow, cascading down the side of the worn motel mattress. The white lace teddy sprinkled with pearls—the one he'd purchased and made her change into—was appropriate for the moment, complementing the rhinestone tiara on top of her head.

"Put it on," Billy had told her earlier.

"No, I couldn't possibly. . . ."

Ignoring her protest, he'd fastened the tiara on her head. Then he backed away and moved toward the portable stereo that he had brought with him for this "romantic" evening. The cassette he had specially prepared was already in place. Soon the music began, and filled the room.

Billy walked back to the bed and reached for her hands. His pulse quickened.

"Let's dance to the perfect wedding song."

The look he'd been waiting for came into her eyes. When she resisted his offer, he sat beside her on the quilted polyester bedspread—standard seedy motel decor. He could now see that first tiny flicker of awareness that something wasn't quite right. Recognizing she was in danger, the near naked showgirl he'd lured away from the strip joint reacted just like all the others. At first she began speaking too quickly, nervously.

"I have to go," she said, her eyes darting around the room, her voice now shaky.

"Just one dance," he whispered as he pulled her up and held her tightly against him. She felt good in his arms. She belonged there, just as they all had. For a moment he felt disloyal, thinking she might feel better than Rose.

Then he felt her panic accelerate. Her body grew rigid and her eyes filled with fear. This was his favorite part, and tonight his enjoyment was intensified. She was particularly satisfying. At the end, she seemed to know it was useless to plead, and in a burst of animal strength, she fought him. He placed his hands around her throat, and when she began to lose consciousness, he whispered, "Till death do us part."

When she was dead, he danced with her again. This time there was no resistance in her lovely, flaccid body.

As the music began to fade, his eyes fastened on the white lace teddy. Was she an angel yet? *No,* he thought; with her sordid past, he assumed she'd be relegated to a demon. Billy turned his back on her and walked to the window. There was a chill coming in from the cracks around the panes. The incoming draft made a soft hissing sound that vaguely pleased him. Outside, the streets were tranquil. He'd have to celebrate this triumphant moment in silence. His eyes closed as the keen thrill coursed through his body. Then he opened them and shifted his gaze toward the sky.

The day dawned blue and wan, the sun only an imagined presence behind a thick blanket of clouds over the city, which from his vantage point looked like one huge gray puddle. The few patches of snow left over from last week's mild storm had turned to dirty slush as the temperature inched up a few degrees. Gray, wet, dirty . . . how befitting the moment, he thought.

Billy reached inside the pocket of the blue flannel shirt he was wearing and pulled out a box of Marlboros and a gold lighter. He lit a cigarette and dragged heavily on its tip. He always savored that first cigarette after one of these strenuous scenes, his version of "afterglow."

The motel room was sparsely furnished. There were a few scattered pieces of antiquated furniture and the few personal belongings the stripper had brought up with her: a purse, a magazine, and a cheap pink umbrella. The cleanup routine had been perfected through experience; already the fingerprints and debris were completely removed. He had played out this same scenario a number of times before.

Billy searched his memory for her name. Was it Roseanne, Rosemarie, perhaps even Rachel? He couldn't remember. Oh well, it didn't matter—not now, anyway. He lit another cigarette and inhaled the nicotine deeply, then turned back to her. A rush of pleasure suffused him. Those luminous dancing eyes, not dancing anymore, pouty lips, enticing, inviting. Except for the red marks around her neck, she looked pristine, a perfect beauty. He'd waited several years for this unforgettable moment—and others like it, with more still to come.

From his pocket he pulled out a crumpled piece of paper, its edges jagged, having been torn from a book. He read it, not once, but twice, and then smiled. He had accomplished his plan scrupulously, right down to the last detail. He focused on the vase resting on the end table, then checked his watch. Three hours, three roses. How perfect. Billy's intense gaze was fixed on the flowers; he was mesmerized for a moment.

Now it was time for him to leave, but not before he'd added the finishing touch. He walked to the end table and removed the roses from the vase. Gently, careful not to prick his fingers on the thorns, he plucked the petals and scattered them around the bed, blankets, sheets, and the showgirl's lifeless body.

In his head he heard the music begin again. Always, it seemed quiet at first, as though whispered in his ear. As the song grew louder, he began softly whistling the lyrics. The subtle fragrance of the petals enlivened his senses. Their touch, scent, and beauty enveloped him, and now he was singing along to the music:

The moment you wake,
Let there be no mistake,
I'll be watching you.

IT WAS IMPOSSIBLE TO BELIEVE ANYTHING SO HORRIFIC COULD HAPPEN AGAINST THE SETTING OF MAUI'S BLACK SAND BEACH, BENEATH ITS MIDNIGHT BLUE SKY. BUT CASSIDY RIMES KNEW OTHERWISE, HAVING JUST WITNESSED THE BRUTAL MASSACRE OF BOTH HER PARENTS. THEIR LIFELESS BODIES WERE COVERED WITH BLOOD, SEAWEED, AND SAND. . . .

2

"Would you like another cup of coffee, Mrs. Miller?"

The young flight attendant hovered over Rose, the metal carafe aimed at her cup.

Rose Miller looked up from her laptop and shook her head. She was finishing a graphic scene in chapter seven of her new novel.

"I haven't finished this one," she replied politely, and covered the mug with the palm of her hand. The young woman nodded, then hesitated just a moment before she withdrew from the 747's first-class cabin.

Rose knew she wanted an autograph. All the signs were there—the ogling, the attention, the lame attempts at conversation. But they were nearing New York now and the attendant hadn't approached her.

The seat belt light was on and Air France flight #139 from Paris began its final approach to JFK. In a by now familiar ritual, Rose logged off and powered down, waited for the blank screen to appear, then carefully tucked her laptop inside the leather carrying case. Next, methodically, she took off her reading glasses, smoothed the skirt of her black Donna Karan suit, and pulled the cuffs of her white silk shirt down to her wrists. Finally, she ran her fingers through her shoulder-length, honey blond hair and drew a deep, cleansing breath.

Rose pressed her forehead against the plane's window, absorbing the gleam of sun reflecting off the Atlantic and distant outline of Manhattan skyscrapers. She loved this moment at the end of a trip. Each time she traveled, when the city came into view, she felt complete, still and serene.

In many ways, coming home was a relief from the hectic schedule she'd followed for the last week. Her publicist, Dario Roselli, had insisted that she stay at the Ritz-Carlton in Paris and had arranged an exquisite suite for her, decorated in high Baroque style with detailed furniture and tapestries. That first night, she'd sunk into the goosedown pillows and fallen into a peaceful sleep, a rarity for her. And it was a good thing, too, because the next couple of days were frantic.

The first morning of her trip, she had met with her French publisher, including the marketing and public relations people. After the meetings at the publisher's offices, they'd whisked her off to the Quai D'Orsay for lunch, where they'd enjoyed an elaborate three-course meal: first a bottle of Château Pétrus to complement an exquisite *bouchée au champignons sauvages;* then *le veau chantelaine,* the restaurant's specialty; and for dessert a *chocolat marquise gâteau,* served with an expensive bottle of Château d'Yquem Sauternes.

Her days in Paris were the antithesis of her routine at home. In Paris Rose could luxuriate in the indulgence of a lavish midday meal and somehow not lose a beat. Paris regenerated her creative spirit and refreshed her soul. Since her French was flawless, her publisher had requested she do a small tour for their edition of her latest novel. Dario had also arranged for several print and television interviews. Rose was delighted and didn't mind adding them into her already busy schedule. Paris seemed to exist in a completely different reality from any place else in the world. The élan of the women—and the men, for that matter—as they walked the city streets, going about their business, spoke of taste, culture, art, and history. In her heart New York was where she lived, but Paris was where she belonged.

Only minutes away from landing at Kennedy International Airport, Rose leaned back, her body comfortably enveloped in the plush leather seat, and took a deep breath. She was exhausted but regretted none of the madness.

Suddenly the pilot announced that the air traffic over New York was heavy and they'd have to circle for about fifteen minutes. Once he'd made the announcement, Rose realized how anxious she was to get off the plane. Whenever she was away she missed her daughter, Alexis, perhaps even more than was considered normal. She missed her husband, Evan, desperately as well. Although theirs was a small family, it was more than she'd ever had growing up. Spending time together was the most treasured aspect of Rose's life, so coming home was always special. The Millers had a family ritual: each time Rose traveled, Alexis and Evan would be at the airport when she returned, no matter when her plane was scheduled to land. Since she'd traveled to Japan and Australia, some of these family reunions had come at ungodly hours.

Rose reached for the phone concealed in the armrest beside her, slid her credit card through the side of the receiver, and ran through the instruction menu.

"Dario."

"Rose, where are you? Did it go well? Tell me everything." Static, then: "It's such a bad connection." More static. Dario needed to know every detail of her life. He was always full of questions, firing off one after another.

"Paris was wonderful, gorgeous as always. Everything went well. The publicity plans went as scheduled. I expect you'll get a follow-up report in the morning," she said somewhat impishly.

"I'm glad you charmed the pants off 'em in Paris," he remarked. "But then I knew you would. I really wish I could have been there to see you in action. But, anyway, while you were gone I booked you on three shows for tomorrow: *Live! with Regis and Kathie Lee, The Rosie O'Donnell Show,* and then *Larry King Live* later in the evening."

"Clearly there's no time for—"

Dario continued as though she hadn't spoken. "I hope you're ready for the book party tonight. I stopped by the Waldorf earlier to make sure everything is in order. The food and flowers have already been delivered. Now all we need is a room full of famous, rich, well-connected people."

"I hope some of these people have actually read my book instead of just showing up to do some air kissing."

There was no one anywhere who could put together an A-list party like Dario. Dario Roselli, Ltd., was considered the most prestigious and successful public relations agency in the country. Dario had scorned the merger-and-acquisitions fever that had led to such PR dinosaurs as Rogers & Cowan and P.M.K. He kept the agency small, the client list select—and elite. He purposefully limited the agency to two branch offices, with three staff members in Los Angeles and two publicists working out of a D.C. office near the Capitol. The main headquarters, located at the Trump International, had been designed with minimalist yet sophisticated essentials. Dario didn't want his clients to think their money was going to pay for interior decorators. At the New York location, in Columbus Circle overlooking Central Park, there were twenty people on staff, including three senior publicists and assorted assistants and secretaries. Dario's client list boasted some of the hottest celebrities, fashion models, authors, and politicians in the country. But it was Rose who received the most attention, service, and, if necessary, hand-holding from Dario himself.

It was obvious to anyone in publishing that Dario considered Rose his prize possession. He hovered over her at tapings and interviews, often even accompanying her on book tours, taking full control of any situation. Rose trusted him implicitly, although Dario had a tendency to cross the line. At some point he had mistaken her admiration of him for something more romantic. Rose had tried to tell him diplomatically that his affection for her was misplaced, fueled by the fact that he had no time for any real, meaningful relationships outside of business. But he'd pursued her, almost obsessively so, until she'd had to give him an ultimatum: "Back off or I'll walk." He had, and they had come to an understanding.

"I should be landing shortly. Will I see you at the party?"

Dario jumped on the edge of her sentence. "Of course. I'll be there before you even arrive."

The connection broke and she replaced the receiver inside the armrest, then checked her diamond-studded Patek Philippe watch. Between the delay in Paris and now here, the plane's landing was off by well over an hour, which meant she'd barely have time to freshen up before going to the party being held in honor of her latest book, *Thorns of a Rose.* It was situations like this that reinforced what a good decision it had been to get her own apartment in the city in addition to the family's luxurious home in Brookville, Long Island. When she was pressed for time or needed solitude, it was invaluable to know she had a space to call her own. Tonight, she could go from the airport to the apartment to change and recharge before heading to the party.

The whole process of publishing a book, from conceiving the idea through the final interview or book signing, was like a roller-coaster ride. In fact, it was a ride that never ended. Rose would have loved to have the opportunity to slow down, but she was on a roll. Her third novel, *Thorns of a Rose,* had just hit the stores two weeks ago and had already found its place near the top of the *New York Times* best-seller list. Tomorrow morning was the kickoff for her national book tour. Her life would now consist of nonstop traveling from city to city, where she'd be dealing with a brutal schedule of signings, cocktail parties, and televised chats with upbeat hosts on morning talk shows.

Her agreement to tour was a requirement of her contract. Do the talk show circuit, sit through grueling interviews, and give your life away for the duration of the publicity blitz. Even if she weren't obligated, she'd push herself nonstop to promote her books, as the tours boosted book sales. Rose cherished each aspect of her work: her voice, her characters, whom she grew to love or hate, and the expression of her innermost thoughts about the way she viewed life. Like children, when those books were sent out into the world, they needed attention and nurturing to reach their potential. After months of writing and rewriting, the time came to get out there and pitch, striving to move books out of stores, battling hundreds of other authors for a spot on the best-seller list.

It was grueling, but she knew there were aspects of a writer's life that could be a lot worse, like never getting published at all. Once she'd completed the arduous journey of becoming a published writer, with all it entailed, she'd felt triumphant, as though she'd fulfilled her dreams and her parents' dreams for her. No words could begin to describe the sensation.

When her first book, *The Devil's Daughter,* was published, Rose had been thrust onto both hardcover and subsequently paperback best-seller lists around the world. Even while she was still writing *Last Rites,* her second psychological suspense novel, her publisher at Boardman Books was pushing her for a new contract. Boardman wanted her to sign for an additional three novels: a substantial seven-figure deal.

But now the deadlines were shortened so each book could be published sooner; "keeping the momentum going," was how Dario had explained it. This meant she had only nine months to write the book after the one she was promoting now. *Thorns of a Rose* was well on its way to being her biggest commercial success so far, and as soon as the tour was over, she would put the final touches on her next novel. *Murderous Intentions* was perhaps her favorite book—though that was like loving one child more than another. In any event, she knew the manuscript was good. No one except her agent and best friend, Marilyn Grimes, had read a word of it. But Marilyn confirmed Rose's opinion: *Murderous Intentions* had that special Rose Miller touch.

Rose had wanted to write for as long as she had been able to read, maybe even before, when she had made the connection between her daydreams and the stories Mama read to her at night. But it wasn't until she was twenty-one that she began to clear a space in her life to sit down and pour out the stories and feelings that had built up over all those years. As she began to commit these thoughts to paper, she uncovered events and emotions from her past that she'd repressed. She wrote two romance novels, and once she had completed them, she eagerly sent the one she considered her best to a dozen publishers. Just as quickly, she collected twelve rejections, not even personal notes, all printed slips that read "We're sorry, but we do not accept unsolicited manuscripts."

Discouraged, she'd decided she was not a writer. But something compelled her to keep going. While her computer lay fallow for several years, Rose began to mine her dreams, and her deepest feelings continued to float to the surface. She found a lot of fear inside that had been hidden from long ago, but just as objects embedded in the ocean floor can begin to rise after a major storm, Rose's old terrors emerged. These were revealed in her third attempt, *The Devil's Daughter,* a suspense novel about Peach Walfred, a struggling artist who makes a modern Faustian deal that forces her in the end to give in to her dark side to gain fame. Writing in the very early morning hours, before her husband and daughter woke, Rose managed to finish it in a little more than a year. This time, a bit more savvy about the publishing world, she submitted her manuscript to literary agents. The second agent she sent it to was enthusiastic.

Marilyn Grimes took Rose on as a client and helped fulfill her dreams. Boardman Books, a prestigious New York publishing house, soon accepted her manuscript, and Rose hadn't looked back since, except to say a prayer of gratitude that her books were successful and well reviewed.

As the plane began its descent, Rose sensed the young flight attendant by her side again.

"Mrs. Miller, could I ask a favor?"

The petite woman, her skin the color of burnished copper, hesitated a moment, as though her courage were faltering. In a tremulous voice she asked, "Would you mind signing my copy of your book?" She held out a paperback copy of *The Devil's Daughter.* "I wouldn't normally be this forward with one of our customers," the flight attendant said, "but I'm a big fan of yours and I may never get this opportunity again."

"Of course I don't mind," Rose replied as she took the book from the young woman and reached inside her handbag for a pen. She considered requests for her autograph an intimate moment shared between herself and a reader, a major payoff for all the hard work.

"Would you like it personally inscribed? Or will 'Best wishes' do?"

"'Best wishes' will be just fine, Mrs. Miller."

She was used to her fans calling her Rose; most of them did, though everyone knew the Miller family name. Rose's husband, Evan Miller, was a top-notch criminal attorney in New York City and soon, with luck, a candidate for governor of New York. The Millers were synonymous with old money and generations of power, mentioned frequently in such magazines as *The New Yorker, Forbes,* and *Time* and favored by columnists and the paparazzi in society columns. Like the Daleys in Chicago, wherever the political action of New York was happening, the Millers were at its center. Evan was considered a standard-bearer for the baby boom generation, and his name and face were ubiquitous. In November *New York* magazine had run a cover story on him about his political plans for the future and his life as the husband of a famous writer. Evan had looked so handsome in the cover photo, dressed casually, photographed in the sweeping gardens behind their estate, Paradiso.

Rose returned the book with a smile, and the young woman tucked it under her arm carefully, as if it were a piece of valuable Steuben glass. "Thank you so much," the flight attendant said. "You can't imagine what this means coming from someone like you!" The young woman stopped. "My goodness, I'm babbling. Thank you again," she said, and went back to her prelanding details.

Inwardly Rose laughed. Her own beginnings couldn't have been more humble, although her readers had no way of knowing that. The whole country would be shocked if they knew of her secret past.

The plane landed with a bump on the runway and began to taxi toward the gate. As she filed out of the first-class cabin, Rose's eyes fell on a copy of the *New York Times* lying on a seat in front of her and she picked it up. The headline stunned her: TRIAL BEGINS LATER THIS WEEK. The subhead read "An irate Judge Judy Knauer denies further postponements in the racketeering trial of multimillionaire Dimitri Constantinos."

Waiting in the long line at passport control, Rose read the article, growing increasingly anxious:

> NEW YORK—Trial begins tomorrow in second circuit court for hotel and casino millionaire Dimitri Constantinos. Constantinos, 35, was arrested last year by federal agents in Las Vegas.
>
> Constantinos, who was charged with racketeering and extortion activity centered in New York, resides in the luxurious Las Vegas suburb Spanish Hills but will be tried in the New York courts, because several of the charges against him were alleged to have occurred in New York.
>
> Witnesses who are key to the prosecutor's case against Mr. Constantinos have turned government's witness. The FBI has linked them to the loan-sharking operation which allegedly was a large source of profit for the millionaire's Moonlight Hotel and Casino in Las Vegas. At least one defendant has provided videotapes of illegal transactions.

> **This evidence is believed to be crucial to the federal authorities' long-standing attempts to connect Constantinos to what they have called "widespread illegal tactics that earned billions of dollars from gamblers around the country and Canada," as stated by William Barney, head of the New York division of the FBI.**

Also on the front page was a blowup of Dimitri Constantinos's face. He wore a cocky grin, and there was a confidant look in his cold, mysterious eyes. The picture was black and white, but Rose could fill in the color of his eyes, skin, and hair, and much more. Suddenly she felt the force of her past and present colliding. Dimitri was back in her life, and she was terrified.

Once she had made it through customs, Rose could see Evan and Alexis waving at her from the front of the international arrivals gate.

"Mom, you look beautiful." Alexis had brought a bouquet of flowers, as she always did on her mother's arrival, tea roses this time. To Rose's adoring eyes, her petite eleven-year-old child had an otherworldly look, almost glowing, with perfect olive skin that set off her glistening dark brown, almost black, hair and blue eyes, sparkling with innocence.

"You're the beauty in this family, my sweet," Rose replied. She embraced her daughter tightly and clasped the bouquet, catching a whiff of the roses' subtle fragrance, a break from the musty airplane smell.

"I've hated every minute you were away, Rose," Evan said as they headed toward the exit.

Rose turned to look at him, reacquainting herself with his boy-next-door good looks, sandy brown hair, and angular features. The media referred to his appearance as Kennedyesque, the ideal look for a politician.

She kept her eyes on him as they walked. "Why didn't you phone me in Paris?"

He stopped just before the terminal exit, letting Alexis move slightly ahead. He didn't need to speak; she read his mind immediately. He hadn't wanted to discuss Dimitri.

Outside the terminal, the Millers' regular driver, Larry, loaded Rose's bags into the trunk of the car. The strap of her laptop carrier now hung on

Evan's tall, nicely toned frame as he turned to question her with his eyes. He gently brushed her cheek with the back of his hand, the scent of his cologne reminding her of all that was familiar. He was ever vigilant when it came to her, and Rose knew that this was his way of checking to make sure she was all right. It wasn't necessary that they discuss today's headline. They both knew Dimitri Constantinos's reentrance into their lives could be catastrophic.

As the limo sped toward the city on the Van Wyck Expressway, Rose, thinking about Dimitri, grew silent, oblivious to the lively conversation going on between her daughter and her husband about Alexis having scored the winning shot at her basketball game earlier that day.

"Are you okay?" Evan asked when Alexis turned to look out the window.

Rose smiled weakly. She must not lose her composure in front of her daughter. She wouldn't express her feelings, good or bad, not now. "It can wait until we get home."

Evan was a dear to be here at all. She marveled at how he never missed one of their reunions, though his own busy schedule required that he work fourteen-hour days. If he got on the ticket for governor, the schedule would be even more hectic. But she knew without a doubt that he would still be there for her always, whether to attend publicity functions or to greet her when she returned. Thinking about tonight's book party and the toll these occasions took on her, Rose could only imagine how much worse they were for him. At least she was the author: these were *her* books being recognized. But none of this seemed to faze Evan. He was secure enough to bask in his wife's success.

After tonight's party they would fulfill another Miller ritual: they would take Alexis to Serendipity, Manhattan's whimsical version of an old-fashioned ice-cream parlor. Under the restaurant's famous Tiffany lamps, the three of them would share Serendipity's famous frozen hot chocolate. Afterward they would return home to Brookville, driving the forty minutes instead of spending the night in her apartment because Alexis had school the next day.

3

The Millers made a quick stop at Rose's apartment on Fifth Avenue and 84th Street. The doorman, Domingo, greeted Rose warmly. "You haven't been here for a long time." He was a relentless charmer.

"You say that so I'll think you missed me." Rose smiled as he held the door for her and Alexis. "And I'm sure you say it to every tenant here, even if they just stepped out for coffee."

Domingo laughed. "Ms. Grimes is upstairs waiting for you. She used her own key."

Evan stayed behind to work out the details of the suitcases with the driver—which stayed here and which went home—while Alexis and Rose took the elevator upstairs. They wended their way through the well-appointed corridor until they arrived at Rose's apartment, number 8B. Before Rose could get out her key, the door was flung open by Marilyn Grimes.

The two women hugged, and then Marilyn chatted with Alexis as Rose walked briskly through the apartment to her airy office, which looked out onto the Metropolitan Museum of Art. She set her coat and laptop on the delicate French writing table that served as her desk. Getting her bearings, she looked around. There were fresh flowers in a sterling-silver vase, undoubtedly from Marilyn. The smell of coffee emanating from the kitchen drew Rose out of her office and away from the pileup of e-mail, letters, faxes, and packages. She joined Marilyn and Alexis at the counter that separated the kitchen from the living room. It wasn't yet twilight, and a small brass lamp that filtered light through a cluster of red and blue pieces of glass was the only illumination they needed. Coffee in hand, Rose turned her attention to Marilyn.

"The trip went well; Dario already told me all about it," Marilyn said. "He also called your editor for next week's best-seller list after he spoke to you. You're going to be number one."

The *New York Times* actually compiled their best-seller list a week ahead and released them the Wednesday before the following week's Sunday's edition. Every Wednesday at about six P.M. publishing houses and other people whose lives depended on the book business waited for the fax of the list to come in from the *Times,* always hoping for good news. For Boardman Books, Rose Miller's success was spectacular news.

"That's fantastic." Rose's answer lacked the usual enthusiasm she had for each of her books' success.

"Are you all right?" Marilyn asked with concern. "You seem distracted."

Rose gave her slightly chubby friend a spontaneous hug without answering. Marilyn seemed to make a concerted effort to hide her assets. Her glasses, gone out of style in the 1970s, hid the liquid softness of her compassionate eyes. At forty, she still had model-perfect skin and would need only a dash of blush to bring out her prominent cheekbones. She didn't bother with makeup except mascara on special occasions like tonight. Nor did she try to minimize her chubbiness with the right clothes or colors. Marilyn reminded Rose of a chunk of clay waiting for a sculptor to release her true beauty.

"So I'm to assume no answer means . . ."

Rose just shook her head, which Marilyn knew meant she didn't want to talk about it.

Alexis, who had left to check her clear lip gloss for the sixth time, poked her head into the kitchen. "Mom, you gotta get ready! It's five-thirty!"

Rose took a moment to study Alexis. Her daughter seemed to grow up an entire year each time they were separated. Dressed in her Laura Ashley purple velveteen dress with its satin sash, Alexis was as different from the adolescent in plaid school uniform Rose had left at home one week ago as the clear summer sky was different from a rainstorm.

"Mom!"

Rose stood, and as she passed Alexis, her fingers grazed the top of her daughter's head. "It will take me thirty minutes, tops." She bent to kiss

Alexis's cheek and said, "I could take two hundred hours to dress and never look as beautiful as you do, darling."

"Go on already," Marilyn said from her place at the counter.

In exactly thirty minutes, dressed and spritzing a little Il Bacio, her favorite perfume, Rose emerged. The simple black sheath dress by Calvin Klein enhanced her clear green eyes and blond hair, now swept up in a French twist.

"No one would believe you've been pushing your tush around Paris for the past week," Marilyn said.

"Mom, you look so cool!" Alexis said.

By six-fifteen the limo carrying Marilyn, Rose, Alexis, and Evan pulled up to the curb on Park Avenue in front of the Waldorf-Astoria. They approached the entrance to the regal old building, its door held open by several liveried doormen.

Holding on tightly to Alexis's hand, Rose walked into the immense Starlight Room and smiled at the first young man to greet her, shaking his hand. "Kent, it's so nice to see you." He was her editor's assistant. Rose had a feeling he was going to make a fine editor himself one day.

Kent and Alexis were buddies, and he was perhaps her daughter's first crush. The young man had a gift for putting youngsters at ease. As Kent and Alexis caught up on the latest celebrity gossip and the most recent MTV videos, Rose took a moment to acclimate. The art deco–designed ballroom was large but narrow. The soft, low lighting gave the room the feel of intimacy. Though hundreds of people filled the room, the atmosphere seemed intimate and convivial, more like a gathering of friends than a crowd. Once Marilyn and Evan appeared, greetings were made all around, then Kent pointed them toward the right-hand side of the room, where Rose spotted her editor. But before she took a step, Kent touched her arm, holding her back.

"Rose, before I forget, there's a package for you. It arrived earlier today."

The young man disappeared and seconds later returned with a long white box tied with a bright red ribbon. Rose reached for the box and ripped off the bow. She had always loved surprises. She lifted the lid, exposing dozens of long-stemmed red roses.

"How nice!" Kent said, standing beside her.

Rose thought they must be from her good friend and colleague Jackie Collins. The best-selling author had phoned before Rose left for Paris to say she was genuinely sorry she couldn't come to the Waldorf party but was scheduled to leave for London the same night. Rose leaned closer to take in the delicious fragrance. She estimated there were three dozen perfectly blooming Victorian roses. After resting the box on the counter, she searched eagerly for a card. On the bottom of the box she found a bright red envelope. Inside was a white card with red lettering.

SUCH A DELICATE, BEAUTIFUL FLOWER, THE ROSE . . .

Rose looked up for a moment to see where Alexis might have gone and then glanced back to read the rest of the note. Not believing her eyes, she read the words over and over again. At first she couldn't decipher the message, but when she did her reaction changed from disbelief to horror. Neatly typed was a message:

SUCH A PITY THEY SHOULD DIE. . . .
I'LL BE WATCHING YOU.

Rose swayed and the box went crashing to the floor. Evan, Marilyn, and Kent rushed to her side. She could feel the blood draining from her face. Suddenly she felt dizzy.

"What is it?" Evan asked suspiciously. "Who are they from?"

Rose steadied herself quickly, not wanting to worry him about the note and spoil the evening. She tried to make light of it, even though she felt clammy and her heart was racing.

"I don't know . . . a fan. I'm fine, really," she said, trying to assure those now hovering around her. "Just a little light-headed." As a way of deflecting their attention, she added, "Point me toward the hors d'oeuvres."

Evan quickly picked up her cue and used his body to clear a path for them through the throng. Marilyn stayed behind, greeting many of the well-wishers while Rose composed herself. Evan led Rose and Alexis over to the lavish spread. Seeing the caviar, bowls of jumbo shrimp, delicately sculptured sushi, plates of various pâtés, little squares of focaccia, and warm sourdough rolls, Rose felt a sudden wave of hunger.

As she dipped a shrimp into a dollop of cocktail sauce, her eyes stayed on Alexis, who seemed to be focusing her attention on any food that wouldn't threaten to dirty her clothes. Her daughter was so much more ladylike than she had ever been, well mannered but not uptight. When Alexis began talking with Marilyn's assistant, Rose marveled at her poise. Later on, of course, at Serendipity, her daughter would indulge her less mature side and order a huge sundae, her eyes far bigger than her stomach. Rose adored every inch of her, from her tiny size four feet to the tip of her waist-length hair. Now Alexis turned and saluted her mother with her glass of Coke. "I love you," her child mouthed. Just seeing her daughter made Rose stop thinking about the flowers with their threatening card.

Rose mouthed, "I love you, too," and then turned back to the party, her eyes sweeping the room. Familiar people gestured at her, holding glasses of wine or champagne, keeping their voices to a polite, low hum. She noticed the publisher and the managing editor from *People* magazine talking to the president of Boardman Books. The Boardman publicity people were now making their way over to her, which suddenly reminded Rose that someone else was very much absent. Where was Dario?

Jeanette English, director of publicity at Boardman, echoed her thoughts as she came to greet Rose, "Where is that persistent public relations man of yours?" The beautiful African American woman smiled. She reminded Rose of an older, more refined Halle Berry. Everyone in the business knew how aggressive Dario was on behalf of his clients and often took light jabs at him.

"I suspect he's directing the kitchen help," Rose said in jest.

"Or maybe he's getting ready to launch those one thousand turtledoves carrying thorned roses in their beaks," Jeanette quipped.

Roses . . . No, she wouldn't think about that now.

"I talked with your French editor this morning, Rose. They adore you over there," added Susan Shapiro, the assistant director of publicity. Susan's personality was perfect for her job, Rose thought. She was savvy, creative, highly attractive, and charming beyond belief.

"Thanks," Rose replied. Just then Evan joined them, and he and Jeanette English began discussing the merits of lecture agents, since Evan was thinking of hiring one.

"Evan, darling, don't take your eyes off Alexis for a second," Rose said. "I'm going to walk around and thank my guests properly."

While she tried to remain attentive and gracious to her guests, shadows lurked in her mind, ominous and distracting. The message on the card stayed with her as she circulated the room, chatting with other writers and complimenting them on their latest books. Rose struck up a long conversation with her idol Mary Higgins Clark, who had been her literary mentor ever since Rose had read her book *Where Are the Children?* When Mary spoke about how happy she was with her new husband, Rose quickly looked back at Evan standing with Alexis. She loved her husband, too. She had adored him when they were children and never questioned they would be friends for life.

But now Dimitri, the only person who, long ago, had uncovered the depths of her soul, had come crashing back into their peaceful existence. She couldn't help but wonder if he was planning on spilling all of the Millers' secrets, taunting her in the process. Could Dimitri possibly be the one who had sent the roses?

"You're a silly goose," she mumbled aloud to herself.

"I'm sorry, what did you say?" Kirby Reed, her editor, peered into her face.

"Oh, I was just talking to myself," Rose said apologetically. She brought a hand up to her forehead and brushed away a few stray hairs. "Writers, you know. It's very warm in here. I'm going to get a club soda. Come, take a walk with me, Kirby."

As the sun outside had long since faded, the famed blue ceiling of the Starlight Room was now dazzling, fully lit. It had been designed to create the image of the night sky, and the effect was staggering. The room seemed suddenly enormous, with the entire sky as its ceiling. If she didn't know this was midtown Manhattan, Rose could imagine that the sky above them was located in Montana, with stars twinkling as far as the eye could see and all seemingly within reach. The ceiling was a magnificent work of art.

Marilyn found her, saying Evan was keeping an eye on Alexis. Marilyn was hovering too close, and Rose suspected her friend was worried. She guessed that Kent had insisted security discreetly recheck the entire room and that Marilyn had made sure she knew everyone in attendance. Soon she managed to calm down. The idea that all this fabulous commotion was for her took over her thoughts, and she gave herself up to the pure pleasure of receiving compliments and being the center of attention, just for tonight.

"You look beautiful," a man's voice said quietly behind her. Startled, she turned and found herself face-to-face with John McClelland, a publisher who had been trying to woo her away from Boardman.

"You like it, John?" she said, giving a little turn to show off the black sheath dress. She liked John McClelland and loved teasing him. She gestured to herself, then to the crowd. "All this could have been yours—the party, the crowd."

"The money Boardman is making!" he said, nodding. "Well, tell me how you can be mine, and I'll call Marilyn first thing tomorrow and start talking."

"I'm teasing you, my dear. Boardman gave me my first break, and as I recall, your beloved house declined both of my first two books when I was an unknown."

"I yield," John said, "at least for tonight. But I'm not giving up on you."

His innuendo didn't surprise her. The fortyish man was handsome, a well-known Romeo, and tonight, as always, he wore his signature suspenders and Armani tie. After some more informal exchanges, John smiled and said, "I'm on my way to the bar, can I get you anything?"

"You'll never find me again in this crowd."

"Tough to be famous," he said. With a wink he excused himself.

The crowd lingered for what seemed like hours. Just when she thought she could smile no more, a figure appeared on the stairs, walking down the steps at the left side of the room and coming very aggressively toward her. Her heart skipped.

Where was Evan? Or security?

Then she saw it was a young man, holding out a copy of her book for an autograph.

"Sign it 'Roses are red . . .' "

Rose's thoughts were becoming cloudy, and she felt herself drifting away. Her hand trembling, she reached for the book while fighting hard to balance herself. Her heart began accelerating; she was gasping for air. The dizziness she'd experienced earlier returned. The floor beneath her seemed unsteady.

"Help, oh God, someone help me. . . ."

When she eventually opened her eyes, she stared into a sea of blurry faces. Why was she lying flat on her back? The starlit ceiling seemed to be circling, and suddenly she was terribly thirsty. She felt the cold spot at the back of her tongue that had accompanied her fearful, racing heart.

Evan took her hand. "Darling, you passed out cold. I'm sure it was just the lack of air. Oxygen can be scarce with a big crowd."

As she looked up into Evan's ever reassuring eyes, Rose wondered if it was the crowd, or the fear, or the thought of Dimitri being back. Her eyes still on Evan's face, she wondered if things would ever be the same again.

4

Billy was watching through the partly open picture window of the master bedroom as Rose slept, observing her in tranquil slumber. This put him into a kind of trance and satisfied his craving for serenity.

The Paradiso estate was glorious, elaborate, and palatial. The mansion was typical of the North Shore of Long Island. The mist was rising up toward the still dark sky, moving out to the Long Island Sound. Acres of manicured lawns, stables, tree-lined paths, a freshwater pond complete with a cascading waterfall—anything the imagination and an endless bank account could conjure up—dotted Paradiso's landscape. But Billy didn't care about that; he wanted only to see Rose.

From where he was standing, Rose was clearly visible through Billy's nightscope binoculars. She rarely slept this late, according to the log he kept. He knew her habits and admired her discipline. At five A.M. every day she was at her computer while the rest of the mansion was dark. Like clockwork, she'd write for almost two hours, stopping only to reread the pages, take a sip of coffee, then go back to her work. The words seemed to flow without stopping. At about seven he would see the lights turn on in her daughter's room and knew Rose was getting the girl ready for school. With all of these details down pat, he considered himself her most enlightened fan, the one who knew her best.

Billy leaned against the grand oak tree behind him, puffed on his Marlboro, and congratulated himself for the plan he'd devised, which allowed him to watch Rose from outside her bedroom window without being caught. He'd simply obtained one of the blue denim jumpsuits the maintenance men wore as uniforms, slipped it over his own clothing, and "borrowed" one of the snowblowers from the wooden shed. In this disguise he could maneuver around the property as he pleased. Once a staff member actually said hello to him, thinking she recognized him.

He looked back at the window; she was still asleep. He threw the lit cigarette to the ground and crushed it with the tip of his boot. He felt euphoric, so elated that he knew the high would last all day and tonight he would lie awake thinking of Rose, her perfect body, her heavenly face. He glanced down at his watch and smiled. It was almost time for his special delivery.

She floats in a cold gray place that gradually takes on shape and substance. It's a sprawling mansion with stables. She feels welcome and safe here. Tilting her head back, she peers up through oak leaves, watching the clouds go by.

"Come here, Rose," he says in a whisper, tugging at her arm. "Let's go into the stable." Over the rocky ground, she follows him willingly. He warns her to watch her step and grips her hand so tightly, her fingers begin to ache. She doesn't care. She follows him into the barn. He places a blanket over a large bale of hay in the back of the barn. He pulls her close to him, so close that she nuzzles her face in the small of his neck.

"I love you, Rose," he whispers. "I'll always love you." He cups her face in his hands, bringing her lips close to his. They kiss as his hands explore her body, her neck, shoulders, thighs, and breasts. His hands are fumbling with her green satin dress, peeling it away, revealing her nakedness.

She loses herself in his touch, the heat of his hands, the exquisite taste of his mouth. He pulls her even closer, pushes her back gently, and rises above her. He enters her slowly. She tries to pull back. She's never done this before. But she is powerless in his arms. He thrusts even harder. There is pain, a sense of tearing. She cries out, first in pain—then in ecstasy—floating higher and higher . . . whatever Dimitri wants, wherever Dimitri goes, she is his.

Afterward she stares into his eyes, absorbing their softness, their vulnerability. Her body at peace, she lies very close to him and lets out a long, drawn-out sigh.

Her face was damp with sweat. Rose awakened to the piercing sound of the alarm clock next to the bed. She searched for the clock on the end table and slammed down the button.

Relief swept over her quickly when she realized she'd only been dreaming. Rose shook her head to clear out the cobwebs of last night—the book party, the note, the roses, the anonymous man with the request for the ironic autograph—then blackness. Her body cooled down, and her breathing returned to normal. The scare at the party last night hadn't yet worked its way out of her system. Then she made the connection between the dream and reality; Dimitri's reentry into their lives had already invaded her mind.

She glanced over to the empty side of the bed: Evan was up and about. She pulled herself to the edge of the mattress, stepped into her slippers, and stopped for a moment to enjoy the view from the enormous bay window in her bedroom. The primordial winter morning sun was forming long shadows across the tranquil pond. The rows of pine trees were carefully trimmed to avoid obstructing the view of the meticulously manicured grounds. The wind, chilly with the fully developed signs of winter, whipped around the corners of the large bay window.

Rose padded down the hall toward her daughter's bedroom, opened the door quietly, and tiptoed to her bed. Alexis's tousled hair spilled down the sides of the pillow. Gently Rose brushed aside her bangs. She loved to watch her daughter in repose.

As she sat on the edge of Alexis's canopied bed, she thought of how each season came and went, and all revolved around Alexis. Every so often Evan would remark gently that he was worried Rose was overprotective. And it was true. Alexis was the heart of Rose's world. She watched her grow, day by day, month by month, year by year; it seemed to Rose a never-ending miracle from the moment she'd begun to develop into her own person. Even before then, starting with the day she was born.

Rose could remember as if it were yesterday: Alexis taking her first steps, her first words, letting go of her bottle, drinking from a cup, giving up her security blanket without a fuss, going off to school for the first time alone.

Everyone who met Alexis was instantly taken in by her sensitivity and concern for others. She was self-contained for an eleven-year-old, just as

Rose had been as a child. Because Alexis had no dark shadows hanging over her childhood as Rose had, she was carefree, innocent of the malice that people sometimes face in the world. And Rose intended to keep it that way for as long as she could.

She contemplated her daughter's sleeping face, her pronounced nose, cleft chin, and strong jawline. But her most magnificent asset was her enormous, sparkling, blue eyes.

Rose closed the door quietly and made her way back to the master suite. In the shower, the image of her child stayed fixed in her mind. As she shampooed her hair, she thought of Alexis's dark coloring and the lush eyelashes that decorated her lids like a row of elongated commas.

Rose was certain Alexis would soon be a ravishing young woman, but all she wanted for her was a normal, happy childhood. More than anything, she prayed and dreamed for her daughter to grow into young womanhood without having emotional baggage to bear—as different from her own childhood as possible.

Rose was the only child of Victor and Sophia Calvetti, a lower-class couple who enveloped their child with warmth and tenderness. Victor was handsome, nurturing, and completely devoted to his family. Rose was his miracle, and he treated her as one, showering her with fantastic stories, bringing her treasures he'd discover during his walks in the woods that would delight her: a robin's egg, a four-leaf clover, a butterfly trapped in a net. Rose worshiped her father, imagining him a prince who could just snap his fingers and make her every wish come true.

Victor Calvetti's misfortune was that he had been born with epilepsy and therefore couldn't be relied upon to make enough money to support his family. It seemed no sooner did he settle into a steady job than he would have a seizure that would cost him days of work and often terrify fellow workers. Medication couldn't control his disorder.

It wasn't until he landed the position as handyman for the Millers that he was able to work around his problem, laboring hard during his good times with his boss's full knowledge that there would be days when he could not be counted on.

Because of her husband's disability, Sophia was the main breadwinner in the family. She worked as head housekeeper for the Millers at the Laurel estate, a massive two-story white brick colonial mansion with large ornate pillars, acres and acres of lush, manicured lawns, and an interior that matched the beautiful edifices. If Victor's legacy to Rose had been to grab for the magic of life, it was from Sophia that she learned about the practical side and how to face reality. Her mother talked often of how Rose must strive to go far. All they worked for was their precious child's future. Although money was scarce, the Calvettis made the best of it. Sophia didn't think at all about her husband's weaknesses and honored those traits in him that were strong and special. At an early age, Rose absorbed her parents' values, and as far as she was concerned, theirs was an ideal family.

Then, on her tenth birthday, the secure world Rose knew came to an abrupt end. Devout churchgoers, her family was coming home from Sunday mass when the brakes of the car suddenly failed. The late-model Chevy Impala collided head on with a tractor trailer. The only survivor was Rose, who miraculously emerged from the accident unscathed. For a while she was taken care of by another maid, who moved into the handyman's cottage. Only sixteen, the girl didn't have the wherewithal to comfort Rose, to help her through her grief.

Rose repressed most of the memories of the accident. For many years only the terror remained close to the surface. Other than that, she learned to blot out all the gruesome pictures. Even in the middle of a nightmare, she would suddenly awaken, screeching in horror, blocking out the horrible images. After calming down, she would replace those thoughts with memories of her parents and all the special times they had shared together.

As Rose got in touch with her inner self and began to write thrillers, she started to remember all the fear she had blocked out. The first image she recalled was that of her mother on the day she died, dressed all in pink, suit, hat, shoes—the spring church outfit that Sophia had made herself from a pattern in a magazine. The most unfathomable aspect of her mother's death was that there was no blood or sign of injury when Rose saw her that last time. One minute Rose was in the backseat behind her mother's broad-brimmed straw hat, the next minute she was outside the car and Rose could see her mother bent, leaning on the dashboard before the shattered windshield. But she was all right. Rose was sure of it. In a dream years later, Rose remembered running to the car. "Mama," she called, trying to open the fractured door.

Rose never saw her father's body, nor did she know how he died until many years later. She was at the local police station doing research for The Devil's Daughter *and got up the nerve to request the report on her parents' accident. The shock of seeing a police photographer's snapshot of the crash scene caused her to kneel to the floor, tears streaming from her eyes. In this close-up shot of her father's body, Rose could clearly see that the steering wheel had penetrated his chest cavity. The accompanying medical examiner's report described his injury. Interpreting the medical language, Rose realized that her father's heart and lungs had been shattered into pieces.*

From then on, Rose could draw from these haunting images when she wrote about the emotional impact of seeing the body of a person who had suffered a grotesque death. Though the sight of her father's body never left her mind, she found that writing scenes of Victor's dying in horrible ways helped her release the memory.

Several weeks after the accident, her father's brother, a virtual stranger to Rose, appeared out of nowhere. "Darlin', I'm your daddy and your mommy now," Uncle Tom said. He parodied a southern accent, perfected while serving time in a military prison at Fort Bragg for raping a female officer. Rose would come to recognize this mean imitation of people he referred to as "rednecks" as a sign he was drunk and nasty.

Rose never thought of Tom as an "uncle" or family in any way. She developed an immediate visceral dislike for him: for his obsidian eyes and bulky body, puffy from too much alcohol and soft from laziness.

Uncle Tom moved into the cottage, took on the job of handyman, and, as soon as Rose turned eleven, forced Rose to accept the position of assistant maid at Laurel to bring in extra wages. By the time Rose was twelve, she was the Miller family's laundress. Perhaps out of a remote sense of obligation to her parents, James Miller saw to Rose's education, even sending her to a local Catholic school. Still, she was expected to work in the house late into the evenings. Haunted by her mother's dreams for her success, Rose pushed hard and finished high school a year early. Surely now she would find a way to go to college; even a community college would do. Instead, at the age of sixteen Rose was promoted to head housekeeper. Her future stretched ahead of her, an eternity of loneliness and unhappiness.

At night, instead of being able to retreat to the comfort of the once homey cottage, she returned to the squalor Tom brought with him. Gone were Sophia's knickknacks, pretty china pieces, the ruby red pressed glass vase Mama loved so much because it was an anniversary gift from her father. Some of her mother's delicate treasures were broken during Tom's drunken stumblings. Once, in a rage, he grabbed the life-size china cat her mother had always kept on the kitchen wall and threw it at her.

Often, at night before she fell asleep, she would summon the memory of her father's rugged hands resting protectively on her shoulder as he walked her to school. She would recall the bedtime stories he had told of faraway places; or she would imagine herself touching her mother's long blond hair, secured behind her head with a small gold clip, another gift from her father.

When her body began to fill out, she was forced to dodge Uncle Tom's clumsy advances. He seemed to leer, hover, and watch her every step. She asked him for a lock on her door, but he refused, saying it could be dangerous if there was a fire. Now Rose became afraid to close her eyes, but when she eventually fell asleep, she'd dream of Uncle Tom's hard, mean eyes enveloping her. She'd awaken with a start, her cotton nightgown wet with sweat.

As Rose became aware of the changes in her body, she also began to realize how different she was from the other kids at school. She was excluded from the socializing that seemed so much a part of their daily lives. For Rose, there was no group of girls she routinely ate lunch with; no one who invited her to come over to their homes after school. She was an outcast. Isolation was an ache, and she was aware of a new emotion: envy. Rose felt cheated. Why did the others avoid her? How could they look down on her when they didn't even take the time to know her?

Once she had graduated from high school, James Miller, his responsibility fulfilled, treated her with the same disregard as he did all the other servants at Laurel.

5

Rose tried to shower away the memories of all the nights she'd been too frightened to sleep. She remembered discovering the peephole Tom had carved through the wall in his bedroom that looked directly into the bathroom. No, she told herself, don't go there. She pushed her thoughts away as the hot water skimmed over her body.

Rose managed to dress and make it down to the breakfast room just in time. Evan's father, James Miller, the millionaire widower and "master of the mansion"—as she'd once heard him refer to himself—insisted that they all meet in the breakfast room each morning at seven A.M. sharp—no excuses. "A calming period," he called it. Rose checked her watch. There was an hour left until Alexis had to be off to school. Today she would have to miss James's mandatory breakfast.

It was a lucky thing, too. As Rose approached the room, she heard James and Evan shouting at each other from the other side of the door. She hesitated, not wanting to interrupt the argument.

"There's nothing I can do. Dimitri wants me to represent him," she heard Evan say. "He doesn't want another attorney from the firm. He could have gone elsewhere, hired the best legal gun in the country. God knows he has the resources. But he insists on me."

"Exactly, Evan, that's why I'm convinced he's up to something. Why us? Why now? I'm willing to bet this mansion his first attorney didn't have to drop the case because he was ill. Jack Lester faked those chest pains. This whole cock-and-bull story of a heart attack is a hoax. Dimitri, that son of a bitch, has something up his sleeve."

There was the sound of a fist crashing onto the table.

Rose had never heard James in such an agitated state. Nearly seventy, Evan's father had the same angular features as Evan. But the older man's were etched with a sharp nose, full mouth, and beaming eyes that still glistened with ambition. James Miller, a man who feared no one and nothing, suddenly sounded frightened.

James continued, "Obviously he decided it's payback time. I'm surprised it took him this long. But it's not going to happen. He won't get the chance to cast a scandal on this family or the firm."

"I'll do what I can," Evan said, trying to calm his father. "I'll try to reason with him today at our meeting."

"Don't try!" James yelled. "Just do it. Find out what the hell he wants, then I'll figure out how to deal with him. I've worked too damn hard to get us here. Your popularity has never been higher. Soon we'll be starting your campaign for governor. Serve a term or two and then we're off to the White House."

Evan's voice lowered. "Don't you think you're jumping the gun a bit on the White House, Father?"

"Not at all," James said. "I've invested all I have in your political career. I've gained the trust and support from all my friends and fellow businessmen, politicians, union leaders, you name it. I bet if polls were taken right now, your popularity would be increasing weekly. People are attracted by your charisma. You are the next Jack Kennedy. Goddamn it, I won't let Dimitri destroy my dream."

It was his father who had whet Evan's appetite for politics. James Miller represented the third generation of powerbrokers, all descended from a contemporary of the Vanderbilts and the Astors. The original Miller, John James Miller, James's great-grandfather, and his family existed on a handful of cattle and pigs that got them through the winters, paid a few bills, but not much more. His son, John James II, had lifted the family out of poverty and into the financial stratosphere by designing an entire system for cattle raising, including feeders, milkers, and efficient systems to transfer fattened cattle from the barns to trucks to slaughterhouses on an automatic conveyor system. By the time James's father, Charles James Miller, was college age, the family was awash in money, social contacts, and the power that accompanies both. In New York the Millers were part of the Astor 400 and Charles Miller was the senior senator from New York. James didn't need to improve their fortune. He could easily live off the interest on investments.

But Charles decided that it would be prudent for the Miller family to gain influence behind the political scene. James went about this by establishing himself as a lawyer specializing in lobby law. He had been raised to believe in one bit of philosophy alone: "Millers can buy anything or anyone." Put into action, this meant whatever James Miller wanted, he got—no matter how many people he dragged down, walked over, and left behind in his wake.

Father and son were still arguing as Rose pushed open the door. Both men jumped at her entrance.

Evan was the first to speak. "Rose, are you feeling better this morning?"

She managed a slight smile. "I overslept."

"You need the rest." He came to her side, gently brushed back a strand of hair from her face, and kissed her on her cheek. "Come and have something to eat. Considering what you've been through the last week or so, it's no wonder you fainted last night."

Rose knew Evan was trying to deflect attention from the conversation with James.

"Boardman Books should take better care of their star author," James added. He was smiling as he spoke, but Rose knew what he was really thinking. Men like James didn't understand why a woman with a rich husband would have ambition or the desire to carve out a place of her own. She held James's gaze long enough to let him know she wasn't fooled by his solicitous pretenses. Then she turned to Evan.

"What were you two arguing about? Did I hear right—you're going to represent Dimitri?"

Evan patted her hand. "Now, don't go jumping to any conclusions. I intend to talk him out of it. We all know it's insane. He's a highly intelligent man. Dimitri will come around."

But his words rang hollow: he didn't sound or look at all confident.

As her mind processed the argument she had overheard, Rose composed herself by looking around the opulent room. Hand-painted florals adorned the walls, and bright peach carpeting covered the floor. In the far corner of the room were two floor-to-ceiling windows, displaying a spectacular view of the garden outside. In the center of the room was a nineteenth-century Biedermeier breakfast table and matching mahogany chairs. The cushions were covered with a paisley print, complementing the elaborate balloon curtains and drapes that graced the room's seven windows. She might have found this sunlit space particularly relaxing were it not for the palpable tension forever pulsating just below the surface of the family's conversation.

Though Paradiso was certainly more comfortable to her than Laurel, the newer mansion had taken on a cold, cavernous feeling. When Rose and Evan had first seen the estate, she was running away from the memories that haunted every corner of Laurel. So she had jumped on Paradiso as the place they, or more specifically she, could start over.

As the years went by, though, the new house failed to become a home. Rose felt alone, especially when Alexis was at school. The household staff, gardeners, and maintenance people who bustled about only augmented her sense of isolation. She longed for a normal life. She wanted Alexis to grow up with her feet on the ground in a less formidable atmosphere, and she wanted to move away from her father-in-law, whose toxic presence hovered over the house, as thick and malodorous as his cigar smoke.

She had expressed her thoughts on many occasions. "Can't we get a place of our own, Evan?" she would say. "Do we have to live in this grand, hollow house?" What she did not add was, "Do we have to live with your father?"

But she dared not ask, as she knew the answer. The Millers, like the Weilsteins, the Kinsolvings, and other wealthy families, tended to live and travel together, a sort of multimillionaire version of nomadic Bedouin tribes.

Silence fell over the breakfast table. Rose looked at James and felt revulsion rise in her. The man was made of dollar signs, devoid of values, morals, or ethics. To him, Evan was just a well-maintained political tool, which James would use to suit his needs, to push the Miller family even further politically, socially, and professionally.

James's face was red. His tirade had no doubt raised his blood pressure, but he acted as though the tension weren't there, never once referring to the argument or his concerns in her presence. Did he think she hadn't heard his fortissimo performance before she'd entered the room?

Rose hated this sport. To her, it was a form of deception. It struck such a false note. Often breakfast became an uncomfortable way to start the day, especially since there was no love lost between her and her father-in-law.

Myra, the housekeeper, a Polish immigrant who had been with the Millers for twenty years, always prepared the breakfast James favored: fruit, scrambled eggs, assorted rolls and toast, and warm Taylor ham. The meal was always served family style and promptly at seven-fifteen. Now that the family was seated, Myra would bring in hot coffee and platters of food on warming trays. The overheard argument and Evan's inevitable submission to his father had spoiled Rose's appetite. No one was talking. The men, their appetites apparently unaffected by what had transpired, ate hungrily. Rose played with a small piece of melon and coffee, but Evan insisted she eat something. To silence him, she nibbled on a croissant.

Even though she knew her opinion wasn't welcome, she didn't care. After minutes of nothing but the sounds of chewing, Rose decided to break the silence.

"What are you going to do?" she asked.

"We all knew Dimitri was on his way back. I've had time to prepare for it. It was just . . ." Evan stumbled for words. "I never expected to be pulled into his case. Who could have predicted that Jack Lester would have gotten too sick to handle Dimitri's defense?"

"I'm sure you can persuade him to see reason," Rose said reassuringly. But she knew otherwise: once Dimitri set his mind to something, he was unstoppable. And she knew that he, more than anyone, didn't have a price. No amount of money the Millers might offer to dissuade him would alter his course. She touched Evan's hand, lying next to hers on the table. "You'll have to get him to tell you what he wants." She thought of Alexis, how important it was to keep trouble away from her. As though from far away, she heard herself say the words she could not stifle: *"Before he destroys us all."*

She closed her eyes. Her thoughts drifted back. The memories flowed.

6

Upper Brookville was home to blue bloods and power mongers. There, people lived a world apart from New York City, though it was only minutes away. Instead of the idiosyncratic mix of most of suburbia or the ferocious beauty of Manhattan's skyline, Brookville had mansions. Some of them, like Laurel, had up to seventy acres of land.

The three of them—Rose, Evan, and Dimitri—had grown up together. Though James forbade the boys to grow close, as teenagers they would disappear into the woods surrounding the estate. Once, curious to see what they did there, Rose followed quietly behind and found them smoking marijuana. Dimitri's idea, no doubt. Evan stubbed out the joint as soon as he saw her. And from that day on, often one or the other would ask her to join them, though they never smoked when she was there. All through early adolescence the boys continued their secret friendship.

Evan, younger than Dimitri by one year, was by far the more easygoing of the two, always making her laugh and offering a compliment when they ran into each other as she went about her chores. It seemed to Rose that Evan had always been there, a constant and kind companion, and she loved him like a brother. Rose had been at Laurel when Evan's mother died in a tragic accident. Mrs. Miller had been in a rush, late again for a charity function, when she lost her footing on the staircase and tumbled all the way down, shattering her skull on the marble floor. Having lost her own parents by this time, Rose knew how hard it was to deal with and admired Evan's ability to put the tragedy behind him rather than letting its shadow haunt his childhood. That was Evan—optimistic, smart, and caring.

Dimitri was more remote. When he first arrived at Laurel, she found him a little scary, but as time passed she learned more about him.

He wasn't rough at all, and as she got to know him better, she started seeing him in a whole new way. Like a mustang separated from his herd, Dimitri could prevail despite the worst of circumstances, yet always inside him would be that place searching for the comfort of his pack. He was like Clark Gable playing Rhett Butler, Paul Newman as Hud. Handsome, dressed always in outdoorsy clothes, he would telegraph messages with his sapphire blue eyes that could frighten, seduce, calm, or pretend.

As Rose began to leave childhood behind, a seismic change occurred among the three of them. Evan went from sneaking looks at her to declaring his affection openly. The closer it got to the time he was to leave for Harvard, the more ardent his advances became. Dimitri, once Evan's closest friend, turned sullen and refused his company. It wasn't until later that Rose realized this behavior stemmed from Dimitri's jealousy. At the same time, she and Dimitri's friendship flourished. He seemed oblivious to her burgeoning womanhood, and they spent long evenings just talking in his tiny room in the back of the stable, sharing childhood stories, filling each other's lonely places. She came to think of this place as a haven away from all her cares.

Dimitri was becoming a part of her. He had settled in an empty space in her heart, and she savored his constant presence there. Beneath Dimitri's tough exterior, he was good, kind, and ambitious. By the time she was eighteen and he was twenty-two, he loved her and she loved him. She knew there would never be anyone else for her.

Then came the night that destroyed any lingering good memories among the three of them.

After Evan had successfully completed his first semester at Columbia Law School, his father planned a dinner to celebrate. Evan used the opportunity to pressure James into inviting Rose to the dinner party. Though she hated the thought of going, she would never hurt Evan's feelings, so she reluctantly accepted.

After all, it was Evan who had intervened on her behalf and eventually convinced James it was in his best interests to help Rose finish her education after high school by hiring tutors for her. "Think of her as one of your charities, Father," he had said, playing right into his father's notion that he was one of New York's most highly regarded philanthropists. After Rose had been out of school a year, he hired tutors to get her up to college level in English literature, French, and creative writing. And now, as Evan pointed out, he could be char-

itable once again by including her at a formal Miller dinner party. Of course, before he'd let her attend, James had insisted that she have a crash course in table manners by an instructor well known for the etiquette classes she taught for children. Rose felt like Eliza Doolittle in My Fair Lady, *with Evan as Henry Higgins, picking out the right kelly green satin cocktail dress and accessories for her to wear to her debut. In the end, despite their efforts, she'd embarrassed them anyway.*

Wine was served with the various courses. As Rose sipped away at one, two, three glasses of wine and counting, she became increasingly dizzy. At dessert Evan rose, lifted his champagne glass to Rose, and proposed. If Rose was shocked, James was apoplectic. The silence that descended over the table of thirty guests was excruciating.

The guests, all good friends of James, had never even met this lovely young woman; nor, strangely, had James ever spoken of her before. They assumed she was just Evan's date for the evening, perhaps even a Radcliffe girl. The only sound Rose could hear was James muttering in Evan's ear that she was "common" and "trash" and perhaps Evan "had far too much to drink to see clearly."

A few minutes went by, with guests clearing their throats, assiduously eating the crème brûlée. Eventually a woman who Rose thought was dressed like Clarabell the clown started an inconsequential conversation. Another guest picked up the small talk. Soon the table was humming politely again. But Rose wanted to die. She could feel thirty pairs of eyes sneaking curious glances at her. Disgraced, she kept her head down, her trembling hands resting in her lap. She could not even look at Evan. She kept thinking James would probably dismiss her over the embarrassment. Then what would she do?

Suddenly she longed for Dimitri's comfort. Rose ran straight to the barn, where Dimitri was already asleep in his living quarters at the back of the stable. He comforted her and held her in his arms. When she calmed down, they made love for the first time—sweet, passionate love—and she felt she was where she belonged. He promised to take care of her forever and that they would leave Laurel together in the morning. She fell asleep in his arms. Still drunk, she drifted in and out of consciousness.

Rose awoke in a strange bed surrounded by curtains. Her head throbbed, and she could barely lift her limbs. After a few moments of feeling disoriented, she realized that she was in a hospital room.

"You're awake," a nurse said, bending over her. "How are you feeling?"

Rose, still feeling woozy, said, "I don't know. Why am I here?"

The nurse replied, "Oh, it's not serious. You'll be fine. You suffered a bit of a shock."

Rose remembered nothing after lying in Dimitri's arms. "What do you mean?"

The nurse was kind, but not about to say more than she had to.

Minutes later Evan came in with a bouquet of flowers.

"Has something happened?" she asked, puzzled by her surroundings.

"You really don't remember, do you?" Evan looked at her in surprise.

She shook her head.

Gently Evan said, "You're a patient. You mustn't be told worrisome things."

But as he spoke, fragments returned to her, images cascading on top of each other, starting with Evan's proposal. But her mind didn't budge beyond lying next to Dimitri. "Tell me what's happened. Help me remember."

He evaded her question. "The doctors just want you here a few days for observation."

After he left, she forced her memory back to the dinner party. She felt again the shame and then a powerful wave of nausea. Rose dragged herself to the bathroom of her hospital room and became violently ill. Afterward she curled into a ball and laid her head against the cool tile of the bathroom floor. Now purged, she recalled in detail Uncle Tom's probing fingers and piercing, beady eyes—then the deafening sound of gunshots and wailing police sirens echoing through the barn—the chilling sound of her echoing screams. "No . . . no . . . Dimitri . . . No! . . ."

Ashamed, she did not ask anyone what Tom had done to her. No matter how awful the truth was, she knew she could handle it only when she was safe again in Dimitri's arms. He would know how and when to tell her.

Evan, of course, did not press her to respond to his proposal in her current state. Once she had regained her equilibrium, she'd be able to compose a diplomatic "no" and explain to Evan that though she cared for him, it was Dimitri she truly loved.

The day she was to leave the hospital, Evan came to pick her up and found her pacing the room impatiently. She had forgotten to ask him to bring a change of clothes, so she'd been forced to put on the same kelly green dress and black high heels she'd worn to the dinner. She felt dirty and ridiculous. If she could only get home to her own clothing, get back to Dimitri, everything would be okay again. But Evan was dawdling.

"Evan, what are we waiting for?"

He led her to the visitors chair next to the bed. Kneeling next to her, he said, "Something's happened. You need to know before we go home."

With uncharacteristic impatience, Rose banged her hand against the arm of the vinyl chair. "Well, then tell me. I'm desperate to get out of here."

Taking both of Rose's hands in his, Evan spoke hesitantly. "After the party there was a shooting in the barn."

Her heart stopped—Dimitri? Her thoughts stopped whirling; he had all her attention. "Was anyone hurt?"

Evan held her hands tightly in his. "Your uncle Tom was killed."

She froze. The jagged memory she'd recalled the day before played out, like a movie, until the end. Tom's repulsive body struggling to restrain her, Dimitri standing over the body, the gun in his hand. She flashed back to the day her parents were killed. Once again her first reaction was to deny the truth. But logic took over, and she realized with sudden clarity that the love she had shared with Dimitri had been destined for tragedy.

"Oh, my God," she whispered. "Will Dimitri be okay?"

Evan shook his head. "He'll probably go to jail for a long time, Rose." He sat on the edge of the bed, still holding her.

"Marry me, Rose . . . I'll never let anything happen to you."

The room grew dark. Outside, the sun became covered by clouds. Only the bright glare of the overhead fluorescent light remained. There were visions and voices in her head . . . Sophia sewing late into the night so Rose would have clothes as fine as those of the other girls in school . . . her father's strong protective arm around her . . . Tom saying, "I'm your mama and daddy now" . . . Evan's proposal . . . James's outrage . . . Dimitri's passion.

Evan's voice interrupted her. "Marry me." He sounded urgent. "Dimitri's future is bleak. Don't let him take you with him. Marry me and you'll have a new beginning."

When Rose didn't reply, Evan continued, "You have to consider the facts."

His voice was more insistent. "You were there. You will be questioned, perhaps interrogated. You'll need protection."

He stood, and she could imagine him arguing a case for someone's life.

Again Evan took her hand. "Rose, I know you think you don't love me, but you're wrong." Rose still did not look at him. Putting his finger beneath her chin, Evan tilted her head to his. "It doesn't matter to me that you're not sure of your feelings right now. But I will give you the world, and in time, Dimitri will just fade into memory."

Instantly Rose saw the way to save Dimitri. "Evan, you're certain you want to marry me?"

"Of course!" There was no hesitation in his response.

The voices inside her head were loud now. Dimitri had rescued her, and now she would do the same for him.

"Well then, I will."

Evan smiled, and it was then that Rose felt his love for her like a safe spot in a raging river. Marriage to him would be stable, even though she didn't yearn for him in the intimate places of her heart and body. Nevertheless, she loved who he was—his essence. And while Dimitri owned her soul, her desperate need for his body on hers would fade in time and she would give Evan all the love she could. She would cling to Evan's love as if to a life raft.

"But there's one condition. I want you to get Dimitri free of these charges. He was protecting me. He shouldn't have to go to jail."

"You're not a lawyer, you don't understand these things."

"I want him cleared, Evan. It's important to me. Please, you must help me. The three of us were close. Weren't we?"

His eyes turned liquid with emotion. His love for her could be dangerous to him. She could see that.

It was in her power to use him any way she wanted, but she swore to herself that this would be the only time. Evan would save Dimitri so she could live with the guilt of causing him pain. And when she explained to him the bargain she'd made, he would understand why she married Evan.

"Please," she said again.

He leaned over and kissed her cheek, her forehead, her long blond hair, and finally he gave her a tentative kiss on the lips. "What have I done to deserve you, Rose?"

One thing his declarations of love did accomplish was to break down the barriers of class between them. To those who had known her before, she was like Sabrina, the chauffeur's daughter who married the millionaire. But when it came down to just Rose and Evan, they were on equal footing—in fact, if anything, she had the upper hand. As for the new people who entered their life: he was right, she could begin again.

As soon as they could get a license, they were married at the Town Hall in Brookville. Evan drove home and carried her over the threshold of Laurel, the mansion where she had days earlier been a servant. When he gathered his courage and told James, his father erupted like a volcano, spewing obscenities, his face beet red and his arms flailing. The men sat in the solarium, and James's voice could be heard in every room of the house. James used every tactic he had employed in his ruthless drive for power to dissuade his son. He tried threats: "I'll disinherit you"; humiliation: "How could you. A nobody! You married her to protect her. Don't you know she'll make a fool of you once her reputation is out of danger?" When that failed to budge Evan, James tried mudslinging: "She's a piece of dirt who belongs right alongside Dimitri."

But Evan found the strength he needed to stand his ground, telling his father he loved Rose, that she was the only woman for him. He flatly refused to listen when James said he would buy her off.

"She's after your money. It's obvious. Get an annulment and I'll see that she leaves with a handsome sum. I'll set you up a meeting with the DA to get Dimitri off the hook."

"You're going to do that anyway, because I promised her you would," Evan shot back. "I've promised her that you would make certain Dimitri was protected."

"Of course I'll do that," James replied, using his most successful gambit, manipulation. "But don't you see, Rose is stained. She'll drag our family's good name into the gutter. Once the tabloids get wind of this, I'll be the object of public ridicule. Your entire future has been carefully mapped out. There's no room for a ludicrous scandal. There will always be talk about what happened here that night, no matter how much we try to keep it quiet. For the rest of your life, Rose's involvement in that mishap will be fodder for rumor and innuendo."

"You're not listening, Father. I love her. Shall I say it again? I love her." Evan was taller than James, and when he stood, he used his size to intimidate his father. "You will do what you have to protect my wife's reputation. And you

will honor my commitment to protect Dimitri. And, Father, I do believe you know how to cover up a scandal."

James must have made the decision to go along for as long as he could until he could find another way to quash his son's feelings for the young housekeeper. For a time, he appeared to acquiesce to Evan's wishes. He arranged for a second ceremony a month later, an elaborate one at the North Hills Country Club in Manhasset. They would hide Rose's background from their elite world. Should someone recognize her, the Millers agreed among themselves to deny her identity. Rose wanted only for Dimitri to be free and agreed reluctantly to everything in return for his safety.

By then, Dimitri had signed a plea bargain for involuntary manslaughter, a deal neatly set up by James. As planned, Rose's presence at the scene was covered up as well. Dimitri was sentenced to six years in jail. James claimed that the furthest he could push his influence was to get the murder charges reduced. For that cruel deception, Rose would never forgive James Miller. He was a snake, a liar, and a fraud. Every time she looked into his eyes she saw a constant reminder of his ultimate act of revenge toward Dimitri.

Despite Rose's letters and pleas to let her visit him in prison, Dimitri answered only once.

His letter read simply, "How could you turn your back on me and marry Evan? Will you ever know what I did for you? I'll never forgive or forget your betrayal. And you will learn to regret it."

7

Rose was in her office, located in the west wing of the Tudor mansion. It was a pleasant room, with feminine touches. There was a sofa upholstered in soft colors where she could rest when she was not writing. She called it her "creative thinking" seat. The silk curtains at the double windows could be drawn back to give her a view of a charming area of the garden, which had a birdbath and honeysuckle bushes that attracted hummingbirds in the summer.

Aside from the bedroom suite she shared with Evan, this was the only room that James could not enter. Rose made sure of that: she had installed a lock, and only she had a key.

She looked at her watch and realized she had to get to the ABC studio for her first appearance of the day, on *Live! with Regis and Kathie Lee.* Frustrated, she thought of the scene she had wanted to write this morning. It was an important one in which her heroine, the stalked victim, hid in panicked silence in the stable, having learned her recent lover was just moments away from killing her. Drawing back on that fateful night with Dimitri and Uncle Tom, Rose had visions of the barn, the gunshots, and she felt a cold shiver move down her spine.

The shrill ring of the phone startled her.

"Hello."

"Rose!" Dario yelled in his usual enthusiastic way. "They called from Paris. You were great. A big hit."

Rose tried hard to match his excitement, but her spirit was clouded by worry as well as a sense of disappointment toward him. "That's great, Dario. I missed you last night. Why weren't you there?"

"Oh, I'm sorry, I got sort of . . . hung up. Couldn't get away. Let me make it up to you," he hurried on. "Lunch, on me. I'll send a car for you. The driver will pick you up after your last taping. We'll meet at Le Cirque 2000."

"No," she said, her tone sharp. "I have too much work to do."

"It can wait. Besides, there are some things we need to discuss. I'll see you then."

Before she could refuse, the connection was broken.

Dario was so damned controlling and arrogant. He ignored her pleas of exhaustion as though she were a cranky child who would feel just fine after a nap. Because Dario fed on whirling activity, he could never empathize with her need for solitude. If she complained that he pushed too hard, he would say that was what set him apart from all the rest. She could almost hear him: "Don't I always do what's best for you?" Which was why his excuse for not being there to work the room with her last night was rather lame.

Dismissing it from her mind, she hurriedly went through her daily planner to make sure she hadn't neglected anything. When she heard Myra's footsteps, she knew the studio's car must be there. She grabbed her coat and handbag and almost ran right into Myra in the hallway.

"The car is waiting for you, Mrs. Miller, but before you go, this was left for you." Smiling, she handed Rose a small blue box wrapped with a white ribbon. "That Mr. Miller, he is so wonderful. From Tiffany's, no less!" Then she asked, "Do you need me for anything else?"

Rose eyed the box suspiciously, then shook her head. "No, Myra, thank you. Wait! How did you say the box arrived?"

Myra looked up at her quizzically. "A delivery man, I guess. The butler found the parcel on the doorstep after hearing the doorbell chime."

"Tell the driver I'll be right down."

To Rose, the box might as well have been a time bomb, and she wasn't going to put off opening it. When the door shut, she unwrapped the ribbon. The world started to spin slowly as her anxiety mounted.

The open box revealed layer upon layer of white tissue paper. Hurriedly she shoved aside the paper to find that the box was filled with dried roses, the heads now dead and brown, the petals scattered around the box. Her eyes welled with tears; fear consumed her. Searching for a card, she put her hand into the lifeless pile of dried-up flowers and felt the sharp prick of a thorn. On the bottom of the box she found what she was looking for. The index finger of her right hand left drops of blood the same color of the message:

LANGUISHED BEAUTY
LONG AGO
A BLEEDING ROSE WILL TELL YOU SO,
I'LL BE WATCHING YOU!

U.S. District Attorney Kevin Allen had black Irish looks, cropped dark brown hair, and emerald green eyes topped by dark eyebrows set against fair skin. In his mid-forties, he was sturdily built, with the remnants of a high school football player still evident in his body and the way he held himself. When he frowned, his brows drew together so that he appeared to have a single eyebrow. It was particularly useful in the courtroom when he wanted to appear menacing.

In fact, he was frowning, but it was not for the same effect. He was furious.

"What the hell is going on here?" he demanded. Kevin Allen had put together this team of ten men and women—three assistant district attorneys, two paralegals, and five secretaries—to prosecute Dimitri Constantinos.

"We have a guy who did time for manslaughter, who's connected to . . . Hell, who orchestrated every dirty detail of that extortion operation in Vegas. We know that, everyone knows that. How does the media make him into some sort of Robin Hood? What the hell gives? I can't pick up a newspaper or magazine without reading about the goddamned scholarships Dimitri Constantinos gives to underprivileged kids."

Kevin's voice was mocking, probably because he had once been one of those poor kids and no one had ever given him anything. "I can't even turn on the friggin' TV without seeing his picture. What the hell is this world coming to?"

He shook his head theatrically and raised his voice. "I won't have it!" Every feature of his face expressed fury. He narrowed his gaze, eyes shadowed beneath those bushy black brows. "We're going to nail the scumbag, no matter what it takes."

He paused to look directly at every person in the room. His staff sat around a long conference table, too intimidated even to touch their coffee cups. "I know I give this speech before each trial starts—my usual pep talk. But this time it's different. I need—" He corrected himself quickly. "*We* need this win. This one's ours.

"I want a conviction. Do you all understand? Illegal gaming, racketeering, laundering, and extortion, the works. I want to take Constantinos down with them all. And I mean all of them."

His gaze shifted back to Chris Knowles, his best and brightest assistant DA. Chris was smart, with a quiet way. He was a Columbia graduate whose nerdy, innocuous demeanor made him the perfect foil for the DA's emotional trial style. "Do what you have to, Chris. Call in all favors, get the best investigators in on this. Dig deep. I want to know everything about our man."

Kevin was well aware that this tactic had backfired when the Nevada DA had gone after Constantinos. Every sordid, tawdry detail of Dimitri's life had somehow gained him a sympathetic reaction from the public. The average man or woman struggling to make ends meet, to put their kids through school, needed a hero to give them hope. And Constantinos was it. After all, he, too, had started with nothing but a rap sheet.

Since he had seemingly materialized into the public eye four years ago as one of Las Vegas's noteworthy "bad guys," Dimitri's every move caused controversy. The government eyed warily his entry into legal gambling. Constantinos had been bugged, followed, questioned, and harassed in every way at their disposal, but to date they had not found him guilty of anything. To the government he was a big fish they wanted to catch. The people, average working citizens, viewed him differently. He was a symbol of hope, perhaps an outlet for their frustration with the government or the boss or whoever was keeping them down. He represented both the good and the bad in them.

His generous philanthropy created advantages for many: there was the pediatric hospital on the outskirts of Las Vegas, to which he'd added a wing for children who were HIV-positive; the summer camp founded close to Lake Mead, where each July inner-city kids got a chance to smell country air; donations to scientific research for AIDS; and numerous scholarships to various universities throughout the country for financially deprived students. As far as the public was concerned, Dimitri Constantinos might have stolen from the rich, but he gave it to the poor. No matter what crimes the feds tried to pin on him, the public had adopted him as *their* Robin Hood.

Assistant District Attorney Chris Knowles, without knowing it, had uncovered one of the tactics Kevin Allen was considering. "Well, we know a lot about Constantinos's infamous father-in-law. The guy's got a list of priors long enough to make a ticker tape. Joseph Braun is a real lowlife, but we haven't been able to nail him on anything substantial."

"Not yet," Kevin corrected. "But I don't think the old man would want to spend his last years in prison when he could be having gimlets at 'Twenty-one.' I want you to lean on Braun, Chris. Subpoena him, and bring Donna and Mike with you to the interview." He gestured to the two other assistant DAs seated around the conference table. "Use threats, intimidation, then offer him a deal. We get off his back if he hands us Constantinos." The DA paused and then said softly, "I want the maximum sentence. I want reassurance that Constantinos will never enjoy freedom again."

"Don't worry," Knowles said confidently, "we'll take care of it."

8

Dimitri Constantinos leaned into a dark blue marble sink in the Vanderbilt Suite at the Plaza Hotel, staring at his reflection in the gilded Baroque mirror. It had become his temporary home for the duration of the trial. As he listened to the morning shows on the television in the master bedroom, his chest bare, his face covered in shaving lather, Dimitri stroked the razor up his long, tanned neck. He could hear his wife, Jewel, mixing a mimosa for herself. Regis Philbin was introducing his show's next guest.

"Ever since her first novel, *The Devil's Daughter,* climbed the best-seller lists," said the talk show host, "Rose Miller has become one of the world's hottest suspense novelists. She's here to tell us about her passion for writing and her latest thriller, *Thorns of a Rose.* Please welcome Rose Miller."

Dimitri was rinsing his face when he heard her name. He straightened and grabbed a towel, dabbing leftover shaving cream from his face as he turned to gaze at Rose's lovely image. Watching her, listening to her tell of her rise as an author, seemed surreal. He hadn't seen her in twelve years, except for photographs in magazines. Once, he had even seen her profiled on *Dateline.* He remembered the time he'd picked up her first novel. He'd been at Logan Airport in Boston on his way back to Las Vegas after a business convention. He'd assumed she'd gone through a change while married to Evan. There could be no other explanation. This was a far cry from the gentle, tender young girl he once knew. Rose, he remembered thinking, must have gotten in touch with her dark side.

Jewel returned to the master bedroom with her drink and settled comfortably on the sofa in front of the television. On the screen, Rose was smiling and gesturing with her expressive hands.

"Thank you, Regis. . . ."

Dimitri came into the bedroom, a large white terrycloth bathrobe now tied around his body, and stood quietly behind Jewel to watch Rose. He felt Jewel's eyes turn in his direction. His eyes never left the image on the screen.

"Did you know that bitch would be on?" Jewel asked. Her voice was piercing, like the yowl of a Siamese cat.

He shook his head, still watching the screen.

"Well, she certainly got your full attention."

Subtlety was not one of Jewel's strong points. Her graceless demeanor was on his mental list of her character flaws. She also nagged and was suspicious by nature. His complex business world was enough of a drain, but coming home to her bickering drove him insane. At first he'd told himself she was the perfect corporate wife. She was beautiful, albeit in an artificial way, with long black hair, sparkling amber eyes, and perfect features, compliments of her plastic surgeon. Jewel had undergone breast augmentation, had collagen injections for her lips, and had even had liposuction—far easier than working up a sweat on the StairMaster. Superficially Jewel lived up to her name. Her wardrobe consisted of Chanel suits, Manolo Blahnik shoes, Ferragamo bags, and jewelry from Harry Winston's private collection. Dimitri knew when he married her that Jewel would be expensive to keep. She was her father's only soft spot and, as such, had been spoiled for all of her twenty-three years. What Dimitri had not planned on when he married her was what a toll it could take to try to keep her satisfied. Jewel had turned out to be a bottomless pit of demands and greed.

Dimitri didn't spend all his time in prison brooding. Great Meadow Correctional Facility, located in rural upstate New York, had a streamlined exterior that belied its dilapidated state. But the warden was progressive, and a program was offered to inmates interested in taking college classes while behind bars. Dimitri had studied all the math, management, and theory of business he'd needed to earn enough credits for a BA in business. When he had served his six years and was finally released, he'd expected his hard work to count. He was wrong. Soon he learned that no one wanted to hire an ex-con, even one with a business degree. Looking for work was a disaster, full of lots of discouragement. Left little choice, he took a job as a runner for a hotheaded but street-smart thug, Joseph Braun, whose name was synonymous with money laundering, prostitution, and racketeering. Too embarrassed to tell Braun the truth about his background, Dimitri told him his parents had died in a fire. He intended to keep his past secret until it was advantageous for him to let his story be told. At first, his job consisted of hanging out nights picking up information from the young men in Little Italy he had known before his mother had left him with James Miller and departed for parts unknown.

When Dimitri had left for prison, these men were teenagers. Now they were as hardened as he was, and they knew what was going on in the neighborhood. What's more, they knew where all the action could be found. For the right amount of money they could be persuaded to tell who might be trying to cut in on Braun's action or, better yet, where more action might be found. Big Tommy's, a bar on Mott Street, was their hangout. Braun arranged for Dimitri to rent a room above it. A seedy, roach-infested box. It was a shithouse, no heat, no hot water, with a bathroom he shared with three other tenants. But it would do for now. He wasn't staying long. He never saw Braun but instead got his orders from an up-and-coming man in the gang, a small corpulent man known as Cougar. Dimitri ran numbers all day and collected markers at night.

His big break happened one night when one of Braun's goons got into a nasty scuffle and had both his arms broken. Dimitri was sent in his place to "take care of" a resistant borrower named Kiki who owned a Chinese restaurant a few blocks from downtown Little Italy. Dimitri figured the transaction would be amicable, but it didn't turn out that way. Kiki was a smart-mouthed, hand-happy gambler and a sore loser. He refused to pay up.

After some heated exchanges, a scuffle ensued. Dimitri was lighter than Kiki, but there was no doubt who was stronger. Dimitri decked him at least four times, but Kiki kept stumbling to his feet. The man was a glutton for punishment, Dimitri thought, willing him to stay down. His face was covered with blood, his stamina visibly affected.

"You're over, old man." As he headed for the door with bundles of hundreds he'd removed from the register, Kiki lunged toward him with a knife, cutting a vicious gash down the side of Dimitri's left arm. The pain was bad, but the indignity was worse.

"You piece of shit!" Dimitri yelled as rage came over him, the all-encompassing fury that kept him awake most nights, the need for revenge. Finally he had found a way to release years of built-up anger.

Dimitri wasn't himself at that moment. All he saw was James Miller's belittling face. He grabbed Kiki's knife arm and pulled it back, twisting, not even hearing the sickening crack or Kiki's agonizing screams. He was a wild animal devouring his prey, pounding, kicking, ripping. It took three waiters to drag him off Kiki. Kiki had ended up out of commission for a year afterward—a long time to miss business in the streets.

That night, as Dimitri left Bellevue Hospital with twenty stitches in his arm, Braun's man Cougar was waiting outside near the hospital entrance. "The boss wants to see you."

I screwed up, Dimitri thought as he entered Big Tommy's bar. At a corner table, across from the bar, four men were playing poker. All eyes turned to Dimitri as he entered, but one man recognized him and gestured for him to go into the back room.

Joseph Braun was sitting behind a large wooden desk. An expensive gray flannel suit jacket hung on the back of his chair, and the knot in his silk canary yellow tie was pulled down, revealing a neck as thick as a bulldog's. Braun was counting money. Without pausing, he motioned with his head for Dimitri to sit opposite him. Cougar immediately moved directly behind his boss. Dimitri noticed the .38 when Cougar pulled back his jacket, and he would have bet there was another weapon, either a knife or another revolver, tucked into a holder on the small man's calf. Turning away from Cougar's unflinching stare, Dimitri watched with sheer fascination as Braun counted hundred-dollar bills into thousand-dollar piles. The pile Dimitri had collected from Kiki had been delivered by Cougar after he'd taken Dimitri to the hospital.

When Braun had neatly packaged all the money, he pulled the thick Cuban cigar from his mouth and took a moment to relight it. The noxious smoke tickled Dimitri's nose. "I guess what the other young guys in the neighborhood say about you is true. You're a wild one," Braun said, half smiling, half smirking. "I need to keep my eye on you, keep you under tight rein."

Dimitri stared back, his unflinching eyes mirroring Braun's cool gaze. He sensed it was crucial that he show the older man he couldn't be intimidated. So the two men stared silently. Finally, as though he'd come to a decision, Braun nodded several times and, sounding like a benevolent uncle, said, "You did good tonight, son. I'm proud of you. In fact, I wish I had ten more guys like you. Hungry, ferocious. From now on, you take orders only from me."

That night, Dimitri's whole life changed. Braun gave him enough room to explore other avenues. In fact, he introduced Dimitri to a whole new world. Fast cars, fast money—and fast women, all of them ravishing and easy to get into bed. They weren't Rose, but they fulfilled his needs just the same. He put the shithouse of an apartment behind him and moved into a two bedroom in a tony West Village townhouse.

The longer Dimitri worked for Braun, the more determined he became to make it in the straight business world. He enrolled nights in the Berkeley Business School in New York and earned his MBA. When he graduated, he suggested that Braun use him to better advantage and start relying on his business know-how.

One night, while having a drink with Braun at the bar, Dimitri said, "I can take you to the top, make you more successful than you ever imagined."

Joseph Braun looked at the impudent young man and decided to be tolerant. "I am successful."

"No," Dimitri corrected. "You just think you are."

"Stop it right there." Braun's patience disappeared with the smoke from his cigar.

But Dimitri kept talking. It was a reckless move, but he saw that Braun had begun to listen, so he leaned forward in his chair and continued to speak. "Pool your resources. Get rid of all the insignificant businesses, the penny-ante stuff. Put it all together into something big, a business that could go national, maybe worldwide. Invest your capital in a hotel, even a casino, a legitimate enterprise."

Braun had moved cautiously at first, testing each piece of Dimitri's advice. Under Dimitri's supervision, within a year Braun had unloaded most of his not quite legal investments for even more prosperous legit businesses.

After three years Braun's enterprise had branched out to include several restaurants, trucking companies, clothing manufacturers, and hotels across the country. Dimitri received a twenty-five percent stake of each deal he helped orchestrate. He became known for finding ailing companies across the country that needed financing and proper management. Then Braun would enter the company as a minor partner, increase his share, and gradually take over. Under Dimitri's direction, the company would increase its profits by using union workers, controlled by union bosses, who reported to Braun. In a one-

hand-feeds-the-other operation, Dimitri created a series of businesses that brought wealth and stature to Braun, pulling his reputation out of the gutter. Eventually, though, Dimitri began to feel it was time to move on. He'd made enough money and had all the material things he needed.

Because he had made Braun so successful, Dimitri was aware he would soon become obsolete. Braun no longer needed him. He had learned all he needed from Dimitri. After those three years, Dimitri knew that his days were numbered. Joseph Braun was a greedy man. Nothing meant more to him than money. When he felt Dimitri was getting too much of a cut, Braun approached him. "Maybe you should slow down, pull back, enjoy all your earnings."

Dimitri put him off; soon rumors reached him that Braun was planning to get rid of him—Jimmy Hoffa style. Luckily Dimitri had seen this moment coming and had a backup plan. Joseph Braun's only daughter, Jewel, was now eighteen. Her mother had died when she was young, and Jewel had been raised by a housekeeper. She was wild and rebellious, a constant source of trouble and upset for her father. He was always having to bribe someone or use other means of persuasion to get her out of one disaster or another. She was constantly overextended financially and seemed to attract car accidents that cost Braun plenty in liability and insurance claims. Dimitri often wondered why Braun didn't cut up her credit cards, take away her Corvette, and maybe let her bail herself out so that she'd get a taste of the real world. But he kept his mouth shut. During Dimitri's apprenticeship with Braun, Jewel had been thrown out of three schools: two were fancy private academies and the third was Mt. Maplewood Junior College in Vermont. Braun had managed to "gift" a seat for his daughter at the prestigious institute, but Jewel was expelled in her freshman year for sneaking out to meet a "townie," a man twice her age.

"What am I gonna do with this kid?" While Joseph Braun was a lowlife and a crook, everything the law said he was, he was also a loving and overindulgent father.

Dimitri met Jewel soon after she was sent home from Mt. Maplewood. At that time she was tall and slightly overweight, with a porcelain complexion and slanted amber eyes. The night they met, Braun was hosting a large dinner party at La Côte Basque. The elegant restaurant, with its blue-and-red decor and enchanting paintings of the Basque coast lining the walls, was the perfect spot for the collection of gentlemen who had made their way up from meals of homemade pasta and red wine in small family restaurants way downtown to the lavish service and ambiance of the midtown classic French restaurant. Jewel was the only woman seated at the table among the twenty-five guests. Dimitri made sure he was seated to her right, but she pointedly ignored him, deigning to talk only to her father.

Over a Waldorf salad, Dimitri managed to catch her attention by stealthily causing her glass of rich, red Opus 1962 to nearly tip over and then "saving" her dress from being ruined by catching the glass just in time. While the entrée was being served, she at least acknowledged his presence. Quickly he charmed her with a combination of compliments and astute, somewhat nasty observations about the other guests, many of whom were barely off the streets of downtown Manhattan. Jewel shared his wicked sense of humor. When fruit tarts and Amaretto were served, Jewel and Dimitri excused themselves to get a breath of fresh air. It was June, and small gardens planted and carefully cultivated at the base of the city's trees were sprouting daffodils and irises. The air was sweet and filled with the excitement of New York City in spring as they headed up 55th Street and strolled down Fifth Avenue.

From that evening on, it was an easy downhill ride to make Jewel fall in love with him. Dimitri, who had tantalized and bedded women more sophisticated and worldly than Jewel, knew exactly what he had to do. He sent her luscious bouquets and took her to the finest, most romantic restaurants, impossible-to-get-into Broadway shows, and other places where she would be surrounded and seen by the so-called beautiful people. He'd break off stolen fervent kisses, saying, "I could never take advantage of you." When they attended a fund-raiser for poor children with terminal illnesses, a charity to which he donated much money, Dimitri made sure Jewel was noticed. That Sunday, The New York Times*'s society page included their photograph, and Monday's* New York *magazine quipped:* DOES ROBIN HOOD HAVE A FAIR MARIAN? *By the time fall came, she had fallen madly in love with him, and Dimitri had saved his life. So while Braun was discussing the best way to get rid of Dimitri, Dimitri and Jewel were planning exactly when to tell Braun they were in love and planned to get married.*

To say the wedding was elaborate was to say a tidal wave might knock you over at the beach. One hundred thousand dollars' worth of partying went for the Rainbow Room, where the reception was held, the Vera Wang gown, ladies' slippers, pagonia orchids, wines from Braun's private stock, food served under the supervision of world-renowned chef Wolfgang Puck, and, to top it off, a four-foot layered wedding cake by celebrated cake designer Sylvia

Weinstock, who had created elaborate wedding cakes for such luminaries as Eddie Murphy, Whitney Houston, Liam Neeson and Natasha Richardson, and Donald Trump. Peter Duchin's orchestra provided the music. It was the wedding of New York's fall season, and no one would ever say that Joseph Braun didn't give his little girl away in style.

As a wedding gift, Braun offered his new son-in-law a bigger piece of the action. Dimitri thanked him, then announced: "It's not necessary. I intend to take over the Moonlight." The Moonlight was a hotel in Las Vegas that Dimitri had resurrected. "I can pump up the property and buy another, then another. I'll make you proud, Joseph, to have been my mentor, and I'll take good care of Jewel."

Dimitri relished watching Braun struggle with his two priorities: to prevent Dimitri from outdistancing him and to keep his daughter happy.

Despite the competition between them, Braun grew to respect Dimitri, if only for the way he controlled Jewel. As far as Dimitri was concerned, for the first year Jewel wasn't so bad, but he knew if she was suddenly out of his life, he wouldn't miss her. He could always find someone else to keep him company and fulfill his basic needs. And there were always his memories of Rose.

After their first year of marriage, the rush that came with matching her sexual prowess and drawing her to him through their shared animal magnetism faded, then ceased. Dimitri turned to one-night stands with other women. The married ones never made demands. They were needy and grateful for any erotic experience other than with their staid husbands. Sometimes he would meet women at one of the gala charity affairs Jewel always insisted they attend in order to, as she said in her poor imitation of the vernacular of graduates from the Seven Sister schools, "meet the right people."

There would never be any shortage of women attracted to Dimitri Constantinos; he knew this. As he matured into his thirties, all traces of the poor, untutored boy had been left behind. He had re-created himself into a sophisticated, engaging gentleman, a magnet for women of all kinds. But attracting women wasn't a problem; feeling something for them was.

Dimitri was working in the master bedroom in the Vanderbilt Suite at an opulent Louis XVI desk. He was reviewing documents for his upcoming meeting with Evan when he heard another television talk show host introduce Rose. Simultaneously, he also heard Jewel's determined steps as she approached from the elaborately decorated living room that separated them. She began to speak even before she got to his door. Her voice had the shrill tone it always took on when she was working herself up into one of her tantrums.

"Why is it your old flame is suddenly all over the city just when you arrive?"

The biggest mistake he'd ever made was to tell Jewel about his young love for Rose. To this day she held it against him.

"Don't start, Jewel. I'm trying to deal with serious business here, legal and financial business that could affect you and your spending sprees. I can't deal with your whining."

Her presence caused him to slouch, as though she were a weight on his shoulders. A fresh mimosa in hand, Jewel stood just a few feet away from him, hands on her hips. In her black spandex unitard and high-heeled boots, Dimitri thought she looked exactly like Catwoman.

"Come to think of it, you didn't come home last night," Jewel bitched. "Were you with her?"

Dimitri shook his head furiously. "Goddamn it, Jewel, not now!"

She paced in front of him, high heels making holes in the royal blue carpet. Then she made a turn that was no doubt planned to be dramatic, à la Joan Crawford, but her ankle twisted and she plopped indelicately on the floor, spattering her drink all over herself. Dimitri was glad of the comic relief, and while Jewel pulled herself together, he turned his attention back to the television and Rose.

Still on the floor, Jewel continued to nag, poking a finger at him. "Well, where were you?" Before he could even answer, she went on, "You came waltzing in at eight o'clock this morning. And don't tell me it was *business.* I've already called Daddy; he wasn't aware of any late meetings."

"Well, *Daddy* doesn't run my fucking life . . . he runs yours. Your father is an old man who only budges himself to try to screw, drink, or gamble. How would he know about my business? But more to the point, why do you check up on me?"

As gracefully as possible under the circumstances, Jewel pulled herself up, placed her glass on Dimitri's desk, and stood to face him, her arms now stiffly at her sides. "You expect me to just forget you once loved her?" She stuck her chin out. "Well?" she said, demanding a reply.

Dimitri removed himself mentally from this moment, this room. If she were a less self-absorbed woman, she would have seen the signs. Soon after the spectacular wedding, Jewel underwent a miraculous metamorphosis from a beautiful, albeit spoiled and reckless, young woman into a shrew. He wondered what kind of man could ever love her—and why she hadn't yet guessed that he never had.

She hadn't stopped her sullen staring, and he supposed he'd better answer.

"That was a long time ago. It's all in the past. I've told you that. Now drop it."

"Revenge will do funny things to a man," she said. "Change him into a totally different person, mostly for the worse. Or make him take his anger out on someone else."

Jewel was right, he did want revenge. But he'd never tell her. "Where'd you read that, Jewel, one of your ladies' magazines? Oh, no, I've got it, you heard it from a guest shrink on that Jerry Springer show. Certainly you didn't put those pieces together all by yourself."

He was still mentally removed from Jewel, participating in the conversation with only a sliver of his mind. The rest of his attention was concentrated on the television. "I wish you luck with your next novel and hope you'll come back and talk to us again." The talk show host pushed out her hand, and Rose shook it firmly.

"Anytime, Rosie. Your show always gives me a lift."

That was the Rose Dimitri knew, so ladylike, grateful and polite.

Dimitri's thoughts lingered in the past with Rose. He could feel her lips pressed against his that very first time, her warm body barely touching his yet making him burn.

Sometimes he found himself remembering the Rose he knew long ago, wondering why she betrayed him and when she had shed the innocence he had once so treasured. How could he have been so wrong about her? She'd made a fool out of him and left a gaping hole in his heart. Now, after all those years, it was the day of reckoning. The time had come.

"Well?"

Back to the present, Dimitri was almost surprised to find that Jewel was still in the room with him. Her face was twisted into a grotesque mask of anger and jealousy. "Are you even listening to me?"

The contrast between the woman on the couch and the young girl in his memory collided. He snapped, "Not now. I'm going to be late for my meeting. It's about the case. So, if you'll excuse me . . ."

He brushed past her on his way to the second bedroom.

"What about me?" Jewel hissed. "I wish we were back home in Spanish Hills. I hate it here. What will I do for the rest of the day?"

He turned to her and thought what an inconsequential and shallow brat she was, an irritant in expensive clothing. "Oh, I don't know, darling. I'm sure you'll find a boutique or a beauty salon you could persuade to take some of my hard-earned money."

9

Evan let out a heavy sigh, then slammed the palms of his hands against the steering wheel of his brand-new dark green Lexus. After inching through the Queens-Midtown Tunnel, he was now caught in a classic New York City gridlock—cabs, buses, and cars all brought to a halt, leaning on their horns as though that would make a difference. These were the times Evan felt he'd rather move to Peoria, Illinois, than confront the daily stress of commuting to Manhattan, or "Madhattan," as he liked to call it. He looked at his watch and realized that he'd be late for his meeting with Dimitri. He picked up his car phone and punched in the number to his office.

"Miller, Miller, and Finch," said the friendly receptionist.

"Extension 2316, please."

Two rings, then Karyn, his secretary, picked up. "Evan Miller's office, how may I help you?"

The sound of her familiar drawl jolted his memory. He realized he needed to apologize to her. Karyn had been working with him for nearly five years, and never had he even raised his voice in front of her; yet in the past two days he had snapped at her more than once for no apparent reason. He was on edge, obviously distracted by Dimitri's sudden reappearance in their lives.

"Hi, Karyn, it's me. I'm running late. If my bro . . . um, if Mr. Constantinos gets there, have him wait in my office. I'm on my way." He pictured his plain-faced, painfully thin, probably anorexic secretary with a mixture of pity and gratitude.

"Yes, Mr. Miller," she replied. "Can you hold on one minute? The other line is ringing."

Boy, that had been a dangerous slip. No one outside the family knew that Dimitri was his half-brother, and it had to stay that way.

The traffic light was red. Evan glanced down at the *New York Post* on the passenger seat. The headline read:

GUBERNATORIAL HOPEFUL EVAN MILLER WINS WIDESPREAD RECOGNITION IN MURDER TRIAL AFTER SUCCESSFUL ACQUITTAL

The case was summarized in a few short lines, as if it were a log line for a movie script:

> **Billionaire toy manufacturer is acquitted of charges that he murdered his elderly, bedridden wife. Miller proves defendant's alibi is true. The son and partner of James Miller seems to be heading for a promising political career. . . .**

The all-news radio had topped the last hour with a bit about the Dimitri Constantinos trial. The line "Who will replace Constantinos's lawyer, Jack Lester?" resounded.

Neither James nor Evan had expected Dimitri to ask for their help. They had relied too heavily on the past as an effective deterrent, assuming Dimitri would not try to reestablish contact. Even when the Constantinos trial was moved to New York, the legal community assumed that he'd retain Jack Lester, who had more experience representing cases involving the RICO laws than anybody in the city. Lester's entire practice for the last fifteen years had focused on representing defendants accused of extortion, racketeering, and money laundering.

The RICO laws were a huge umbrella under which New York had convicted an array of people on tax evasion. The collection of laws was originally conceived as an instrument through which to attack major organized crime. Activities that fell under the jurisdiction of the RICO laws included money laundering, extortion, tax evasion, and bootlegging. This was

Lester's bailiwick, but by quirk of fate, or perhaps machinations by Dimitri, Lester had suddenly announced he was "too sick" to go through the trial.

Karyn came back on the line, her voice a comforting interruption to Evan's thoughts. "That was Mr. Braun. He's going to call you any minute on your car phone. Sorry, Mr. Miller, I couldn't put him off."

"No, of course not. Thanks, Karyn, I'll see you soon."

Evan hung up, groaning. His father was in denial about how injurious handling Joseph Braun was to Evan's bid for the governorship. Kevin Allen had made no secret of the fact that he'd like a chance at the governorship. This trial would give Allen an optimum opportunity to tie the Miller name to Braun and all that he represented. Aside from the prosecutor's desire to run for office, the district attorney's office had been trying to put Dimitri's father-in-law away for the last ten years, as long as Evan had been in the firm. In that time, Joseph Braun had been arrested twice for tax evasion and once last year on racketeering charges. The DA never could get anything to stick on Braun because the government did not have the resources to come up against Miller, Miller, and Finch's high-priced legal talent. Evan knew Allen's tactics, and he assumed the DA would attempt to go after Braun yet again, this time to turn him into a star witness against Dimitri. But it wasn't going to happen. And if they didn't get Braun, or someone close to Dimitri, to talk, they'd never convict either one of them.

Nevertheless, Evan had tried to convince James that representing Joseph Braun wasn't good business. "He makes us look bad, Father. We need party support. We're representing the wrong client. Let's get rid of him."

"I don't want to, Evan. And I can't do it."

James had a blind spot when it came to Braun, and Evan had an inkling why. Joseph Braun and James Miller must have some connection. Evan often wondered how the firm had gone from lobby law and its notorious high-class clientele to defending Joseph Braun and now Dimitri Constantinos.

Evan's thoughts switched back to Rose. She hadn't looked good this morning. She seemed tired and worried. He dialed her office number on his speed dialer, but the voice mail picked up. "I love you," was the simple message he left.

The cell phone rang. His caller ID displayed Joseph Braun's home number. Evan let the phone ring a few times while he put a finger to his temple to stop the pounding that had started there. On the fourth ring, he answered, "Joseph, how are you?" remaining, as always, courteous and polite.

Braun ignored the pleasantries. "I read about your big win this morning. You're the lawyer of the moment," he rasped, his laugh a revolting combination of morning phlegm and fractiousness. "But I didn't call you for that. I'm assuming you'll take my son-in-law's case. The jury's all picked, and before he had to leave the case, Jack said there wasn't a more favorable jury in Manhattan. So we have to proceed quickly, and I know you're the best at picking up the ball." He paused, perhaps waiting for a reaction; but when there was none he continued, "Anyway, I assured Dimitri that you wouldn't refuse any request of mine."

The sound of the signal breaking up as Evan finally entered the tunnel gave him a chance to think. Braun's strong-arm tactics were as offensive as James's unreasonable behavior at breakfast. Between the two of them, he couldn't win. A sunken, helpless feeling came over him, and he felt his stomach twist into a knot. James had created this mess. Now it was up to Evan to try to maneuver through it. At this moment, his fury at James was the strongest emotion he felt. Why wouldn't Braun assume they'd oblige him? They'd never denied him anything in the past.

"Evan?" Braun said.

"Sorry, I lost you there in the tunnel. The traffic is just unbelievable."

"My son-in-law's case?"

"I . . . I'm not too familiar with the case, Joseph," Evan tried to hedge. "Perhaps one of the other attorneys in the firm would be better suited." Out of all the partners, Miller, Miller, and Finch had three defense attorneys including himself. The others specialized in lobby law. Evan was now resigned to having the firm take Dimitri on—but at least he could distance himself.

"You'll take it, my boy. He wants you." This time Braun's tone was harsh. "I'll talk to you tomorrow morning. Oh . . . and give your father my regards." The line went dead.

The light turned green and Evan inched up a few more feet. How ironic, he thought—two half-brothers, their blood ties kept secret all of these years, would now have their different worlds entwined in public. If his own life were not so dominated by James's worship of the Miller family destiny, he mused, he would probably want to handle his brother's case, if only out of a feeling of obligation. He had never been comfortable as the so-called chosen one. Life had always felt too easy for him. Money had never been a problem; he'd skated through school, graduating with honors; and once in the world, he'd quickly advanced to an outstanding career any man would envy. His entire life had been carefully orchestrated by his father, except, of course, for his marriage to Rose. And in this one victory over his father, Dimitri had been cheated by Evan again.

Finally, Evan pulled into the garage beneath the firm's building at 501 Park Avenue. He stepped out and nodded to the parking attendant, a young Hispanic man named Juan. Evan had once struck up a conversation when Juan had shyly pointed out how much he admired Evan's Lexus. An earnest young man who had started working in the garage when he was sixteen, Juan was now attending City College while working full-time.

"Good morning, Juan. Busy day?"

The young man smiled. "Yes, sir, Mr. Miller, busy as always, but you know you'll get the best spot in the garage." He pointed with his finger. "Right up front so I can keep an eye on it all day for you."

Evan nodded appreciatively. The special treatment was unnecessary since he had his own reserved spot, but it made Juan feel good and Evan made sure to tip him extra for the service. With a wave, he headed toward the elevator.

Evan would first try to convince Dimitri it wasn't in his best interests to be represented by him, given the firm's association with Braun. He hoped to appeal to Dimitri's pride and play off the built-in rivalry between the two men. Be careful, he warned himself. Explain it in the best possible way—use gentle tactics. Don't step on any toes. He expected to appeal to Dimitri's common sense. He went over the main argument in his head: it might not be a good idea to have his father-in-law in his corner since Braun was always under suspicion.

If that didn't work, he might appeal to Dimitri's humanity—if he still had any. Perhaps he should just lay it on the line and tell his brother that James did not want the firm to represent him and could make it very difficult. If that worked, he'd have to figure out what to do about Braun's insistence that he handle Dimitri's case. The logistics were making Evan feel like a ball of twine in a kitten's paw.

When the elevator doors opened, he stepped into the lobby of one of the most prestigious office buildings in New York. He entered the glass penthouse elevator reserved for Miller, Miller, and Finch and rode to the top of the world. The windows in the waiting room of the firm looked out onto the top of the Empire State Building. The colors of the lights of the formidable landmark building were changed frequently to signal a holiday, ceremony, celebration, or visit from a foreign minister. The nights he worked late, Evan habitually glanced at the building to admire its lights, allowing his eyes to take in Manhattan's splendor. This ritual never failed to pump him up.

He rushed past the row of cubicles that housed law clerks, office temps, paralegals, and special-case investigators, until he reached his office. Karyn was seated at her desk right outside his office door. She didn't smile this morning but instead unconsciously pulled on her neat brown braid, which held her hair off her face. Her serious look brought Evan down to earth. In an instant, he felt his confidence slip away.

"Mr. Constantinos is waiting inside."

Evan cleared his throat, straightened his shoulders, and entered his office.

Dimitri was settled comfortably in a corner of the plush black leather sofa. A San Pellegrino water with lime was placed on the sleek chrome-and-glass coffee table next to him. His eyes were stuck on a silver-framed photo of Rose. So the best man had won, Dimitri thought. Evan had locked himself into paradise with Rose. Beautiful, gentle, deceiving Rose. Evan had the ideal wife, the faultless daughter, the consummate career, the completely perfect life . . . It should have been his life.

10

Dimitri had arrived at Laurel when he was sixteen, having been used as a bartering tool between his mother and his father, James Miller. Marie was tired of living on the Lower East Side. She was up to here with being an escort and a single mother. James would either take Dimitri off her hands or she'd expose the existence of his "secret son." Dimitri overheard the phone calls between Marie, his mother, and someone he would later grow to understand was James's lawyer. It was clear they were throwing money at her, but no amount would do. She wanted out.

Dimitri listened and tried not to care. Still, a little voice inside was asking why she had to get rid of him in order to leave the city. Or why the money he gave her from running odd jobs around the neighborhood wasn't enough. Why wasn't he enough? When the duel was over, arrangements were made and James's driver picked up Dimitri at his mother's apartment and drove him the forty minutes to Laurel. He never rode in the Miller limousine again. From that moment until he went to jail, Dimitri was a constant reminder to James of an inappropriate affair, a miscalculated peccadillo.

James had agreed to raise him because Dimitri was old enough to know the truth about his father and possibly reckless enough to reveal it. James couldn't take that chance. All his life he had successfully avoided public scandal, and he intended to keep it that way. From the time he arrived, Dimitri was known in the mansion and to those who asked as an orphaned teenager Mr. Miller had taken in—another one of Mr. Miller's charities.

Constantinos was his mother's name. She was of Greek descent, which accounted for his dark hair and tanned Mediterranean skin color. Before Dimitri left their apartment for Laurel she made it very clear that she didn't want to hear from him. His mother left no forwarding address, and he never heard from or about her again.

Dimitri began work as a groom in the Millers' stables, often putting in twelve-hour days. He was paid a small wage, which he spent on trips back to his old neighborhood, where he'd keep up with his gang. He had no one else. The tightly packed tenements with mothers gossiping on the stoops and small, nearly hidden restaurants that "outsiders" never knew about became his world. Dimitri loved the energy that differentiated Little Italy from any other community in Manhattan. The combined chemistry of passion, danger, family loyalty, and an overarching code that bound the people together would not easily be replaced.

But slowly he adjusted to James Miller's world. James was part of New York's powerful elite, and the members of that select crowd were constantly attending parties, meetings, and intimate dinners at Laurel. Dimitri would find out through the other servants' gossip when one of these events was planned, and he'd make certain to be in attendance at staff dinners on those evenings. The cleanup duty was always divided among the staff, and Dimitri would volunteer to clear the tables. It was easy then to engage the cook, Sinead, in small talk. As the serving staff passed in and out, they'd invariably gossip about the guests at the party: who was tipsy, what the guests were talking about. Dimitri drank in these details. On the nights he worked as a valet, he would observe how the rich dressed, smelled, what jewelry they wore, and what small talk they made. He knew that one day he'd make his mark. He was sure of it. But for now he would be patient and not draw any attention to himself from the old man. When the thought of running away crossed his mind, he'd remember what he'd seen happen to guys his age on the street. He would bide his time, save money, and make plans. But then he met Rose.

Evan went to the Dalton School in New York City, so he was not around all the time. To Dimitri's surprise, his brother was the one to initiate their friendship. It was Evan who first brought up the blood tie between them, saying his father was a coward and a phony for not recognizing Dimitri as his son. "I'll never do that," Evan said more than once.

Fat chance, *Dimitri would say to himself. But Evan would always surprise him. He was loyal and generous with his spirit, and if Dimitri had let him, he would have been generous with his money.*

Several neighboring young ladies either boarded horses at the Millers' stables or rode James's horses for hunts and shows, and Dimitri saw and heard enough to form some strong opinions about these teenagers. They were boy crazy, loved horses, and were eager to perfect their skills handling both. Obsessed with their looks, clothes, and status with their peers, they could be charming. Mostly they were demanding, catty, and conceited. To his amusement, or perhaps astonishment, when he turned seventeen, the girls went from treating him like a stable hand to practicing their man-trapping skills on him. One girl, whose name was Daphne, an heir to the Bellisima cosmetics fortune, could ride like a demon. Her long red hair, which flowed out her hunt hat and down her back, exactly matched the color of her Thoroughbred gelding. One Saturday, at dusk, when all the other boarders had bedded down their horses and the adults had retired to the mansion for cocktails, Daphne found him in the tack room putting away saddles. Without a by-your-leave, she kissed him—a French kiss. How this thirteen-year-old had developed such skill didn't cross Dimitri's mind. Mostly he concentrated on disentangling himself gracefully. From then on he was careful that no one snuck up behind him in the stable.

Dimitri remembered the day he first met Rose. Two months after he arrived, he was currying a particularly skittish horse named Maxwell when he heard a noise and looked over his shoulder to find a young girl hovering in the open doorway. Mistaking her for one of the daughters of the rich and having learned his lesson from Daphne, he put on his sternest face and asked if he could saddle up a horse for her.

"No, thank you." Her voice was soft.

He remembered how she'd looked over one shoulder, toward Tom the caretaker's cabin, and wondered if perhaps this was the niece he had heard about from Evan. She matched the description his brother had given him: she was wholesome, beautiful, and fresh. She had hair the color of honey streaked lightly with gold and a pair of startlingly large, long-lashed, luminous green eyes that regarded him and the rest of the world with genuine interest. They were expressive eyes, bright with intelligence, glowing with life, yet filled with what seemed a bottomless sadness. Before he could engage her in conversation, she was gone, and it felt as if she'd taken the fresh air with her.

Later that night she returned, this time with a bowl of piping hot stew, two apples, and a glass of milk.

"I didn't know if you had already eaten, so I fixed you a plate."

"Well, aren't you kind," he said.

She nodded, her cheeks blushing, then quickly disappeared into the stillness of nightfall. After that she returned every night at the same time with food. At first he guessed she did it out of sympathy, since he was by himself all the time. But after a few months he could tell she regarded him with genuine concern and care. Her kindness caught him completely off-guard. Her simple offerings touched a place inside him he hadn't known existed. And it was easy for those feelings to become something else. Though he knew she was only thirteen, it was hard to keep his hormones under control. But he did. It was soon after that Rose caught Evan and Dimitri smoking marijuana in the woods and they became a threesome. This was the happiest time of Dimitri's adolescence, perhaps in his whole life.

Rose and Dimitri's friendship consisted of their talks at night, which included what she called "read-ins." She shared with him all that she was learning from the education James was providing for her.

In exchange for teaching him the basics of history, literature, and math, Dimitri taught Rose how to ride Monterey, a sixteen-hand German warmblood, and marveled at how graceful she looked saddled up. Never mind the expensive jodhpurs, blazers, and boots of the other girls. In her patched jeans, flannel shirts, and sneakers, Rose presented such an elegant portrait that she and the magnificent horse seemed one.

Dimitri set up the jump course at the most advanced level, and the young woman and powerful horse flew over the fences, Rose never missing a beat, Monterey never refusing. Rose seemed to derive sustenance from riding, and as the years moved on, the sadness he once saw in her eyes began to disappear.

Some nights she couldn't come because she got off work too late, and he found himself missing her. Rose was like a burst of sunshine in his otherwise dreary life. Four years passed until Dimitri put a name to what he felt for Rose.

One night in the little annex off the barn, she lost her footing while reaching for one of the books they were reading together. He quickly came up behind her, catching her in his arms, and seconds later he found himself pulling her closer, locking her in his embrace, not wanting to let her go. In his head he heard words of warning, a voice screaming at him to stop, to stay away from trouble; but he couldn't fight back. She was at that perfect point between seventeen and eighteen, where adolescence and young womanhood meet. Every move she made captivated him. In his mind he had made love to her a thousand times. He pressed his lips against hers with a fervor he knew was passion, though he never had experienced a kiss like that before.

Growing impatient, Dimitri stood and began to pace, stopping to check the view from the windows behind Evan's desk. The office building was located in the old PanAm building, now Metropolitan Life. The tower straddled Park Avenue. Grand Central Station was directly beneath Dimitri's line of vision, and he could see commuters scurrying in and out of the landmark building. He could see the distinctive art deco top of the Chrysler Building. Dimitri had heard that James had been one of the bidders on the Chrysler Building when it recently went up for sale. Why he had decided to play in the New York City real estate market was anybody's guess. Dimitri thought that perhaps James had grown tired of paper investments. Knowing how tenacious the old man was, Dimitri was certain that now that his father had caught the real estate bug, he would pursue this avenue until he owned some of Manhattan's valuable properties. Of course, Evan would inherit that along with everything else the Millers owned. Evan was the last Miller man, unless he and Rose had a son.

The thought disturbed him, and he walked away from the window. Amid Evan's college and law school degrees hanging on the wall were framed photos, mostly of James or Evan or both with some celebrity. Ronald Reagan smiling as he clasped James's hand. Lyndon Johnson and Evan at a White House ceremony when Evan was just a child. A signed photo of Nelson Rockefeller. It was this that made Dimitri feel cheated, not the money, not the future in politics. He envied the ease with which

Evan took all his life for granted because he was the golden one, the son who hadn't been a source of shame.

The door burst open and Evan entered, offering apologies about traffic. The men shook hands perfunctorily. Dimitri's palm was cool. Evan began to perspire. How many years had it been since they'd seen each other? Evan could see that, as he matured, Dimitri looked more like the ne'er-do-well with the chivalrous manner and romantic streak that Marlon Brando had played so successfully in *On the Waterfront.* The resemblance was pronounced, particularly since Dimitri's face was stripped of any semblance of friendliness. He was all business.

Evan dropped his briefcase on the classic mahogany Chippendale desk with its inlaid black leather blotter. He had taken over the desk, as well as the office, from Albert Finch, the man who had been James's first partner. Finch had died a few years back, but the firm still carried his name. Dimitri returned to the sofa across the room. Evan was suddenly worried and tired.

Dimitri, on the other hand, was obviously very composed, and he let out a relaxed sigh and paused to scrutinize his brother before speaking.

"So, Evan, we both know why I am here, you have all the details. What's your strategy for me?"

Evan stared at him, not saying a word. Their phone call yesterday had been stripped of all civility, and today was the same. Dimitri didn't seem interested in catching up on the years since they'd seen each other, and Evan, though used to playing by society's rules, was damned if he'd break the ice.

"Is something wrong?" Dimitri asked. "Surely you've given some thought to my case."

There was a moment of silence in which Evan glanced reflexively at the photo of Rose on his desk. When he spoke, the words came out in a rush: "It's Rose. I don't think this is such a good idea. In fact, I'm convinced it will take a huge toll on her."

Dimitri's eyes widened for a moment. "Am I supposed to feel sorry for her? For either of you?" He cleared his throat, a signal Evan recognized even now as his half-brother's way of buying time to gather his thoughts.

"Look, I'm not oblivious. Did you think I hadn't considered all the angles before coming to you?" Dimitri's voice was smooth, conversational, but otherwise he seemed like an automaton, his expression devoid of emotion. "The fact is, Lester had to leave the case."

Evan raised his eyebrows.

"No, I didn't make him fake a heart attack. He's still in the hospital, in fact."

This information eased Evan's mind. That Lester really had to bow out validated Dimitri's reason for coming to the firm.

"Did you consider how difficult it was for me to come to you? I need a great lawyer and a great defense." He rose from the couch and stared out the window at the Manhattan skyline. "I've read all the press releases concerning your wins. In fact, I've been following your entire career. And you are, after all, family." Dimitri smiled in a facetious way.

"I'm very impressed. In fact, I find it all quite fortuitous—the entire chain of events that led me to be tried here rather than in Nevada and then Lester having his heart attack. You might say our new association was preordained." He took a large gulp of San Pellegrino. "I want you, no one else. Explain to your wife that she'll have to put her fears and her personal feelings aside for now. We both know business is business. Right, brother?"

Evan knew there were hundreds of prominent and capable defense attorneys in New York City. He wanted to believe that Jack Lester had not been manipulated by Dimitri. This morning he would have sworn that was the case, but now, seeing his brother face-to-face, he had the distinct feeling that whatever had led them to this juncture, it was not Dimitri's doing. Maybe it was preordained. Still, he had other arguments to make.

"Well, I didn't want to bring this up, Dimitri. But as your brother, I think it is my duty to appeal to your intelligence. I know Braun wants us to represent you." Evan smiled for emphasis. "My strong opinion is that the prosecutor is going to use him to get you. They're going to get Braun any time now. It's inevitable. From their point of view, they can get two birds with one stone. If the government comes after Braun, who are we going to choose and who are we going to sacrifice?" Evan was speaking from his gut now because he knew James would sacrifice Dimitri if it came to that. In fact, James would relish it. And, for Dimitri, that was dangerous.

Dimitri swatted Evan's words away. "I'll take the chance."

Karyn could be heard on the intercom: "Your wife is on line one." Their eyes met.

Evan watched as Dimitri exited, closing the door behind him.

11

Kevin Allen glanced around his cluttered, stuffy office, whose standard-size window, streaked with grime, looked out over Centre Street not far away from Wall Street, where the legal community conveniently mixed with their criminal clientele. DAs were not supposed to have impressive offices. Leave that to the Johnnie Cochrans or Raoul Felders of the world. Taxpayers didn't like to see money spent on leather sofas and expensive ficas. But that never mattered to Kevin. He'd started at the bottom as an assistant DA, had risen to the top, and would go further if he could. Specifically, he had set his sights on beating Evan Miller in the primary for governor. There weren't any other notable contenders for the ticket, and the incumbent had served his two terms. Even though all the vultures would come out for the job, there were just two serious candidates. The only obstacle was Evan Miller, with his old-moneyed, politically connected, millionaire, powerhouse father.

So far, all bets were on Miller. Evan was a brilliant attorney, no question. He always managed to win the most visible cases, the ones that struck at the heart of the city. He defended a Hasidic Jew arrested for killing a Hispanic man who Evan proved was selling drugs outside yeshivas and had caused a number of deaths from overdoses in the ultra-Orthodox neighborhood. That was a big press lightning rod and a tremendous score for Evan. Then, back to back, he turned around and defended an African American schoolteacher who killed her white husband. The state argued the killing was premeditated. But Evan convinced the jury that "cold-blooded" murder was relative, as was premeditated. Evan argued successfully that the husband had been killing his wife for over twenty years, spiritually, mentally, and physically. He turned the concept of premeditation on its ear. While Evan was a brilliant attorney, Kevin was convinced his silver-tongued opponent did not have the right political background to be governor. He had never held public office. But then again, Kevin figured, voters didn't really care. Evan could step out of his law practice and right into the governor's mansion just as John F. Kennedy Jr. could step down as publisher of *George* magazine and make it right into Congress or possibly the Senate. Generations of money, power, and connections were what turned constituents' heads.

Kevin wanted the governor's seat for all the right reasons. Twenty years of working hard for the legal system had taught him that crime control was winning. The media cheered the drop in violent crime. In the city, and on the streets, life was becoming safer. But on a larger, more insidious level, the law's foundation was being undermined by intelligent and powerful criminals. What did Evan Miller know about crime?

The closest people around Kevin kept telling him he was kidding himself: "Don't make yourself into one of those kooky candidates who just divide the party," his personal attorney, Robert Sanders, had said. But Sanders had agreed nevertheless to manage the preliminary stages of Kevin's campaign before he threw his surprise hat into the ring. It was a start.

Kevin licked his lips, then traced the label affixed to the folder in his lap with his forefinger and read the word silently: "Constantinos."

The newest information it contained on Dimitri was explosive, if it was true, but he didn't trust the source. It came from Sheila, an escort who worked for a service allegedly owned by Braun, and he wondered where she had come up with this evidence. Sheila had come through before with information on Braun in exchange for immunity—some of the evidence had been good, some unusable, all of it penny-ante stuff. It was Sheila who had informed him that Braun had a silent partner in the business, a partner who Kevin had learned from the new documents was James Miller. An interesting aside. Now she claimed a boyfriend of hers had been one of a crew employed by Dimitri to shake down deadbeats. Sheila didn't have any hard evidence—not yet. But she said she was willing to get it on tape, or maybe they could bag the boyfriend and make a deal.

Kevin needed more. He either needed to corroborate Sheila's information about Dimitri's extortion activities or he had to decide whether or not he could live with himself if he used evidence he didn't trust. If he used both the information she'd given him on the shakedowns and her claim that James Miller was a partner in an illegal escort service, he'd not only bring down Dimitri Constantinos, he'd expose the Miller family as well. He'd probably get something on Braun in the bargain.

Kevin checked through his daily log of incoming calls until he found the number he was looking for. This just might be the person who could back up the evidence that could be as explosive as C-4. He dialed the number. When the woman answered she spoke in a whisper, as if she were not alone, and suggested that she call him back again tomorrow.

The call gave him a positive feeling; he was going to win and smear the Millers.

Not too hasty, he told himself. Be careful. In the case of the *People* vs. *Dimitri Constantinos,* every player had something to hide, including U.S. District Attorney Kevin Allen.

Rose was behind schedule as she ended her segment on Rosie O'Donnell's show. After thanking the audience during a commercial break, she exited the small red carpeted stage, with its tasteful plants and light colored wooden desk for Rosie with the visitor's chair close by. Thankful to get away from the hot lights, Rose quickly replaced the heavy stage makeup with a dash of lipstick and blush, grabbed her black-lined Burberry from the coat rack in the green room, and hurried into the car Dario had sent for her.

She climbed in and slid across the seat. The driver pulled out into the late morning traffic and whisked her across town. Rose tried to focus on her hectic schedule. Lunch with Dario, a signing, two more live interviews, and then a sit-down interview at her apartment for *In Style* magazine. Her mind kept returning to the two packages she had received—a box of live roses and then this morning's box of dead roses. Last night at the party the thought had crossed her mind that Dimitri was behind the nasty messages. But in the light of day she realized how preposterous that was.

So who would play such a sick game? And what if it wasn't just a sick prank? What if someone really was watching her, taking in her every move?

12

Dario Roselli's childhood, in downtrodden Newark, New Jersey, could be described as deprived. As an only child in a family subsisting just above the poverty line, Dario decided early on that what he needed to make him happy was money. While his mother took in sewing jobs from neighbors, his father drove from county to county, calling on small independent bookstores to sell a line of vanity press books, poorly written novels, and self-serving collections of advice by amateurs. Dario's father was one of many "commission reps" struggling to make an honest living. By the time Dario was thirteen, he had realized that the only way to get ahead in life was to hustle. He needed a plan.

Dario spent most of his time at strip malls, where he would lift as much merchandise as he could conceal beneath the bulky clothes he wore. He stored the goods in a trunk in the back of an alley close to his home, using a simple combination lock to protect his stash. At the end of the week he would cart his supply to a nearby indoor flea market where he had rented a spot and would unload the goods for a decent price. By the time he turned sixteen he was running one of the biggest fencing operations from Newark to Manhattan. Dario was a one-man operation: he did the stealing, the carting, and the fencing, giving money to his parents, who did not ask any questions about where it came from, and saving the rest of his money for tomorrow.

His success made Dario come alive; it made him feel high. At seventeen he drove a shiny new Mustang, wore expensive clothes, and always had a wad of cash in his pocket. But then he got his first taste of the downside. He was caught lifting a Sony color TV from Sears. Six months in the juvenile center cured him of his craving for big money from fencing. In fact, his time there was actually good for him. He spent the time thinking, plotting, and reading books like Dale Carnegie's How to Win Friends and Influence People. *His mind was opened to the possibilities for making money in legitimate business, money even bigger than he'd made by fencing. He realized there were legitimate businesses to which he could apply himself with just as much success as fencing. Once released, he re-created himself. Every day he read* The New York Times, The Washington Post, The Wall Street Journal *and magazines like* GQ *and* Forbes. *He read anything that could help him acquire taste and knowledge of rich men's interest and lifestyle. During those years Dario cleaned up his image. When he finally made it, his only regret was that his father never lived to enjoy the rewards of Dario's success. When Dario was just eighteen, six months out of the juvenile detention center, his dad died of a heart attack while on the road.*

Realizing that he was now financially responsible for his mother, Dario got serious about moving into a career. He responded to an ad in The New York Times *and was hired by a prestigious public relations firm in Manhattan. The ad had read "Assistant needed for busy public relations firm; no experience needed; will train." Well, that was good—it meant he wouldn't need an impressive résumé. When he showed up for the interview, he met with a man in the personnel office. Dario would learn to recognize this type—a "suit." The personnel manager, a man named Frank, was easy to read. He was rigid about company requirements. And he liked to think the agency, Brogel & Co., could not get along without him. After reviewing his application, Frank said, "So, you want to be a publicist?"*

Dario smiled modestly. "That's right, the best."

"Okay, you're in luck. We can use someone like you."

Dario was psyched. He had already made a mental list of the kinds of celebrities he would handle: musicians, actors, politicians, maybe even some writers.

"I know I can't start at the top," Dario said, "but as soon as I learn the ropes . . ."

"Right," Frank answered, not really listening. "First thing in the morning, you'll see to it all the executives have coffee. And then you can run the copy machine, answer the phones, deliver packages, take lunch orders—that sort of thing."

Dario was disappointed but not discouraged. He was quite certain that he would be the best PR guy in town. And it wouldn't take long.

Within months, according to feedback from his superiors and from Frank, Dario was considered the best gofer the firm ever had. He was at work an hour early and always volunteered to stay late if one of the publicists needed his help. In these after hours he would listen to the agents' phone calls and pick up important tips on how to conduct himself and how to handle clients. He got to know the four senior publicists by making small talk in the elevator or delivering mail to their secretaries. Dario remembered how many children the secretary to the senior publicist had. He knew all of their names, their ages—even their favorite toys. He learned that the assistant publicist, just above him on the totem pole, was a heroin addict in recovery and needed someone to cover for him if he got crazy and needed to get to a Narcotics Anonymous meeting. He knew that personal information and stroking egos was the way to get ahead in publicity.

The problem was that at the end of one year, Dario was still a gofer. He took a trip down to personnel to see Frank.

"I think I'm ready to move forward—take on a client or two of my own," Dario said earnestly. "If you give me a chance, I'm sure I could . . ."

The suit did not even look up from the paperwork he was attending to. "There's nothing yet. Get me a cup of coffee, son."

Dario realized he wouldn't get far at this rate. He needed a plan.

One morning as he was making coffee, the phone rang. The client, obviously quite upset, mistook him for her publicist, Roger Reeves. She dove right into spilling her story about a crisis that needed immediate damage control.

"Roger, I need help. If those photos get out, I'll . . . I'll be ruined." Gina Kellogg, a rising actress playing a serious role in the latest Merchant-Ivory film, sounded frantic. "My movie premieres in a week. You can't let them print those photos."

"Calm down," Dario said with confidence. "Roger's out of town. Start at the beginning, tell me everything."

Two hours and four phone calls later, Dario had everything under control. He reached out to an old friend from Newark: George DeSantis, nicknamed "Ugly George," was a major publisher and distributor of pornographic publications, including the magazine Inside Peep, *which had purchased extremely hot photos of Gina Kellogg taken when she was just starting out. Dario begged DeSantis for a favor.*

Dario explained his dilemma. "I need you to withdraw the pictures. I'll pay you back one day, big time."

Of all things, it was through his association with Rose that Dario did indeed return the favor. DeSantis was later busted on a narcotics charge. As distasteful as it was to Dario, he prevailed upon Rose to get Evan's firm to represent DeSantis. DeSantis served no time.

At the time of Dario's "save," Roger Reeves was the most senior publicist in the firm, and Gina Kellogg was his newest and hottest client. He was more than grateful when he learned of Dario's intervention. "How did you do it?"

"I know some people." Dario shrugged it off as if it were nothing.

"You can expect a bonus in this week's paycheck," he said to Dario.

"Actually, I was thinking more along the lines of a promotion," Dario replied without hesitation. Who knew when there would be another window of opportunity like this?

Reeves studied Dario a moment, then said, "Okay, I'll give you a chance. You'll start out as my assistant and work your way up from there."

In six months Dario had acquired twenty clients. His MO was to combine charm, appropriate intimacy, and proof of his cunning at optimum times. Probably the most important asset in his toolbox was his gift for making all of them feel that they were his most important. Furthermore, he was a damn good publicist. He kept all of them in the news, at the front of the public's mind.

One day he approached Roger's office and asked for two weeks off.

His boss looked at him curiously. "Dario, I have to hand it to you, you've got nerve. Most people who work in publicity or advertising are afraid to leave their desks for five minutes. You know how public relations firms operate. We're all disposable. Aren't you afraid you'll be replaced?"

"Why should I be? You know what I'm worth. Besides, I'm not taking time off, I'm heading out to L.A. to bring us back a stable full of impressive new clients."

And he did just that. Rock stars in need of damage control, aging actors in need of a comeback, and young models looking to secure their wholesome image or make it in the movies. Within one year Dario Roselli was bringing in more revenue than any of the senior publicists. His career was in motion.

At Le Cirque 2000, Dario was seated at his usual table, the one in the corner with the spectacular view of the room. He loved its chaotic swirl of colors in the futuristic circus motif; it calmed him. Now he watched Sirio Maccioni, the owner, usher Rose to the table. Normally the well-known restaurateur stayed behind the scenes, but when he knew in advance that one of his favorite celebrities, such as Rose Miller, was coming, he was always there to greet them. Dario stood up as Maccioni helped Rose to her seat. He noticed the worried look on her face.

"What's wrong, Rose? You look a bit off."

Rose pretended not to hear him. "Have you seen my schedule for the rest of the day?"

Dario pulled out a black folder from his attaché case and skimmed through some papers.

"Nonstop," Rose persisted.

"You know the program by now, Rose. Boardman Books has the right to decide how much time and money they'll spend. Your contract guarantees them you'll tour, and they insisted you do absolutely every appearance I could get. You're my prize client; you know how well I've always handled you. I know what's best for you, Rose. Can I help it that every show and magazine wants you? You're a hit!"

And you're a snake charmer, she thought, looking back at him. If he knew how busy she was, what had been the point of this lunch? And if he was so concerned about her, how would he justify missing her own book party? Something in Rose's stomach twisted.

"Do you know what's best for me, Dario?"

"Are you doubting me?" He shot her an angry glance.

"You still haven't explained why you missed the party last night."

"Something extremely important came up. An executive of Mishibuto was in New York for just one night. He wants me to represent him. We met for an early dinner. We had a few glasses of wine, one thing led to another. I lost all track of time. Honestly, Rose, if it wasn't of major importance, you know I would have been there."

Rose shrugged it off. "Relax, Dario, I'm just tired." She wished she were far away.

"You know, Rose, I'm worried about you. Lately every little thing seems to bother you. You seem distant. What's going on? Is it Evan? Are things okay at home?"

Dario tried to hide his jealousy of Evan, but every once in a while he wanted to break his agreement with Rose to keep their relationship all business and tell her how he really felt about her marriage. She was shortchanged. Evan was rich, well connected, blah, blah, but it was clear he wasn't touching something inside Rose. She had always seemed to have a sadness beneath her surface, but lately it was more pronounced. He knew what Rose needed, the woman inside the woman she presented to everyone, including her husband. She'd be much happier with a partner who had a different temperament from Evan's.

They ate in silence, Rose picking at her Caesar salad, Dario scoffing down a plate of broiled red snapper.

When the waiter cleared their plates, Dario was the first to break the heavy silence.

"We have the awards ceremony tomorrow night for the Mystery Writers Guild. You do remember?"

"We?" Rose asked.

"You and I," Dario returned. His coal black eyes bored into her, issuing a challenge. Undaunted, Rose stared back. Dario suspected that on some level Rose was attracted to him. Objectively speaking, he knew he was a handsome man, though his dark looks were interesting in an unconventional way. He did his best: he kept his wavy jet black hair off his face, revealing a high widow's peak, and wore elegant Gucci horn-rimmed glasses to offset his rather pronounced nose. Dario's reputation as a ladies' man was founded on the string of ambitious executives he dated and discarded. Sally Hanson, publisher of *On Top,* a new 'zine, was this month's latest. Before Sally there had been a woman with a seat on the Exchange. The list of hearts Dario Roselli had broken was long. But it was essential they be smart and well connected. Rose had once observed that there never seemed to be a break between them, which, she said, told her none of them had touched his heart. And she was right.

"What about Evan? I'm sure—"

"No," Dario announced. "It's better we go alone. Less for me to deal with, publicity-wise." As he spoke his fingers were toying with the red rose in a bud vase that sat at the center of the table. His fingers lightly cupped the bud in a caress.

Rose tried to ignore the agitation rising within her. *Stop it. You're overreacting.* But the questions about him still nagged at her. "What did you need to see me for, Dario? Couldn't we have discussed this over the phone?"

A gloomy look came over Dario's face. "Well, I thought it would be nice to see each other." He lifted the rose bud tenderly from the vase. "And I wanted to give you this."

He smiled a teasing smile, and Rose wished she could go back to two days ago, when this gesture on his part would have been just that, a joke between friends. But now her heart was banging out a warning. The cold, dull feeling deep down inside told her she was in danger.

Heading uptown in the limo for her signing at Madison Avenue Bookshop, Rose dialed Evan, needing the comforting sound of his voice. Karyn put her through immediately.

"Hello, darling."

"Rose, what a delightful surprise."

"I was just thinking maybe we could meet tonight for dinner."

"You don't want me to come to the signing? I was planning on it."

"I think it will be easier if I just plowed through the rest of the afternoon and evening. Then I thought we could have a romantic dinner."

"That sounds lovely. Shall I make a reservation at Match?"

"Yes. Make it for six-thirty so that I have enough time before I go on *Larry King Live.*"

"Fine. I'll see you then. Bye, love."

Feeling totally spent, Rose stepped out of the car and headed into the restaurant. It was six forty-five, and she was sure that Evan was already seated, a bottle of Cristal champagne waiting. Rose loved Match Uptown for its size. Like its name, the restaurant was small and narrow. The intimate space and subdued lighting made her feel as though she were dining alone with loved ones, friends. The menu, the care that went into each dish's preparation and presentation, and the genteel service reminded Rose of romantic bistros she and Evan had enjoyed in Paris. Usually it took months to get a reservation, but she and Evan came here regularly and the maître d' always found room for them.

After completing a meal of Osetra caviar, sweet corn bisque, and roasted monkfish, Rose started to feel human again. In the safe presence of her husband, the stalker had also receded from her mind. She leaned across the small round table to caress his cheek. "This was just what the doctor ordered."

After a moment, Rose registered that Evan was not responding, or rather he was attempting to be attentive, but they were on different wavelengths, out of tune with each other. "What is it, darling?" She removed her hand from his cheek. All of the signals he was sending were telling her to brace herself.

"Dimitri is joining us any minute for dessert."

Rose waited, but he didn't say anything more. She went numb, momentarily deprived of reason. She couldn't think clearly enough to ask why he was coming and why Evan had waited until the last minute to tell her.

Only one question penetrated the fog in her mind: What should she do? Should she smile? Act nonchalant? Before she could resolve this dilemma, the other diners in the close space all looked to the door, and Rose knew it was Dimitri moving toward them. She turned ever so slightly to watch him approach their table.

Even though she was seated, Rose could feel her legs begin to weaken, and she leaned into the plush burgundy velvet banquette. She was transported out of the present, unaware of the whispers of the other guests, who now recognized her as well as Dimitri. She felt her champagne glass begin to slip from her fingers. She knew Evan was here, but it was only Dimitri she saw.

"Hello, Rose." Dimitri's voice was deep, though he spoke barely above a whisper as he approached the table. "It's good to see you again."

Rose watched in silence as Evan stood to greet him, taking the hand Dimitri offered in both of his own.

She had often wondered what her reaction would be if she ever came face-to-face with him again. Would she be terrified, embarrassed, euphoric? Now she was all three.

The newspapers and television didn't do Dimitri justice. His charisma enhanced his arresting features. For a second their eyes met, and the air of mystery, that anything might happen, was still there.

"You look well, Rose." His words shot through her, piercing her heart.

She remained still, her body frozen. Her arms and legs felt like chunks of concrete. She had the feeling he was relishing her discomfort. It was Evan who broke the silence. "Let's sit, shall we."

"Rose, I . . . I . . ." He turned to Dimitri as if asking for help, but Dimitri remained totally silent and still. Rose thought he was letting Evan struggle on purpose. Dimitri and Evan each took a seat on either side of her place at the banquette. Evan started to say something, but the waiter rushed over and the whole business of cleaning the table, taking their orders for coffee, and running down the list of desserts took so long, Rose was convinced that the sweet little Frenchman was never going to leave. Finally, he was gone. Rose turned quickly to Evan.

"I haven't had a chance to explain things to Rose," he said, then paused again. At last he said nervously to Rose, "Dimitri needs my representation. We need to protect him, as my brother, as part of the family."

Evan was telling her this as though the argument in the breakfast room had never happened. Evidently he wanted Dimitri to think that the entire sequence of events was news to her.

"Normally I wouldn't . . . I mean, under different circumstances, I would never take the case, but when Dimitri called . . . well, you understand?"

Rose didn't say anything. Instead she took her time studying the two men looking for her reaction. The similarities between them were minute, practically invisible. One would find it hard to believe they were half-brothers.

The years had chiseled Dimitri's face. If Evan were a watercolor, Dimitri had been painted in oil. The passage of time had not mellowed him; just the opposite. As a youth he'd had an aura of strength but was approachable and kind. Now there was a cynical edge to him and a coldness in his eyes. He was battle hardened, toughened. And though this changed his looks superficially, he was actually closer to the image she'd had of him when they were young: strip away the expensive wardrobe, the meticulously coifed hair, and he remained like a character from one of her novels. The underdog, a loner who took care of himself and hurt those that he had to, but whose eyes still reflected a soul with a gentle streak left for anyone he might love.

He lowered his eyelids. "By now, I'm sure you've heard of my predicament, and the jury's all set. I need the best attorney possible, and that's your husband." He spoke the last two words with a curious neutrality. "Evan is worried this might be a problem for you, which is why I've come to discuss it."

It was obvious that Dimitri was up to something, and for reasons she didn't understand, Evan didn't have the power to stop him.

Dimitri reached inside his suit pocket and pulled out a cigar. "It will just be a minor inconvenience," he said calmly, twirling the Partagas with his long fingers. His tone was so matter-of-fact, she wanted to scream. "When it's over, we can all go back to our everyday lives."

He cast his gaze on Rose and let it linger awhile as though absorbing her, assessing her black crepe suit against the pale highlights of her hair and striking emerald green eyes. Eyes that had once promised him paradise—so long ago. "Are you okay, Rose? You look a bit pale," Dimitri asked in the same deep, throaty tone barely above a whisper.

Dimitri had been the love of her life. A first love that ends abruptly leaves deep emotional scars, no matter what the circumstances. Being in the same room with him electrified her. Her feelings shifted moment by moment: she distrusted him, loved him, was afraid of him. And she wanted him. All these emotions bubbled together in a spicy stew that might boil over at any moment.

She couldn't answer whether she was okay or not. She only found the strength to nod. Go back to their everyday lives? Never—her present and future no longer existed. She was trapped, locked in her past, in the forbidden pool of her desires.

13

Later that night Rose lay awake in bed, burrowed into the champagne-colored Frette sheets, staring at the flickering lavender-scented candle she often lit for its soothing aroma. She watched the small bright vari-colored light dance wildly, reflecting off the hand-carved mahogany four-poster bed. Cream-colored moiré fabric, striped with spiderweb-thin strands of silk gold threads, was draped from the ceiling over the bed's posters, puddling the cream-colored Karastan carpet. The draped bed was the only elaborate touch in the room. The armoire and bureau had been built to her specifications, clean lines of bleached oak bordered in narrow strips of gold leaf. She had chosen dignified *gris* pewter table lamps that sat on colonial-style end tables made of simple distressed pine, stained the same color as the lamps. Rose found comfort in the glow of her candle as she tried to unwind from the day's events.

Evan lay beside her, sifting through some legal briefs. He had accompanied her to her last interview after dinner, but they had not yet discussed the meeting with Dimitri. Dared she bring it up? What was the point? If he chose to, Dimitri would get even with them all—one at a time. Evan was first, by being forced into taking Dimitri's case. She wondered what was in store for her. Was Dimitri her stalker? Could he actually do that? Now, after she'd seen him face-to-face, her mind and heart pulled in separate directions.

Rose glanced over at her husband, who looked so content. His nature was so unlike hers, so uncomplicated. It was hard to imagine that someday soon he could be governor of New York. He deserved it. Never mind the Miller family money and James's political connections. Rose was convinced Evan could have done it all on his own. Though his prominence in his field entitled him to the highest fees of any of the other "name brand" lawyers, Evan made it a point to take at least five pro bono cases every year. He was apt to defend men like the accountant Jonathan Dundy, who embezzled money out of desperation to afford the bone marrow transplant his wife's insurance wouldn't cover; or Jesse Adams, the mother accused of killing the man who sexually abused her young daughter. Evan kept in touch with the other side of life—with ordinary people who had real problems and real dreams. And this was a quality, Rose knew, that would get him far in politics.

"Evan . . . ," Rose started, her voice shaky, as she turned in bed to face him. Where would she begin? Stick to the basics, she told herself, the other stuff can come later. She needed to rely on their years of quiet comfort together.

"Last night at the party, the roses . . ."

Evan propped himself up, his eyes instantly focused on her face. "What about them?"

She forced herself to face him directly. "There was this message that was also in the box. It said, 'I'll be watching you.' I don't know who sent me those roses. I was spooked, but I let it go because I didn't want to get anyone upset at the party. Then, this morning a box from Tiffany's was delivered here. It was full of hundreds of dead rose petals. I was horrified. A similar message was written on a card in the bottom of the box."

Evan pushed the blankets away, bolted up, and swung his legs over the side of the bed, his feet fumbling around on the carpet for his slippers. "Jesus, when the hell were you going to tell me?"

Rose could tell her husband was past angry. His voice was sharp and loud. It was the tone he used to intimidate witnesses, a sound like a battering ram against a metal door. He had never spoken to her this way before. Evan's temperament was mild. His anger was usually expressed in well-chosen words.

"Why the secret?" Already he was getting himself under control.

Rose sat up next to him. She reached over and ran her hand across his back. She understood that his emotion was an extension of his overprotective feelings toward her. His outburst was predictable, as was his quick recovery.

"I wasn't trying to keep it a secret, Evan," she said. "But this is exactly why I didn't mention it at the moment. I thought you might react like this."

He turned his face to meet hers. "What do you expect? You're my wife. Did you think I'd just act casual and let it go?"

She pulled back and let out a sigh. "Evan, please. I need you to be practical."

He got up from the bed, padded across the room to the sitting area, then spun around.

Rose stared at him for a moment, guilt creeping up inside her. How much more to confide in him? Did she dare tell him that she had a tiny fear it might be Dimitri stalking her? No, not now. Perhaps she was wrong. At some level she knew that Dimitri still loved her. While they were entangled once again, the less Evan knew about her fears concerning Dimitri, the less trouble would be stirred up. Joining him at the sitting area, she ran her fingers through his hair, sorry she'd brought it up. She looked away from him and said, "I'll handle it, Evan."

Evan shot back an angry glance. "Not alone, you won't," he replied.

Rose felt a sense of foreboding. She never should have told him.

"First thing in the morning, we're going to the police." He went to the nightstand, opened the top drawer, and pulled out a black leather Filofax. Flipping through the pages, he said, "I have an even better idea. There's a great PI I know. I'll call him first thing in the morning."

"No!" she interrupted. "You have an important court appearance. I'll handle it. I'm going to contact John Falcone. I'm sure he can help out."

Detective John Falcone was a member of a task force that combined cops from the tristate area. John had helped Rose with her research for *The Devil's Daughter,* and ever since then they had become friendly. John had no family. When his wife was diagnosed with a rapid-growing breast cancer, Rose called the local hospice and made other arrangements John couldn't handle. To Rose, John was part father figure, part friend.

Hesitantly Evan nodded, then said, "I want to talk to him. I have early morning conferences and court appearances all week concerning Dimitri's trial. I should be free any afternoon. Have him come and see me."

Rose sat on his side of the bed, taking the phone book from his hand to command his complete attention. "The trial already?"

"Things have moved quickly."

She shook her head back and forth, as though rejecting the information. "But I thought you just agreed to be Dimitri's lawyer?"

"Yes, but the jury was already selected. We have all of Lester's files and notes."

She understood now that Evan was shifting into defense attorney mode and that his commitment to Dimitri's trial would be uppermost in his mind until he had won an acquittal. Rose was always amazed at her husband's ability to compartmentalize. Evan belonged completely to the trial. It didn't matter anymore what Dimitri may or may not have done. Evan had agreed to take the case, and now he would throw all he had into it. Since they'd been married, he had drilled into her head that a lawyer's responsibility was to the law and not necessarily to the truth. Evan would let nothing come between him and winning acquittal for his brother, no matter what events had separated them over the years. Had she really believed for one moment that Evan would refuse Dimitri? Maybe it was true that blood was thicker than water.

14

It was a typically perfect January morning, cold and bright. The forecast had called for snow. How wrong those weathermen were, Rose thought as she stared up at the picture-perfect, cloudless blue sky. Inside her black Mercedes the heat was turned up high, the automatic temperature control read "75° F." Why then did she feel such a chill? Nerves, she realized.

"You okay?" Larry asked.

She nodded, and he threw the car into drive. Larry Martin had been hired as her driver-cum-protector since she'd become recognizable a few years ago. Evan had insisted. As often as possible, she made excuses to drive herself, but today's visit was too nerve-racking. They moved slowly away from the familiar, warm exterior of Paradiso. She watched outside the rear window, drawing peace from the home she had grown so familiar with. Constructed of brick, with animal gargoyles set into the exterior in unexpected places, the mansion combined the classic that was Evan with the whimsy that was Rose. The car came to the end of the long winding driveway lined with imported French chestnut trees and headed out onto the open road.

Maybe I should call first and tell him I'm coming, she thought. She pulled the cell phone from her purse, then checked her address book. She punched his number into the keypad and waited, listening impatiently to the distant ring. On the fifth ring she reached the watch officer's desk.

"I need to speak to Detective Falcone," she said, and was transferred to his extension. What was she going to say to him? She feared she was being . . . stalked, hunted, terrorized? All of the above? It could be a nasty practical joke, after all. Somehow, though, she couldn't rid her mind of dread. The truth was, she was scared. Someone was out there, watching her, relishing her discomfort. The one person she could count on to help her find an answer to the situation was Detective Falcone.

The telephone came alive now.

"Falcone!"

Rose gripped the receiver with both hands. "John, it's Rose—" Before she could finish her sentence, John Falcone interrupted.

"Why, Rose, how are you? Long time since we talked. Say, I've been following some of your television interviews. You look great; I'm looking forward to reading your new book."

Rose felt the tension in her hands disappear, and a sense of security swept over her.

"I need your help, John." A tiny voice whispered in her head that she might be making a complete fool of heself. Was she getting hysterical over something as trivial as an ardent fan? She couldn't allow herself to take the chance. After taking a deep breath, she said, "Can I come down to the precinct? I'd rather not discuss this over the phone." She waited for his reply.

"Why do I get the feeling this has nothing to do with research?"

"I can be there in a few minutes. Will that be okay?" she asked, hoping he'd say yes.

"I'll meet you out front and escort you inside," he replied.

John Falcone had been with the police force for twenty years. His record was unblemished. He'd started his career in Manhattan and earned a transfer to Nassau County, which included a much higher salary. Then, as a way of inching toward a comfortable retirement, he'd asked for and received a comfortable position in Brookville's police department. Then the task force position had come up and he couldn't say no.

Rose got his name from a local newspaper. The reporter had compared John Falcone to John Douglas, the famous criminal profiler from the FBI's behavioral science department, most associated with his work on the Jon-Benet Ramsey case. In a newspaper interview, Detective Falcone had hit it right on the mark when he profiled serial killer Joel Rifkin, who had murdered a number of women on Long Island, all of them prostitutes. Falcone concluded that the psychopath would have trouble separating himself from his victims; possibly he'd keep the bodies close to him for a while. And in fact this had proven to be true. When Rifkin was stopped for a major traffic violation, the body of his latest victim was discovered beneath a tarpaulin in the rear of his pickup truck. When Rose was working on *The Devil's Daughter,* she remembered the piece and contacted the detective.

They had spoken briefly on the phone, then arranged to meet for coffee. Rose had arrived at Starbucks on Northern Boulevard in Greenvale first and taken a booth in the back. When he walked through the door, she knew immediately it had to be Falcone. He was a carbon copy of Dennis Franz playing Detective Sipowicz on the television series *N.Y.P.D. Blue.* Like Franz, he was bald and heavyset. From the first minute they recognized each other that day she was drawn to his deep brown, assessing eyes. As time went on she learned those eyes never missed anything that they had seen.

Rose had warmed up to John Falcone instantly, and they started working on what became the most intricate research-driven plot she had written: the story of two orphan girls separated at birth and reunited when one is kidnapped from her prominent family. The twin realizes for the first time that the "voices" she hears, which her parents feared was schizophrenia, had been her sister's voice all those years. The detective work needed to find the missing twin was elaborate, and John Falcone had been a godsend to Rose, enabling her to construct an intricate, plausible, and utterly fascinating tale. It had been the beginning of a mutually satisfying alliance.

The Brookville Police Department was located in a long, low, white brick building off 25A, exactly half a mile west of Paradiso. The station had been built soon after World War II, when Brookville was home to gentlemen farmers, and the station still reflected the rural community of that time. The three-story structure was made of wood—a "firetrap," as some called it. With the advent of technology, coaxial cables, fiber-optic telephones, and fax machines had littered the first floor, where the officers worked, with Gordian knots of wires that no one would ever be able to straighten out or conceal. Falcone had told her that when he worked late at night, once in a while he could hear the mice scurrying among the files on the second floor. The jail on the third floor was more or less a drunk tank or used as a scare tactic for rowdy teenagers, since Brookville was nearly as safe as it had been when the station was built. The station house stood out on the quiet intersection next to a gracious old estate, like a sentry guarding the castle.

Rose entered the building with trepidation. She had been here many times before, but this was different. It was personal. It wasn't about researching other people and their lives. Now she was like a character in one of her own novels, scared, desperate, and searching for help.

Falcone met Rose in the lobby and quickly ushered her down the hall and into his office, obviously protecting her privacy. His office was completely utilitarian, no frills, though she noticed the once wooden floor had recently been covered with black linoleum. He closed the door behind them, wheeled a chair from the corner of the room, and gestured for her to sit down. As always, his desk was totally organized, with current files arranged neatly one on top of the other and a paperweight kept on top, a souvenir from Gracie Mansion. She knew the framed photo turned toward John was of him and Sylvia on their twenty-fifth anniversary vacation in Veracruz.

Falcone gave Rose a moment to let her get her bearings and then said, "So, tell me what's going on."

Rose straightened her back in the dilapidated wooden chair, cleared her throat, and began. But she couldn't get started, couldn't get her wording right. The whole ordeal was taking more of a toll than she'd realized.

Falcone stared at her, concern in his eyes. "Do you need a cup of coffee? It might make you feel better."

Rose shook her head. "No, I'll be okay. I'm not sure, but—" She broke off and started over, this time determined to get words out. "It's just that, well, I don't quite know how to say this, so I'll just spill it out. I think someone is stalking me." Saying the words aloud to Falcone had a far greater impact than the minimizing she had given them last night with Evan. The words spiked through her veins like a shot of adrenaline, reminding her of how she'd felt those nights years ago when she'd spent hours lying awake, terrified Uncle Tom would enter her room.

Her hands dropped from her lap to her sides. "I didn't know where else to go, who else to tell."

"Rose, you know you can always count on me for help." His voice was kind. "Start from the beginning, tell me everything."

Then she told him the story—the roses, the dead petals, and the cryptic messages.

"I know what you're going to say. It's probably just an overeager fan. Actually, I feel the same way, but just to be on the safe side, I wanted to talk to you." When she finished, she reached inside her coat pocket, pulled out an envelope, and handed it to him.

He tore open the envelope and read each of the two cards twice, his eyes scanning the words.

"Dried rose petals," Falcone mused, "as in dead Roses?" Already she could see his cop brain clicking into action.

"Look," he said, frowning deeply, then running his finger across his lips. "This is probably nothing, Rose. Being in the public eye attracts all kinds of crazies."

His words were meant to soothe her, but Rose found them unsettling. She imagined what he might be thinking despite his blasé attitude.

"Let's go over some details. Any chance you remember where the first box of flowers were sent from?"

"No, but I could check with my editor's assistant. He gave them to me the night of the book party, and I do remember asking my housekeeper about the Tiffany box. It was delivered by hand." She paused, recalling her brief conversation with Myra that morning. "At least I think so. My housekeeper found it on the doorstep. I didn't have the time to consider how strange that is until just now."

"Don't think too much, you'll scare yourself, especially with that imagination of yours." Falcone came around the desk and sat on the edge. "Let me handle it from here on. Anything happens, you call me immediately. You got my beeper number?"

She nodded, then stood and put her arms around him in a grateful hug.

"Can I keep these?" He waved the cards.

"Yes, I've already made copies."

He walked her down the corridor to the station door.

He opened the front door and showed her the way out. "One last thing, Rose." She turned to face him. "I know it's hard, but try to live a normal life, go about your business as usual."

"I'll try," she replied.

Getting in and out of Rose's office at Paradiso was easier than Billy had imagined. He wouldn't have believed that one could actually pick a lock using a credit card these days, but it was true. Rose's lock wasn't a heavy-duty exterior lock, and all he'd had to do was run the card through the bolt and open the door. Billy stood in the center of the large, beautifully furnished room, gazing around him, taking in every detail. The ivory-colored walls and carpet. The French cherry writing desk, antique armoire, and elaborate silk curtains at the windows. *This is where Rose works, soft and feminine, just like Rose.*

He placed the tiny chip inside the receiver of her phone. Now he scanned the room, looking for the perfect hiding place for the little unidirectional microphone and its activating mechanism. He needed somewhere inconspicuous to conceal the receiving device. He glanced at the ivory-and-taupe damask roll arm sofa, then at her desk. Perhaps the sterling silver day calendar? Too small. He picked up the ornate desk lamp and affixed the device in its interior. Next, he opened Rose's laptop computer on the desk, pushed the power button on, and waited. When the screen cleared, he went into the file manager. When the files appeared, he sifted through them. Soon he came upon *"Murderous Intentions."* He was certain this was her latest work in progress, and when he opened it the rough appearance of the draft confirmed his suspicion. He slipped the floppy disk from his pocket into the computer and copied the file. Seconds later he had what he'd come for. Time to go. He shut the door behind him and heard the bolt go back into the lock. Billy's mouth twisted into a smile.

A cough, shoes scraping against the floor, papers rustling. From the prosecution table, Kevin studied Dimitri Constantinos, who was seated across the aisle just a few feet away from him. The defense table was a duplicate of his in every way, from the rickety legs to the scarred top that had seen so many other bored attorneys fretfully awaiting their turn on stage. Kevin had learned early on that being a lawyer was two-thirds law, one-third drama. Today it was drama. This could be his chance to make his name known throughout the state, maybe even the country, and he was relishing the opportunity to put Constantinos away and replace that bum's name in the headlines with his own.

Kevin had fought a hundred battles, but this was an exception. There was much more at stake than just a conviction. He thought of the numerous humiliations he'd suffered each time he failed to get a conviction on Braun. But that just made him even more determined to heap all that stored-up indignity onto Constantinos. He'd get him good, no matter how he had to do it.

Two tables, two teams. Only one would walk away victorious. He visualized himself winning. The press conference, cameras flashing, a row of microphones before him. He turned to study Constantinos.

The man seemed fearless, he'd give him that. Constantinos was leaning back against the old wooden chair with assurance, almost as if he were posing for the cover of *GQ*—and under different circumstances he very well could. The custom-made black Brioni suit, the elegant, hand-painted silk tie, handkerchief, and Gucci loafers were all part of his image. He looked more like a movie star than a man accused of racketeering and extortion. Kevin was convinced that men like Dimitri did not acquire their magnetism—they were born with it. Dimitri's looks, charm, wealth, and celebrity status all combined to create a figure everyone wanted to know more about. Dimitri, the consummate enigma. It was precisely for this reason—Constantinos was an icon—that Kevin wanted to take him down. This trial had nothing to do with justice. For all Kevin knew, Dimitri was not guilty. In fact, a part of him thought the man was completely legit. But that was immaterial. To Kevin, the trial was *Allen* vs. *Miller* rather than the *People* vs. *Dimitri Constantinos,* because it was the Millers who stood between him and what he wanted. Constantinos's trial was just the vehicle to get him there. A shame, really, but that was U.S. justice for you.

For a moment their eyes locked, fierce opponents preparing to enter the ring for the ultimate fight championship. Dimitri held Kevin's gaze, and Kevin felt a momentary sense of doubt about the dangerous game he was about to play. No, he thought, fighting hard to keep his composure, I won't let him stare me down. He will not, cannot, intimidate me. Kevin needed to prove to the party and the public that he was worthy of their respect and noble enough to support the best of them. While some evidence may have been doctored or perhaps tainted, did it really matter? He pushed aside his guilt. He could live with it. It was done all the time. Wasn't it?

Kevin Allen shook his head. He couldn't think of that now. Back to the present. He felt Constantinos turn away from him. A guilty verdict would surely catapult him to instant fame and celebrity. He would be as well known as Rudy Giuliani was before leaving the prosecutor's office to go into politics. The DA threw back his shoulders. Slowly his confidence returned. Victory would be sweet indeed.

15

Rose left the police station and told Larry to head for Alexis's school. There was a faculty meeting today, and classes concluded at eleven o'clock. Ordinarily she wouldn't interfere with Alexis's schedule, but she'd been away and felt it important they spend time together. No, that wasn't it. She chided herself for even pretending. Telling John Falcone had made the threat against her feel all the more real. And if she were in danger, it made sense that her loved ones were also at risk. She had to have Alexis close to her right now, to see her and make sure everything was all right. Then she would meet Marilyn in the city for a quick shopping spree.

The bell sounded just as Larry pulled the car up to the front entrance of Greenvale Academy. The campus consisted of three buildings—the lower school, the middle school, and the high school—situated on twenty acres of manicured lawns divided by graveled paths that led to tennis courts, a baseball diamond, and, of course, the football field, which also served as the soccer green.

Rose exited from her car as hundreds of students emerged, all with their own individual "take" on the blue blazer and skirt or pants that was the school uniform. One young girl had knee socks and platform shoes. Another wore a hand-painted denim vest beneath her blazer. The boys tended to leave the building, while the girls stayed in groups on the stairs of the low building that housed the middle school. Rose spotted Alexis with Gale, her best friend of the moment, just as Gale turned in the direction of the tennis courts. Alexis began meandering toward the buses waiting in the parking lot. Larry honked and Rose called simultaneously. Alexis looked up, waved, and ran toward the car.

"Mom, why are you here? Is everything okay?"

Rose wrapped her arms around Alexis, hugging her tightly. "Everything is fine, sweetheart. I just thought I'd surprise you before I left for Manhattan."

Rose marveled at how each day her daughter seemed to mature, and then, when Rose had accepted the new evolution, Alexis would change back to a little girl again. Just now, for example, before she knew Rose was looking, Alexis had been walking slowly, obviously practicing a new sultry walk. Yesterday she had insisted that she braid five or six tiny little braids into her waist-length hair, for a more preteen punk look. Tomorrow Rose would not be surprised if Alexis wore pigtails and high-tops instead of the collegiate penny loafers with Ralph Lauren fashion socks she wore today. Rose squeezed her daughter one more time as Larry held the door open for them. This child was her raison d'être.

When Rose first found out she was pregnant, she was torn between keeping this tiny speck of life inside of her and destroying it. She had gone to a clinic in Manhattan and, under an assumed name, arranged for the procedure. Her baby would die anonymously.

On the day the abortion was scheduled, Rose took the Long Island Railroad to Manhattan, then a taxi to the clinic downtown. Inside she was greeted by a nurse, who led her to an examining room and handed her a gown and slippers.

As she changed into the gown, she felt as though she were putting on a hair shirt. She imagined the life inside her. In her mind, her hands became splattered with blood, and she began to tremble.

A voice said, "We're ready."

She looked up to find the doctor hovering over her. A burly man with a bald head and horn-rimmed glasses, dressed in a white lab coat, he examined the chart in his hand without emotion.

"We'll give you a sedative. It will be over shortly. Place your feet in the stirrups."

The nurse reappeared, holding a needle. Seconds later Rose felt a pinch. As the doctor's voice filtered through her mind, she felt herself drifting, although she fought the sudden sensation of forced sleep. She felt the cold speculum being inserted inside of her, and she began to cry. A wave of ineffable loss, a deep sorrow, enveloped her. Visions of a beautiful child came into her mind.

The clock on the wall was ticking. It became louder and louder, filling the room. She was crying harder, and she couldn't shut the baby out of her mind. It was warm, safe, and secure inside of her, but not for long. A sleepy feeling was stealing over her. Her thoughts became clouded. My baby is going to die, she told herself. This man, a complete stranger, was going to destroy her child. She had to stop him. Then, with all the strength she could muster, she pushed herself up onto her elbows.

"No!" she screamed. "Don't kill my baby."

She awoke an hour later, lying in the hospital bed. Through the window she could see it was dark outside. Her thoughts were blurry. She reached for the call button and summoned the nurse. When the nurse appeared, she cried, "My baby! Is . . . ?"

The nurse shook her head and smiled. "No, Mrs. Smith. Your baby is fine. I do hope it's a girl, because you kept calling her 'princess.'"

Seven months later, Rose awoke to a flare of pain in her abdomen, a pain so intense that she jerked around wildly in the bed as though somehow she could escape its hot, punishing grip.

Hours later at the hospital, voices telling her to push filtered through the roar of blood pumping in her ears. Just when she thought she couldn't take it anymore and she felt her body about to split open, the pressure eased abruptly and the baby slithered free.

She heard a tiny gurgled cry. Rose sobbed, in part from relief, mostly from elation.

"A girl," she heard someone shout. A moment later the baby was thrust into her arms, tiny and still covered with blood.

Rose blinked back the tears as she looked down at the fuzz on the baby's head. The nurse took the infant from her for a few minutes, then returned the baby swaddled in a soft blanket. "Why don't you two take a few minutes to get acquainted, Mrs. Miller. Your husband is waiting outside."

Rose nodded, her eyes never leaving the baby's tiny features, her button nose and red bud of a mouth. She caressed each finger, and when the baby began to whimper, she held her to her breast. "Shhh, Alexis." She didn't know where the name came from. It was as though the baby had told Rose what she wanted to be called.

"Alexis," she said again out loud. Just as Evan came to her, the baby opened her piercing sapphire eyes, which dominated her face. At that moment any suspicions she'd had about who the baby's father was evaporated. This precious gem was Dimitri's child. There was no question.

A day hadn't passed over the last twelve years that she hadn't thanked God for giving her the courage to make the right decision. Rose hugged Alexis's warm, fragile body, pushed the dark hair out of her eyes—Dimitri's eyes. If Dimitri set eyes on Alexis, he would surely know she was his.

Instinctively she grabbed Alexis's hand and got her into the car. Forcing herself to act naturally, she reverted to a long-standing exchange they had been repeating since Alexis was old enough to talk:

"Do you know how much I love you, sweetheart?"

Alexis smiled back at her and opened her arms wide. "Yes, because you always tell me—'as big as the sky and more than life.'"

Larry drove mother and daughter home safely.

Billy listened to her voice coming from the tiny transmitter.

"Rose, I'm just checking up on you," a male voice said.

"John, I did a stupid thing. I picked Alexis up at school. Now I'm scared he followed me there."

Billy shut his eyes dreamily. Good. She was scared. That meant he was succeeding. He was getting closer to his dream. The more frantic she became, the more she would give away. People in a panic tended to talk—just see how she'd gone to the police so soon after she'd received his gifts. How she had spilled her guts to the detective about the little game between them, exactly what he'd hoped she'd do. He'd pushed the right button.

The bitch thought she was untouchable. He would get to her.

She thought it was a sick joke. He would show her.

She would be his. And then he would kill her.

His eyes snapped open.

16

Bergdorf Goodman had never been just a department store to Rose. Her first trip to Manhattan had been with Evan, shortly before her sixteenth birthday. She had stood outside the building, gawking at the astonishing window displays. The store represented a lofty dream, an unreachable fantasy in her threadbare and lonely world. No matter how hard Evan tried to coax her inside, she refused. She was too intimidated, certain she didn't belong there. Evan did not notice that her knee-length red skirt was a size too big and rolled up at the waist or that her white angora sweater had started to pill. The young woman who had stood outside, staring into the windows, never quite left her, and now, as she walked into the store, that same adolescent wonder returned.

The delicious scents, the array of colors, the beautiful, cultivated models parading in sophisticated clothes through the elegantly furnished departments, completely transfixed Rose. Even the shoppers fascinated her as they clutched expensive clothing and accessories in their arms and were whisked about the store by attentive personal shoppers.

Rose checked her watch. Marilyn hadn't arrived yet. They had agreed to meet at one o'clock on the first floor, near the 57th Street entrance. Rose was to be the guest of honor at the annual Mystery Writers Award Ceremony. *Last Rites* was being awarded Best Psychological Suspense Novel of 1997, an honor she'd never believed would be bestowed on her. After searching her closets, she'd realized it had been a long time since she had bought herself a new dress, so she'd enlisted Marilyn's help in choosing one to wear to the ceremony. The odd thing about Marilyn was that she had a great eye for what looked good on everyone except herself.

Rose circled the cosmetics counter, perusing the vast selection of lipsticks, eye shadows, creams, and powders. She stopped at the Clarins counter to pick up moisturizer and self-tanning cream. The sight of the Christian Dior counter reminded her she was running low on foundation, but before she could catch the salesman's attention she heard a voice behind her.

"Someone as gorgeous as you doesn't need makeup," Marilyn said.

Rose laughed and turned around. "You're late, but then again, you always are."

Marilyn ignored her teasing and said, "C'mon, it's Valentino for you."

They spent an hour sorting through the gowns, holding up this one or that one, discussing colors, cuts, and designs. Rose selected six evening dresses to try on: a Valentino, two Oscar De La Rentas, a Christian Dior, and two Armanis. A saleswoman chose another three, then directed them to a private dressing room.

As Rose considered a black satin De La Renta, Marilyn picked that moment, probably figuring Rose's guard was down, to question her. "Honey, are you okay? Dario and I were talking about you earlier. Ever since you returned from Paris, you've seemed distracted."

Their eyes met in the full-length mirror. Rose was the first to look away.

"I'm okay. Between the tour and Evan's involvement in a new trial, there's a lot of pressure on me. It will all calm down soon."

Marilyn persisted. "Something tells me otherwise."

Rose shook her head. "No, I'm fine . . . really."

She peeled off the de la Renta and slipped on the Valentino, a long column of black silk crepe with a single rhinestone clasp on the left shoulder.

"Now, that's definitely you," Marilyn blurted as she put one hand on her hip and stepped backward.

"It is nice," Rose said, forcing herself to focus on her reflection, on the fit of the exquisitely draped dress. Clean lines, a simple elegance. Yes, this would do.

"Rose, what's going on? It must have something to do with those roses you received at the party. I could see it in your face."

Rose shook her head. "It's nothing I can't handle, Marilyn." Her hands fumbled with the dresses as she put them back on their hangers. "It's probably someone playing a prank. Or, for that matter, a harmless, disgruntled fan. It happens."

"Exactly what happened?"

Rose tensed up. Now was her chance to lessen her load, share her fears with her best friend. But should she drag Marilyn into it? She decided she really needed some comfort.

"The card had some sort of sick poem. It ended with 'I'll be watching you.' Then the next day there was another delivery, dead roses in a Tiffany box, with another cryptic message."

Marilyn was silent, then said, "Have you gone to the police? You can't take the chance that it's just a harmless fan."

Rose, who was putting her street clothes back on, paused, and said, "Yes, you don't have to worry about that. John Falcone, remember him? He's on the case, and even he said it happens all the time. You know that when people are in the public eye, they become targets."

Marilyn's eyes widened. "Maybe, but I've heard too many horror stories about 'harmless' stalkers who didn't turn out to be so innocent in the end."

At Rose's request, they stopped to have an early dinner at Il Cantinori, a Village fixture. It was a cozy Tuscan restaurant with handsome glass front doors that opened onto the street, making the entire flower-filled restaurant feel like an Italian summer garden. Rose loved to dine on the outdoor patio during the warmer months, where she could look onto the quiet street and be surrounded by windowboxes full of glorious flowers.

"I love the risotto here," she said when they were settled at her regular table, nestled cozily in the rear. She glanced around, adding, "I think this is one of New York's most romantic restaurants. The perfect choice if you're staging a seduction. Evan and I spent our last anniversary here." Rose looked tentatively at Marilyn, whose lack of romance in her own life made her sad for her friend.

"So that's why you picked this place," Marilyn said with a hint of humor in her tone. "Always campaigning for me to find someone. Well, just because you and Evan have a perfect marriage doesn't make every relationship a fairy tale."

Both women were silent. Of all people, Marilyn knew Evan and Rose didn't have a perfect marriage.

Frank Minieri, the restaurant's general manager, stopped by their table to greet them, and shortly after, Phillip, Rose's favorite waiter, arrived to take their orders. When they were alone, Marilyn said, "Rose, I want to know everything that's going on."

Rose tried to make small talk, hoping to divert Marilyn's attention from their earlier conversation at Bergdorf's, but to no avail. Marilyn persisted: "No tricks, my friend. I'm not letting up until I know everything that's going on. Flowers, cards, psycho—that's not a good mix."

Rose's heart sank. She knew Marilyn was right. Since Dimitri had forced his way back into their lives, nothing seemed the same.

Trying to sound nonchalant, she said, "Now that John Falcone is on the case, I'm not at all worried."

Marilyn's eyebrows rose skeptically. "Oh, sure."

When the appetizers arrived, grilled calamari for Rose and asparagus vinaigrette for Marilyn, they sampled each other's choices and gossiped about publishing, giggled over how pompous Dario could be, and caught up on any news regarding their mutual acquaintances. Just when Rose thought she'd diverted Marilyn from her questioning, her friend grew silent, pulled her chair in closer, and stared pointedly into her eyes. Marilyn wasn't one to leave well enough alone: she had to know every last detail and wouldn't stop until she'd heard the truth.

"Talk to me, Rose."

Rose hesitated, acutely aware of the other guests and the attentive maître d' hovering nearby. How could she speak freely and risk being overheard? Then several glances at the other patrons convinced her they were all engrossed in their own conversations. She and Marilyn were safe from prying eyes and ears; there was nothing to worry about.

She leaned in closer to Marilyn, took a deep breath, and began: "I know this might surprise you, but when I was a teenager, I worked as a housekeeper for the Millers. . . ."

Marilyn remained silent, sipping her Chianti, only nodding occasionally. Unable to stop herself, Rose revealed the long and twisted turns of her past at the Laurel estate, including her uncle Tom's physical and emotional abuse. She studied Marilyn, watching as different emotions played across her face: empathy, sadness, fury, horror.

"My God, Rose, you poor thing. Wasn't there anyone you could turn to?"

Rose stared straight ahead and answered softly. "Yes. Dimitri Constantinos."

Marilyn looked astounded, completely taken aback.

At that moment the waiter brought their risotto and refilled their glasses from the bottle of wine they had been sharing.

Marilyn ignored her entrée. "What does Dimitri Constantinos have to do with you?"

The distant sound of glass shattering in the kitchen momentarily distracted Rose. "Dimitri lived on the estate. He tended the horses. He's James's illegitimate son."

"What?" was the only response Marilyn could muster.

"Oh, don't be shocked, Marilyn, the Miller family is besieged by scandal." Rose quickly ran through just a few. First was James's cover-up of arrests for drunken driving, including one in which a little girl was hurt, fortunately not too seriously. She pointed out, "In that case he paid the family off handsomely." Next she told Marilyn about rumors surrounding James's silent partnership in Joseph Braun's escort service. "He does this just so he can have whatever woman he wants when he wants her. He's battered a few of them, and these women have little recourse, so it's easy to cover up. For the right price, you can buy anyone's silence."

Marilyn raised an eyebrow. "I guess you hear about scandal in every high-profile family. Ordinarily, it wouldn't shock me, but coming from you . . . I mean, I know James Miller and I never thought . . ."

Rose began talking faster as she sensed Marilyn's disbelief. "There's only one reason I care about James's ugly secrets. If the press digs hard enough, eventually the scandals will surface and that would ruin Evan's dreams. I never thought he'd want to serve in politics, but he's increasingly into it. I don't want my father-in-law's private life to haunt Evan."

"And Dimitri?" Marilyn leaned in closer.

"Dimitri is a different story. Like me, he had nothing and no one. Imagine one son raised in the lap of luxury, the other living, literally, in a barn. I was drawn to him, out of pity at first, but then . . ." Silence filled the air. "If the truth be told, he was the only part of that whole horrible time, after my parents died, that is worth remembering."

"Dimitri Constantinos?" Marilyn placed her elbows on the table, cupping her chin in her small hands and looking squarely at Rose. "Why am I not completely surprised? There's always been this space between you and me, as well as between you and others. It's as though you were hiding something." She shook her head. "Dimitri Constantinos and Rose Miller. Hmm."

The waiter returned and cleared their now empty plates. Rose waited until he'd disappeared, then continued. "Marilyn, you don't know what he was like back then. Trust me. Dimitri paid so much attention to me. He doted on me. He taught me how to ride a horse, swim, even how to hit a baseball. Before I knew it, I was madly in love with him. To everyone else he was hard and distant, but with me he was gentle, loving, and compassionate."

Thinking back to that time in her life, Rose felt a pang of despair.

"Around that same time Evan began to pursue me. . . ." She described the events leading up to the infamous dinner party and what happened afterward. "When I came to I was in a hospital and Evan was there. He was so kind, but I really needed to get back to Dimitri. We were planning on leaving Laurel together."

"And?" Neither woman looked up when the waiter arrived with the dessert tray. He set it down, then withdrew to the kitchen.

"This part gets tough." Rose kept her head down, but she couldn't hide the tears that streaked her cheeks.

Marilyn took Rose's hand in hers. "You don't have to say any more. I didn't mean to—"

"No, I want to tell you. I need to finish." She told Marilyn about the "deal" she had struck to try to save Dimitri and how it had backfired. "James arranged for Dimitri's plea bargain, six to ten if he pleaded guilty to involuntary manslaughter. I wasn't even questioned. After the wedding, everyday life resumed."

Marilyn's eyes filled with disbelief. "As though nothing had happened?"

Rose took a long breath. "That's right—as though nothing happened. Except that Dimitri wasn't there. The newspapers carried stories of a fight between two servants in which one ended up dead. James covered everything up. Soon the Millers sold Laurel, and we moved into Paradiso."

"But Dimitri is his son?" Marilyn broke in.

Rose shook her head. "He didn't care. James is a monster. Dimitri represented an affair he wanted hushed up, a regrettable mistake. He thought nothing of getting rid of him. I'm sure he could have gotten him off the hook and chose not to. You know, out of sight, out of mind."

Marilyn put a hand on Rose's arm. "I'm so sorry you went through all of it. I had no idea."

"Dimitri saved me and paid for it with six years in prison. God, Marilyn, I looked into his eyes yesterday and I could see how he's hardened. It terrifies me."

Rose closed her eyes for a moment. Marilyn couldn't possibly know how deep her exhaustion went. Yes, she was tired, tired of being torn apart, of bearing such a heavy secret. Her nerve endings felt raw and exposed. Her world was beginning to unravel all at once, and she wasn't sure what to do. Last night, sitting across from Dimitri had seemed unreal. All these years later she'd assumed she'd be pretty much steeled against feeling anything for him. But just the sight of him across the table had been enough to convince her that what she'd felt for Dimitri years earlier would never die.

Marilyn's forehead wrinkled. Rose knew her friend was worried.

"Are you thinking Dimitri is the one stalking you? Shouldn't you tell this to Evan?"

The Dimitri she knew a long time ago wouldn't; he would have confronted her squarely. However, the Dimitri she'd come face-to-face with last night . . . Rose nervously ran her fingers through her hair.

"I don't know how much to tell Evan. I don't think it would occur to him that his brother would be so twisted. Maybe I should try to sort things out myself."

Marilyn shook her head. "Are you crazy? If you think he'll just go away, you're wrong. With all the publicity surrounding Dimitri's trial, his past is bound to come out—his relationship with you, the manslaughter, even the fact that he's James's son."

Rose scanned the restaurant, still nervous about being overheard. "When he joined us last night, I felt my throat closing up. My whole body was trembling."

Marilyn leaned forward until no more than a few inches separated their shoulders. "I . . . I don't know what to say," she murmured.

Rose cleared her throat and stared straight ahead of her. "There's nothing to say. I'm in trouble, and I have no clue how the hell to get out of it. I guess I'm telling you all this not just because you're my dearest friend, but also, in case something happens to me, someone should know that Alexis is Dimitri's child."

Marilyn's mouth dropped open—and stayed there.

Dimitri pushed past the people in the crowded lobby. He found the public phones located in the far corner behind the bellhop station. He checked his watch, then fumbled inside the pocket of his cashmere overcoat for change. He didn't want to use the phone in his suite for fear of being overheard by Jewel or a maid, maybe even by a bug. One couldn't be too careful. He punched in the number and waited. One ring, two rings, then on the third he heard a voice say, "Yes."

He clutched the receiver with both hands. "It's me. When can I have the information?"

A pause, then, "Give me a few days. You'll know everything there is to know about Rose Miller."

He heaved a sigh. "Make sure. I want to know every detail about her life, every aspect. Past and present, I want her upcoming schedule, as well as what kind of coffee she drinks in the morning. How many sugars, how many times she stirs it. Do you understand? Details to the nth degree. That's why I'm paying you so much money."

"I've already taken care of it." The line went dead.

Dimitri glanced around the Plaza's opulent lobby. When he was convinced no one had seen him, he left the phone booth and headed for the elevator, catching a glimpse of Central Park through one of the revolving doors of the hotel's 59th Street entrance. *My world,* he thought, lavish, filled with beautiful and powerful people. In this world he could afford the best of everything—the expensive suits, the yachts, the expensive cars, a fleet of helicopters—the good life. Surrounded by the accoutrements of his success, he might have found it easy to forget the cruel turn of life that had brought him to this particular point in time. But he could never blot out the past, because at his core he was lonely. Long ago, he'd thought that loving Rose would fill the chasm inside him that had opened when his mother abandoned him. But his feelings for Rose had only intensified the emptiness, and his years in prison had finished the job: the abyss had never been—would never be—filled. Now he faced another sentence, this time on a trumped-up charge of racketeering.

At first he had dismissed the indictment as merely a bump in his carefully calculated plan, a typical government ploy. Then he'd realized he was being framed. He had to admit, the evidence seemed overwhelming. When his corporate books were seized and scrutinized, they showed doctoring. But not by him. Someone had switched his books. Of that much he was sure. Now he faced the roar of the lion, another prison sentence. If the pendulum swung his way—great. If it didn't, he was ready. He'd face the music once again. But not until he took those responsible with him. This time, he wouldn't go down alone.

17

At eight P.M. Rose arrived at the ballroom on the third floor of the Sheraton New York on Seventh Avenue and West 52nd Street. Gilbert Spalding, president of the Mystery Writers Guild, greeted her at the door. The middle-aged, balding man was dressed in a black tuxedo with a red bow tie and matching cummerbund.

"Rose, congratulations. It's great to have you here. Mr. Roselli has been lurking by the door waiting for you. I believe he's gone off to get a drink."

Rose managed a smile, her eyes darting over his shoulders at the guests already assembled inside the ballroom. She began to make her way through the crowd, stopping to greet Sue Grafton, who looked adorable in a sleek black pantsuit. Patricia Cornwell smiled and waved from across the room, and Rose made a mental note to tell her later how much she'd enjoyed *Hornet's Nest.* Robert Parker's bulky frame barely fit into his tuxedo, and with him was his beautiful wife of many years, Susan, who was dressed more casually than most of the other women. Then she caught sight of a young man with shoulder-length brown hair whose face looked familiar—was it Caleb Carr, author of *The Alienist*? He was wearing black jeans with his tuxedo jacket. Mentally Rose applauded his resourcefulness in bending the rules that governed the social aspect of her work. Sometimes she felt that she was going through life in a disguise and yearned to be herself, to wear jeans or sweats—casual, the woman she really was inside.

Exquisite fresh flowers adorned the steps leading to the dais where the winners would make their acceptance speeches. In her present mood, the lonely gloom of the dimly lit coat check would have been preferable to the romantic excitement of the ballroom. Reluctantly Rose made her way to the center of the spacious room. Dario was already seated and waved her to the table they would share with other award winners.

"You look stunning," he said as he put his arm around her waist and pulled her closer to him. Then he planted an affectionate kiss on her cheek. "How do you feel?" he asked. "Is my favorite award-winning client nervous?"

"I'm fine," she managed to say while simultaneously moving a bit away from him. Her eyes instinctively swept the room. It was still haunting her: the feeling of being watched. She knew it seemed paranoid, but she couldn't help it.

Dario was smiling. "We'll take this room tonight, Rose, have them eating out of our hands." He looked around and checked out the crowd. "Have you seen all the press?" Rose turned her head slightly to follow his gaze. "Look, there's Richard Johnson at table number four, facing the podium," he said quietly. Rose eyed the handsome blond man engrossed in conversation with a woman Rose thought she recognized as Nancy Taylor Rosenberg. Johnson headed the tantalizing gossip sheet known as "Page Six" for the *New York Post.* "He wants to speak with you after the ceremony. I think it would be a great boost for *Thorns of a Rose.*"

She didn't hear him. She was thinking about the roses.

The cocktail hour was ending, and those guests who had decided not to stay for the long award ceremony were drifting out of the room. Now the crowd was more intimate—the core of mystery writers and those who supported their work in one way or another. Still, Rose was on edge. It's just because you have to speak before the group, she told herself.

Conversation came to a halt as Rose made her way to the podium to accept her award. Despite her cool appearance, her voice was low and throaty, and she sounded nervous.

"La-Ladies and gentlemen, I'm honored to be here this evening . . ."

As Rose fought her way through the speech she had rehearsed earlier, she began to fumble. Each time she corrected herself quickly, trying to come off at least somewhat presentable, but she couldn't focus. No matter how hard she tried, she couldn't shake the uncomfortable feeling that he was out there, watching and waiting. Her stomach began to churn.

"Thank you once again," she finished at last, and the applause rippled like thunder. Her smile was sincere, but so were the twinges of anxiety.

Once the applause died down, she left the ballroom discreetly and made a beeline for the nearest ladies' room. Inside, she turned on the cold water and dabbed at her forehead with facial tissues from her purse. She had thought she could get through the evening without feeling panicky, but the setting, another ballroom like at the book party, had made her sweat. She had obliged Dario and insisted Evan stay home.

"There's no need for you to come," she had said last night over dinner. "You're working too hard, Evan. I can take care of myself. Besides, Dario will be with me."

Now she was sorry that Evan wasn't with her. Just his presence, or even Marilyn's, would have settled her nerves. But Marilyn couldn't come, either. She had a meeting with a lawyer, who was flying in from Los Angeles to finalize a contract between a client and the author's publisher.

Rose stared at her reflection in the mirror and was shocked at what she saw. Yes, the features were the same, but she looked drained. Her complexion was pale. Deep circles darkened the skin beneath her eyes. Little lines crimped the sides of her mouth, where she'd never had lines before. Her face had always been thin, but now her cheeks looked hollowed out, her lips pinched.

Hastily she emptied the contents of her Judith Leiber bag on the counter, spilling out the small makeup compacts. With quick, expert strokes she dabbed on more pink lipstick, applied a touch more concealer under her eyes, and then brushed on a heavier stroke of blush above her high cheekbones. With her hands, she fluffed her shiny blond mane gently around her shoulders. After the touch-up, she watched the color return to her face. The churning in her stomach had stopped, and her wobbling knees felt stable again. She threw the tissue in a wastebasket, turned the door handle, and walked out into the now empty hall. Still not ready to deal with the crowd in the ballroom, she headed for a nearby sitting area with two peach-colored sofas, a coffee table, and a watercolor of the Hudson River. There she sank into the velvet softness of one of the sofas.

The bang of a distant door slamming made her jump. She looked up, fully expecting to see Dario. He'd want her to come back into the party and "work the room." In the low-lit hall, all she could make out was a tall man in a tuxedo who seemed to be coming in her direction.

Cloaked in the shadow and silence, he kept coming toward her, his steps slow, purposeful, his arms bent at the elbows. She bolted off the sofa and noticed that the man seemed to be holding something in each hand. For a split second her fired-up imagination conjured up a gun, maybe even a knife. Then he passed through a pool of glassy light, and she recognized Dimitri. In one hand he was holding a copy of *Thorns of a Rose,* in the other a glass of champagne.

When he was in front of her, she looked first at him, then at the crystal glass in his hand. He towered over her. His stern face, with its square chin and iron jaw, and the line of thick, dark brows made him seem that much more threatening.

"Hello, Rose," he said in his deep, resonant voice.

Her heart began to pound. Her brain desperately ordered her body to flee, but she couldn't move. "What are you doing here? How did you get in?" she demanded.

He held out the glass. "Champagne?"

Rose shook her head.

A change came over Dimitri's face. "Evan gave me his ticket. He thought I might enjoy seeing you get an award. I thought it was rather generous of him."

Suddenly the feeling of fear left her, and she turned angry. "Evan wouldn't give you a ticket!"

"Why not? We're all one big happy family again, and I'm also an important client. Besides, last night we didn't really have a chance to catch up. It was so stifling with Evan present."

He brought the glass of champagne to his lips and took an exaggerated sip. "I wanted to tell you that I've been following your career in the newspapers and on television—quite impressive." He held out the copy of her book. "I don't have a pen, but if you do, perhaps you'll autograph it for me."

Rose could tell his smile was totally insincere. She shook her head, forcing her gaze to some invisible distant point so he couldn't tell how much his coolness tore at her.

Dimitri went on: "You're truly talented. But we always knew that, didn't we? Always so sweet, so polite. You had me fooled, Rose."

He set his champagne glass and the book on the coffee table and looked at her intently, almost leering. Did he sense her fear? She knew he was deliberately trying to intimidate her. But she'd be damned if she'd let him.

"You turned out to be quite an actress, a show-stopper, in fact."

Rose whirled around to leave, but Dimitri grabbed her arm and pulled her back.

"Not so fast, darling. We have lots to talk about."

She tried to wrestle free, but his grip was too strong. "Let go, Dimitri. You're hurting me."

He let out a hearty laugh. "Hurting you? Rose, I couldn't possibly hurt you. You proved that when you picked yourself up from that barn floor, brushed yourself off, and married Evan. Now that I think about it, you never even bothered to say good-bye."

"Damn you, Dimitri. If you think you can just come here and wreak havoc in my family's life, you're crazy."

Dimitri pulled her closer to him, digging his fingers into her skin. His free hand slid around her waist, curving her body into his arms.

All the fight began to drain out of her, but she forced herself to keep it alive. "I mean it, Dimitri. Goddamn it, let me go!"

Rose felt her legs press into his thighs and her breasts against his chest, followed by the sudden shock of his warm lips covering hers. It happened too quickly to resist, and then it seemed to happen in slow motion. His arms were taut around her, flattening her body against his. Dimitri kept his eyes open and on her face. When his tongue slid between her closed lips, she stiffened. Even if she wanted to protest, she couldn't. He took complete control of the kiss with a force that devastated all her resistance. His lips were hard and angry. His mouth was hot and wet and tasted of champagne.

She pulled back, just enough to see his face. He lifted her head a fraction, his eyes looking into hers, and she thought he was going to let her go. Instead he squeezed her so tightly, she cried out. She could feel the urgency in him, the telltale hardness pressing against her abdomen.

"Ah," he murmured. "The familiar taste of your mouth, the incredible warmth of your body. It's been a long time, Rose."

Her head began to spin, and her breathing grew shallow. Then her rational side kicked in. With a sudden motion, she jerked her head back and pushed him away, separating their bodies.

"Don't touch me." She could hear the warning in her own voice. Her head was swimming with uncertainty, confused by his actions, unsure of her feelings.

"You're still the same on the outside, Rose. Your luscious lips, your body, your touch, even your scent."

She stared back at him. Instead of tenderness, she saw rage in his eyes.

"And oh so easily led, so eager to please. Which one's the puppet? You or my brother? Does he bark and you bite? Have you fooled him into thinking that he's in charge? Tell me, Rose, how did a simple girl like yourself master the art of manipulation? It's made me start thinking about all those years ago at Laurel. Perhaps you manipulated me then, too. Did you?"

"You son of a bitch." She spoke out of hurt as well as rage. "Don't you ever come near me again."

This time, when she looked into his eyes she saw cynicism instead of anger.

"Funny, Rose, a minute ago, it didn't seem to bother you."

"Leave me alone, Dimitri. Stay out of my life, our lives, or else . . ."

He tilted his head just a bit, an unreadable look on his face. "Or else? Is that a threat, Rose? Are you trying to scare me?"

He took a step closer and grabbed both her elbows this time, pulling her face inches from his.

"Just remember, Rose—now that I'm back in town, I'll be watching you."

She let out a sob, unable to hold back. When he finally let her go, Rose ran through the hall, down the steps, and out the front entrance. It no longer mattered to her that she was the guest of honor. She had to get away. His parting words reverberated in her mind and confirmed her suspicion. First the card, then the petals, and now this. All that mattered was getting away from Dimitri. If only she could get him out of her life, forever.

Jewel reached over to the nightstand, grabbed the phone, and dialed her lover's number. After four rings she got a recording. She left a cryptic message, and two minutes later the phone rang in her Plaza suite.

"Is there a problem?" he said without preface.

"A potential problem . . . Rose."

"Is he seeing her again?"

"I don't know. But it sure looks that way."

"Why's that?"

She explained quickly, her voice hushed yet urgent. "Dimitri didn't come home last night. In fact, he walked in at eight this morning. No explanation. And he's out again tonight. He left in a tuxedo. In this morning's paper I read that Rose was receiving an award at some writers' shindig at the Sheraton. I'd bet all my jewelry that's where—"

"I'll need more proof than that," her lover interrupted, "and I'll need information about his other activities as well."

"I'll keep you posted. So help me God, if he . . . I'll see to it she . . ."

"Now, now, settle down," he said soothingly. "Don't get hysterical on me. I need you to remain calm. The right information could nail him." He was silent, then added, "We'll talk in the morning. Sweet dreams, darling."

18

Once back at her apartment, Rose stripped off her gown, washed her face, and reached for her most comfortable robe, a luxurious black cashmere that nearly reached the floor. When the phone rang, she let the machine get it. *It must be Dario,* she thought, *wondering what happened to me.* She didn't feel like talking to anyone right now. Her taped message ran its course, the machine beeped. Silence, then the sound of heavy breathing on the other end. She hurried over to the machine and turned up the volume, listening for background noises. A car horn, that was all. Then there was a click and the line went dead.

Evan—she needed to call him. She hoped that Dario had not called the Long Island house looking for her. Though she often stayed in the city when she had engagements at night, if Evan learned she had vanished from the awards ceremony, he would be frantic. Her gaze shifted to the mantel clock . . . eleven-thirty. *Too late to call,* she thought, *he needs the sleep.* Back in the bathroom, she tied her hair in a ponytail and applied some moisturizer to her face, hoping the soft cream would soothe her.

The mahogany bed that dominated the small bedroom was the first piece of furniture she had bought for the apartment. She'd come across it while shopping at ABC Carpet & Home, a multilevel emporium of European antiques and furnishings—and then she'd returned a few weeks later to purchase a mahogany dresser and two matching nightstands. They fit right in with her Victorian theme. The room was warm, tasteful, and comfortable.

She crawled under the mound of blankets and sheets, sinking into their cool softness. She was exhausted, but far from sleep. Dimitri's cynical chuckle replayed in her ears as she clutched her pillow. Could it be she alone who inspired such rage? More likely it was everything that had happened, an accumulation of all the insults and injuries he'd endured. Whether he hated her or loved her mattered less than the guilt she was feeling. Almost worse was her own sense of responsibility. Although she hadn't initiated their embrace, she had responded to his kiss. And she'd enjoyed it.

The peal of the phone interrupted the volatile mixture of feelings churning inside of her. She let the machine pick up. This time the caller left a message.

"She's dead. Soon it will be your turn." Then the line clicked off.

Rose sat up in bed as if pulled by some magnetic force. She ran to the machine and hit the rewind button. She did not recognize the caller's voice. Instinctively she hit *69, but a recording came on. The number was blocked and could not be accessed.

"She's dead." Who? Rose thought.

Immediately she reached inside her desk drawer, pulled out her phone book, and dialed Detective Falcone's number.

Billy crossed the room and stood to the side of the window, peeking out from behind the blinds. Outside, light snow was falling. *A typical late night in New York City*, he thought, watching the red and yellow lights of taxis as the drivers maneuvered recklessly through traffic.

He turned his gaze back to the white damask sofa, now splattered with blood. Marilyn's twisted body sprawled across it. A pool of blood leaked obscenely on the celadon green wool carpet. A bloodstained knife lay beside her. It had been so easy to break in. He had merely lurked outside until he'd seen her come out of a taxi and then had followed her to the apartment on the Upper East Side, right down the street from Rose. He had worn a simple disguise, just in case she saw him. But she never looked behind her. The doorman, the idiot, must have assumed that he was with her. While she searched for her keys, he hid in the enclosure created by a bank in the wall. As soon as she unlocked her door, Billy pushed his way inside. The look of shock, then terror, in her eyes kicked up the hunger inside of him. She tried to scream, but he covered her mouth with his hand, held the knife to her throat, and whispered, "Surprise, surprise!"

Seconds later he thrust the knife into her neck, making contact with soft tissue, just enough to make her bleed, exactly what he had intended. He didn't want to kill her too soon. He stabbed her with the knife again and again, in those places certain to bleed but not kill. Then, when he'd had enough, he severed her carotid artery and she no longer struggled. Finally her body went limp. After it was over, it was time to set the stage and make all his preparations. He knew Rose would be impressed.

Scattered around the living room were pillows he had stabbed until they bled feathers. He had ransacked her closet with unmitigated rage—stabbing her clothing, her leather pumps, even her handbags, until everything was in pieces, scattered everywhere. His eyes caught sight of two Victorian pewter frames, each holding a photo of Marilyn and Rose, obviously taken a few years apart. He threw them to the floor and stomped them into the thick carpet, breaking the glass. Then he tore Marilyn's image from both of them. On the corner end table were seven hurricane candles, which he lit. Now that they were burning brightly, Billy took the opportunity to incinerate the photo of Marilyn's face. As he looked into the flames, he imagined Rose's shock when she discovered his massacre. He was certain that Marilyn's murder would send her over the edge.

19

Rose paced the floor nervously as she watched Falcone hit the rewind button on her answering machine. John had, by a stroke of luck, been off-duty and only twenty minutes outside of the city when he responded to her page.

Falcone played the message back once more, then shut off the machine. "I'll take this," he said, waving the tape. "My friend Charlie Dawkins is a sergeant here at the Twentieth Precinct. He's specially trained in voice analysis. The caller most likely used one of those automated voice enhancers, but you never know. We might get lucky."

"I'm scared, John. Do you think it's true that someone, perhaps someone I know, is dead?"

"I wish I could answer that," Falcone said as he put the tape inside his pocket.

He then gestured for Rose to sit on the sofa and he took a seat for himself on one of the stools at the counter directly across from her. "Let's go over some details. Where were you tonight?"

"I was at an awards ceremony at the Sheraton." How unimportant that accolade seemed now.

"Tell me anything you think I should know. Who was there? Evan, I assume."

"No," she corrected him. "I was with my publicist Dario—Dario Roselli. He insisted I leave Evan at home."

Rose looked down at her lap as she felt her face flush. John was quiet for a moment, obviously thinking over this piece of information as he jotted down Roselli's name.

Tell him, Rose reasoned with herself. He needs to know. But how could she possibly explain?

"Anybody else?" he continued. "Did anything suspicious or out of the ordinary happen?"

She twisted her hands in her lap, stalling for time, and then said, "What do you mean?"

Falcone searched her face for a reaction. "Is there something more, Rose?"

She let out a long, drawn-out sigh, took a sip of the chamomile tea she'd made for them both, then haltingly she told him. "Dimitri Constantinos was there. He approached me when I was alone in an alcove."

Falcone's eyes widened. "Well, Evan is handling his case. Right?"

John was fly-fishing, using innocuous questions as the lure.

Rose put down her teacup and traced her finger around the gold-rimmed Lenox saucer. "I haven't been completely forthcoming with you about my past. He—I mean, Dimitri and I were involved before I married Evan. We left off on bad terms. There was an incident at the Laurel estate twelve years ago. Dimitri killed a man in self-defense. He had been protecting me. He went to prison, and I married Evan. I'm sure Dimitri's never gotten over my betrayal."

With this small piece of her secret out, Rose felt some relief. She was able to look at John directly instead of cringing.

"Did Constantinos threaten you tonight?"

Rose ran her fingers through her hair as she collected her thoughts. "I don't know. He grabbed my arms, spoke for a while—"

"What did he say?" John interrupted.

Rose looked around the room, trying to get grounded.

Dimitri's voice resounded in her mind. "He was angry—bitter about . . ."

Suddenly Rose was compelled to move around. The room seemed too small. She stood up and walked into the kitchen to make herself more tea. John turned around on the counter stool, his eyes following her every move.

"Rose, tell me. If you want help, I have to know everything."

She turned to him quickly, her black robe swirling around her ankles. "Well, I remember the last thing he said after he let me go—he said, 'I'll be watching you.' "

Falcone sat still, seeming unmoved. "So you think he's the one stalking you? Do you think he's also the man on the tape?"

"Well, remember the roses I told you about at my book party? They were delivered the day after Dimitri arrived in town."

"That hardly incriminates the man," Falcone said matter-of-factly. "Why would a guy like Constantinos stalk you? If he wanted to kill you or anyone, he'd hire someone to do the dirty work. Besides, when would he have time? He's on trial."

Rose felt a part of her mind detach, and when she answered her voice seemed not to come from her. "I don't know what makes a man dangerous." Even as she spoke, the real Rose didn't want to believe that the cards, the phone call, or the threats were from Dimitri. But she was terrified nonetheless. John's gaze followed every motion of her eyes, hand, and face. She saw him studying her for clues. She wondered what he was thinking.

"None of this makes sense, Rose. I'm still not convinced that Dimitri could be a suspect."

With something akin to relief, she accepted his statement instantly. "Oh, you're probably right." She put her hands in the pockets of her robe and examined her bare feet.

"I've got a lot to process about all of this." John lifted himself off the stool, gathered up his belongings from the sofa, and headed toward the door.

She found herself following him, not wanting him to leave. Suddenly Rose was petrified to be alone.

When he turned to say good-bye, she clutched his arm. The story she'd kept hidden from him and had shared only with Marilyn was wrapped around her, tying her into knots. At that moment she realized that keeping these secrets could prove extremely dangerous. Screw James Miller and his desire to bury all the old Miller family scandals. She realized she needed Falcone to stay.

"Wait, John, there's more. . . ."

20

As Rose stepped out of the shower, the feel of the cold marble beneath her feet sent a shiver through her body. She grabbed a towel and wrapped it around her. The day was going to be another hectic one. Dario had given Rose a wake-up call at seven A.M. It had been close to three when Falcone finally left her apartment, and she had been groggy when she spoke to Dario.

He was worried about her sudden disappearance last night. Rose had placated him with the excuse that she didn't feel well and then changed the subject quickly.

"So what does my schedule look like this morning?" she had asked.

"You have a live radio interview at eight o'clock," he'd replied, and she'd begun to protest. In her present state of mind, there was no way she could go on the air.

Dario had told her about the interview just days earlier. She remembered the conversation explicitly, because he had interrupted her train of thought in the middle of writing an important scene. She had written it down in her appointment book, but last night's events and the intense conversation with John Falcone had eclipsed the memory of her commitment this morning.

Right after she hung up with Dario, Rose pressed the speed dial on her phone to call him back and force him to cancel, but then she released the button. She would never do something so unprofessional. She called Marilyn at home. She needed one of her friend's pep talks, but all she got was the voice mail. Checking the time, she realized she had only about one hour to shower and get her thoughts together. She'd be lucky to do her interview in her bathrobe.

Staring at her reflection in the bathroom mirror, she was shocked by what she saw: the destructive effects of ever-present fear. It had become a shadow that pursued her in her dreams at night, the invisible wolf that crouched in the darkened corners everywhere she went. *He is out there, waiting and watching for the right moment to strike. He's killing me slowly, and probably getting his pleasure watching me squirm.*

The phone startled her—her interview. She ran, and on the fourth ring she picked up the receiver.

"Hello?" she said, out of breath.

"This is WWNH in Connecticut. Is this Rose Miller?" The man's voice on the other end was loud, abrupt.

"Yes, yes, this is she—I'm ready—"

"You die next!"

Then the receiver on the other end crashed down and there was only silence. She froze, the phone still in her hand. Shock waves raced through her body as she dropped the receiver. How did he know she had an interview?

Billy read the *Daily News* article with intense fascination. WOMAN FOUND MURDERED IN LONG ISLAND MOTEL ROOM, read the headline. It was splendid. Journalists certainly knew a story when they saw one—the front page, no less. He wondered what had taken them so long to discover Rachel's body. Although he had paid for a two-night stay and requested no maid service, he'd thought for sure one of the maids would watch him leave the room, then go inside and snoop around. He was wrong. The article said the body was badly decomposed. His pulse was racing. A burst of adrenaline shot through his body, and he felt pumped, just like the elation he experienced after each "seduction." The power struggle; the elaborate plan always working just as he wished; the thrill of victory; finally the euphoria.

The very thought of Rose, her body cold and limp, had a mystical hold on him, so much better than the bodies of those he was using as a substitute for her. Mary, an ash blond actress from Parsippany, New Jersey, had felt good in his arms. Shelley, the showgirl from Manhattan—feisty. She'd fought him so hard in the end, he'd had to tie her hands behind her back.

And then Rachel, so exquisite, so fragile . . . He closed his eyes, and when he held her tight against his body, he was lost. She was Rose . . . they all were. Except for Marilyn. She was just an example, a point he had to make. He needed to prove to Rose just how serious he was. He thought about Rose now and imagined her reaction, the look of horror in her face when she saw what he'd done to Marilyn. His heart began beating faster. Soon it would be her turn.

What would that moment be like? The moment he'd been waiting for? He imagined her body in his arms, their dance, the wedding song. All the other women were simply practice. Rose was his ultimate bride.

Billy's mirthless laughter filled the room.

21

Falcone pushed his way through the crowded hallway. He shook his head in disapproval at the nosy New Yorkers, always glued to crime scenes. Now they wanted a look at the corpse, as if they'd been invited to a viewing. The press was already there in droves, with photographers snapping away at the apartment building and anyone who entered.

He threaded his way through the crowd and ducked under the yellow ribbon that blocked entry to the apartment. When Falcone had beeped Charlie earlier this morning to discuss Rose Miller's case, nothing had prepared him for the return phone call minutes later, telling Falcone to get to 73rd and Fifth Avenue—"Immediately!"

Inside the victim's apartment, forensic technicians hustled around, busily collecting carpet samples and blood samples and dusting for prints. He saw Charlie in the corner of the room. With his burly body and shock of gray hair, he always reminded Falcone of Santa Claus.

"John." Charlie walked toward him as Falcone moved farther inside. "I thought you might need to take a look at the corpse. Her name is Marilyn Grimes. She's apparently Rose Miller's friend and also her agent."

"Jesus Christ." Falcone winced as he walked over to where Marilyn's body lay sprawled on the sofa. A pool of blood had drained onto the carpet. A bloody pillow covered her face. She was wearing a pair of slacks and a black bra, the latter exposing ample cleavage.

Falcone made a gesture with his hands. "May I?" he asked. Charlie nodded, and Falcone hesitantly lifted the pillow covering Marilyn's face. Detective Falcone was used to the sight and smell of death and was surprised at his own emotional reaction. Marilyn Grimes was obviously a stand-in for Rose Miller in the stalker's mind, and it got to him. Slash marks crisscrossed her once lovely neck, and her bottom lip was split in two. The murderer had not touched her face, so the split lip might have been an accident, perhaps the result of her falling onto the glass cocktail table. Her hair was in disarray. Her black-tie tuxedo pants remained intact, untouched. No one had violated this victim, except to kill her.

"What time was she found and by whom?" Falcone asked.

Charlie scratched his head, then answered, "Around ten A.M. It seems like we're dealing with a real nut case. The killer called 911 himself from a pay phone and reported that he'd murdered Rose Miller's best friend. I guess it's safe to say he wanted Mrs. Miller to know as soon as possible."

Falcone pulled out a Polaroid Instamatic from his duffel bag. "Do you mind if I take a few shots?"

"No, take as many as you need," Dawkins replied.

Falcone focused his lens on the body, snapped three pictures, then moved the camera around the rest of the room. First, the closet full of torn clothing, tattered shoes, and ripped handbags. Next, the blood-splattered sofa and carpet, then the torn, burned photographs, and last, the seven burned-out candles on the end table.

The scene reminded Falcone of a sacrificial slaughter, a ritualistic slaying. He was looking at the work of a deranged mind, and he would bet that the psycho would become a serial killer, if he wasn't already. His rage was too hot to be extinguished by just one woman's murder. But what was the killer's connection to Rose? Someone was sending her a powerful message. Falcone knew it was his job to be the messenger.

Marilyn had only one sister, who lived in London, so there was no one but Rose to identify her body. In his car on the way to the morgue, Rose grasped Falcone's hand, clinging to reality in this surreal moment. She had spent time in morgues, watching autopsies on strangers, seeing their naked tagged bodies wheeled out from the refrigerator. She was no stranger to pathology labs and the telling evidence of what one man can do to another man. But those experiences might as well have happened to another woman in a different lifetime. Under the circumstances she was beyond feeling all together.

She kept seeing Marilyn's concerned face over dinner at Il Cantinori. *"You have to go to the police,"* Marilyn had said. Now her best friend's words rang in her ears, a long wailing echo. Was it only last night that they had shared that intimate dinner? If she had known it would be the last time she'd see her dearest friend alive, would Rose have done anything different? She had agonized over this question since John had told her the unbearable news.

Falcone hadn't been in the station house when she returned his call, so she had asked one of the officers to page him. When he showed up at her door twenty minutes later, she heard the sirens in her head and knew something was wrong. At first she didn't grasp what he had told her. Marilyn, dead? Impossible.

Rose had gone immediately on automatic pilot. There were no tears; she was anesthetized. Now, sitting beside Falcone on their way to the hospital's morgue, she reflected that Marilyn's death seemed so unfair, and all the more tragic because *she* was supposed to be the victim, not Marilyn. Then she remembered the anonymous caller's voice: "You die next."

"I have some pictures I want you to look at." The sound of John's voice brought her back to the present.

"Pictures?"

He picked up a large manila envelope, opened the clasp, and pulled out some photographs.

"I took these at the murder scene. I know this is hard on you, Rose, and these photos will make it even harder, but I need to show them to you. Maybe you'll recognize something in the background. Something that might lead us to the murderer."

Her pulse quickened as she took the photos from him and sifted through them slowly.

"Block out her body, Rose, concentrate on the background."

She followed his advice and found that she actually was so numb, she could ignore the figure on the couch.

One photo showed a close-up of Marilyn's face partially hidden beneath a shredded pillow. In another, her face was visible, the pillow removed. Rose tried to move quickly past this one, but her resistance broke down. She focused on Marilyn's expression. Even in death there was a look of horror in her eyes. Tears streamed down the sides of Rose's face, uncontrollable sobs made their way up from her lungs. Shots of the bloodied sofa, the bright red stain on the carpet, the candles. The candles . . . She studied the photo closely, then bolted forward.

Gasping, she said, "Oh, my God!"

Falcone reached out, keeping one hand on the steering wheel, and grabbed her shoulder. "Rose, I . . . I know how hard . . ."

She only nodded. "I set this up," she said with disbelief.

"What?"

She didn't look at him. Her fingers gripped the photographs. She pointed to the candles, then the shredded pillows. "My new novel . . . the one I'm working on." She fought hard to continue. "There's a scene toward the middle of the book—a murder . . . it's setup, carried out just like this."

She turned to face Falcone and saw the disbelief in his eyes.

"Rose, now come on. How can—"

"No, John, I'll show you the pages from my manuscript. It's set up exactly like this—the sofa, the clothing, the candles . . ." Her hand flew up to her mouth and she nearly choked, remembering in vivid detail. The victim, Amanda, a lawyer, had come home to find her elegant apartment ransacked. And for some inexplicable reason Rose had decided that seven hurricane candles would burn brightly in Amanda's living room.

"Were there torn photos near her body?" she asked John, her voice tremulous.

After the stalker stabbed Amanda repeatedly, he left her to bleed to death as he tore up photographs of her beloved family and friends. In the pathology report, the medical examiner in *Murderous Intentions* had surmised that the position of the victim's head would have allowed her to witness this desecration until she lost consciousness.

John pointed out the violently slashed pieces of photos on the floor. Until this moment she had written about her villain's rage but she never could have conjured up a real-life scene that oozed such evil. She thought about the eyes of such a psychopath moving across the pages of her manuscript, and she felt nauseated. How had he gotten hold of her work in progress? Did he find it in Marilyn's apartment? Rose thought this over. No. She had made Marilyn promise to throw out each draft, and Marilyn would never have broken this trust.

"Rose," John said, "what are you thinking?"

Falcone's expression told her he thought she was confused, mixing up the murder scene with her own writing.

"No, really listen to me," Rose begged. "The slashed throat . . . the ruined photos"—she paused to take a breath—"and the seven hurricane candles burning at the murder scene. I wrote Marilyn's death scene. Oh, John, what am I going to do?"

"Rose, you're drawing conclusions without enough evidence. Stop torturing yourself."

"You don't understand. Marilyn's murder isn't the end of this story. In the final scene, the villain destroys the woman he's really after."

22

Falcone's eyes followed Evan as he walked across the library of Paradiso, a book-lined, mahogany-paneled room whose most arresting feature was its stone fireplace, presently generating a roaring fire.

"A little brandy before we start?" Evan asked. His voice was shaky, revealing his reaction to the insanity that had marked this day.

John Falcone nodded and watched as Evan opened up a mahogany cabinet, intricately carved and inlaid with jade. He pulled out an exquisite decanter and filled two brandy snifters.

"Beautiful decanter," Falcone said.

"Rose collects crystal pieces of all kinds. She likes the way the glass refracts the sun into rainbows."

"That sounds like Rose," Falcone said.

"Rose is special; her way of looking at the world is unique. And her values have integrity. She's a natural, you know? Everything about her is real. She lacks artifice, thank God. Not like most of the others in our circle."

Evan walked toward Falcone, seated on the custom-made leather sofa, and handed him a glass of brandy. Then he sat on the other side of the detective. Both men took a sniff of their brandy and swirled their glasses. Falcone sipped the amber liquid. It was beyond smooth, almost sensuous. *Definitely not the house brand*, he thought. But then again, the rich lived large, the best of everything.

Evan continued. "Even the trophy wives, the second wives of the men I associate with, don't have much in their lives—not like Rose."

Evan's eyes darted through the open doorway, out into the hall, and up the stairs. Once Rose had positively identified Marilyn's body,

Falcone had called Evan from the morgue. The judge had granted a recess, and Evan was at the hospital in less than an hour. Falcone recalled the expression on Evan's face when he saw Rose, looking small and defenseless in a chair in the medical examiner's office. He admired Evan Miller's unconditional love for his wife. It was clearly expressed on his face, which reflected her anguish. He had soothed her the way a horse trainer might calm a frightened Thoroughbred. The three had driven back to Paradiso in Falcone's car.

"You can imagine the torment my wife is going through."

Falcone took another sip from his glass, listening intently.

"Although I'm devastated by Marilyn's death, I have to admit, Detective Falcone, that I am most concerned about the safety of my wife. This is all a little too close for comfort."

"Yes, I'm extremely alarmed. We're following up some leads." Falcone unconsciously copied Evan's formal way of speaking, then added sincerely, "As her friend and not just as a detective, I'm also concerned about your wife's safety."

"I need to be kept informed about everything," Evan interjected. "If she's pursuing something, a scene that needs research, a book signing with an unmanageable crowd—she needs to be watched. I need you to assure me that there will be the best protection for my wife. I know you'll need assistance. I want a bodyguard assigned as soon as possible, and a private investigator. Can you arrange these things for me? If you're in charge, I know Rose will feel more secure."

Falcone nodded. "Absolutely. If I were in your position, I would do the same."

"Guarantee me you'll do your best to prevent anything from happening to my wife," Evan insisted.

"You have my word," replied Falcone.

As Falcone put on his coat, he turned to Evan and said, "Oh, one last thing. Do you think Dimitri Constantinos could possibly be the one stalking Rose?"

"Dimitri?" Evan asked, puzzled. "He's my client. She doesn't even know him."

Getting in to see Dimitri Constantinos was much easier than getting his attention, Falcone realized when he was admitted to his elaborate suite at the Plaza. For the past ten minutes he had been seated across from Dimitri, listening in on a conversation between Dimitri and his press secretary, a middle-aged man with a receding hairline and small, close-set brown eyes who was trying to convince him to agree to a press conference. At the same time, Dimitri signed contracts, talked to his assistants, made numerous phone calls, and ignored Falcone.

All of a sudden Dimitri's eyes leveled on Falcone. "You were saying, Detective?" he asked in the clipped tone of one issuing a command. The press secretary left the room discreetly.

"I need to discuss Rose Miller with you. There's a situation, and it may concern you. You do know her?"

Dimitri's face was blank.

Then, as though sharing his problems with a colleague, Dimitri gestured to the paper-strewn desk, the bank of phones with each line lit up. "You see how it is, John. May I call you John?"

The detective didn't respond.

"Six years ago my company didn't exist. I worked for my father-in-law. But I'm sure you know all this."

John nodded. Who didn't know the story of this man?

Constantinos leaned his elbows on the desk, chin resting in his enormous workingman's hands. "Now Constantinos Enterprises is pursued by hopeful buyers—corporations that would like to consume us—or, rather, me."

Falcone had no idea where this was going, but he knew whatever Dimitri said should be remembered.

"Mr. Artlow on line three," his assistant spoke into the intercom.

"Will we be long?" Dimitri asked courteously, and Falcone shook his head no.

"I'll get back to him." His assistant started to protest, but Constantinos cut off the intercom.

Gesturing to the phone, Dimitri said, "Jack Artlow—perhaps you've heard of him? He's the chairman of Hotel and Resorts International and also serves on my board of directors. So does Tyler Livingston and Marcus Regan. Do these names mean anything to you?"

Falcone thought the other man's attitude was leaning toward contemptuous. So he took control of the conversation.

"Rose Miller, Mr. Constantinos?"

"Please call me Dimitri. Yes, Rose and I grew up together."

"That would be on James Miller's estate?"

Constantinos paused and then said, "That's correct."

"You've known her a long time as well as her husband?"

Dimitri pulled his elbows off his desk and placed his hands behind his neck. "So you're not interested in the ins and outs of Dimitri and Co.?" He sneered his trademark semismile.

"No, frankly," replied the detective.

"Well, we're thinking of going public. I'll give you a tip, John—buy early."

Falcone had to admire him, he was stunningly deft—reclaiming the conversation, changing the rhythm so the pressure of his questions couldn't escalate.

Falcone continued. "Rose has received several deliveries of 'gifts' with cryptic notes, as well as threatening phone calls."

Dimitri shrugged and raised his eyebrows, looking surprised.

Faking? Falcone wondered.

Dimitri leaned back and raked his fingers through his glistening black hair. "Oh, I get it, Detective. You think it's me. Rose has convinced you I'm stalking her." He sounded cool, maybe even amused.

"No, not exactly, but she did tell me it was a possibility given the circumstances."

"What circumstances?"

"I mean, your history."

Dimitri focused on the clock hanging near the door. The loud ticking seemed magnified. For a moment Falcone thought he caught a glimpse of remorse in the man's eyes, as though he had struck a chord in the unreachable Dimitri Constantinos. But then the look changed.

"Our 'history,' as you call it, is long past. It certainly has nothing to do with Rose being stalked." He paused meaningfully. "If she is being stalked, that is, and not just getting paranoid from writing all those scary stories." At this he smiled at Falcone, but the detective kept his face blank. "What is it you want, Detective? I have a full schedule. I'm afraid I don't have time to placate Rose Miller's fantasies."

Falcone was at a loss for words. Was he crazy thinking he'd come here this morning and get full cooperation? From Dimitri Constantinos? The man was impenetrable, and Falcone had no solid proof of anything.

Falcone stood. "I'll show myself out."

The door closed and Dimitri stood up, his hands jammed in the pockets of his slacks. He opened the top drawer, unlocked the steel box he kept there, and removed a recent photo of Rose taken by Annie Leibovitz for *Vanity Fair* magazine and an old photo he had taken of Rose when she was about sixteen. She was sitting atop a beautiful black horse. Her blond hair hung long and loose on her shoulders, and she was smiling at Dimitri. He passed his thumb lightly over her face and for a moment sought the right adjective to describe her. Luminous? Captivating? Extraordinary? *Yes,* he thought, *extraordinary.*

The clamorous ringing of the phone broke his concentration.

"Ah, Dimitri—you didn't come home last night."

"Business, Jewel." He was hardly listening. He could tell from the background noise that she was calling from a salon.

"What kind of business would keep you out all night? Your side of the bed wasn't slept in. Daddy says you don't spend enough time at home—with me."

Daddy this, Daddy that. If she only knew how he had pulled Daddy's ass out of the gutter years ago, she'd be shocked. Yet despite the respect he'd earned Joseph, the old man insisted on keeping his hands in the till, hanging out with the worst of them, loan sharks, pimps, and prostitutes. *You could take the man out of the street,* he thought . . . *but oh well, it didn't matter.* There were things in Braun's past that Jewel would never know, things her father had done when she was still innocent, just a child. For some time he had not only laundered drug money for South American cartels, he'd also overseen his own drug distribution: cocaine and speed. Lately Dimitri heard Braun was heavy into heroin. But Jewel never knew the worst parts about her daddy. As the only child of a widower, he'd made himself her hero. Her father was a knight in shining armor, always there to catch her when she fell. Braun had protected her from the truth, and Dimitri Constantinos kept up the charade. It didn't seem necessary to tell Jewel that "Daddy" was a dirty lowlife.

He wanted to tell her that he knew all about her own forays, but why let her know how much he had on her? It went against his philosophy. Right now his primary concern was the drop in last weekend's earnings at his Vegas casino. One reason Dimitri's net worth hovered around $400 million was that he kept track of every business decision, every dollar spent, and every dollar earned—whether it be his new line of specialty cigar stores or his major hotel and gambling operations. Everything counted. That had always been his philosophy and the key to his success.

"I have to go, Jewel. I have more pressing things on my mind." He broke the connection before she could respond.

He slipped the photos back into his drawer, grabbed his suit jacket from the back of the chair, and buzzed the concierge. "Please have my car ready. I'll be down in a few minutes."

Constantinos had an appointment, one he couldn't be late for. At least not if he wanted to find out more about Rose.

23

Dimitri looked around the low-lit bar, below street level, and knew he wouldn't be recognized here because of its upscale clientele. Pravda, on Lafayette Street in lower Manhattan, was a luxurious Russian-influenced cigar-and-vodka bar.

The man he was meeting sat with his head down at one of Pravda's red banquettes, a shot of one of the finest vodkas in front of him, a cigar burning slowly in a nearby ashtray. His hands rested on a folder.

"You work fast," Dimitri said, sliding into the booth.

"That's what you pay me for."

Dimitri gave him a curt smile. "What do you have for me?"

"Plenty." The man opened the folder and emptied a dozen snapshots of Rose.

Dimitri went through them slowly, relishing each one:

Rose leaving the mansion with her daughter; Rose picking her daughter up at school; Rose having lunch with a man who the investigator said was her publicist, Dario Roselli.

"She stays at her apartment in the city at least two times a week." He shoved a piece of paper at Dimitri. "Here's the address. She's always there alone."

Dimitri cleared his throat. "What else?"

"She eats at Fresco, Serendipity, and Bruno's. Lunches at Le Cirque, Michael's, Cipriani's, and Balthazar. Those are the regular places, though she and her husband sometimes dine together at other, more romantic spots."

Dimitri thought about the evening at Match—yes, you could call that romantic.

"She spends weekends on Long Island. Takes her daughter to the Celebrity Diner every Saturday morning at nine A.M. At eleven the kid has a ballet class in the area, Rose accompanies her. Sometimes they're driven by the old man I told you about before, Larry. Usually she does a little shopping while the girl is in class. At one, latest, they're on their way back home. Sundays, the family, including James Miller, go to the nine o'clock mass at St. Paul's Church, also in Brookville."

Dimitri stared down at the photo of Rose and Alexis entering church. Rose had her arm around her daughter's shoulder protectively. He focused on the girl, realizing he had never seen a picture of her before. She was stunning, extraordinarily beautiful. But unlike her mother, the little girl had dark hair.

Dimitri collected all the photos, shoved them back in the folder, tucked it under his arm, and handed the man three grand. As he slid out of the booth, he said, "I'll be in touch."

Kevin Allen rolled up the sleeves of his white Brooks Brothers shirt and looked down at the notes he had taken during the phone conversation. He had not been all that shocked when James Miller called, though the defense usually didn't call the prosecution unless they wanted to switch sides. But he wasn't prepared for the surprise Miller dropped in his lap.

"Just tell me this: How do I know for certain that this information on Constantinos is true?" he asked James, referring to a tape Miller had messengered to him.

"I'm a man of my word."

"Unfortunately, Mr. Miller, I need more than your word."

"Listen, you won't be sorry," James replied confidently. "I promise you, I'll pay you back twofold. Take Dimitri down and you'll earn my respect."

"Why take down a man your firm represents?"

"Don't ask questions," James said impatiently. "That information I just sent you will nail him. Isn't that what you want?"

"I can't promise to protect you if your son, his lawyer, discovers the source of this information."

James laughed. "Oh, don't worry about his lawyer. When my son gets into office, a lot of favors will be returned, if you know what I mean."

"*If* your son gets into office," Kevin corrected Miller.

James cleared his throat. "When my son gets in office," he admonished the DA, "we'll all be fat and happy. We're going to ride this thing to the top. Once he's governor, the next step will be plotting out his presidential run."

"Sounds like a carefully mapped-out plan." Kevin thought about the obviously false information. Miller's evidence now corroborated Sheila's information. The stories these witnesses told were so similar that they had to be trumped up, especially given Sheila's and James Miller's vested interest in Madam May's Escort Service. But Kevin didn't care. He had made up his mind that he was going to use whatever he could to get Constantinos, ethics and conscience be damned.

Kevin pushed Miller harder. "None of us can be certain Evan is a shoe-in. What promises do I get if he doesn't succeed?"

"That's impossible," James said. "The people want someone young, someone fresh. By the way, is it true what I've heard? You're considering running against my son?" James continued on mockingly, "Now we both know how absurd that is. I don't mean to insult you, but you know you have no chance of getting a place on the ticket on your own."

Kevin read through the insult but held back his words. In the long run he knew his court victory would win over old man Miller's checkbook.

"And there isn't anyone else," James continued. His voice became louder, as though he were talking closer into the receiver of the phone. "My son is the perfect choice. You'll see. When he's in office, we'll have the world on a string. You just keep up your end. Get Dimitri—and I'll take care of mine. Play your cards right and you'll be part of the winning team—maybe even lieutenant governor?"

Kevin hung up the phone and smiled. Not only would he be able to nail Dimitri Constantinos, he'd also be able to get an inside line from James about his strategies for his son's political plan—a look into the enemy camp. Then he could use what he had against all of them to make the Millers put him on the ticket. Never mind James's vague promises. When it was over, Kevin would demand exactly what he wanted. This was more than twofold—this was a triple win for him, absolute pay dirt. Perhaps Evan Miller could be his lieutenant governor.

Falcone decided the best way to get to know his prime suspect was to spend a day in his life, so he hired a private investigator that the department sometimes worked with to tail Dimitri Constantinos for a day.

He glanced at the diary opened on the table at a greasy spoon in Astoria, Queens, near where the PI, Ingrid, lived:

7:05 p.m.: Inside Pravda, sitting with heavyset man—sifting through photos, gave man money for folder.
7:20 p.m.: Hops into a black Mercedes limo; heads downtown to the Holland Tunnel, toward New Jersey.
9:35 p.m.: Arrives in Atlantic City at his casino, the Ivory Palace.
9:45 p.m.: Valet tells me he rarely leaves until early a.m.

And so went Ingrid's report. A day in the life—or, in this case, a night in the life—sometimes gave away much of the suspect's secrets. There was no other way he would learn about this intensely private man. He thought about the conversation he had had with Rose about her past. While she was very open, Falcone sensed there were even more layers to peel through. Now it was his job to uncover them. Where would he start?

Falcone pulled out his cell phone and punched in Charlie's home number. After three rings he got a recording. At the beep he said, "Charlie, it's John. I need a favor. What do you have on Dimitri Constantinos's background? I need a list of priors—his addresses, before and after prison, anything you can dig up. It would take the boys out on the Island a week to get it, and I need it now."

24

You need some time off," Evan said to Rose as she lay curled up on the chaise longue in the far corner of the master suite. Rose didn't respond, merely stared blankly at the television screen. She could think about nothing other than Marilyn's murder.

She'd had a restless night, tossing and turning, caught up in a series of nightmares, awakening herself with her own screaming. Just before dawn, Evan convinced her to take another sedative, and she settled into a drugged slumber. She felt haggard, spent, and try as she might, she could not focus. In reality she didn't want to. Maybe if she stayed in this zombielike state, she wouldn't be able to think about what was happening around her. Just a short while ago her world seemed nearly perfect; but now everything she had was crashing down around her, and she found herself fighting desperately to remain stable. She had to hold on for Alexis's sake.

She sipped a cup of coffee slowly, her hands wrapped around the cup, soaking up the warmth. Ever since Marilyn's funeral the image of the coffin being lowered into the ground wouldn't leave her. Rose felt like a robot; she proceeded minute by minute mindlessly, dazed and sedated.

There were dozens of messages she had to return. Dario kept calling, imploring her to call him and assuring her that work would help keep her mind off Marilyn. There were police officers who needed to speak to her, reporters pushing for a story, and condolences from friends. What could she possibly tell them? Confide to them that she was responsible for Marilyn's death? That the killer used Marilyn to get her attention?

"I would feel more comfortable if you had better security," Evan was saying. "I spoke to Detective Falcone right after Marilyn's death. In fact, he's been looking for the right bodyguard. At the moment there's already twenty-four-hour security in place, but those guys are only temporary."

Rose heard Evan's voice but could barely take in the meaning of his words. Other voices were streaming through her head. Marilyn's: *You need to tell the police. . . .* Falcone's: *Is there something more, Rose? . . .* Dimitri's: *I'll be watching you. . . .* The mysterious voice on the phone: *You die next!*—

"Rose!"

Evan's hands gripped her shoulders as he shook her. "Are you okay? You're scaring me." He touched her face gingerly, as though she were made of glass. "I know this is a hard time for you. The shock still hasn't passed. But there's something I need to ask you. What exactly did you tell Detective Falcone about Dimitri?"

Rose wasn't sure where the words came from, they just rolled off her tongue. "Why? Evan, do you realize how serious this is? Marilyn's been killed and someone's stalking me. I'm not about to jeopardize our lives because of James's buried secrets." It was difficult to dredge up interest in either his question or the answers.

"Rose, what were you thinking?" Evan asked. He could only imagine what her revelations may have included. "Surely you know that the right words in the wrong hands could devastate us—you, me, Alexis's future. I know this is not a good time to ask, but I have to."

Rose shook her head. "Evan, I was scared." She paused for what seemed liked an eternity, then finally said the words. "I panicked, and I told him everything."

She realized how harsh she must have sounded, and she put her hand over one of Evan's, now resting on her shoulder. He quickly pulled back.

Alarmed by his distance, Rose immediately tried to explain her reasoning. "Darling, the moment Dimitri walked back into our lives, the die was cast. Certain things—who knows what—were bound to be exposed. The deeper we get involved with him, the worse it will be. That's why I think you should drop this case. Please, Evan, I know him better than . . ." She stopped, not wanting to hurt him.

"You think you do," he finished her thought. "But I understand him the way he is now. I've tried so many cases with men like Dimitri—people just as hard and determined. You leave Dimitri to me. My only concern is you. The police say you could have been the one murdered instead of Marilyn. From now on, we do things my way."

Rose stood and came to his side behind the chaise longue. "The security is necessary, I agree. But we don't have to overexpose ourselves, or flaunt our involvement with a man accused of illegal activity."

"How do you know he's guilty?" Evan asked defiantly.

"I didn't say he is, but why are you being so obstinate? If I recall, you didn't want this case to begin with."

Evan drew her down beside him. "I'm trapped, Rose. Firing a client is as good as throwing him into jail. The legal system, the jury, everyone would perceive this as an admission that the lawyer knows the truth, whether that perception is right or wrong. But let's suppose I did walk off the case and threw him to the wolves. What do you think he'd be capable of then?"

Evan's words spoke to her heart, and she sighed, resigning herself to the situation. Without waiting for her response, he left the room. Down the hall, she heard stirring. Alexis was awake. Rose glanced over at the nightstand. It was now seven-fifty. Then it registered . . . school! Alexis would be late. Seconds later the horn from the school bus sounded, and Rose panicked. She called Myra on the intercom and told her to dismiss the bus. For as long as she needed, she would take Alexis to school herself.

Within minutes Rose was showered and dressed. She and her daughter climbed into the backseat of the black Mercedes. Rose snuck a glance behind and saw that the unmarked car that had been parked outside the house was following them. She had decided not to tell Alexis about the tight security around them. Her daughter's life must not be disrupted.

"Mommy, why did Aunt Marilyn get killed?"

Alexis's question jolted Rose. Children, no matter how sheltered, no matter how rich or poor, were becoming more exposed to violence. Evan had delicately explained to Alexis the simplest details of Marilyn's death, but it was Rose who now had to answer the hard questions.

"Because sometimes crazy people find their way into our lives." Rose looked over to see how her daughter would absorb this response.

"You mean like that man who leaves mean messages on your answering machine?" her daughter asked as she crisscrossed her feet nervously.

Dumbfounded, Rose said, "How do . . . I mean, what did you hear?"

Alexis shrugged. "I heard you and Daddy talk about it. Is that who murdered Aunt Marilyn?"

"I don't know, baby." Tears slid down Rose's face.

Alexis moved closer to Rose on the seat. "Don't be sad, Mommy. I'm here, and I'm not scared." She might still be young, but Rose always knew her daughter had an old soul.

Rose reached out for Alexis's hand. "You mustn't worry, that's the main thing. I know you're sad and so am I, but no one will hurt us." Alexis put her head in Rose's lap, her hair covering her face. They were silent until the school building came into sight.

Rose had a sudden inspiration. "How would you like to take a vacation? Just you and me."

A smile lit up Alexis's face. Her joyful expression melted Rose's heart. She was so caught up in her own despair, she'd forgotten the last time she saw Alexis smiling.

"You mean it, Mommy? Just you and me? Where will we go?"

The car pulled up to the front entrance. Alexis unbuckled her seat belt but kept her eyes on her mother.

"I'm not sure yet. Maybe we could go someplace warm."

Rose held Alexis's hand in hers for a moment, not wanting to let go of her daughter's enthusiasm.

"Can you get time off from work?"

Rose caught some of Alexis's excitement, and her heart lifted a bit. "For you, anything. Besides, I can bring my work with me. Now you run along or you'll be even later. We'll talk more about it over dinner."

After making sure Alexis entered the school safely, Rose instructed Larry to drive north on Route 25A until they reached Huckleberry's, a gourmet coffee shop. There she ducked inside for a caffe latte and a raspberry scone. No matter how much she grieved for Marilyn or how scared she might feel, Rose had to maintain her composure. She needed to stay focused and carry on with her daily routine. Getting out of her house today was a start.

Dario had made it very clear she must keep up appearances. "People are vultures," he had said. "They'll feed for weeks on the bizarre connection between your being a psychological suspense writer and your agent's grotesque murder."

After Rose finished her breakfast, she decided to head back home. On her way out, she grabbed a copy of the *New York Post.* She glanced at the headline and gasped: SECRET DALLIANCE: DIMITRI CONSTANTINOS ROMANCES BEST-SELLING NOVELIST ROSE MILLER. There she was with Dimitri's lips on hers, and in this shot she wasn't pushing him away.

"Oh, my God," she gasped.

Dario Roselli had arrived at his office shortly after seven A.M. The place was dark and quiet, the way he liked it. He found more than a dozen messages on his voice mail. *It will be one hell of a morning,* he thought. He sifted through the messages one by one. All pertained to Rose and this morning's headline. "Oh, Rose," he murmured, "that was stupid." He shook his head. Rose needed him right now, and she needed him desperately.

He sat back heavily in his chair and began rubbing his forehead, which was suddenly covered with icy beads of perspiration. He was caught up in the excitement of the moment—his moment. Where to begin? Should he call or simply wait for Rose's call? No doubt she was apoplectic. And Evan . . . Dario let out a pleasurable sigh. He must be beside himself. His prim and proper wife had fallen from grace. He imagined Evan's reaction to the headlines. Shock? Disbelief? Anger? He guessed all three. He glanced over at the clock on the wall, its sound magnified to his ears. Tick tock, tick tock. The day was young, and he was sure it still held many surprises. He stared at the phone and waited for it to ring, thinking of the day years ago when Gina Kellogg had called, saying, "I need your help—those photos can't get out. My career will be ruined." He had saved her, and she'd been most grateful. Now he would save Rose. The thought of her repaying him was immensely arousing.

"Maximum damage control," he whispered.

25

Long, narrow shadows shot across the grounds of the estate as Rose and Larry returned to Paradiso, driving up the seemingly endless winding driveway. On the outside everything looked peaceful, predictable, just as it had when she'd left. The one thing she had always counted on was Paradiso's stability. Seasons passed without a whisper of change.

Not anymore, though. She was sure that news of the photo in the *Post* had reached Evan and James by now. Once inside the house, she stood outside the study room and listened to the two men's voices. They spoke quietly, though the tone of the conversation was edgy.

"That's enough." Evan's voice was strained. "I won't let you talk that way about my wife."

James's voice rose. "Do you know what this means? The embarrassment she's caused all of us? I've received twenty calls already this morning, and I've returned none. I'm at a loss. How do I explain this?"

Rose heard the sound of paper rustling. She could picture James waving the newspaper at Evan.

"How can the people trust you to run their state when you can't even control your own wife?"

"Don't go there," Evan said, now more under control. "I'm sure there's a perfectly reasonable explanation for this. Rose would no more—"

"Are you that stupid, son? You'll be an object of ridicule if you don't get rid of her!"

"Get rid of her? Father, she is not some possession—she's my wife, and you're out of line!"

Hearing Evan have to defend her, once again, galvanized Rose into action. She pushed open the door.

"As usual, James, you seem to be reveling in anything negative that happens to me." Rose forced him to look at her. She positioned herself so that she and her father-in-law were practically toe to toe. Never before, no matter what had happened to her, had Rose felt so much the need to defend herself against an assault. Obviously incapable of winning this contest of wills, James looked away, dropped the newspaper on the desk behind him, and turned to Evan.

Rose was not going to be put off so easily. "Can I have a word with you alone, Evan?" She tried to keep her voice steady and reasonable.

Evan looked at his father, who rose from his chair and walked out of the room.

"You don't believe this photo, do you? You can't think I simply fell into Dimitri's arms for a kiss?"

Evan shrugged. "I don't know what to believe anymore. Damn it, Rose, you're so evasive and so secretive about everything."

"It's not what it looks like." She approached him. "Please give me a chance to explain." Standing just inches from her husband, she could feel the chill in the air between them. "That night at the—"

Evan's hands flew up as he mocked her. " 'Stay home, Evan, don't bother yourself with another boring function.' It was all about Dimitri. You knew he'd be there."

"No!" she yelled. "In fact, he said you gave him your ticket!"

"*I* gave him my ticket! That's preposterous!"

Rose put her hands on his shoulders. "Listen to me. After giving my thank-you speech, I was a little anxious, so I went to the ladies' room. When I came out, Dimitri was there. He was quite clear on the fact that you gave him the ticket because he was such an important client. I even argued with him, telling him you would *never* do this. Then . . ."

"Then he kissed you," Evan finished her sentence sarcastically.

"He only did it to make a point, Evan, can't you see that?"

Her husband's face underscored his skepticism. "Oh, and the press just *happened* to be there. Rose, do you think I'm naive? Did you think for one moment about me? Our marriage? Are you so wrapped up in yourself that you lose sight of those you love?"

"We were arguing. God, Evan, you know how he can be. Before I knew it, he grabbed me and he kissed me. I pushed back, then broke free. That was all. I never saw a camera."

She looked into his eyes and knew he didn't believe her. Didn't he see? Dimitri had set her up. The family should be pulling together now, using Dario to express their outrage and prove, somehow, that it was a trick. She glared at Evan, as he picked up his briefcase from the desk and walked to the door. She opened her mouth to speak, but Evan cut her off.

"I have to go, or I'll be late for court. Don't forget about tonight."

Rose remembered that they were scheduled to attend a party for Tom MacGregor, the toy czar for whom Evan had won an acquittal.

26

The shiny limousine pulled up to the curb outside the courthouse, and the car came to an abrupt halt. Within seconds a horde of reporters flocked around the dark tinted windows, eager to get a glimpse of Dimitri Constantinos, hoping for a quote or at least a photo opportunity. Reporters and photographers fought to be first in line to catch his attention.

Inside, Dimitri winced. This wasn't going to be easy. Since the trial had started, he'd been able to tune out the constant presence of the press. But today he was tired.

Within seconds the chauffeur leaped out of the driver's seat, scurried around to the back, and opened the door slightly before standing erect, seemingly waiting for a sign to proceed. A nod from Dimitri and he opened the door wide. Then the grilling began.

"Dimitri, do you think you'll get an acquittal?" shouted one reporter.

"Dimitri, is it true your casino laundered money for the Medellín cartel?" asked another.

"Sir, how do you feel about District Attorney Allen's being accused of trying the case in the media?"

A smartly dressed reporter elbowed her way to the front. "Mr. Constantinos, how does your lawyer feel about your having an affair with his wife?"

Cool, an amused look pasted on his face, Dimitri ignored this and all questions, waving one hand, the other tucked neatly in the pocket of his cashmere overcoat. With a confident smile, he gave the media their daily dose of ad-libbing.

"How do you like this weather?" He raised his hand to the gray skies above. The crowd charged at him once again, shoving microphones and cameras in his face.

"The forecast calls for snow," he continued. "Though I'll lay three to one odds it doesn't."

"What are the odds you'll beat this, Dimitri?" yelled another reporter.

Dimitri turned back to the crowd behind him, flashed another magnetic smile, held two fingers up to the crowd, and announced confidently, "Two to one."

Most of the crowd laughed as Dimitri pushed past them and made his way up the courthouse steps. Out of the corner of his eye, he saw Joseph Braun and Jewel arrive in a separate car.

Like it or not, Dimitri was a headliner. Anything that had to do with him was news. If he was seen out on the town, in a restaurant, at a sporting event, or just strolling down Madison Avenue, he always managed to grab a few lines in the daily papers. Because of this, Dimitri also knew that he was a thorn in Kevin Allen's side. This trial had become a personal vendetta.

Jewel was ushered through the crowd by her father.

"Mrs. Constantinos? Do you believe your husband committed the crimes he's accused of?"

And then another reporter: "Do you know Rose Miller? How do you feel about this morning's headlines? Will you stand by your husband?" Jewel fumed inside but kept her smile in place.

Although their marriage was a charade, Dimitri served Jewel's purposes more as her husband right now than if they were apart. But try as she might, all she saw was Rose's image, smiling at her from a television screen, and that got her blood boiling.

"Mrs. Constantinos, the photo of your husband kissing Rose Miller, what was your reaction when you saw it?" a young man shouted as he shoved a microphone in Jewel's face, daring her to answer.

If she told the truth, the media would have a field day, an all-out frenzy. She was sick to her stomach. How dared he? How dared she? Miss model wife and mother. Jewel was determined to have the last laugh. Rose and Dimitri would be sorry. For now she would have to save face—hold her head high, ride the wave, and minimize the damage. For the three years in which they'd been married, Jewel had come to see her husband as nothing more than a hunter gunning for his prey. He had a "screw the world" attitude. Nothing worked unless it worked for him. His power, his position, his way. All this time she had succumbed to it, but enough was enough. She would get Dimitri where it hurt. In the meantime she'd fool him into thinking she was still under his thumb. Since he had warned her over and over, "Never talk to the press—never respond—never fuel the fires," she would play it his way. But the situation between Rose and Dimitri had pushed her to the edge. And before too long she would answer the press. Perhaps she would even do a sit-down interview with Barbara Walters.

Jewel reached the last step of the courthouse, then gracefully, and with as much dignity as she could muster, announced, "My husband is innocent of all charges. He will be exonerated. As for Rose Miller, it's not what it seems. They are merely old friends, that's all. You're making much too much out of nothing."

Silence fell over the crowd as they hung on her every word, hoping for a sound bite. They needed a great headline.

She tilted her head back slightly and thrust her chin forward, lifting her sunglasses just above her eyebrows. She stared with deliberation at the crowd of reporters. "These accusations are lies. The DA is searching for dirt that he won't find. As for the state of my marriage, I can assure you Dimitri and I are *very* happy."

The reporters charged toward her, tripping over one another, thirsty for more. But she said nothing, only turned and followed her father through the courthouse door, escaping the microphones, cameras, and intrusive questions.

The fluorescent light flickered in the tiny courthouse office set aside for private conversations. Dimitri rose impatiently and turned it off. Then he faced Evan, who was seated on one of the government-issue steel folding chairs, one that teeter-tottered unevenly.

"Don't you see this was planted?" Dimitri's voice was low, but sharp and effective. "We had words—argued. This newspaper photo is bullshit. Someone set us up."

Evan stared back at him, disbelief turning his once kind eyes frigid. "I trust Rose enough to know she's blameless, but the photo doesn't lie. I think you set it up, just to cause Rose pain and embarrassment. Hell, you got back at both of us with this. Isn't that what you wanted? Why did you tell her I gave you my ticket? Why did you lie?"

Dimitri shook his head, then replied, "Okay, so it was a lie. What was I supposed to tell her?"

"How about the truth. Why were you there—how did you get a ticket?"

Dimitri looked away. "I thought the two of you would be there, perhaps the three of us could have enjoyed the evening together, so I had my secretary get me a ticket."

"You put your hands—your lips—on my wife! I want to strangle you. Instead, I'm supposed to go into that courtroom and defend you?"

Neither of them spoke. Evan tried to compose himself by sipping a glass of water. "I'm going to ask the judge for a postponement until you can find other counsel."

It was ironic that he had just explained to Rose why he couldn't—they couldn't—do this to Dimitri. But that was before his brother came on to his wife.

"I don't want other counsel." Dimitri's voice was forceful, his eyes raging. For a moment Evan registered the piercing sapphire orbs.

"Don't you see how this looks?" Evan replied, almost pleading. "For God's sake. Rose's fans expect a certain gentility from her. And I don't think people would vote for a man whose wife openly flaunts infidelity. I'll be perceived as a fool. My dream of being governor could be over. Need I go on? You wanted effective representation. I can't give that to you now. I don't want you to win. I'm not on your side anymore."

"Well, Evan, I'm sorry if your Hallmark card world is caving in. But you're wrong. I didn't set it up. Nothing went on between me and your wife. We got into an argument . . . Rose was angry that I was there. I tried to calm her down . . . but . . ." Dimitri paused for a moment, turned away from Evan. "If truth be known, it was Rose who came on to me. I'm sorry to be the one to tell you this, but as far as I'm concerned, Rose is your problem."

Just then the door opened and Jewel appeared. She felt the turbulence in the room. Something was terribly wrong.

"What's going on?" she asked in a disdainful tone.

Dimitri glanced at his wife standing in the doorway, then his eyes returned to Evan.

"You need to ace this case as much as I do. I suggest you put this business aside and focus your energy where it counts. And remember, you need to win—for you and for me."

With Jewel in the room, they couldn't speak openly, but words weren't necessary. Both knew that Dimitri was right. He held the trump card, and Evan was certain that he wouldn't hesitate to use it.

Thirty minutes later everyone assembled inside the courtroom—spectators, reporters, and counsel for both sides. Eventually Kevin Allen approached the jury box and began his opening argument.

"Your Honor, ladies and gentlemen of the jury, there is plenty of testimony about Dimitri Constantinos's involvement in racketeering, money laundering, embezzlement, and perhaps other criminal activity. . . ."

Kevin looked into the faces of the jurors. "These are not crimes of passion. They are motivated not by human feeling, but by pure avarice and lust for power." He turned to look at Dimitri, and when he spoke again, he was talking directly to him as though they were the only two people in the courtroom. "Some people abuse their power and position. They take for granted the income from these business dealings. They want more. It's a high for them, an overwhelming sense of being in control, staying on top. They lose sight of reality, they give up their morals. Ambition takes over, consumes their every thought and decision. Dimitri Constantinos wasn't satisfied with his enormous financial success. He wanted more. And it didn't matter what he had to do to get it." Kevin turned his attention back to the jurors.

"Ladies and gentlemen, you'll read transcripts of secretly recorded conversations and meetings with Dimitri and underworld masterminds. You'll hear him make illegal business deals, plot to launder money, even rig his own casino parlors for his own personal gain." He pointed at Dimitri.

"Don't be fooled by his charm, his smile, his movie star appearance. He is the devil in disguise—a common street thug, a hooligan, hiding behind two-thousand-dollar suits, expensive leather shoes, and important, influential business associates. After you hear the evidence, you will know that this is a greedy man, a dangerous man, and a criminal who belongs in prison."

Kevin paused for a moment, his eyes resting briefly on each juror's face. Then he walked to the prosecution table and sat next to Chris Knowles and the rest of his team.

Dimitri whispered in Evan's ear, "The guy's a buffoon. Now show him what a real attorney looks like." At that moment, Evan was transported back in time: Dimitri leading him downtown on the subway to Little Italy; Dimitri daring him to walk through the woods, smoking a joint. Back then, Evan's brother's confidence meant the world to him. He would have done or said anything to win Dimitri's approval. But now . . . none of it mattered. He didn't want Dimitri to win, but if he lost the trial, he would be humiliated and risk having Dimitri reveal all the Miller secrets. Dimitri had him by the balls, no matter how he looked at it.

Evan rose and stood before the jury. His navy blue Paul Stuart suit, white shirt, and subtle red paisley tie stood in contrast with Kevin Allen's wrinkled brown Filene's Basement attire. Maybe Evan was a snob to think that clothing mattered. Still, he felt the jurors sitting up straighter, paying attention to him.

"Greed? The devil?" He looked over at Dimitri, shook his head, then turned back to the jury. "Ladies and gentlemen, I've been practicing law for almost ten years. I've been in courtrooms for more trials than I can count. And I have never, ever seen a more transparent performance by a prosecutor. Mr. Allen is making a desperate attempt to portray the defendant in an unfavorable light. His problem is, he has absolutely no solid evidence to support it. Wait and you will see, he will produce no tapes. I know because I haven't reviewed them, and if they do exist and I haven't seen them, that would be reason enough to dismiss the case." He turned to face Dimitri, who gave him an indecipherable nod.

"District Attorney Allen is right. Dimitri Constantinos dresses in two-thousand-dollar suits. He wears expensive shoes. He has influential associates. But is that a crime?" He turned back to the jury.

"No. What it is, is an image that men like Kevin Allen don't like, that of a successful businessman, the image of a man who started from nothing and by sheer force of will scratched and clawed his way to the top. Should we condemn him? Ostracize him? Deem him immoral? No."

Evan crossed to the defense table, picked up a piece of paper, then turned back to face the twelve men and women. "This is a list of Mr. Constantinos's businesses. It will be entered as evidence, and you will review it and see that every aspect of Constantinos Enterprises has been studied and approved by the IRS. If they never questioned Dimitri Constantinos, why should the prosecution? Why should you? Just because of his expensive clothes? I don't think you're that easily fooled, ladies and gentlemen. Kevin Allen is, but I'm not. I know you'll see through his smoke and mirrors and take a hard look at the shabby evidence he presents. And I know you'll find my client not guilty."

Dimitri was smiling, and when Evan returned to the defense table, he whispered, "I'm impressed, brother."

It was late afternoon when Dimitri arrived in Atlantic City. With this morning's court appearance behind him, he walked through the lobby of his new casino, the Ivory Palace, to check on the final preparations for the grand opening Friday night. Everything seemed to be coming together at once. Carpets were being installed, paintings were being hung. Dimitri inspected every public room, accompanied by a staff of seven, which included the architect, designer, manager of the hotel, and assistants to take notes for each expert. It was just what he had imagined. The lobby, with terrazzo floors, mahogany hardwood walls, and a huge Venus fountain in the center, boasted a twenty-three-foot ceiling with ridgeline skylights and elevators with glass doors that went down one floor into the casino. Once in the gaming room, there was a VIP entrance to the right for the high rollers who came for serious gambling. On the second floor there were restaurants, shops, bars, and nightclub entertainment. The Verandah, the hotel's premier restaurant, was already finished, as was the nightclub, Bogie's, complete with a private members-only club, cigar bar, and private sky boxes, ensconced in glass, suspended over the stage and dance floor. Bogie's was designed in art deco style. The walls were white, with aqua moldings. Tables covered with aqua cloths and fringed-shaded lamps completed the 1930s look.

"Get me all the receipts for the club's furniture," he fired off to Daphne Malloy, the hotel's manager.

"Right away, Dimitri." Dimitri had hand-picked Daphne to oversee the casino's decorations. With her bobbed brunette hair and black framed glasses, she looked completely up to the task, not to mention the fact that she had graduated top of her class from Harvard Business School.

To another staff member he said, "I'll be up in my suite. Send me up my usual."

"Yes, sir."

Speak and they jump, he thought. There was a time when he'd relished such power, but lately he'd found himself bored with it all. He had more pressing things on his mind, such as the gaming commission. The members were all eagerly awaiting the result of his trial. Would they pull his license? Only time would tell.

The most important lesson Dimitri had learned from working for Joseph Braun was to keep all his business dealings strictly legal, which was Braun's greatest failing. That was why Dimitri spent over a half million dollars a year in legal fees: he had a large team of lawyers watching over each business decision he made, keeping a paper trail a mile long. It was for this reason that he knew Kevin Allen's charges were false. He just had to find out who had changed his books to make it look as though he had been skimming.

Right now Dimitri needed to clear his mind, channel his thinking, and concentrate on this new casino/hotel he had bought and renovated in Atlantic City. One of the ironies of having to face trial in New York—and probably the most fortuitous result—was the fact that it brought him so much closer to his latest project. The Ivory Palace, which stood on the Boardwalk facing the ocean, adjacent to the Trump Castle, only two hours out of New York City, was built to outshine all the others along the strip. Its magnificent white facade, columns, and gold-domed portico made the Ivory Palace the most elaborate showcase in Atlantic City. But when the architect had first shown him a rendering of a pink-and-white castle, Dimitri went ballistic.

"This is ornate and gaudy. I want class and elegance. I want the building to exude stateliness. It's meant to attract dignitaries and celebrities as well as ordinary people who want to feel like royalty—a mixed bag."

Soon after, on a short business trip to Boston, Dimitri had passed by the State House in Boston and noticed its regal portico, accented with a gold dome that could be seen by anyone driving through the city. When the second set of blueprints was completed, the chief architect said, "Let me explain some points of interest—"

"That won't be necessary," Dimitri interrupted. "Turn these plans over to an artist."

The architect gasped, "What?"

"I want an artist's rendering of the building, every detail exaggerated. I want to see color, fabrics, wall hangings, everything."

The architect obviously thought he was crazy. But Dimitri got his "State House look," complete with a portico.

Satisfied that everything would be completed in time for the opening, Dimitri slipped into his private elevator and was whisked up to the penthouse. Using his private card, he gained entry to the suite of offices and his private apartment. When he entered, he found to his annoyance that he wasn't alone. Janice Slocum, a leggy blonde who had been hired to dance in the scheduled nightly cabaret show at Bogie's, was draped seductively over an armchair, waiting for him. Dimitri frowned. At one time he'd been attracted to her all-American good looks and the sensuality her pouting lips promised. But she had misunderstood his intentions, misinterpreting what to him was a dose of instant gratification. This was the second time she'd talked her way past his secretary into his private office.

"Hello, handsome." The young woman came to him swiftly, wrapping her arms around his neck and pulling his head toward her. The smell of her perfume suddenly repulsed him. He recalled Rose's subtle floral scent, and his heart lurched. He pushed the blonde away.

"Not tonight and not tomorrow. Don't push me, Janice." He escorted her to the door.

But when she was gone, he felt the need for release. The reminder of Rose had started him yearning. He dialed the private number of a very exclusive service.

"May, it's Dimitri."

"Darling, how are you? Are you calling for company?" Without waiting for an answer, she said, "I have the perfect girl for you. When do you want her?"

"As soon as possible."

He hung up.

Dimitri sighed. He was resigned to the fact that his marriage to Jewel was a farce. He could barely look at his wife, much less have sex with her. He had recently decided to turn to the hassle-free pleasures of Madam May's service. After all, paying for sex had its advantages—he didn't feel guilty, he didn't have to worry about the women growing attached, and he didn't have to worry about his own feelings.

He had one more call to make before his guest arrived. He dialed Evan's office number, and a young woman answered. "Miller, Miller, and Finch. How may I direct your call?"

"Evan Miller," he said.

"Just a minute, please. Who may I say is calling?"

"Dimitri Constantinos."

Click, hum, click, and hum. Over and over again. *The netherworld of hold,* he thought. Dimitri wasn't a man to be kept waiting. Then Evan's voice boomed over the line.

"Dimitri, what is it we need to talk about? I have to get to an engagement."

"Friday night is the grand opening of the Ivory Palace. I'll expect you and Rose at eight sharp."

"No, I think that would be a bad—"

"Eight o'clock," he repeated, and this time his voice was firm, an army sergeant issuing a command. "I'll send my private helicopter."

Just then the door to the hotel suite chimed. His guest. He hung up the phone, walked to the door, and opened it to find his favorite girl. Chloe was a striking, tall woman with long blond hair, a sensual mouth, and long hands that promised pleasure. And she played right along when Dimitri called her Rose.

The blonde struck a provocative pose. "I've been waiting for you to call again."

Dimitri walked to her and thrust her back against the door. He was in no mood for small talk tonight. He began to kiss her ferociously, stroking his hands through her golden hair.

Just then the phone rang.

"Excuse me, gorgeous," Dimitri said, leaving Chloe leaning against the door. He went immediately to the telephone. Business always came first.

"Mr. Constantinos?" It was the main switchboard downstairs.

"Speaking." His voice loud, he cursed the interruption.

"I have a call from Rose Miller. Shall I put her through?"

Dimitri paused and then said, "Tell Mrs. Miller I'm in a meeting."

Dimitri hung up abruptly and returned to the pleasures at hand. The real Rose would have to wait.

Rose hung up the phone. She knew he was avoiding her, and it stoked her frustration. She'd called earlier in the day and received the same response. If he wouldn't take her calls, she didn't have a clue how to reach him. There was so much they had to settle between them that no legal maneuverings or hostile confrontations could resolve. If he wouldn't take her call, she would have to find another way to get to him. She was determined. It was time to face him and ask the questions foremost in her mind. A part of her no longer feared him; too much anger consumed her. *Two can play this game. And no one knows how to reach Dimitri better than me.*

27

"You can't hide, Rose, or they'll think you're guilty. Put on a smile and play with everyone's mind." Dario had convinced her to attend the cocktail party in honor of Evan's victory in the MacGregor case, an event that could start the rehabilitation of her image.

Rose thought she was used to photographers chasing her, but the tacky story of her and Dimitri at the awards had turned those reporters into hungry beasts, their photographers into stalkarazzi. And tonight Rose was forced to confront them.

Now the flashbulbs popped as she arrived at the restaurant on Evan's arm. The Top of the Tower, on Beekman Place, looked out over the East River. Lights from Roosevelt Island and the Tip-Top Bakery sign across the bridge in Queens diverted her attention. Rose stayed close to Evan as he stopped to shake hands with some of the New York political machine's most important players. MacGregor was a major contributor to both parties, and these people were his friends. As Evan made his rounds, smiling and shaking hands, Rose thought, He's where he feels most comfortable, in his own element.

She imagined their future together as Evan climbed the political ladder. They'd spend many hours in rooms like this, beautiful settings, the lighting dim enough to complement their aging skin. Their nights would be spent playing host and hostess to these people: major contributors, sports figures and Hollywood leaders, media kings and queens, do-gooders, philanthropists, and perhaps a few people from her world—authors and publishers. She would do it well, do it for Evan. When this fiasco was over she would owe him that—and so much more.

Rose let go of Evan's arm to find a quiet spot. She tucked herself into a shadow near the floor-to-ceiling windows. Her hand pulled at the collar of her opera-length pearls, wound tightly around her neck.

"You look beautiful tonight."

Rose spun around and came face-to-face with Dario. "No, I don't. I look tired and shaken. You just can't see thanks to the low lighting."

Dario took a step backward, his eyes appraising her from head to toe. Then he gave a nod of approval. "No one wears black the way you do, Rose. You have just the right combination of sexiness and sophistication—a sometimes dangerous mixture." He laughed, and Rose was grateful he was just teasing.

After her argument with Evan over the newspaper article, Rose had locked herself in the bedroom for two hours, upset over hurting him and trying to process all that was going on around her. Still, she'd ended up in the same place as before—nowhere. When she could no longer put off getting dressed for the party, she had sluggishly searched her closets for something appropriate to wear. She'd pulled out a simple black Richard Tyler gown and a pair of black satin evening pumps and hoped for the best. While Evan had said nothing, judging by Dario's lingering gaze, she'd managed to pull it off.

"Dario, everyone's staring. I can't wait to get out of here."

"Just keep smiling," Dario said as he turned to face the crowd. "You have an obligation to the public and your husband. Besides, there's nothing to do but put a good spin on things. You're front-page news. Your little tryst with Dimitri will cost you, but I'm doing my best."

Rose gave him a searching look. Sometimes she stumbled across Dario's more cynical side. It worried her—if ever they became enemies, she didn't know that he could be trusted to keep her confidence.

"It was *not* a tryst." She wanted to slap him.

"Just weather the storm, Rose. As they say, this too shall pass. Although I didn't get a chance to ask you earlier, what were you thinking when you kissed Dimitri?"

"Don't start, Dario." She grew strident. "Don't forget who pays your bills." This was the first time she had ever used her leverage against him. Immediately she felt contrite. "First of all, you don't know the whole story. It wasn't a kiss so much as Dimitri's form of a slap. It's obvious he staged the incident. If I can't get Evan to understand, at least I should be able to get you in my corner." She hesitated. "Why would you, of all people, misjudge me?"

"Well, Rose, pictures don't lie," he answered, then slugged back the rest of his cosmopolitan.

Rose wanted to scream. Marilyn would have understood instinctively. Now there was no one she could trust. Not about this. Evan's attitude was understandable. She didn't expect him to be on her side for this one. He hadn't so much as smiled at her or uttered one word the entire ride into the city, and now, after politely escorting her in front of the cameras, he acted as though she weren't in the room. He was embarrassed, and she didn't blame him. Somewhere in this room, James was following her every move with malevolent eyes, she was sure of it.

She had to get out . . . now. She squeezed her satin evening bag with her hands and felt the impression of the key to Marilyn's apartment. She'd excuse herself, say she was going to the ladies' room, then make a beeline to the elevator and disappear.

Billy watched her leave from his inconspicuous spot. She climbed into a late model Lincoln limousine. Billy had listened to her discuss tonight's plans with Evan over the telephone, and her abrupt departure didn't fit precisely into his plans. But that was okay, he could adjust. He would let her go. He would catch up with her later. Besides, he had something more pressing on his mind. It was almost Rose's turn, and the detective was getting too close. He'd have to create another diversion, he decided as he pulled out his Marlboros and lit up.

That same night, Falcone and Charlie Dawkins were in a booth at Taormina, an old-fashioned Italian restaurant with great marinara sauce on Mulberry Street in Little Italy. Dawkins had called earlier, saying he had some new information. Now they sat over a meal of sausage and peppers.

"I can't tell you how much I appreciate your help, Charlie," John said, biting into a piece of garlic bread.

Charlie nodded. "Hey, we're compadres. Besides, I owe you. What are friends for?" For a moment there was a hint of sadness in his voice. Years earlier Dawkins's son was killed in a botched attempt on his life. It was Falcone who finally nabbed the creep responsible, and Charlie never forgot.

"How would you feel if I told you there's a connection between Rose Miller and Dimitri Constantinos?" There was a smug smile on Charlie's face.

"One only needs to pick up the *Post* to find that out."

Charlie shook his head. "No, this goes way back."

Falcone managed to conceal his disappointment. He thought back to what Rose told him: *"We were involved. He went to prison, and I married Evan."*

While it was all information he knew, John wouldn't burst Charlie's bubble, sure he'd worked hard to get the information.

"Dimitri Constantinos killed a man, Tom Calvetti. The murder took place at the Laurel estate—back then it was owned by James Miller. The murder happened a week before Rose married Evan."

Again, all stuff Falcone already knew.

"Now check this out." Charlie flipped through the pages impatiently until he found what he wanted. The file included a transcript of Constantinos's plea. "Obviously the old patriarch had some reason to cover it up. The cover-up has James Miller's stamp written all over it. But there's one strange piece."

Charlie pointed with one meaty finger to the ballistics report, which had been sealed. The coroner reported the entry wound was in the victim's chest.

John flipped through the written reports in the folder. "Where'd you get this, Charlie? That record was sealed. I checked it myself."

Charlie had used either his knowledge of the data bank or his connection to someone he knew to open up the files.

"This is strange," John said, sitting up, suddenly very alert. "The report says here the murder was self-defense, though no other weapon was found in the barn. And Constantinos did time for manslaughter."

Charlie smiled. "Exactly. Something's very wrong with this picture, and here it is."

Falcone felt Dawkins's eyes on his, waiting for him to get it. *Front entry,* yet the transcript of Constantinos's plea said he shot the victim in the back. Presumably that was why the self-defense plea wouldn't wash.

John stuffed the folder and its contents in his jacket pocket, then stood up and playfully punched Dawkins on his shoulder. "Hey, you're the best."

"Don't mention it, buddy."

"Come back to my secret place," he whispered in her ear.

Jewel's current lover was more enamored of her than she had anticipated. That could prove to be a problem once she'd gotten what she wanted and was ready to split. Still, the sex was intoxicating, and at this moment she didn't know what time it was or where Dimitri was. Nor did she care. Not tonight. She was hungry. "Yes," she said. "I'll come."

She gave her driver an address, and minutes later Jewel and her lover were in his suite at the Pierre.

As soon as he closed the door, he began to kiss her, and Jewel didn't resist. He started with her mouth and moved down her neck, his hands wrapped tightly around her waist. Jewel leaned back, falling into his hold on her. She needed him tonight, wanted to feel her lover's body close to hers. For spite, for lust, she didn't care. And this time there was no guilt as she thought about Dimitri's public tryst with Rose Miller.

"One question," he whispered with heated breath.

"What?"

"Does your husband kiss you like this?"

Through labored breaths she replied, "No." And she pulled him closer, clinging even tighter. It was her way of blocking out the humiliation Dimitri had caused her. She pushed the image of him and Rose from her mind. *I'll get you, Dimitri. Just wait.*

28

She gave the doorman a nonchalant nod and proceeded toward the elevator bank. Outside Marilyn's door, Rose hesitated for a moment as an eerie feeling combed her entire body. She took a deep breath, turned the key into the lock, and entered the apartment.

Marilyn's apartment was cold, and a damp musty odor filled the air. Only a few days ago the place was cheerful and bright. There had always been fresh flowers. The scent of Marilyn's perfume still seemed to linger in the air. Yet her absence was unmistakable.

Rose stopped to pluck the now aging sunflowers from an exquisite Verdigris vase that had somehow escaped the psycho's rampage, and discarded them in the garbage pail in the apartment's bright yellow kitchen. In the living room, a faint edging of dust was visible on the windowsill. The gloominess that fell over the apartment made Rose angry. Marilyn craved sunny spaces. The gloom made Marilyn's death that much more irrevocable.

Although the crime scene had been cleaned up, the sofa removed, there was a large, dark brown spot on the carpet. Marilyn's blood. It made Rose cringe, and she fought back tears. She promised herself she wouldn't break down. This was something she had to do. If she was going to find out who was responsible for Marilyn's death and who might be stalking her, she needed a starting point. The only place she could think to start was here. She put her bag on top of the dining room table.

She went to the uncovered window to look out. From up here on the fourteenth floor, the sky looked like a delicate curtain of dancing snowflakes. It would accumulate; soon the ground below would be covered. She had to hurry before driving home to Long Island became too hazardous.

Seating herself swiftly, her black gown draping over Marilyn's comfortable desk chair, Rose drummed her fingers on the oversize, walnut arch-shaped desk. She thought about Marilyn's tiny dumpling of a body, which always seemed swallowed up by this huge desk.

Rose got up and walked down the hall into the bedroom and opened the closet door. Inside, some of Marilyn's things were still intact, the rest removed as evidence. Rose sifted through the clothing left on hangers, a pile of shoes and handbags strewn about the floor, and some boxes of old photos. On the highest shelf, pushed to the back of the closet, was a box wrapped in festive paper, a large red bow tied neatly around it with a gift card attached.

"Dear Rose, Happy Birthday to my best friend. Love, Marilyn."

Rose started to tremble. Tears flowed, and loud sobs followed.

Oh, God, Marilyn, I'm so sorry. Rose had made up her mind before she came here that she would examine everything in her friend's apartment, no matter how painful the memories. It was possible the police had overlooked something. Now she tore the wrapping paper off the box, hoping to find anything that might help.

Inside there was a music box, a glass statue of the Eiffel Tower. Rose wound it up and listened to the melody: "La Vie en Rose."

She clutched the statue to her chest, still sobbing, rocking back and forth to soothe herself. Marilyn's image was so vivid in her mind, Marilyn in her silly seventies glasses at Rose's first book party, smiling; at Alexis's tenth birthday, without makeup and looking as young as any of the children. Her expression when she'd walked into the surprise birthday party Rose had thrown for her last year.

Her voice echoed in Rose's mind: *I'm worried about you. . . .*

Rose sobbed louder now, then whispered, "I never meant to hurt you. God, I'm so sorry."

She placed the statue, her last memory of Marilyn, back in the box, tucking it carefully beneath the tissue paper. As she rushed to put the lid back on, she accidentally knocked over a box of photos. Bending to pick them up, she saw the sparkle of a gold lighter against the white carpet of the closet. Rose picked it up with tissue and turned it over in her palm. Marilyn didn't smoke. Why would she even have a lighter? In the bottom right corner, she saw the faint monogram on its gilded surface. Rose's eyes widened and she sucked in her breath, then clutched the lighter in her fist.

Yes, her trail had begun.

Billy watched the limo drive past the gates, up to the front entrance. The driver got out and opened the door. Rose, cloaked in a silver satin wrap and clutching a gift box, dashed from the backseat into the mansion. She had been away longer than he calculated, and this made him mad. The need to see her was overwhelming. He'd passed the time thinking of the others—all of them smiling at first, then panic—it had been so satisfying. His only regret was that he hadn't given Marilyn a chance to beg. He loved the look of horror in their eyes when they pleaded for him to spare them. Anyway, Marilyn's murder served a different purpose. It was probably the most important so far. He hadn't even been remotely attracted to her. He'd done it for effect—he needed to get Rose's full attention. Over the past few days he hadn't observed any change in either her or her routine. She was going about her business as if there were nothing more important than getting her hair cut and nails manicured in time for her next appearance. Maybe she didn't grieve for Marilyn enough; maybe he had to get even closer before he claimed his prize—Rose.

The light in the master suite went on, and seconds later he saw her lovely silhouette behind the sheer drapes. She was still clothed, but he imagined her naked. His hands touching her body, moving slowly over her breasts, her throat, and then her mouth and eyes. . . . But he was being pulled back by that other force now. His powerful body went limp and he leaned against the iron gate, ignoring the chill of the icy metal. "Oh, Rose," he whispered. "Sweet, sweet Rose . . ." Then Billy disappeared.

29

"I saw the cover for *Murderous Intentions,*" Dario announced into the receiver. "It's fabulous! I'll messenger it out to you right now."

Rose nearly pulled the phone from her ear.

"This one's gonna be terrific, Rose. A real eye-catcher."

"That's great, Dario." She tried to sound enthusiastic. It was Marilyn who had handled all her publishing matters, but Dario had stepped in eagerly as he said, "just for the meantime."

"Now, for the bad news. Have you seen this morning's papers?"

She was terrified to ask. She could just imagine the buzz around Manhattan's "A list" circle.

She's sleeping with him.

She's leaving her husband.

Gossip had a hard time staying put. What fun everyone had with rumor and insinuation.

"I'm trying my best, Rose, but this time . . ."

Rose wasn't in the mood for patronizing. "Give me the worst."

"Okay, here's the rundown. From Liz Smith: 'Socialite mystery writer Rose Miller forced to choose between husband and lover.'" A pause, "*USA Today:* 'Divorce likely for socialite author and top criminal attorney.' The *Daily News:* 'The strain on the Millers' marriage was apparent at Tom MacGregor's celebration dinner. Luckily for him, the gubernatorial hopeful has obviously learned to put on a good public display.'"

A public display, Rose thought. *Evan didn't have it in him; one thing he wasn't was hypocritical. He wore his heart on his sleeve*

"Dario, can't you put a muzzle on these people? Evan is sensitive. Those ridiculous headlines get to him. He's got an image to project. His future is on the line."

"All the more reason for you to put up a front."

Rose couldn't bear to continue the conversation. "I really have to go."

"One last thing, Rose. The upside to all of this is that every show across the country wants you for an interview."

"I'm not talking about any of this scuttlebutt," Rose said. Her voice was unusually high-pitched, even to her own ears. She took a deep breath to calm herself.

"You have a book to promote, an image to maintain. Rose, it's my business to sell you. You still have the Miami swing of the tour left to do—you leave Monday."

"But—"

"No buts. You've committed to this tour." He had said all the right things: how working would help distract her, how her fans needed to see she was still the Rose Miller they loved, and then the clincher: "You've got to do this for Evan, for God's sake."

Rose knew he was right about that.

He concluded, "I'm faxing over your schedule for Miami. I have to grab the other line. I'll call you later."

She held the phone receiver in her hand as she glanced at the partial manuscript for *Murderous Intentions* on the desk. Somehow she would figure out the killer's next move. Though she had written and rewritten every line of these pages at least twice, she was convinced that something beneath the surface—some subtext that she had written without thinking but that was apparent to an objective reader—was contained in these pages. If she could find it, she could figure out the killer's next move. If it took combing through the book line by line, word by word, she'd do it: somewhere there'd be a clue. He was playing a deadly game, and she was the pawn. *Not if I get to him first,* she thought. She pulled out the gold lighter, now protected inside a Ziploc bag, and studied it for the hundredth time. The bold Gothic letter "D" stared back at her. Of course, Dimitri was the logical owner. But if she had seen it the night at Match's, the only time she'd seen him smoke, she would have remembered it, wouldn't she? Something didn't click. Or maybe she could not accept that the man she had loved all these years was a psychopathic killer.

Rose sat back in her chair, staring out the window onto the estate's landscape. Her mind drifted. She saw herself as a girl, a teenager, exuberant, contentment and love written in her smile. The girl rode a horse, an

Arabian the Millers used to keep. She snapped back to reality and reflected, ironically, that despite her newfound wealth and fame, she could never be as happy as that young girl on the Arabian. But Alexis could. If Rose worked at it, Alexis could hang on to the ebullience of young womanhood. And it would start with the trip she'd promised. She was taking her daughter with her on tour. Alexis would go crazy over Miami.

She had noticed that although Alexis hid it well, her daughter was beginning to behave like a person under siege. She would get them both away from this madness.

She dialed Dario's number and got his voice mail. She left a message.

"It's Rose. Make two more plane reservations for Miami. I'm bringing Alexis and Myra with me."

30

Falcone sat at his desk at the station and studied the police files he'd pulled from the old record room in the Nassau County Police Department. He noted the names of the officers at the scene the night of Dimitri Constantinos's arrest. There were two, both now retired. He had to get a background on them, their protocol, commendations, citations. But even more important, where were they now?

"Hello? Anybody home?"

Falcone looked up. Dick Choffey, the senior desk lieutenant, stood glowering down at him impatiently.

"I'm thinking," Falcone said curtly as he pushed the files underneath some mail. He didn't want Choffey getting too curious. As yet, no one was privy to any of the information he had obtained from Rose or Charlie. He'd promised both that he'd keep it all confidential.

"Nassau County put a tap on the Millers' phone this morning," Choffey said, still looking at Falcone suspiciously. "Manhattan is going to take care of Mrs. Miller's apartment on Fifth Avenue." The murder of Marilyn Grimes and her connection to Rose Miller had brought the NYPD in on the investigation.

Falcone feigned enthusiasm. "That's great. Maybe we'll get some leads." He watched as Lieutenant Choffey walked away. *I need one important clue,* he thought, *one piece of the puzzle to get me started.* It would be something he knew was there, right in front of him, but that he just couldn't put his finger on. *It'll come to me,* he told himself, *the minute I stop focusing on it.*

He dialed Charlie Dawkins's number, then asked for his extension. Seconds later, Charlie's voice: "This is Dawkins."

"Charlie, it's John. Listen . . . the police report lists two officers at the Laurel estate crime scene. Can you get me some background? I'll fax the sheet over."

"Consider it done."

Falcone gathered up his papers, grabbed his pen and pad, and stood up. As he turned to walk away from his desk, the phone rang.

"John, I need to see you right away." Rose sounded wired. "Can you meet me at Starbucks in half an hour?"

"I'll be there," he said.

Once inside the Wheatly Plaza Starbucks, Rose spotted Falcone sitting at a table for two in the back. She went to get her tea before joining him, getting in line behind a couple, obviously high school students, both wearing one diamond earring stud and faded baggy jeans. But when she glanced around, she saw him waving at her to come over.

"I hope you don't mind, I bought you chamomile tea. You sounded like you needed it."

Detective John Falcone, homicide, specialty serial killers, could turn instantly into a big teddy bear, always there with open arms, when she needed him.

"What have you got for me?" Falcone said.

Rose reached inside her purse and pulled out a small Ziploc bag containing the gold lighter. "I found this in Marilyn's apartment last night."

He looked at it intently, then shrugged. "What does it mean?"

Rose plunged on. "Look on the other side, on the far right corner. The letter 'D' . . ."

Falcone, still unruffled, continued to stare at the lighter.

"It's probably Dimitri's," Rose blurted.

"Probably." But his expression and tone of voice were skeptical.

In the back of her mind, Rose felt sure Dimitri was the prime suspect, and the lighter would firm things up. But Falcone's nonchalant reaction threw her.

Falcone took the bag with the lighter from her and flipped it a few times in his hand. "It was smart thinking to put it in a plastic bag, but you should know, any chance we'll find prints is long gone. So if I seem less than enthusiastic, you can understand. I'll see what I can make of it." He hesitated. "Rose, I need to ask you some questions. Can we pretend it's not friend to friend?"

Rose was alarmed. Had something else happened? She put one hand around her throat, feeling exposed in her baby blue V-neck sweater. "Sssure," she answered hesitantly.

"I need some more information about the murder of your uncle Tom."

Rose stared back at him. She was aware of James's work behind the scenes to cover up what he could about that evening, though she had pushed it far back in her mind, filed away, like all the memories of Tom. She waited to hear what he wanted from her.

Falcone leaned forward on the table. "Rose, I've been a cop for twenty years, I've seen the worst side of humanity—people brutally murdered, women, children dismembered, buried alive, cannibalized. I've handled rape cases, robbery cases . . . the list goes on and on. I've made some very important and near impossible collars. I like to think of myself as both capable and effective. Hell, I'm a damned good cop." His eyes smoldered momentarily. "Don't play with me and don't insult my intelligence."

Rose stiffened. She suddenly felt like a suspect under interrogation. She took in how ruffled Falcone looked. Usually very put together in his basic homicide detective brown suit, today he was just plain wrinkled. Obviously he had been up all night doing his homework. What was on his mind?

"Are you sure you've told me everything?"

She nodded emphatically. But it was clear in his expression that he wasn't convinced. "What are you driving at?" she asked. "Maybe I can be more helpful if you give me more insight."

John sipped his black coffee. He said nothing, just watched her.

"So?" Rose prompted, impatient to get on with it.

"Who was in the barn that night?"

"We've been over that. Dimitri, Tom, and me. But I wasn't exactly coherent. I was pretty drunk."

"Could someone else have been there?"

"I don't know. I have no reason to think so."

"Could James have followed you there? Evan?" He was pressing, once again an unusual tactic for him to use with her. Rose could feel herself growing flustered.

"John, I don't know! You have to believe me. It never occurred to me before."

"But is it possible?" He wasn't giving an inch. He was going to push until he got an answer or believed her.

Rose studied her hands in her lap, twisting her wedding band. She thought back through the distance of years. She had no answer. "I have no idea," she replied at last.

Falcone curled his upper lip, then said, "Constantinos's story doesn't match the ballistics report. Do you know why he lied?"

Now Rose was agitated. "Look, John, all of this is irrelevant. You know my side of the story. You read the report. You probably know more than I do."

"Have you ever spoken to Constantinos about that night?"

"No!" Her reply was quick and firm. "I never spoke to him about it. In fact, regardless of what the gossip columnists would have everyone believe, I've had very little contact with Dimitri."

Falcone wasn't convinced. He had a questioning look in his eyes.

"Look, I've told you all I know."

He gave a long, drawn-out sigh, then said, "I feel the need to tell you, I'll be investigating this further. The murder of your uncle, your role in it, and whether or not there's a connection to whoever's stalking you. I'm a detective first and foremost. No matter who the trail leads back to, I've got to follow it."

Rose realized she'd opened a can of worms by going to him in the beginning. But what choice did she have? She needed help, and John Falcone was a man she could trust.

"By the way," he added as he pulled a piece of paper from his shirt pocket, "the security detail from the Nassau County Police Department have to go back to regular duty. I found a bodyguard for you. This guy is perfect. He has a military history, worked ten years for the NYPD, and now he's known as one of the best bodyguards in the country. If he's good enough for visiting royalty, he's good enough for you."

Rose took the paper, glanced at the name and number, then shoved it in her purse.

"Call him, Rose—immediately. Don't take this lightly," Falcone said as he got up from his chair. Rose wondered if her hand felt cold as he squeezed it gently when he said good-bye.

31

There was one word to describe Evan's dedication to law and politics—passionate. When he'd started with the firm almost ten years before, he had fulfilled the duties expected of all junior attorneys, putting in twelve- to fourteen-hour days, six days a week. He met clients at night at their favorite restaurants or watering holes, at their homes, at their vacation retreats—even at their masseuses'. He was determined to be the best attorney in the city and forge his destiny without the help of James Miller and his fortune. His reputation was hard-earned. Now, as he headed into the East Coast Health and Racquet Club to meet Joseph Braun, he wondered if his earlier methods had turned on him, making him too accessible. When Braun had called earlier that morning and said it was urgent, Evan had suggested they meet at the office. Braun had declined. "Too formal," he said. When Evan had suggested a nearby diner, Braun had said, "Too visible."

Then Braun suggested the health club and Evan thought, What a pain in the neck. But, as always, he indulged his client.

The gym was attractive and well equipped with a good supply of Cybex and other weight-lifting paraphernalia, a large lap pool, running tracks, airy rooms for aerobics classes, racquetball cages, an entire floor devoted to treadmills, rowing machines, exercise bikes, and large punching bags, and a fully stocked juice bar. Young, scantily clad women were on hand to assist members. The obvious attraction for his client, Evan thought. Certainly Braun wasn't a health buff. Hell, he smoked two packs of cigarettes a day, plus his cigars, usually consumed four Scotches and several gimlets, and hardly ever got to bed before three A.M. Part of the life, he'd rationalize to Evan. "I have to do what

I have to do, you know." Evan had nodded, not caring one way or the other. The less he knew about Joseph Braun's "doings," the better.

The young blond ponytailed woman behind the reception desk had flawless skin and a smile "whiter than white," as the commercial used to say. She was almost a parody of good health and fitness. Evan, overworked, having spent too many recent days and evenings in musty conferences and courtrooms, was almost put off by her sunny disposition.

"I'm here to meet Joseph Braun," he said abruptly.

"Mr. Braun is in racquetball cage seven." She pointed to the back of the room. "Just behind the juice bar."

Grinning, Evan thanked her and headed off to find his client. It was too ironic: any day in the life of Joseph Braun could easily qualify him for a cage—a federal one.

Then, in the next few moments, thoughts of Braun faded as Evan made his way across the room and became uncomfortably aware that he was out of his element. It wasn't the Harris tweed suit or the Coach leather briefcase. Lots of guys came in here dressed that way. Rather, it was something about his attitude, he decided. He felt more like an FBI agent serving a subpoena than an attorney on his way to a business meeting with his client. Whatever it was that set him apart, he felt awkward.

He was met outside the court by one of Braun's goons, a rotund man with a bald head and a proclivity for loud ties.

"Mr. Braun will be right with you. He's just finishing up his game."

Evan glanced inside the glass cage. When he caught a glimpse of Braun's partner, his mind began to race. District Attorney Kevin Allen, dressed in navy blue sweats and swinging a racquet, was running wildly around the court, his face dripping with sweat.

Braun, clad in the club's signature white shorts, provided to members only, was panting like a wounded tiger and fighting fiercely to keep up with Allen.

Evan thought to himself, If this isn't a Kodak moment.

When the game was over, the bald man opened the door and Braun emerged with Allen just a few steps behind.

"You win some, you lose some," Braun said, talking to Allen.

But the prosecutor's eyes were glued on Evan.

"You must be nuts—what's he doing here?" Allen gesticulated with his racquet, waving it around as though he could make Evan disappear. "You said this would be private!"

Joseph threw an arm around Evan's shoulder, pulled him close, and let out a hearty laugh. "You didn't see nothin', did ya, Evan?"

Evan didn't know what kind of game Braun was playing with the DA, but it was apparent he had staged this confrontation. Obviously embarrassed, Allen looked like a man with a bad case of whiplash.

On impulse, Evan offered Allen his hand and said, "See you in court." Then he turned his back on the prosecutor, and Allen quickly disappeared into the locker room.

Once Allen was out of earshot, lawyer and client sat down at the club's juice bar. Evan waited for Braun to speak first, not sure what their meeting was about. After the older man had finished his drink, a fruit energy shake with concentrated protein, he turned to Evan and said, "So, how do you think my son-in-law's trial is going? Give it to me straight."

Evan's mind ran through all the angles Braun might be playing with this question and replied, "Fine." That seemed like a safe bet.

Braun wiped the red stains of strawberries from his lips. "This stuff stinks. Wanna try it?"

Evan didn't reply. Instead he said, "What am I doing here, Joseph? Obviously you staged this performance for my benefit—worked it out so I'd bump into Allen here. Is there something I should know?"

"I think it's safe to assume that we both know how much influence I have in this city." His smile was inscrutable. "I just wanted you to, let's say, see it in action." His voice turned sharp. "That's why I'm only gonna say this once. Keep your wife away from Dimitri."

Braun's words almost floored Evan. He remained silent, not sure what to say.

Braun continued, "My daughter is very upset about all this nonsense in the newspapers. I have to tell you, I'm a bit embarrassed myself."

Evan turned to Braun with a frown and said, "Newspapers inflate things—if anyone should know that, it would be you. Besides, Rose tells me Dimitri came on to her and she resisted. Why not keep your son-in-law away from my wife?"

"I'll take care of my son-in-law, you worry about your wife. Remember, Evan, it takes two to tango." Braun squeezed Evan's shoulder, hard.

His quick dismissal of the topic convinced Evan that Braun's command performance with Kevin Allen wasn't just his way of flaunting a "buddy-buddy" relationship with the prosecution or to warn him about Rose and Dimitri. It was about something else. But what?

One more sip of his drink and Braun came to the point. "It might be in everybody's best interests if you lost Dimitri's trial," he said casually. "Kevin Allen has been kind enough to let me know that he's got a lot on Dimitri. Of course, I don't know what that is, but I think it would serve you to change my son-in-law's plea to guilty and plea-bargain."

Evan felt a vein at his temple start to throb. Wheels within wheels: the Millers, the Brauns, Dimitri Constantinos—where would it all end?

"No, Joseph," he answered curtly, his usual diplomacy in tatters. "I'm not throwing a case. Dimitri will never cop a plea."

"There's enough information in Allen's hands to force him. Remind him what all those years in jail were like." Braun smiled, and Evan suddenly pictured him morphing into a shark.

"I've got nothing else to say, Joseph. My client, even if he is your son-in-law, isn't someone you can push around." Evan's eyes wandered around the room, then back to Braun. "I'd think you would have learned that by now."

Everywhere Rose went, people stared—at the salon, in the grocery store, the fancy bakery where she loved to buy treats for Alexis . . . The last straw was when she went to pick up a pizza at Bertucci's and the woman ahead of her in line started to whisper to her companion. Rose was used to being in the public eye, but never as an object of ridicule. Putting on a brave face at the fund-raiser for Evan had taken a bite out of her hard-won self-confidence and proved what she'd suspected all along. If lines were really drawn between her and Evan, few people could be counted on to take her side. But truthfully, in the grand scheme of things, the only person she really needed was Alexis, who knew more than any eleven-year-old should about the gossip surrounding her mother. While she also needed Evan, in the deepest part of her, she wasn't sure he would stand by her when the chips fell.

When she'd married into a prominent family and become a successful author, she had shed the images of the past in her own mind, if not in the Millers'. She'd become somebody. Rose Miller was the woman Rose Calvetti had dreamed of becoming. But the photo of Rose and Dimitri—the gossip and insinuations—had destroyed all she'd learned from life's important lessons. Women, many of them her cherished readers, had lost respect for her. This was evident in the recent drop of her book sales. Men seemed to watch her in a lecherous way now instead of with the admiring looks she had grown used to. The values she'd internalized from Sophia and Victor were what she held dear and how she lived her life. Now her values were being questioned.

As she walked briskly down Fifth Avenue, her golden blond hair hidden beneath a black wool beret, her green eyes shielded by large Jackie O dark glasses, Rose was just another face in the crowd. For the first time in days, she was outside, free to walk wherever, with no one chasing her, snapping photos, or screaming intrusive questions, thanks to her disguise. *How long do I have to hide?* she wondered. Doggedly she determined to clear her mind of all but work. Rose was not one to suffer writer's block, but the novel was coming very slowly since Marilyn's murder. There was no way she was going to make her deadline. Ordinarily Marilyn would have intervened with her publisher to gain more time. Every day some thought or other would make Rose suddenly miss Marilyn with bitter sadness. She couldn't work in the mansion; she couldn't think clearly there. Tension between Evan and her was like a fungus, growing thicker by the moment. Her apartment was her sanctuary, the only place she had any hope of clearing her thoughts.

As she walked back to her apartment, she could see Dario waiting out front, talking to the doorman. For a moment she wished Dimitri and Dario would quietly drop off the face of the earth and take James with them. Some men you could simply live without.

Inside, the apartment was warm. Rose was in the kitchen putting on a pot of decaf coffee. Dario could see her from where he sat, as he made himself quite comfortable on the living room sofa.

"How are you holding up?" he asked.

"The best I can."

He leaned back and rested his head on the plush crushed velvet brown sofa, absorbing the delicious surroundings. *A Norman Rockwell painting, Rose in the kitchen, fixing me coffee. I could get used to this.* Judging by her appearance, how ruffled she seemed, he guessed she was at the breaking point. Right where he wanted her.

"How did you like the cover?"

Rose appeared, carrying a tray with two mugs, cream, and some sugar. "To tell you the truth, I really didn't give it a good look. I was preoccupied."

"Of course you were." He smiled sympathetically, then said, "You've been under a lot of pressure." He leaned forward. "Speaking of which, how is Evan handling things?"

Rose set the tray on the coffee table and took the chair across from him. "Not well," she replied.

Good, he thought. "That's too bad," he said.

Rose handed him a mug, coffee black, no cream, no sugar. Rose knew how he liked it, but then again Rose knew a lot about him, and he loved the ever-present familiarity between them. *Soon she'll learn more,* he thought.

"How can anyone expect him to be otherwise?" Rose said. "I don't think I would be the least bit understanding, if I were he."

She looked so vulnerable, he wanted to embrace her, wrap his arms around her tightly, and never let her go. He couldn't count the times he'd come so close to trying just that, soothing her the way one might calm a wild child. That was the side of her he saw—beneath the lady, the celebrated writer, the wife of a prominent man. His Rose was spontaneous, able to give and take of love without inhibition—and she would, as soon as he could free her.

"Evan and Alexis are the most affected," Rose continued, oblivious of Dario's mental wanderings. "I just wish I could ease their pain. At this point, I feel helpless." Her eyes darted to the window. "It's like I'm waiting for doom to . . ." She stopped, turned her attention back to him, then said, "By the way, Dario, what *are* you doing for damage control?"

"I'm trying," he lied lamely, feeling uncomfortable. Her world was tumbling down, her career was on the line, and all she thought about was

Evan. It was a jolt. *I'm going to lose her. Then again, who am I kidding? I could never have her, at least not willingly.*

The sound of the phone ringing distracted him and caused Rose to jump. But she didn't move to answer it. On the fourth ring he asked, "Would you like me to get it?" Inwardly he thought, *She's so paranoid, she can't even answer the damn phone.*

Rose remained frozen, staring at the phone. "The machine will pick it up."

Then the ringing stopped and there were a few seconds of silence, followed by a beep, then: "Rose, it's me. . . ."

Evan's voice . . . *The bastard was interrupting their time together,* Dario thought as he watched Rose jump up and dart across the room to pick up the phone.

"Rose—don't forget. Tomorrow night is the opening of the Ivory Palace. We're expected to show." Then a click and silence.

Rose was obviously eager to speak with him. *Damn him,* Dario thought, and couldn't help feeling a bit amused when Rose, knocking over a chair in her haste, missed Evan's call.

He paused and considered the message. The opening of the Ivory Palace? That was Dimitri's casino. Was Evan crazy? The press would have a field day if they could get Dimitri and Rose in the same city on any given day, let alone at the same party. A plan began to take shape in his mind as Dario sipped his coffee and smiled sweetly at Rose. Another big headline would break out. It would make the first scandal look like the work of an amateur. Then she would come running to him—willingly. He would be all she had left. As soon as he left Rose's apartment he would call his secretary and have her contact Constantinos's office. He needed to guarantee himself a place setting.

Dario watched her staring at the phone, waiting for a show of emotion. Instead all he got was, "Dario, I need to get back to my work. Would you mind leaving?"

32

Falcone was waiting at the airport gate at La Guardia when Timothy Houston returned from what he guessed was a family vacation in Disney World. He spotted the large man immediately, although now, with his salt-and-pepper hair, he looked much older than he did in his picture. The ex-cop's arms were filled with packages; his wife trailed a few feet behind him, clutching their toddler's hand.

"Timothy Houston?"

He turned. "Yes?"

"John Falcone. I'm with the Brookville Police Department. Can I have a word with you?"

"I'm not really free at the moment, I have—"

"Here, let me help you," Falcone said as he took some packages from him. "Lighten your load."

Houston half smiled, then said, "What department did you say you were with?"

They started walking side by side toward the terminal exit.

Falcone said, "Brookville, your old stomping grounds."

"What can I help you with, buddy?"

"I need to ask you some questions about the murder of Tom Calvetti back at the Laurel estate years ago."

Falcone saw that Houston immediately made the connection, but that didn't mean much. Everyone knew the old Laurel estate.

"I understand you were on the scene that night." Falcone kept his voice casual. They exited the terminal, and the Houstons were first in line for a cab. Minutes later, when the luggage was loaded in the trunk, Houston turned to his wife and said, "Wait in the cab, hon, I'll just be a minute." Then he turned to Falcone and nodded toward the entrance of the terminal. "Why don't we go stand back over there and talk?" he suggested.

Falcone nodded and followed the big man. Houston, he noted, must have been 270 pounds and at least six four. He would have been some bruiser twelve years ago.

"I have a copy of the report that was filed that night." Falcone produced a crumpled piece of paper from his coat pocket.

Houston looked wary. "The case was, what? Thirteen, fifteen years ago? Why are you asking me questions now?"

"Actually, it's been twelve years. This is informal. I need some information about the murder. It might help me with a current case I'm working on."

"What kind of information?"

He shoved the paper at Houston. "Why don't we start at the beginning, like why this report was falsified?"

Falcone waited for a reply, an expression from Houston. Instead all he got was silence.

"Something stinks. That report can't be accurate. Look, it says here 'self-defense.' Yet only one gun was found on the scene. A gun that was kept in the barn. It's the same gun used to kill Tom Calvetti."

Houston's forehead creased, and beads of perspiration formed above his brow. "I'm not sure I follow you."

Falcone rubbed his forehead with his index and forefinger. "The autopsy report states Calvetti had an alcohol level of point three. We both know when a man drinks that much, he's in no condition to put up a fight, especially not against a younger, stronger guy."

Houston didn't look so good, and Falcone could smell the nervous sweat on him.

"Listen, uh, Detective . . . what did you say your name was?"

"Falcone, John Falcone."

"All right, Falcone. I can't remember specifics. There was a struggle between two men. One died, the other went to prison. What's your point?"

Falcone could tell he was lying. He knew more, but he was holding back.

"My point is that the murder didn't happen the way the report states. There's no way Constantinos could have shot Calvetti from a distance. Not according to ballistics. The medical examiner's records dispute the facts in your report. The bullet was fired at close range. The position of the body, the site of the bullet wound—nothing in this report makes sense. You and your partner, Vince Hogan, were the first on the scene. Hogan died two years ago in an automobile accident. That leaves you holding the bag."

Falcone leaned in closer to Houston, their faces just inches apart. "I'm on this case, and I won't stop until I get all my questions answered." He turned his gaze on the cab parked at the curb. "Looks like you got yourself a nice family. Any man would kill to be in your position. Why risk losing it all? Who are you protecting? Why don't you make it easy on yourself and tell me what really happened that night?"

"Look, I have to go . . . my wife's—"

"Yeah, yeah, sure. I understand." He reached into his pocket, took out his pen and pad, and scribbled his phone number. "Call me, Houston. If you don't, you're gonna fall."

He watched as Houston stuffed the piece of paper in his pants pocket, then joined his family in the cab. If Falcone had any doubts before about a cover-up, he was convinced now. Houston had turned white as a ghost as soon as he'd mentioned the murder. He's gonna crack, Falcone told himself. He has too much to lose.

Falcone's next stop was at the Belleville shooting range, which Wells, the desk lieutenant on duty the night of the murder, had purchased after his early retirement. He made his way past the rows of shotguns lining the walls and the gleaming handguns inside their cases, all for sale. Ray Wells was just coming out of the men's room when John approached the counter.

"Hi, I'm Detective John Falcone." Falcone realized he already knew that by the spark of recognition in the other man's eyes. Maybe Houston had tipped him off, though he wouldn't have had much time to make the call.

"I understand you were on desk duty the night Tom Calvetti was murdered out at the Laurel estate."

Ray Wells didn't flinch. By all rights he should be away somewhere relaxing, going fishing, collecting his pension. Who knew what made guys like Wells hang on?

"I have some questions. Maybe we could go into your office, where it's quiet." Falcone's eyes scanned the shooting gallery. "Impressive. You've come a long way from desk lieutenant. You must have worked your butt off—or perhaps you knew people in high places."

This last remark seemed to move Ray and he quickly ushered Falcone down the corridor through double doors and into his office.

Ray shut the door, then said, "What can I help you with, Detective?"

"I need to know what really happened that night." Falcone took the police report out of his pocket again. "This is a copy of the report." As Ray Wells watched in disbelief, Falcone tossed it into the wastebasket near the desk.

"It's garbage."

There was silence for a few moments, then with a smug look on his face Ray said, "Are you aware, Detective, that I can have your badge for this inappropriate behavior?"

Falcone let out a hearty laugh. "Are you aware, Wells, that I can cause you a shitload of trouble?"

He was wasting his time. It was obvious that Wells wouldn't be the one to crack. Falcone threw his telephone number on the desk and said, "I doubt you'll use it, but call me if anything comes to mind."

Under ordinary circumstances, neither man would be having it this easy. Houston enjoyed expensive vacations with his perfect family—second family, according to his records—and Wells had also established a nice solid life for himself. The shooting gallery he ran was only one of four that he owned—the 21,000 feet rent on this location alone could have run about fifty grand a year. Wells had retired soon after the Laurel estate incident and was now living in a brand-new five-thousand-square-foot ranch house in Port Washington, with a built-in swimming pool. John wondered what he'd lived on until the shooting galleries got going. Houston was by far the weaker of the two, as well as the one with the most to lose. His kid went to a private school, and his wife drove a brand-new candy apple red Jaguar XJS.

Dawkins was right: there had been a cover-up, and it had James Miller's prints all over it. What did Miller have to hide? Two of his employees had gotten into a fight, and one had died. Miller had no liability, no stake in the matter at all. Unless he knew more about that night than what was in the case files.

33

The white Saks Fifth Avenue box with its familiar gold-and-white logo had been brought to her apartment by the doorman. Once she had been a woman who loved surprises, but not anymore. Now any gift she received might be a Trojan horse. She eyed the box warily as she moved from the foyer to the living room. Sun swept the room's feminine floral motif, and Rose decided nothing bad could happen on such a beautiful day.

Rose cautiously lifted the lid off the box, pushing aside layers of tissue paper that soon revealed a black beaded Cynthia Rowley gown. She held the dress up to the sunlight. It was a classic, with a high neck, low-cut back, and a slit up the side; it was made for her. There was only one person who would have known her this well.

> *Dear Rose,*
> *I'm sorry, please forgive me.*
> *Evan*

Who else but her husband could have made such an exquisite choice for tonight. *Dear, sweet Evan,* she thought. She had been so afraid, he had been so distant. But she should know him better than that and put more trust in his good heart. She read the card once again, smiling for the first time in days. She needed to tell him it was she who should apologize. Holding the gown against her body, she twirled wildly around the room, and for the moment she forgot all the madness.

She would go to the Ivory Palace opening tonight and have her final words with Dimitri. Tonight, when she came face-to-face with him, he would have no way of avoiding her any longer. The negative images and thoughts began to recede as she carefully hung the gown in her closet. Evan's thoughtfulness had soothed her. His forgiveness made all the recent bad events seem trivial, insignificant. Now, she decided, a long bath would chase away all remnants of her sadness and fear.

Rose stepped into the claw-footed antique tub and allowed her body to relax and her thoughts to wander. Warm water scented with lavender oil trickled over her skin. Baths were the luxury she indulged in when her stress level reached an unbearable high. Normally she turned off the lights, lit rows of scented candles, and basked in the flickering, serene ambiance. But ever since Marilyn's death, she couldn't bear to light a candle.

Rose emptied her mind of everything but her life with Evan and their future. Everything would be okay. He'd forgiven her. He had built his world around her and Alexis. Despite her turbulent feelings for Dimitri, she still loved Evan, in her own way. He was her sanctuary, a safe and stable place in the world for her and her child. And once she straightened things out with Dimitri, she would tell her husband everything—no more living as a prisoner of the past.

She wondered what Evan's reaction would be if she told him Dimitri was Alexis's father. Although she believed she understood Evan completely, no one could know every nook and cranny of a loved one's thoughts and feelings. Evan might be stable, but he was capable of unpredictability—look at the impulse that had driven him to invite Dimitri to join them for dinner at Match, no matter what the consequences. While she was certain the truth would not change Evan's feelings toward their daughter, there was no way of calculating ahead of time how angry he would be at her and for how long, or if their marriage would turn to dust over such an admission of so many years of living a lie.

The thought sent an icy shudder through her soul. She heard a warning voice inside telling her to let sleeping dogs lie. But no, that was a coward's way out. She couldn't live with the lies anymore. She should have come clean from the start. Marilyn was right: her honesty would have spared everyone a lot of pain. The truth was, though, it had all seemed so complicated and ugly that she didn't know where to begin. With Dimitri gone, it was easy just to go along with the charade. But his reappearance rocked her world and stripped it of its equilibrium.

She stepped out of the tub and reached for a towel. A cold, damp draft seemed to emanate from the crevices of the marble floor. A chill rushed through her body as she padded into her bedroom. Silence filled the air. Normally she craved the tranquillity. But lately it drove her mad, made the apartment feel spooky, and heightened her paranoia. She heard noises, imagined intruders, created dreadful scenarios in her mind. She was always on guard. But not tonight. Staring at the gown, she thought of Evan and imagined the two of them gliding along the dance floor, while the orchestra played one of their favorites. *I'll get my business with Dimitri over with, then Evan and I will enjoy the evening,* she thought. In the morning, she would tell Evan her last secret.

Dimitri's office window looked out onto the boardwalk and, beyond that, the ocean. There had been a snowfall early in the morning, and now crows left their claw marks in the dusting of sand mixed with snow as they went about their never-ending job of scavenging. He turned from the window, thinking that he had fallen prey to the other form of scavengers. The DA, Jewel, Braun . . . the list was long.

Don't think about that, he told himself. Tonight he would be in his familiar role, king of the hill. The opening party for his casino had been meticulously planned. First there would be gambling for his four hundred invited guests. The slots were fixed to give out frequent jackpots. Then, in the ballroom, through the formal dinner, an orchestra would be playing music from the big band era. Tony Bennett would be headlining later in the evening. Dimitri's favorite. Dimitri had overseen every detail, right down to the lighting picked to show women of a certain age at their best.

No, not quite: one detail had gotten away from Dimitri. Seated behind his desk, he fingered a copy of the *Post,* remembering the unwilling kiss that had made him want her more. His obsessive feelings for Rose were not under his control. *"Damn her,"* he whispered, despising the hold she still had over him. Her absence from his life had brought out his ruthlessness, and he hated her for it. Yet, at the same time, he knew he wouldn't have been so driven if she hadn't infuriated him by her betrayal. There was a good chance his rage was the propulsion that fueled his climb to succeed.

And now she needs me, he mused, unable to contain the mix of emotions that her plea for his help was stirring inside. He'd avoided her calls for the sole purpose of ensuring that she would come tonight. He glanced down at his watch. Just two more hours.

A knock on the door interrupted his thoughts. The door opened and Joseph Braun appeared.

"Where's Jewel?" he asked. His bland tone clashed with the vibrant royal blue Versace tuxedo he wore. Braun had a tendency to overdo it, just like his daughter.

Dimitri walked to the desk, opened the top drawer, and pulled out two vintage Macanudo cigars. "Join me?" he asked matter-of-factly.

"Sure," Braun said. "Is Jewel getting ready?"

Dimitri nodded. "She's in the bedroom deciding on a gown. You know your daughter. She doesn't buy one gown for an affair; her minimum is three. She had designers coming and going all day today." He clipped the tip of the cigar, then struck a match, held it to his mouth, and lightly swirled the Macanudo as he took a long, smooth puff. Braun did the same.

Dimitri pushed the talk button on the intercom. "Bring in a pitcher of martinis, please."

The men sat opposite each other on two burgundy leather sofas. Dimitri sensed something coming from Braun that he couldn't figure out.

"So," Dimitri said, his tone ebullient. "Tonight's the night. My guests, the critics, the celebrities, everyone will, no doubt, have an opinion when they exit. Will the Ivory Palace be a hit? What do you think, Joseph?"

"You forgot to add the feds to your list of attendees," Braun said, smiling coldly. "Come on, Dimitri, cut the bullshit. Everything you touch turns to gold. It's part of the reason I hate you!" He winked. "A week from now, this place will be so crowded, you'll be turning them away at the door."

Dimitri was disgusted by Braun's insincerity, his ill-disguised enmity, but he kept his expression neutral. "I never brag. It's like spitting into the wind."

"Anyway—"

Braun was interrupted by a faint knock on the door. An attractive young woman, one of the rotating twenty-four-hour staff, entered carrying a tray with the martinis and a dish of green olives. Both men nodded thanks, and when the door closed behind her, Braun continued, "Actually, I'd like to discuss some business with you. Is this room secure?"

"It's clean. My team is very thorough. What business?"

Braun sipped his martini before going on. "I received a message from some friends from the gaming industry in New York. They're bowled over by your latest venture. As far as they're concerned, the Ivory Palace is gonna blow the other casinos off the strip. Forget Trump's casinos, all three of them. As for the new Hilton and Merv Griffin's joint, well, none of them stands a chance."

Dimitri could tell by Braun's intensity that this was a conversation he didn't want to have.

"They want a piece of the action. Just a small percent. Think of it as insurance. You know what I'm talkin' about, Dimitri."

Was Braun crazy? Dimitri had left his father-in-law's business in order to legitimize himself. "No," he shot back, splashing his drink onto the Lucite coffee table for effect. "You tell your friends that the answer is no!"

Braun popped an olive in his mouth, then rested his elbows on his knees and knocked his fists together silently, like a prizefighter.

He's buying time, Dimitri thought. Now he really was starting to get angry at the old fool. Dimitri shut his mind to whatever else Braun had to say.

"Calm down, Dimitri, you're my protégé—my son." Braun projected a demeanor Dimitri was positive he didn't feel.

"Stop it right there, Joseph. Look at me." Dimitri waited until he had Braun's full attention. "I built this empire. I made it happen, and no one, *no one,* gets a piece. You tell them that!"

Braun's entire attitude changed. He moved forward, leaning directly into Dimitri's face. "I'm afraid it's not so simple. You don't tell these people no. There could be repercussions."

"I'll deal with whatever comes my way." This time Dimitri leaned forward and spoke softly, staring down Braun. "I work alone—here and in Vegas. I take all the falls, and I get all the profit. I won't let anyone muscle their way in."

"They're willing to pay," he said. "They can buy in for a small price and then—"

Dimitri put his hand up to stop him from speaking another word. "Last time, Joseph—no way!"

Braun's face twisted, turned nasty. "Dimitri, these people are *friends* of mine. You understand, don't you? Quid pro quo. They don't go away because you ask them to."

"I'll worry about my back if it comes down to it." Dimitri suddenly stood. "I have to get ready, my guests will be arriving."

Braun changed tactics. "Dimitri, I'm scared, these guys can hurt me—hurt us. They know things, they could go to the DA."

"Well, they have nothing on me, Joseph. I'm clean, and this trial will prove it. When I left your business everything was totally legit. I can't help it if you went back to those rodents."

His face flushed, Braun tossed back the rest of his martini. There was a warning note in his voice. "Don't play with these guys, Dimitri. I'm trying to help. They're dangerous."

"I'll take my chances," Dimitri retorted as he opened his penthouse door, signifying it was time for Braun to go.

Joseph followed his son-in-law to the door, then said, "Don't forget where you came from, Dimitri. I took you off the streets."

Dimitri turned to Braun and chuckled. "Great line, Joseph. Sounds like it came from one of those old James Cagney movies."

"Will I see you after the party?"

Jewel clutched the receiver, her eyes darting around the suite's enormous aqua-and-blue master bedroom. Gowns were everywhere—piled on top of each other on the bed. As Jewel talked, her personal maid held up a black-sequined, form-fitting Geoffrey Beene gown. Jewel shook her head, turned her back to the maid. "I . . . I can't talk now."

"Then I'll do all the talking. You just listen. Remember last night, how great it was? Will you meet me tonight?"

Jewel felt a rush of heat. "How could I forget?" Just remembering made her hungry for more. The deal struck between them was as seductive and rewarding as the sex.

"Of course I'll come," she whispered. "We'll meet after it's over. Your place."

When she hung up, Jewel took a short, sheer, red Versace slip dress and held it up to look at herself in the mirror. *Yes!* Her red stilettos would give it that extra touch, along with the enormous ruby earrings Dimitri had surprised her with for the opening. The thought of wearing his gift while she made love to another man made it all the more exciting.

Rose opened the door to her apartment and found Evan standing there with twelve long-stemmed roses in tissue paper cradling his arm. A smile curved his lips. And at that moment he waved away all the vultures circling their marriage, the hurt and madness that was driving them apart. Time disappeared, and somehow they were together again.

"I see you got my surprise," he said as his eyes roamed over her approvingly. The slit up the gown's side revealed one beautiful leg, and as she moved, the gown seemed designed to mold each gorgeous piece of her.

Rose stared back at him, and for reasons unknown to him, her eyes filled with tears. "I've missed you," she said, her voice barely above a whisper.

Then his lips were on hers and they were kissing passionately. Evan held her in a fierce embrace. Several minutes later she pulled back. Although she wanted nothing more than to spend the evening wrapped in Evan's arms, she had to think rationally. It was important that she get closure with Dimitri, and then she and Evan would be healed. Tonight was her chance.

"We'll have time for this later, dear. Right now we have to go."

Evan was lost in her beauty. In the heat of the moment, all the pressure he felt from James and Braun was banished by his love for Rose.

"Keep your wife away from Dimitri," Braun had warned, but he had to bring her to the opening. Dimitri had insisted, and Evan understood when not to push him. He knew too many family secrets. Between Braun and Dimitri, Braun was the easiest of the two for him to handle. Dimitri was holding a much better hand of cards than Braun.

"Before we go"—he held her against him—"I want to say I've been unfair. Please forgive me? Of course you were set up for the photo. What could I have been thinking?"

34

So far, the celebration was a success. Dimitri Constantinos's name was big enough to attract the press in droves and a *Who's Who* list of the biggest entertainers, actors, actresses, and politicians. Yet his most important guest of the evening had not yet arrived.

As Dimitri walked through the casino, tending to his guests, he spotted Donald Trump accompanied by his young blonde of the moment in a far corner of the room. Dimitri and *the* Donald made eye contact and exchanged smiles. Trump gave him a thumbs-up sign, and Dimitri thought, *You bet, buddy.*

Hors d'oeuvres and drinks were being served in the ballroom by waitresses in white thigh-high sarong skirts, high heels, and aqua body suits. Deftly Dimitri worked the room, answering questions from reporters, greeting associates, and complimenting their wives. *Keep them happy,* he thought. When he was thirty, he'd had an affair with an older woman, a notorious Texas socialite, who taught him that if enough liquor and food flowed and everyone was comfortable, either seated or standing, a host could throw his guests into the room, slip away, and never be missed. She was right. He saw that now.

A jackpot bell sounded and the manager pushed over to tell Dimitri that Senator Darcy's wife had just scored $1,000. Dimitri dragged his eyes away from the door and went to congratulate Grace Darcy, who remained ensconced at the video poker machine. He bent over and kissed Mrs. Darcy's hand, giving her his most charming smile.

"Would it be illegal to give this to my husband's reelection campaign?" Mrs. Darcy asked in a giddy manner.

Dimitri laughed, pecked her on the cheek, and said, "Congratulations." He excused himself politely, and as he walked away he began to obsess. *Where is she?* He had explicitly told Evan to be on time and had sent the newest and fastest Constantinos Enterprises helicopter to pick them up. He glanced at his watch. It was well past eight. He knew he was behaving like an adolescent, and he hated her hold on him. In prison he had vowed no one would ever dominate him again, but he hadn't counted on being a prisoner of his own feelings.

Dimitri felt a hard tug on his elbow. Joseph was with two men he assumed were the "associates" they had quarreled about upstairs.

"Dimitri, this is a great turnout," Braun commended as he put his hand on his son-in-law's shoulder. "You did one hell of a job." His eyes darted toward his daughter standing near the bar, entertaining a wealthy sheik and his wife. "Jewel looks great, doesn't she!"

Dimitri winked back at Braun and said, "Joseph, there isn't another name in this world that you could have picked that describes your daughter so appropriately."

"Why, thank you, son," Braun replied with overt pride yet internal skepticism. Quickly turning back to his guests, he said, "By the way, these are my friends, Mark Kelig and Ralph Manard. They're also in the gambling business."

Dimitri got the picture. Braun had made promises on his behalf. Now he couldn't come through. Part of Dimitri felt sorry for the old man, but the fighter in him spoke loud and clear. *That's his problem.*

The taller of the two men, Kelig, shook Dimitri's hand. His face was a map of a brutal past, his mouth set in a permanent scowl.

"Great place you've got here," he said.

Dimitri nodded but said nothing. There would be no small talk.

The other man, Manard, added, "What I wouldn't give to own a piece of it. Perhaps we—"

A commotion broke out among the reporters at the entrance. Dimitri knew Rose had arrived.

Clutching her husband's arm and smiling brightly, Rose Miller made her way through the crowd of photographers and journalists, maneuvering around the gaming tables, stopping to greet acquaintances while avoiding the reporters.

From where he stood, Dimitri could see a towering, burly bodyguard following the couple's every move. He watched as Rose stopped to shake every hand and sign a few autographs. Behind him the casino noise resumed, the neon lights flashing in many colors, but he was oblivious to all that. He saw only Rose and felt her gliding toward him. At that moment he realized he'd never stop wanting her.

He tore his attention away and turned back to Braun's goons. "You must excuse me, but I'm afraid I have to circulate. I hope you have a wonderful evening," he said, and left before they could get in another word.

Dimitri remained at bay, drinking in the sight of her. *Exquisite,* he thought. Rose suddenly found him in the large room, and for a moment their eyes met. Just the sight of her heightened his senses. She was the only person to ever bring Dimitri Constantinos down. Yet he wasn't going to let her get away with it. Under different circumstances he might have forgiven her, but she was a Delilah to his Samson, and her betrayal had killed something deep inside of him.

Minutes later Evan squeezed Dimitri's shoulder. Instinctively Constantinos pulled away. He gave Rose a slight nod and then said to Evan, "I'm glad you both could make it."

He was afraid his voice would give him away, so he made believe for a moment that he was someone else—a trick he'd learned when prison life turned too ugly. It worked. For that moment she was just another guest.

Evan, now glowing at Rose, said, "I'm sorry we're late." As Evan leaned over to give his wife a kiss, Dimitri noticed his brother kept his arm securely around Rose.

He shows her off like she's his most prized possession. He wants me to know things are fine between the two of them. She's convinced him nothing happened. That might work—at least for the time being.

"The night would have been a total loss if you hadn't come," Dimitri said gallantly as he focused his attention on Rose. She grew visibly uncomfortable, and this pleased him immensely.

Dimitri turned back to Evan. "You'll have to excuse me, I have some other guests I haven't said hello to yet. I do hope you enjoy the evening." This time he forced himself to give Evan an affectionate hug. In public, defense lawyers had to pretend they liked their clients.

Rose left the casino and opted for the relative serenity of the ballroom. The invitation called for dinner at nine o'clock, which was when the other four hundred guests would move away from the gambling floor. She entered the room, found their assigned table, and realized they were seated dead center, where everyone's eyes could find her. To add to the disgrace, she and Evan were seated at Dimitri's table. She felt unnerved, but she wouldn't let the rest of the world know that. Squinting in an effort to read each place card, she saw that Evan was seated to her left, Dimitri on her right, and his wife, Jewel, next to Dimitri. *How interesting,* she considered, convinced Dimitri had staged it this way. *Another attempt to make me feel uncomfortable, but it won't work, not tonight.*

Baccarat crystal chandeliers hung from the ceiling. Prisms of light reflected a sparkling, diamondlike brilliance. The settings were Limoges china, each dish with a beautiful gold-and-blue border. Elaborate candelabras adorned each side of the white lily centerpiece. One thing was evident: Dimitri adored opulence. White linen napkins with fine blue-and-gold stripes were arranged like fans and placed in each empty crystal water glass. The tablecloths matched the napkins, but on the skirt of each, just like the signature of a famous artist, there was a small replication in blue of the Ivory Palace's silhouette and an inscription of the casino's name in gold. A red cloud in her peripheral vision got Rose's attention and she saw Dimitri enter with the woman she presumed was his wife on his arm. The guests followed in their wake. Rose wished the orchestra would start soon. The silence was stifling.

Jewel Constantinos broke away from Dimitri's side and strode purposefully over to Rose. *Brave woman,* Rose thought, assuming Jewel was defying rumors about Rose and Dimitri.

"So, I finally get to meet the one and only Rose Miller." Jewel's expression was inscrutable. Rose offered Jewel her hand, but Jewel only nodded and picked up a glass of champagne from the tray offered by a waiter who had materialized next to her.

"You know, Rose, I've *always* been a great fan of yours," she slurred in a lockjaw vernacular now emboldened by the booze. "But don't you think the ending for *The Devil's Daughter* was a bit extreme?"

Rose was taken aback but knew Jewel was just trying to unsettle her. "Well—"

Jewel interrupted Rose's reply. "And what the hell is this new title? *Thorns of a Rose?* Now that sounds like some trashy romance novel. I mean, the cover should have been one of a bare-chested stable boy rescuing his fair maiden."

The overpowering scent of Jewel's perfume, mixed with the alcohol on her breath, made Rose think of how a hybrid hothouse flower might smell. She did not let her gaze drop from Jewel's amber eyes as she carried on.

"As for *Last Rites . . .*"

Finally, getting a little tired of Jewel's "critiques," Rose decided to change the subject. "Why don't you sit down, Jewel? Your shoes are fabulous, but they must be killing you."

Jewel gave her a cunning smile and sat.

A moment later Evan joined them, and Rose thought, *Thank God.* She didn't want to waste energy trying to draw Jewel out anymore. She would let him steer the socializing. As she faded out of the conversation, her mind went immediately to the confrontation she was planning on having tonight with Dimitri. She watched him circulating the tables. More than anything, Dimitri's demeanor, low-key and unpretentious, told her that he had made it. He had fulfilled his dreams. He had nothing to prove to anyone. A jolt, like a synapse in her brain short-circuiting, took her mind way back. The image was completely clear: Dimitri, holding her against him: *One day I'm going to be big, Rose. So big, I'll forget all this mess—my mother, James, this whole plastic world they live in. I'm gonna break out, you watch.*

And he had in such a big way, Rose could hardly believe his success. She was happy for this part of his story. But she also felt sorry for the ugly streak that had surfaced in the man she once knew. She continued watching until Jewel nudged her.

"He's quite charismatic, my husband," Jewel said with more than a hint of sarcasm. "It's really a shame how the press ambushed you the other night."

Rose had the feeling the other woman was speaking lines she had rehearsed in order to get her through the humiliation she must feel. Instinct told her to disarm Jewel, tell her exactly what she wanted to hear.

"The press distorted the whole incident." She paused, not knowing how much Dimitri had told his wife. Keep it simple, she warned herself. "Nothing happened. I'm sorry if it caused you any distress."

Jewel stared back at her. She was a hard woman, certainly tougher than Rose, that much was clear. Everything Rose had perceived about Dimitri's wife, whether in the media or through the little Evan had said of her, told her that Jewel could be an insidious enemy to deal with. *How can I make her believe me?* Rose thought. But it was obviously too late. Everything about their exchange told her this woman was already her foe.

Evan watched them intently. She could only imagine what was going on in his mind. He'd always been so easy for her to read, but lately his emotional state was nearly opaque. Other than the sweet moment tonight, they'd been strangers roaming around in the same space.

"It looks like the evening is off to a good start," Dimitri commented to the guests at his table.

He had done this to them—all of them—including Jewel, and that made Rose feel sorry for the other woman. Tonight she would do whatever it took to stop the torment and the games. This entire evening she had been thinking how best to get Dimitri alone. It wasn't going to be easy. Guests stopped by their table constantly, and she could barely get his attention long enough to say anything. Now Joseph Braun approached with another guest in tow, obviously to introduce the man to Jewel. The waiter was serving oysters Rockefeller just as Evan's beeper went off. He apologized, then excused himself to find a nearby phone.

Seizing the moment, Rose leaned to her right, tugged gently on Dimitri's jacket sleeve, and said, "I need to speak with you."

He looked back at her with Alexis's eyes. There was a long pause, and then: "In my private suite at ten o'clock."

Evan returned and, with a worried look on his face, said, "I'm sorry, Rose, I've been called back to the office for an emergency meeting."

Dimitri raised his eyebrows. "It can't wait until morning?"

Evan reached down, gave Rose an affectionate kiss on the cheek, and said to Dimitri, "No, it can't. I've called for a limo to take me back to the city." To Rose he said, "The car will continue on and take you back home and I'll meet you there later. Unless, that is, you want to stay?" His tone was caustic, and Rose should have agreed to leave with him, but she couldn't. She needed to speak with Dimitri.

"No, Evan, if you're going back to the office, I can stay a bit longer and—"

"Don't take a car, Evan," Dimitri said, barging in. "I'll have one of the pilots take you back in the same helicopter you came in on. And then I'll send Rose home in one of the others. She'll get home safely."

Evan bit his lower lip, a sure sign he was hiding his feelings. She could only guess what he was thinking. Perhaps she should go with him. But as she considered this, looking from her husband to Dimitri, Evan turned abruptly and left.

35

The note was handed to Evan by Fred Grapple, a paralegal, when he arrived at the office.

I'm not sure why I'm writing this letter. I have no interest in the Dimitri Constantinos trial, nor do I have anything to gain. I am, however, a big fan of Dimitri's and, therefore, I feel the need to tell both of you there is an inside informer. Someone you'd least suspect. Someone has "flipped" and will be a surprise witness for the prosecution, someone very close to Dimitri.

Sincerely,
A Friend.

"Shit," Evan said loudly. "This is disastrous. How was it delivered?"

"By messenger," Fred responded. "The man said it was urgent. It was lucky I was still here. I thought you'd want to see it immediately. I'm sorry if I pulled you away from—"

"You did the right thing," Evan said brusquely.

"It could be some nut who has read about the trial and—"

"I can't take a chance. This could destroy my defense." Then Evan had a thought.

"Do you remember that private investigator, Duke Farina? The ex-FBI agent?"

A look of recognition crossed Fred's face. "Yes, he worked on the Bridgewater case."

"Get him on the line. Get this note to him, put it in an evidence bag so it doesn't get any more contaminated than it is. Tell him to check it for fingerprints."

Fred studied him. "It's a long shot."

"Farina has access to all the equipment at the FBI headquarters. If he needs to speak with me, tell him to call my cell phone. I'm headed back to Atlantic City."

Evan needed to tell Dimitri about the possible informer in person. Quickly he gathered his things together, making sure he had all the files he needed in his briefcase. He'd most likely stay at the Ivory Palace, then come in with Dimitri from Atlantic City in the morning.

"If anything develops, call me."

Dario slipped into his Givenchy jacket, straightened his cuffs, then smiled approvingly at his reflection in the mirror in his room at the Ivory Palace. Eight-thirty. By now the tips he'd faxed to every single newspaper in the tristate area, let alone the national news stations, would have arrived. By midnight the press would be climbing all over her, picking clean the carcass of the story. The *real* Rose Miller story. He wanted to make sure he was downstairs at the party to witness Rose's humiliation. All of the reporters covering the opening were certain to be there when the story hit the wires.

Soon the world would know the true story of Rose Miller, the fairy tale of a servant girl who slept with Dimitri Constantinos. His source was unimpeachable, he was sure of it. And he hadn't even had to pay for the information. Tony Gardner, a writer who had a contract for an unauthorized biography on the Miller family, had been researching the book for two years. No one knew who Gardner's sources were, but he'd exposed the secrets of many prominent families. And lucky for Dario, Gardner had a crush on him. Despite Dario's notorious reputation as a ladies' man, he had been able to manipulate Gardner's feelings and get him to dish the dirt. Rose had tried to pass herself off as somebody else, but he would expose her. And then she'd come running to him to control the damage. *This time* she wouldn't be so surly. *This time* she'd realize he was all she had left.

He checked his watch: nearly nine. He had to get moving or he'd be late. But first the warm-up. He'd make one stop before hiding himself in the crowd down in the casino.

Breaking away from the crowd was not nearly as hard as Rose had anticipated. The biggest obstacle would be slipping away from the bodyguard Evan and Falcone had insisted upon. She couldn't believe he'd fallen for the old "ladies' room" ploy, but he had. Obviously the guard, Malcolm, didn't read her books. The rest was a breeze. She didn't have to say good-bye to anyone. Jewel had left the table a while ago. It was safe to assume no one saw Rose sneak into the service elevator and ride up to the penthouse floor.

The penthouse corridor was quiet. Rose made her way to the end, until she was face-to-face with a set of large wooden doors. A hundred emotions stirred inside, but her resolve won out. So she knocked. No answer. She knocked again, hard enough that her ten-carat diamond ring scraped the wood. She checked her watch. It was a few minutes past ten. Obviously this was another one of Dimitri's games. Angrily she grabbed the doorknob, and to her surprise, it turned easily. Inside, the penthouse was dark. Rose called out to Dimitri but received no answer.

There was a creak, and then the door slammed shut. Rose remained still.

"Dimitri?" Her voice trembled, and she stayed rooted to the spot just inside the door. Steps made crunching sounds in the thick new carpet. Then she felt a hand on her shoulder.

"Don't hurt me," she pleaded.

"Just relax." *It didn't sound like Dimitri.* Then he was all over her, all of his weight pushing down on her. *He's going to kill me,* she thought. *I don't want to die.* She felt a sharp pinch in her upper arm . . . a needle.

"Don't move," he whispered, "and you won't be hurt."

If he wasn't going to kill her, then what?

"Seven, six, five, four, three—there you go, feel better?" he asked.

Rose felt warm all over, then sleepy.

Billy popped the trunk latch of the car and stared into the wide, tear-filled eyes staring back at him.

"Hello, my pretty one," he said to Janice.

The twenty-two-year-old Atlantic City showgirl was tied up. Her hands and feet were bound with two leather belts. Her mouth was taped and gagged, but from the look of horror in her eyes, he could tell she was screaming inside. It simply delighted him. She tried to scream despite the tape.

"Shhh," he said, putting two fingers to his lips. She glared at him, and he slapped her, hard. The bruise from an earlier punch was blossoming into a purple-and-blue circle surrounding her left eye. Tears spilled from the corners of her swollen eyes, filled with panic—horror and the unknown.

"Soon it will be over," he whispered. Her baby blue eyes showed fear. Predictably, he let out a pleasurable sigh.

Janice had turned out to be a tough one, a real fighter. She didn't want to play the game, and for that she would be punished. He would kill her slowly, not like the rest. Because she fought him, he would revel in her suffering.

He had taken her to a secluded motel he knew about, given her some Asti Spumanti—deserving of the celebration—and then showered her with kisses. But when he'd asked her to put on the silk nightie he'd bought, she'd refused. They'd struggled, and with her long red nails, she'd nearly clawed his eyes out.

"Bad girl," he'd said softly. Then he'd hit her so hard, she had fallen against the dresser, hit her head, and lost consciousness. Even though it had made his job easier, he'd been disappointed. The game had to be played by his rules, and she was not cooperating. So he'd tied her up, carried her limp body to the car, and thrown it in the trunk. Now they had reached their destination—in her case, the final destination.

He took out the black duffel bag first, then dragged her naked body from the trunk onto the dirt. She began to moan. He made no effort to be gentle. Her moans of pain only heightened his pleasure. He slung the duffel bag over his shoulder and, with one hand, continued to drag her along the ground.

The sand was surrounded by thistle and weeds that were up to his knees. He had to take each step carefully, lest he scratch himself on the naked wintry fauna. At some point the bush line stopped and all they had to get through was the wet, clammy sand. The sound of the crashing waves was almost as good a backdrop as the music.

"You didn't listen. You refused to play with me. Now you have to die," he said aloud.

Billy dragged Janice another hundred feet, then stopped. He threw the duffel bag to the ground, unzipped it, and pulled out two sharp steak knives. He brought his eyes down to meet hers. She was crying. The tears streamed down her face.

He held a knife in each hand, raised his arms above his head, and slammed each knife into her shoulders. Two dark rivers of blood began to flow, slowly at first, then picking up speed as she bled into the sand. He pulled out the knives and watched her squirm. He repeatedly stabbed and pulled, stabbed and pulled, each time hoping to make the thrust hurt coming out as well as going in. Even in the dark he could see that her upper torso was nothing but flapping skin and blood. He reveled in her agony. When it was over and she no longer squirmed, she looked just like a big pinned dead butterfly. He felt a sense of satisfaction and euphoria.

Billy chuckled as he headed back to the boardwalk.

36

The whirling sound of the helicopter nearby jolted Rose and snapped her awake. Her thoughts were clouded, her surroundings fuzzy. She'd been drugged. But by whom? She was being dragged by her arms along the ground. She struggled wildly against the two men holding her, but she was no match for them. They dropped her, and the cold pavement made her shiver. She clawed at it, grasping handfuls of something in her hands. Dirt? No, it was coarse, prickly—straw.

Rose opened her eyes and fought hard to focus. She saw two men recede into the shadows, switching on a light positioned so that it blinded her. She tried to figure out where she was, but there was little to go on except for the straw and a familiar smell she couldn't immediately identify. Somehow she managed to pull herself up and rest on her elbows. The light was glaring, making it impossible for her to focus. She had known many feelings in her life, but never this kind of terror—so all-consuming, she was lost to it.

"Feel familiar, Rose?" The voice was a whisper—it was Dimitri's. Paralyzed and struck dumb with shock, she did not move.

The light grew brighter. He had moved the hurricane lantern so she could see her surroundings. The wooden walls were chipped, and above her the flat roof was caving in on one side. Rose realized that beneath the straw the floor was stone. It was the barn—they were back at Laurel. She realized the odor she couldn't identify came from the horse stalls, still replete with the smell of horses from so long ago.

Outside, she could hear the relentless drumming of the rain and the moan of the wind.

She brought one hand up to her eyes in an attempt to block out the glare. Resting all of her weight on one elbow proved to be too much, and she collapsed against the ground.

"Be careful, Rose, you're disoriented," Dimitri said, but he made no effort to help her. "I'm sorry they drugged you, but there was no other way to get you here."

She curled her body into a ball and began to sob. "Why are you doing this to me?" Her speech was still slightly impaired.

"Look around, Rose. Is it all coming back to you?"

Everything came crashing down on her at once. The memory of that night. The wine, her flight from Evan's proposal into Dimitri's arms. Though she couldn't see him, she felt Dimitri forcing her to dredge up the haunting memory. And she did. She relived every feeling from that night until her mind stopped and was unable to go beyond the memory of Uncle Tom's wretched body on hers, then darkness.

She knew Dimitri was going to kill her and had gone to much trouble to carry out the task here, where it all began.

Time passed slowly for her, and the drug was beginning to wear off. Dimitri, still dressed in his black tuxedo, was standing a few feet from her. His body blocked the torturous light, and she saw that his eyes were hard and hateful. He started to walk toward her, gliding through the light like an angel or an apparition.

"Get up," he demanded. She tried to force her body forward. It was no use. She couldn't muster the strength. Her body flattened against the ground.

"Discombobulated?" he asked. "Our elegant Rose?" His voice was edged with sarcasm.

Another sob exploded from Rose's mouth. Her nails clawed the dirt floor and she waited, heart pounding, for Dimitri's next move.

"I said get up!"

Rose, shivering from fear, dopey from the drug, somehow managed to push her body up. On her hands and knees she began to crawl toward him, catching her legs and arms repeatedly on the long gown. In front of her, just a few feet away, she could see a bale of hay. She moved faster, and when she reached it, she sank her body deeply into the mound.

"Just like that night, Rose. Remember? You were completely out of it, totally unaware of what happened."

Now his voice sounded gentler. Somehow, though, it was more frightening. She couldn't predict what would happen.

She tried to reach him. "I have never forgotten making love for the first time in my life, with you."

Dimitri didn't respond. There was a deep gash across his cheek. He noticed her staring and said, "I wrestled with a tree branch outside. Nasty, isn't it?"

He placed his hands beneath her elbows and pulled her up, his face inches from hers. She could see the feeling return to his eyes, and his scent enveloped her.

"So you remember that night, Rose?"

She tried to steady herself and managed to stand without his assistance. Somewhere along the way she'd lost her shoes, and her stockings were tattered. Desperately she fought to break free from his grasp. But his arm moved around her waist and he pulled her even closer.

"Remember how it felt? It was magic. I've never felt that way since." He paused. "Have you?"

Before she could reply, he went on, eyes far away, caught up in the last sweet memory they had shared. "You were so pure and soft." He raised his hand to her cheek. "You still are." He stroked her hair with his hand, then brought it down to her face. His fingers traced the outline of her eyes, then her mouth, moving gently across her lips. "I was you and you were me. When I saw Tom . . ."

"Stop!" Rose held up her hand. She stared back at him through tear-filled eyes and whispered, "Why are you doing this to me, Dimitri?"

His eyes were now filled with passion. Romantic or vengeful? She couldn't tell.

"I loved you so much, I would have died for you," he said. "You were mine. I would never let anyone hurt you. I protected you till the end. You knew that, didn't you?"

She couldn't answer but only found the strength to nod.

"When I was first locked up, all I thought about was that night. It was the only thing that kept me going. Then I saw a newspaper and read about your wedding to Evan."

His grip tightened, and she flinched.

"The thought of another man's hands on you . . . of you loving him back . . . it nearly drove me insane. I stopped thinking about wanting you and thought about killing you instead."

"Dimitri, don't do this." She was trying to find the password, the way to reach him.

He couldn't hear her; he was caught up in his own whirl of devastating memories. He continued rambling.

"When I walked in here that night and found your uncle . . ."

"Stop," she begged. She had to grab hold of her senses or she'd be lost in that memory and in him. She thought about Uncle Tom, his hands on her body, the glint of the cold metal against her throat, and she shivered again. She despised the memory of his touch. The very thought of that night only reminded her of what could have been, if Dimitri hadn't been so foolish.

"Why did you have to kill him?"

There was a moment of silence, then Dimitri's shrill laughter.

"You mean you still haven't figured it out?"

"Figured what out?" Rose blurted through sobs.

Then his eyes turned glassy. "I didn't kill your uncle, Rose."

She curled her lip, her forehead creased, tears spilled down her cheeks. She couldn't speak around the terrible lump in her throat. Her head raced. That night . . . Dimitri had gone to get a blanket, and suddenly Uncle Tom was on top of her. The smell of alcohol, and the warm stink of his breath, the feel of the gun. She struggled. The ugly pieces slid together, forming an even uglier and more terrifying whole. Even though she knew the answer, she needed to hear him say it.

"Who . . . who killed him?" she stammered.

His answer was a thick silence she couldn't read.

"You did, Rose," Dimitri said. "When I returned with the blanket, I found you passed out with the gun in your hand, your uncle's body next to you."

Shock brought back a memory she had repressed all these years. In an instant, she recalled groping for the gun she knew Dimitri kept beneath his bed, just in case anyone tried to break into the stable. Tom was pawing at her, his hands touching where Dimitri had so tenderly loved her just moments before. And she remembered suddenly that she had killed him with one shot and managed to roll out from under him so that his blood never touched her.

Her tears fell like rain. Rose reached out her hand and caressed Dimitri's face, letting it linger. Dimitri wiped her eyes with his handkerchief. But Rose gently pushed his hand away. She didn't deserve his caring.

All these years she had blamed Dimitri for their misfortunes. His one fatal mistake—only it wasn't his.

She pressed the back of her hand to her mouth to stifle her sobs. "You took the blame for . . ." Then the last horrible piece fell into place. "And James went with that story, just to get you out of the way."

Something must have snapped inside Dimitri, because his entire demeanor changed. He pushed away from her.

"You certainly had a strange way of expressing gratitude, dear, sweet Rose." Dimitri stood and left her sitting on the barn floor. He seemed to hover above her, his eyes hard as blue diamonds.

As she struggled to get her balance, he said coldly, "The helicopter is outside to take us back. I suggest you clean yourself off."

As she watched him walk toward the door, she screamed, "Dimitri . . . wait! . . ."

The helicopter descended on the roof of the Ivory Palace. From the rain-soaked window, Rose could see a crowd below, waving them on. She turned to Dimitri. "Another one of your surprises?" she asked. But when she took a closer look at him, she could tell he was just as puzzled. He didn't answer, nor would he look at her. They had not exchanged a single word the entire forty-minute ride back from Long Island, and Rose had thought, *Just as well.* The sound inside the chopper made any further questions on her part irrelevant. She could hardly hear her own thoughts. A good thing, under the circumstances. The rain pounding against the window made it difficult to see the faces in the crowd until the helicopter landed on the casino's roof.

Her eyes lit on Evan, and she wondered what had brought him back. She could not see the expression on his face, and that was a relief. She didn't see Jewel. In fact, she doubted anyone in the horde had been a guest at the opening. From their frenzied activity, Rose deduced that much of the crowd comprised media people, gossip columnists, and photographers rushing for a story. If she had any feelings, she would be horrified to make this grand entrance with Dimitri Constantinos, but she was still numb. Everything inside her was empty and dark. Shards of the pieces that had been Rose Miller scratched against each other. *So this is what it feels like to be shattered,* she thought. Nothing about her would ever be familiar again. She was guilty of murder, and at the moment the sweet, stable world she had cherished was destroyed. Only one thing mattered—Alexis.

As the pilot cut off the helicopter's engine and the noise stopped, an unnatural silence enveloped them. The faces outside the window came into focus. What was Dario doing there? she wondered. Someone was shoving a microphone into Evan's face. She saw him shake his head and push the microphone away. His eyes were glued to the helicopter door, his expression unreadable.

Rose preceded Dimitri out of the helicopter, and the press descended on them, screaming questions, snapping pictures. Rose's gown was ripped, and she was barefoot. She alighted to a crowd that was momentarily silent as they gawked. But she didn't care. She was an empty vessel carrying only pain.

Evan ran to her, grabbed her hand, and led her inside. He was silent. When the door was shut, he turned on her, his whisper a hissing sound. "How could you do this to me?"

What could she possibly say? It was Dimitri who broke the silence. "It's not what it looks like." Neither of them had heard him enter, and in the dark beneath the escalators leading to the casino, only Dimitri's white shirt and the glow of his cigar were visible.

Evan was in a rage. "Really?" he asked incredulously. "I rushed all the way from Manhattan to tell you that the government's got an informer. I rushed here because I thought you should know. And you were off flying around the fucking city with my wife?"

Dimitri glanced momentarily at Rose, as though he hadn't heard Evan, as though he didn't really care. And Rose understood. For the first time since that dreadful night, they shared a common ground. The inexorable sense of death that had consumed Dimitri all these years now invaded her body and her mind. She would never be the same. She finally, profoundly, understood all of his pain and loss.

She had died tonight.

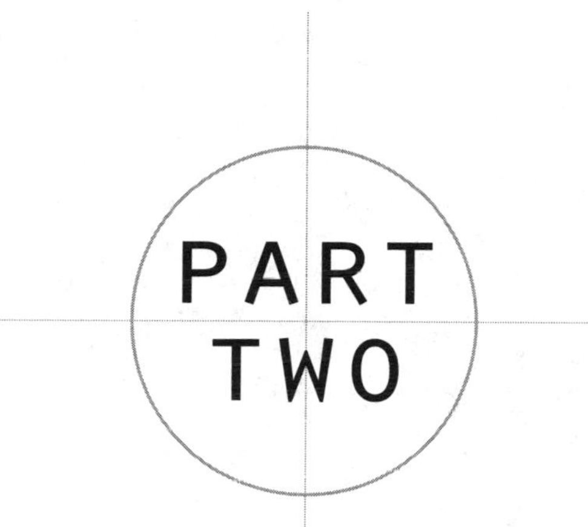
PART
TWO

37

The sun, unencumbered by clouds, rose over the windswept ocean in an explosion of golds and reds. Rose peered out the window of her hotel suite to glance up and down the strip of beach at the famed Fontainebleau Hilton Hotel Resort and Spa, an elegant white crescent reaching seaward and skyward. Dario had changed the reservations to allow Rose, Alexis, and Myra to arrive on Sunday instead of Monday, to escape the fallout of Friday night's fiasco. When the bellhop had let them into one of the sixty lavish suites, they were thrust into the elegance of the Victorian era, with a breathtaking ocean view. Both bedrooms, as well as the living room, had windows that overlooked the majestic Atlantic Ocean. As Rose tipped the bellhop, Alexis and Myra took in the sights, including the palm tree–lined landscape that led to a half-acre rock grotto swimming pool, complete with a cascading waterfall, a scene as soothing as a David Hockney painting.

Within minutes of their arrival Myra began to unpack their suitcases. Alexis had picked out all her own travel clothes during a spree at Bloomingdale's. Now, instead of the long quilted skirt that she'd worn with clogs on the plane, she opted for the more funky look of droopy jeans and a half-cropped top.

"Mom, can we go shopping on that street we saw from the limo?" Alexis had already spotted the allure and excitement of Ocean Drive in South Beach, its shops beckoning with merchandise that would bedazzle any adolescent.

Rose hesitated. Although she trusted Malcolm, her newly assigned bodyguard, and had noticed nothing untoward since leaving JFK, the sensation of being watched persisted. It surpassed mere paranoia. Ever since Friday night, when Dimitri had revealed what she'd subconsciously suspected all along, she couldn't shake a terrifying feeling of doom—that she deserved to be punished. Although his revelation had been shocking, somewhere it had been gnawing at her, hidden in the far reaches of her subconscious. The experience of not being able to recall events and of losing control that night so long ago had haunted her. She had wondered what was missing; now she knew. She didn't know when or how to start, but when she returned home, her first priority was to begin making amends to Dimitri.

"Mom, can we?"

Alexis's voice pulled her back to the present. Her growing conviction that Dimitri was not her stalker didn't change the fact that someone was out there. As far as she was concerned, there was no such thing as being too careful.

"I don't know, honey."

"Malcolm will come. Please, Mom?" Alexis pleaded.

Just then Malcolm, an odd-looking, stocky man with a boxer's scarred face, knocked at the door, and Myra let him in. The bodyguard looked as though he were dressed for South Beach rather than the posh, mostly formal crowd of the Fontainebleau. His short-sleeved, navy blue polo shirt revealed a huge tattoo, and not one of the pretty ones favored by today's kids. No, this was a skull and crossbones and one of the hand-drawn variety prisoners often decorated themselves with. Malcolm had on cutoff jeans with high-topped white sneakers. To conceal his gun, he wore a denim jacket with cutoff sleeves.

"Hey, I bet you ladies want to look around."

Rose realized this must also be Malcolm's first visit to Miami. How could she say no?

"All right . . ." She looked at her watch. It was still too early for dinner. "But, Malcolm, follow Alexis and Myra into every single shop."

"No problem." He patted his holster to reassure her his charges would be safe.

"Okay, guys, have a great time. Be back by six, we're all going out to dinner." Rose had Dario call ahead to make reservations for the ultrachic Italian restaurant Joia.

"Thanks, Mom!" Alexis threw her arms around Rose's neck, kissing her on the cheek. Then the three departed.

Alone, Rose sat by an open window. The light breeze off the ocean made her shiver. In her solitude, she thought back to her last moments with Evan, after she'd alighted from the helicopter with Dimitri. Though he'd kept his face expressionless, she could feel his turmoil. He had trusted her, despite the fact that it had forever driven a wedge between himself and his father.

"How could you do this to me, Rose?" he'd asked. Instead of answering him, she'd acted like a coward. She'd said nothing, offered no explanation, given no argument. Evan had walked away, crushed and heartbroken, leaving her to face the vultures alone. He'd returned to the mansion and she to her Fifth Avenue apartment. Now their lives were separate. *Is he going to divorce me?* she wondered. *He has every right to.*

Since that night, she'd locked up all her feelings. I've hurt all the people around me, she thought despairingly. Marilyn, Dimitri, and Evan. Even here, in a resort that was supposed to be a haven, she remained haunted every minute by all that had happened and all that was still to come.

Mommy, why do you look so sad?
Your daddy's not coming back.
I love you, Rose, I'll always protect you. . . .
Marry me, Rose. I'll protect you.
Why did you have to kill him?
You . . . you killed him, Rose . . .
I'll be watching you. . . .

Her past was a kaleidoscope of disturbing images, changing shape each minute. Rose realized that even the serenity and beauty of Miami could not heal her. *I can't escape,* she thought. *I'll never break free.*

She stared out at the sea.

"I'm sorry, Dimitri," she whispered. But she knew "I'm sorry" wasn't enough. Rose straightened herself in her seat: somehow she would put the pieces together and rebuild her shattered world.

The file on Timothy Houston that Charlie Dawkins had sent to Falcone had one piece of information that piqued Falcone's curiosity—Houston's frequent visits to the OTB in Jericho, Long Island. Everyone had a weakness, and Houston's was spending his Benjies on the ponies.

Falcone had followed him here, deciding not to use Ingrid for this job. Though it made him feel ridiculous, he had worn a fake beard and glasses as a disguise. Standing ten feet from Houston, he could see that the noise, the smoke, and the press of the crowd of bettors were unimportant to the ex-cop. His eyes were glued to one of the many monitors overhead. Leaning against the counter, Falcone kept a log of all Houston's wins and losses. If Houston got on line at a window, Falcone made sure he was just one person behind him: enough distance to enable him to hear the man's bets—most important, the dollar amounts. After the fifth race, one thing was clear: Houston was not only a heavy bettor, he was a heavy loser as well. There was no way Houston could possibly survive on a cop's pension with this kind of gambling. He had gambled away one week of a cop's salary in the first three races. Someone was funding Houston's habit.

As the bell sounded and the horses left the gate for the sixth race, Falcone came up to him. "An expensive sport—horse racing."

Houston whirled around. He recognized Falcone despite his disguise and dropped the program to the floor.

"Oh, don't bother. I've already picked up all your losing tickets." Falcone reached inside his pocket and pulled them out.

"The first race—two hundred down. Impressive. The third, one hundred and fifty lost on the exacta." Falcone raised his eyebrows. "Looks like you gambled away a pile. How do you do this on a pension? Or do county cops get a better deal than us poor Brookville guys?"

The other man, caught by surprise, was vacillating between fear and anger. "Why are you following me? I told you already. It was a long time ago, I really don't—"

"I thought perhaps you could remember something that may have been overlooked, or inadvertently left out of the report," Falcone said as he removed the fake beard and glasses and stuffed them in a garbage pail. "You know, stupid things like a motive? Or why Dimitri couldn't subdue Calvetti without a gun, given the high level of alcohol in Calvetti's system?"

Houston's shoulders sagged.

It can't be a good day for him, Falcone thought. Three hundred and fifty gone in one hour and a bug on his ass.

"Who are you working for?"

"I'm working for the police department. That's all you gotta know. Of course, if I can't get information from you willingly, I could always go to the newspapers. I have a good friend, a top criminal justice reporter at the *Post.* I'm sure he'd be interested in this story, considering the cast of characters."

Fear won out. It was written all over Houston's face. "Wait . . . you don't have to get the papers involved. I mean, I . . . Can we get out of here?"

Falcone kept a straight face, but secretly he gloated. *I knew he'd crack.*

Outside, winter showed its strength. The air was frosty and dry. The gusty winds whipped around the corner of the small brick building, and the parking lot offered no shelter.

"Come on, let's sit in my car—it's warm," Falcone said as he pushed his collar up around his neck.

Houston stood still. "How do I know your car's safe? Maybe you have a bug."

Falcone kept walking and yelled over his shoulder, "You don't have to worry. I don't operate that way."

He opened the door of his white 1978 Chevy Impala and climbed behind the wheel. Seconds later Houston slid into the passenger seat.

Falcone expected he'd have to pull the information out of him, bait him, at least. Instead Houston opened his mouth and the story came pouring out.

"I was working the late shift that night. A call came in saying there was a shooting at the Laurel estate. My partner, Vince, and I responded. When we arrived on the scene, we found Tom Calvetti on the floor, face up. The gunshot wound was just below the left shoulder, close to the heart."

Falcone turned on the ignition and switched the heat up high. "Who was in the barn?"

The radiator blew out cold air, and Houston began to shiver. "Three men and a young girl, Rose Calvetti. She's Rose Miller now."

"Where was Dimitri Constantinos?"

Houston wouldn't look at him. Instead he stared directly ahead.

"He was standing a few feet from the body."

The cold air slowly turned warm. Falcone noticed Houston was beginning to sweat, but it wasn't from the heat, that was for sure.

Houston's big face was getting redder and redder, and Falcone cracked a window. He was starting to breathe too fast, suddenly gasping. *Just my luck, he'll have a heart attack. Better get the story out of him fast.*

"Come on, Houston, give it up." Falcone put his face right in Houston's, who instantly pulled away.

"My partner cuffed the suspect, and I was gearing up to question the girl, although it was apparent she was in shock. The next thing I knew, a call came over the radio. The desk lieutenant, Wells, told me to leave the girl out of the report—to make believe I didn't see her."

"So you falsified the report."

The guy had the look of a trapped animal. Falcone felt sorry for him—almost.

"Look, I was young, I was getting married. You know how that goes. I didn't falsify. I just didn't report what I saw."

Falcone nodded. "What happened next?"

"We took the suspect back to the station, and the report was already written up. All we had to do was sign our names to it."

"But you knew it was a cover-up."

"Like I said, I was young."

"Didn't you question it at all?"

This time Falcone detected a hint of remorse in Houston's voice.

"I thought about it all night. I couldn't sleep. I realized the story Constantinos told me was ridiculous. Nothing matched up. Constantinos claimed he shot Calvetti in the back as Calvetti reached for the rifle hanging on the barn wall. Yet it was clear, judging from the entry of the bullet, that Calvetti was shot in the chest, at close range. The next day I was prepared to go to my superior and tell him about the discrepancy. I arrived at the station an hour earlier than usual and found James Miller and Lieutenant Wells waiting for me in the conference room."

Falcone hesitated for a moment. "Who do you think really killed Calvetti?"

Houston shrugged. "I could be wrong, but my money is on Rose Miller."

Falcone's insides cringed. There was yet another layer to this story—but he was sure Houston didn't know.

"Did you tell anyone? More specifically, James Miller?"

"No, I kept my mouth shut, and did what I was told. They read me a script, told me what part I had to play, and handed me fifty grand." Houston turned to Falcone. "Do you know how much fifty grand was back then? To someone my age?"

"Was that the only payoff?"

"Back then, yeah. But then they started again. Two grand a week. When I received the second envelope, I didn't understand why, nor did I question it."

"When did the payments begin again?"

Like a rock crashing through the windshield, Houston announced, "Two weeks ago."

The telephone sounded shrill in the cavernous room, causing Rose to jump. She reached for the receiver.

"Rose, it's John Falcone. I hope I didn't disturb you."

"No, of course not. I'm glad to hear a friendly voice."

The tenor of the conversation, though, was hardly friendly. Even before Falcone spoke again, Rose sensed something amiss; he seemed distant, his tone edgy.

"I need to talk to you, Rose, but not over the phone."

Rose paused and took a deep breath before she answered.

"Frankly, John, with all the gossip flying around New York, I can't come back right now. If it's not too much trouble, could I send you a ticket?"

"Let's make it as soon as possible."

38

The next morning Rose awoke to the sun glowing on the horizon over the Atlantic, right outside her bedroom window. Surfers were already in the water, their agile forms weaving and swaying in tune with the waves. She made a cup of coffee for herself in the small kitchen and sipped it outside on the terrace. By the time she was finished with her first cup, the sun was up and sparkling off the ocean. She could hear Alexis and Myra stirring.

Rose was scheduled for two book signings this morning and a quick appearance on a live local morning show. Dario had assured her it would be a nonconfrontational interview, as he had spoken at length with the show's producer. The first signing was a short drop-in at a Barnes & Noble on Collins Avenue. Then it was on to the local CBS affiliate and finally to Waldenbooks in Coconut Grove.

Even though a long line of fans formed from the front of the store well into the street, Rose didn't feel the claustrophobia she'd been suffering over the last few weeks. Before she made her entrance, she suggested Malcolm, Alexis, and Myra have the driver, Keith, take them on a tour.

"Make sure they have a good time. Drive by Madonna's home and Gloria Estefan's estate," Rose whispered to the driver as she slipped him fifty dollars.

She spotted two security guards at the entrance in blue uniforms, wielding shiny brown batons tucked neatly in their holsters, assigned to keep the crowd in check. This added to her feeling of safety. Yes, it had been a good idea to get out of New York.

The sidewalk was filled with local television crews who would send reports throughout the Miami area. Rose thought, *They've come to capture the real Rose Miller, subject to real pain and ridicule.* Though she realized not all of these faces and cameras were benign, Rose still believed that most of her fans supported her. As she approached the entrance, the crowd began shouting her name, cameras blinded her, and the intrusive questions from reporters began.

She took her place behind a podium near the front of the store. The store's manager introduced her to the crowded room. Folded chairs were filled with fans who stretched toward her eagerly. People squeezed into every available inch of the store.

Rose took a deep breath, then began. "I'd like to welcome all of you. Thank you for coming. I hope you enjoy this excerpt from my new novel, *Thorns of a Rose.*"

The crowd didn't stir. The TV cameras whirred. *They're waiting for me to break. I won't let them see me fall apart.* Willing herself to concentrate on the approving faces in the audience, she turned to a page and read a passage she had decided on the night before.

"HE LEANED CLOSER, ONLY AN INVISIBLE LINE OF AIR SEPARATING THEIR FACES. SHE STARED BACK AT HER STALKER, A LOOK OF HORROR IN HER EYES. SHE WAS THE PREY, HE THE SUCCESSFUL HUNTER. NOW THE GAME WAS OVER—HE HAD WON . . ."

Rose read on, losing herself in the scene, forgetting everything else. Minutes later, when she finished, the crowd applauded. This time she focused on the smiles. She took a seat behind a table where customers would bring their books to be autographed.

Two and a half hours later Rose retired the Mont Blanc pen to her purse. Although her hand ached from all the writing, she felt refreshed, triumphant. Her ardent fans, it was clear, were going to stand behind her. A number of book buyers had given words of encouragement.

"Don't you pay any attention to those ugly stories," one woman said. "We know what a wonderful lady you are—just like one of your heroines." Rose looked up gratefully into her soft, smiling eyes.

She thanked the store's manager, a young woman in a suit wearing big hoop earrings. "I'm so thrilled at the turnout," she enthused. "We sold five hundred copies! Can you come back after your next book?"

"Perhaps," Rose responded, pasting a smile on her face. Though she was eager to break away, the manager kept talking. Her eyes looked out over the sea of fans, and she saw that Alexis, Myra, and Malcolm had returned and were waiting for her at the front entrance. The two security guards she'd spotted earlier were standing behind them. Rose realized she hadn't felt uneasy for the entire time she'd been there.

"I really do have to go," she said to the young woman, "I'm afraid I—"

"Sure, Mrs. Miller. But before you do, I have something for you." The manager thrust a plain white envelope in her hand. On the back it read "GIVE TO ROSE MILLER—URGENT!"

She felt a sudden chill. Slowly she tore open the envelope. Her heart was racing. She pulled out a note card. It read:

I KNOW WHAT YOU DID!
YOU CAN'T KEEP ME AWAY MUCH LONGER!
I'M GETTING CLOSER—TO YOU AND ALEXIS!

The two men met in a deserted building in the outskirts of downtown Miami.

"Don't make it look like an accident. Let her know someone's sending her a message. Can you do that?" the older man asked.

That was an insult. Anger crackled inside him. This was not a question you asked of someone of his caliber. After all, he had been trained to kill. Back then he'd answered to the U.S. government. Now he reported to the highest bidder. He considered himself a gun-for-hire, and among this elite and secretive profession he fancied himself the best. His reputation preceded him. How dared this old man question his ability? He was tempted to reply with sarcasm, "I think I can manage that. After all, do you know about the poisoning I arranged to look like a heart attack that killed an Iranian diplomat? Or what about the nasty fall down a flight of winding stairs that the young heiress from Morocco suffered?"

Instead he said nothing. He never bit the hand that fed him. As the older man handed him an envelope with a down payment of fifteen grand, all he said was, "Yes, I can arrange that."

The older man was studying him with cold, assessing eyes, a long pause. When he finally spoke, he said, "I'll leave it up to you. My boss doesn't want her hurt badly, just enough to scare the living daylights out of her."

"Everything will be to your boss's liking. No one will ever connect him to the accident."

"Why did you have to kill him?"

Rose's words still buzzed in Dimitri's ears. For six long years he'd paid the price for her crime. He'd lost his innocence and any good name he might have made for himself. In the bargain, he also lost her. He was glad to let her finally know the truth—to let her suffer over it. There had been many times—and there still were—when he wondered how much she really remembered about that night, how much she pretended to forget. Now, though, there would be no more forgetting. He was here as a reminder of what had come before, and he wouldn't stop reminding her until she had paid as he had.

On Friday night in Atlantic City, he had taken a calculated risk. A woman is never more dangerous to a man than when she has to be saved. Although he had to admit, if only to himself, he did feel the slightest bit of remorse watching her squirm. But then he thought about how she'd betrayed him, and the feeling quickly subsided. He had endured too many personal betrayals: his mother, James and Rose.

Meanwhile there were other women to dally with until the time was right to make his move on Rose. Tonight he'd invited two women to join him as he checked up on the new croupier at one of the blackjack tables. After Janice he was careful not to use other employees to satiate his physical needs. The young brunette on his left, Julia, was a cocktail waitress at Bally's. The other woman, Serena, was an "aspiring actress." She was in Atlantic City looking for work, probably not acting work, Dimitri figured. Serena was the more attractive of the two, with dark brown hair and a body made for sin. Dimitri knew in all likelihood he'd choose her by the end of the evening, and he'd pay her, either with money or an expensive gift, just to keep it simple. *That way,* he figured, *I'll never have to hang around till morning.*

The cocktail waitress assigned to the crap table brought another round of drinks, margaritas for the ladies and a shot of chilled vodka for him. Dimitri kept his eyes glued to the table, counted every chip, and watched each toss of the dice.

As he slugged back the drink, from the corner of his eye he felt the sensation of being watched, and as he turned to his right, he saw Detective Falcone making his way to the table. Dimitri expected the detective would be back after the night he and Rose had slipped away. In fact, he wondered what had taken him so long to get here. Dimitri stared momentarily at Serena and thought, *So much for tonight.*

The view of the Boardwalk from Dimitri's private office was magnificent. His floor-to-ceiling windows overlooked the lights of the Ferris wheel and other amusement rides located on a strip that jutted into the Atlantic. The brightly lit outline of entertainment palaces reflected the white crests of rolling waves as they gently met the beach. Within his private sanctuary the floor was marble, the furniture mahogany and leather. On the walls were Dalís, Keith Harings, and a prized Picasso. There was an enormous wooden partners desk, a classic of inlaid leather surrounded by brass studs.

Dimitri, dressed in clothes as exquisite as his office decor, took command of his space, seating himself behind the desk, arranging the cuffs of his pinstripe light-blue-on-white shirt so they fit perfectly under the sleeves of a gray suit jacket that only a man like him could buy. *All style,* Falcone thought. *The guy reeks of class.*

Falcone spoke first. "Forgive me for disturbing you again, Mr. Constantinos. But I have to leave town in the morning, and if I can have a minute of your time, I'd appreciate it."

Dimitri checked his watch. "I'll give you a few. What can I do for you?" His face appeared relaxed, more accessible than Falcone had seen it before. It seemed Dimitri had been expecting him, and Falcone didn't like being anticipated. The element of surprise was a far better tactic.

Falcone plunged on. "I hate to dredge up your past again . . ."

He waited for a sign, but the man didn't flinch—didn't even blink. Constantinos must be some poker player, John thought.

"On the night of Tom Calvetti's murder . . . can you tell me why Rose's name was left out of the police report?"

Dimitri smirked and replied, "Who says she was there?"

"Officer Houston, who was at the scene. According to the police report, the story you gave the officers on duty that night doesn't match the ballistics report. It's apparent you didn't kill Calvetti. Why don't you tell me who did? Who were you protecting? Is it Rose?"

Dimitri rested his elbows on the desk and brought his fingers up to his lips. "I have nothing to deny, and I don't want to discuss the murder with you or anyone else. So unless you're arresting me, Detective Falcone . . ." And with this Dimitri's expressive eyes went blank.

Falcone ignored the man's signal that their meeting was over. It was at that moment that the last piece fell into place. If there was one thing he'd learned about Constantinos, it was that he could not be bought; loyalty and devotion would take precedence over money any day. He must be covering for Rose.

"The night of your grand opening for the Ivory, the body of a young woman, an employee of yours, was found about a hundred feet from the Boardwalk."

"What?" Dimitri asked, a surprised look on his face. "Who?"

The detective flipped through the pages of his pad. "Her name was Janice Slocum. I checked with personnel. She was one of the showgirls at Bogie's."

"Yes," Dimitri said. "I'm familiar with the name."

It was impossible to tell if Constantinos was toying with him. He was a pro, a master manipulator.

"How familiar?"

Dimitri waved his right arm as though to dismiss the importance of the acquaintance. "The same as all the other girls. I've heard her name. Said 'hello' as we passed in the casino. Are there any suspects?"

Falcone shook his head. "No, not at the present time, but there's a full investigation going on." The detective opted not to repeat the gossip he'd heard about Janice and Constantinos's brief, torrid affair. When questioned by the Atlantic City police, a close friend of the victim's, also a dancer, was quoted as saying Janice was in love with him.

"Tell me, Detective, why is a Long Island cop asking questions about a New Jersey showgirl?"

Without waiting for an answer, Dimitri stood and walked to the door. *Touché,* Falcone thought as Dimitri opened the door. Now the meeting was definitely over.

Falcone gave him a nod on his way out and said, "Thanks for your time."

At that moment he noticed the track of scratches on the other man's face. "That's a nasty cut. Where'd it come from?"

Dimitri put a hand to his face, obviously uncomfortable. "My wife and that damned cat of hers."

"Better take care of it," Falcone said.

In the kitchenette of his small house in Williston Park, John Falcone made himself a cup of coffee, then settled his tired body in the well-worn La-Z-Boy recliner. The living room, where chaos and clutter reigned, was his haven. *TV Guide*s and old newspapers littered the floor, the couch, and the coffee table. A twenty-seven-inch television filled one corner of the room. A folding snack table held the remains of the night's frozen dinner.

Ever since his wife's death, Falcone had found himself becoming increasingly reclusive. If he wasn't working, he was home, nestled in his favorite chair, leafing through a magazine, or channel surfing. Tonight he was tired, but he needed to study some information before meeting up with Rose. *Forget sleep,* he thought, *I need to stay focused.* He sipped the hot coffee and turned his attention to his work. There was nothing more he could do about the conversation with Houston—not yet. More pieces had to fall into place.

On his lap, resting in a neat pile, were three Rose Miller novels: *The Devil's Daughter,* which he knew pretty well from working with Rose on its research, *Last Rites,* and her most recent one, *Thorns of a Rose.* He would get to know Rose Miller even better. If she was correct about the killer acting out a scene she had written, he just might find some new evidence—possibly a crucial clue.

Falcone put on his reading glasses, switched on the table lamp, and leaned back comfortably. He skimmed *Thorns of a Rose* with fascination. The novel was a psychological thriller, chronicling a week in the life of a serial killer. William Adams, a handsome Wall Street broker, would stalk his victims, get to know them, romance them, lure them to a seedy old motel, then rape and kill them. After each murder he would sprinkle rose petals over their dead bodies.

He read on, then something struck him. He'd read this story before, he was sure of it. He recognized the scenario, remembered the roses. Then, like the flash of a powerful camera, the image came to him. *Newsday* had run a piece about a Long Island woman found dead in the Norwich Inn, not too far from Falcone's apartment. Her body had been badly decomposed, but she had been wearing a white lace teddy and there had been something about roses.

After positioning his battered laptop computer on the snack table, Falcone switched it on and pulled up the *Newsday* Web site. After a few minutes he dug up the story he was looking for.

There it was: WOMAN'S BODY FOUND IN L.I. MOTEL ROOM.

Falcone studied the *Newsday* article, then found other reports of the murder on the Net. No doubt about it, some nut job was copying Rose's murders. The body of the woman, a showgirl named Rachel Larson, was clothed in a white lace teddy, with a rhinestone tiara fastened to her hair. And—this was the part he remembered—rose petals were scattered everywhere. The killer carried out the murder ritual right down to the last detail. Rose's instincts had been on target, that much was clear. The fact that both murders were obviously committed by the same person meant that the task force he and Charlie were assigned to would be put on the case. He'd feel better knowing that Charlie was officially part of the investigative team. His friend had a great mind for weaving together seemingly unrelated clues. In this case, though, one victim was an unknown showgirl and the other one was Rose's best friend. Charlie was apt to find out what linked them in the murderer's mind. Maybe it related to the Laurel estate murder and maybe not. But with this information, Rose Miller's stalker case had grown into a search for a serial killer. The big question was, did the murderer want to kill Rose next? Or was he simply satisfied for the moment, reveling in her discomfort.

39

Normally Rose would have been absorbed in the bustling crowd of South Beach, a people watcher's haven. Beautiful, scantily clad women Rollerbladed past bodybuilders, musclemen, Hare Krishnas, and street musicians, mostly bad ones, playing for change. Not to mention the vast variety of cross-dressers. Rose recognized one man, a well-known venture capitalist from Manhattan who favored long flowing skirts, see-through cotton shirts, and red espadrilles with laces that tied up his shaved legs. The limo passed him as he bargained with a street vendor. Ordinarily Rose would have been admiring the funky old hotels that were South Beach's hallmark, but all the sights were lost on her as she thought about the note from yesterday's signing.

"You can't keep me away much longer. I'm getting closer—to you and Alexis."

The thought made her insides turn to Jell-O.

Keith, the driver, said, "The airport is only ten miles away." She had thought about having him go alone to pick up John but decided to face him as soon as possible. She had left Malcolm home with Myra and Alexis. What would she say when she came face-to-face with John? The revelation of secrets had multiplied over the last few weeks, and there was no way she could contain them. Nor did she want to anymore. She'd spent her adult life living underground. Tired of the subterfuge, Rose welcomed the opportunity to come clean.

Last night, as Alexis slept peacefully, she paced the floors of the suite. After hours of grueling decision making, Rose decided she would tell John everything. She had no idea what the consequences would be. All that mattered now was that she come into the light. She would tell the truth, even if it meant going to prison. She simply could not live with the guilt any longer.

Rose spotted Falcone standing in front of the Delta terminal. The limo rolled to a stop, Keith put his bag in the trunk, and the detective climbed in next to Rose. He looked like hell. Rose assumed that he hadn't slept or eaten much as he'd spent time piecing together the confusing Miller puzzle. He was a cop's cop, she knew. Ironically, it seemed that now, his dedication and persistence might not be exactly in her best interests.

She started to speak: "John, I—"

He put up his hand and silenced her. "Not here," he said, staring at the back of the driver's head. "Somewhere safe."

All through dinner he had touched her, awakening her. With every caress, Jewel yearned to feel his body on hers. He pleased her so, pushed her to the edge of paradise. She went into this relationship with only one thing on her mind—to bring Dimitri down and relish his fall from grace. But her clandestine affair had an added asset: great sex.

"Shall we go upstairs?" he asked, his voice barely above a whisper. He leaned across the table, put his hand behind her head, and pulled her to him, so close that she could feel his hot breath on her face as he panted like the tiger he was.

"We really should finish dinner," she said, but the truth was, she wanted only to taste him. She led him out of the sitting area, up the stairs, and into the elaborate bedroom of the suite. A king-size brass bed canopied with wispy white fabric, delicate as angel's wings, beckoned invitingly. The huge casement windows, swagged in gold Salamander velvet, were open a crack, and the night breeze fanned the fire in the large brick fireplace.

The room was Jewel's fantasy come to life with Dimitri's money. The thought that she betrayed him here made her smile. *Two can play this game, Dimitri.* Sleeping with her latest lover heightened her pleasure. And she felt a rush of power. The game was growing exciting. *You'll lose, Dimitri, and all of this will be mine. . . .*

The phone in the living room of the suite shrilled just as Rose opened the door.

"Rose, am I disturbing you?"

"No, Dario, it's good to hear your voice. I'm just sitting here with a friend."

Her voice sounded strange, hesitant. *A friend?* he thought. It had to be Dimitri. He felt anger rise up in him.

"The tour going well?"

"Great," she said, a bit too quickly.

Dario had expected to find her despondent. After all, it was apparent her marriage was over. According to everything he knew as a publicist, her career was marred, her fans jarred by the news of their fallen heroine. The photo of Rose and Dimitri getting out of the helicopter decorated the cover of every tabloid in supermarkets from New York City to Tokyo. He had heard from one of his sources that Stone Phillips was going to do a piece on *Dateline,* examining Rose's past—the real one that the world's media had learned about from his fax.

He wanted so badly for her to need him and for her to crawl to him. Yet here she was, holding herself apart from him as always. Why hadn't she learned over the years how good they could be together, how much further her career would go if only she would surrender to the obvious? They belonged together. But Rose was forcing his hand.

"How was the signing?" he asked in a normal tone.

A pause on her end, then, "Can we talk later? I'm in the middle of something."

"Sure, Rose." He replaced the receiver and thought, Bitch.

Dimitri chose the Palm for his dinner with Evan. The no-nonsense, upscale restaurant on Second Avenue in Manhattan, with its caricatures of patrons drawn on the wall, was a favorite of Dimitri's. The acoustics of the restaurant provided a din that ensured them of privacy.

After taking a sip from his drink, Dimitri went straight to the point. "So, who do you think the informer is?"

Evan studied his half-brother. *Not only has he entered my life again, stolen my wife, and put a dent in my political career—all he's concerned about is his case. But that's fine. I'll play the game for now.*

"Well?" Dimitri asked again. "Who do you think it is?"

Evan looked into his brother's eyes. They reminded him of the icebergs that littered the waters around Prince Edward Island: unyielding and glowing with a light from within. Dimitri's eyes held him for a moment as he considered the question. The truth was, he suspected Joseph Braun was the informer. He had the most to offer the government. And knowing the way Kevin Allen operated, Evan was sure it was an equal exchange. He couldn't believe Dimitri didn't also suspect his father-in-law, although other possibilities easily existed.

"You must have your suspicions," Dimitri prompted.

Evan shook his head. "It's hard to say. Could be anyone. You've got plenty of people around you who might wish you ill."

"Joseph is the most logical suspect. He has everything to gain if I go back to prison and a lot to lose if I don't."

As Evan watched, Dimitri's eyes changed to blue black and then filled with anger. "Two of his goons approached me at the opening the other night. Joseph had promised them he'd get them in on the proceeds."

"How could he do that? He has no say in the matter."

He's not afraid to tell Braun no. For this, Evan gave him credit. But then, he guessed Dimitri wasn't afraid to say no to anyone.

"You got that right." Dimitri leaned across the table and in an angry tone said, "I built this empire myself."

Evan could sense the flint that ignited Dimitri's anger, a feeling he'd grown used to in his years of defending rich, indignant clients. Dimitri's fury pushed his own resentments aside for the moment. More than anything, Evan feared a public outburst. There had been enough scandal lately.

"So, you're sure it's Braun?"

"Without a doubt," Dimitri said, smiling crookedly. Evan flashed back to the meeting with Braun at the health club. Dimitri knew the score. And that being the case, Evan would never be able to live with himself if he wasn't totally straight with his client. It wasn't ethical, and Evan was "cursed" with integrity, unlike his father. He was bound by oath, and blood, to give Dimitri's case his all. Afterward he could deal with his personal rage over Rose's apparent betrayal.

"I've been mulling over how best to tell you this. I was *invited* to a meeting by Joseph."

"Let me guess—at his masseuse's?"

"No, you're close—at the racquet club. But here's the thing. He was playing with Kevin Allen."

Evan waited for a reaction but saw a change only in Dimitri's posture. Nothing else gave away his half-brother's feelings.

"They offered you money to throw the trial."

It was a statement, not a question.

"Actually, they didn't even offer me money. Your father-in-law just issued a command. Obviously I didn't agree."

"What are you going to do about it?"

"I'm not sure. But, believe me, I'll come up with a plan."

The waiter returned with their meal. He set the plates on the table, and when he disappeared, Dimitri said, "Listen, with all the bullshit going on between us, I appreciate your loyalty."

Loyalty, my ass, Evan thought.

"We both know this win will help you counteract the negative publicity you've been receiving—no thanks to me." Dimitri ignored his entrée, and leaned his elbows on the table. "I know you don't believe me, but Rose has not been unfaithful to you."

"You're right, I don't believe you."

Dimitri raised his eyebrows. "So, Counselor? Can I still count on you? Are we going to win this case?"

Evan knew how much he needed this win if he wanted to be governor, though lately, now that his life was in shambles, that ambition seemed less important.

Evan said, "I'll do my best."

Kevin Allen was the last person at the office sitting in the law library, located on the building's first floor. The musty smell of old, worn books reminded him of why he always venerated the law. He felt a jolt of guilt: he was betraying his profession. But then the guilt subsided. He had crossed some personal line with this case, compromised himself, and there was no turning back.

He had locked himself in to avoid the cleaning crew and telephone while he contemplated his problem. The evidence he held in his lap could destroy Dimitri Constantinos and his entire defense. But it had been obtained illegally, and now he had to weigh his options. There were the ethics of the situation to consider; but that had never been a major obstacle in Kevin's book. Still, using illegally obtained evidence was dangerous. It could backfire. Then, not only would his case against Constantinos go out the window, but he could kiss his future good-bye.

Kevin thought about Constantinos and his apparent nemesis, James Miller, for a long time. He thought about Constantinos's cocky attitude, his cold, assessing stare when their eyes met in court. If personal hatred were enough to want to bring a man down, then Kevin would have no problem making this decision. But, of course, those considerations were not enough. James Miller's agenda had to be factored in as well.

Kevin knew precisely why James Miller needed Constantinos to "disappear." There were other former staff members of the Nassau County DA's Office who knew the truth, but they were all gone—retired, dead, whatever. But the once gawky prosecutor named Kevin Allen was still on the scene and very much aware of the cover-up James Miller had manipulated all those years ago. The scheme Miller paid for to keep his son and daughter-in-law from scandal and pin Tom Calvetti's murder on Dimitri Constantinos.

The papers in his lap seemed to draw Kevin toward a conclusion. If he gracefully slipped this illegal evidence into the trial, he would be free of worry for quite a while. Who would believe Dimitri Constantinos, a convicted racketeer? And how could Evan Miller continue the fight when his own father was involved?

The hell with ethics. Constantinos was going to fall and James Miller was going down with him. Kevin had all the ammunition to do it.

Myra and Alexis had retired hours before to Alexis's suite. The remains of room service littered the table, along with an empty bottle of white wine.

"I need to tell you the whole sordid truth, John. Listen to me. Dimitri did not kill Tom."

Falcone studied Rose. Though her world was coming down around her, she still looked great, even more beautiful than he remembered. The golden cascade of hair fell loosely past her shoulders. Her creamy skin glowed with a hint of bronze from the Florida sun. The public Rose Miller was done to perfection, projecting the woman every one of her readers would like to be and every man in those women's lives would covet. Even her surroundings complemented her: the colorful room, furnished with two oversize sofas and silk pillows, antique tables, lamps with silk shades, and three Impressionist prints on the walls. The suite was a far cry from the dump he called home. Still, he knew his life was easier than hers, and if being at the top included all this misery—he would pass on it. He enjoyed his simple life. He felt sorry for Rose as she paced the room.

She had already rehashed the events in the barn that night and her liaison with Dimitri Constantinos. When she told him Constantinos was James's illegitimate son, the motive for pinning a murder on Constantinos made sense. At that moment, Falcone decided he didn't want to hear the rest. To him she was like a child who had been thrust into a world she couldn't handle. He felt protective toward her, like the father she'd lost at an early age.

"Rose, don't," he interrupted. "Don't say anything that might incriminate you."

She stared back at him, confusion in her eyes.

"I'd be forced to go to the DA's office with whatever you tell me. If in fact there is proof that Dimitri Constantinos didn't commit the murder . . ." He paused for a moment, then continued. "I'd be forced to give new evidence to the D.A.'s office and go through all the proper channels."

He stood and walked across the room to the picture window overlooking the ocean. The waves crashed against the surf, and the rumbling sound soothed him. They were caught up in a dilemma. He knew most of what she had told him before he arrived in Miami, and though he'd tried so long and hard to get at the truth, now he didn't want to hear it. He knew that the outcome for her would be grim.

"I went to see Dimitri." His announcement caused Rose to gasp. "Don't worry." Falcone turned to face her. "He didn't admit a thing."

Rose's eyes expressed a hundred feelings.

"Are you surprised?"

She shook her head.

"He wants to protect you."

When Rose had told him what she and Dimitri shared went way beyond passion, Falcone wanted to believe that the love between those two young people, defenseless against James Miller's malevolence, still lingered in the adults they had become. Constantinos's instinct to protect Rose, even now, was proof that he would not hurt her.

Still, there were things about his demeanor and behavior that nagged at Falcone. Constantinos's cold expression and calculating eyes hadn't changed, even when he'd been informed of Janice Slocum's murder. He was a hard man. Men who came out of prison generally lost whatever humanity they had going in. Most troubling to Falcone was that although Constantinos was a millionaire many times over, who could have any woman he wanted, he picked Janice Slocum, a showgirl, for a brief affair. The woman found in the motel had also been a showgirl.

"If Dimitri doesn't make a claim that he falsely confessed to the murder, if he doesn't point a finger at . . ." He paused to rephrase his words, to stay within bounds without putting his career on the line. "If there's no confession from the real murderer, the DA's office has nothing to go on. Things remain the same. A man was arrested for murder, he confessed, he went to prison. Justice was done. It's as simple as that, so far as the DA is concerned. Besides, no one likes to admit he's made a mistake."

Falcone walked over to the minibar, opened up a small bottle of Scotch, and poured himself a shot. "Leave it alone, Rose. From one friend to another, you have a child to raise." His eyes darted down the hall to the bedroom where Alexis was sleeping. "Don't cheat that kid. She needs her mother. . . ."

He checked his watch, swigged another shot, and said, "It's late, I gotta get going. There's a lot more we have to talk about."

Rose nodded and, as though waiting for the other shoe to drop, asked, "Is there something else you're not telling me?"

Falcone came to stand behind her at the sofa. He put a hand on her shoulder to steady her. "I did some research. It seems this psycho has killed before. I have a list of four unsolved murders, all carried out exactly as you wrote them in your novels. In fact, Chief Smalts has assigned the task force to Marilyn's case and grouped it with the other unsolved ones."

For a minute or two silence prevailed. It was broken only by the sound of Rose's slight groan. "I've hurt so many people I love, and I know I put Marilyn in death's path. Now you're telling me I've been the catalyst for the murder of strangers?"

"I didn't say catalyst. Whoever this killer is, he would have murdered them anyway. It was only a question of how."

Rose looked up into Falcone's kind brown eyes and added, "Right, but I'm telling him exactly how to do it. How can I keep writing? Each time I'll only think that my fictional murder scenes could become actual time bombs." She leaned her head back against the couch. "I can't do this anymore."

"Stop it, Rose. Right now! Quit feeling sorry for yourself and carry on."

He was right, of course. The best thing she could do now was to help the investigation by going through material with John.

"Okay, then, where do we start? And how?"

"We'll go over all of it in the morning. Try to get some sleep. We have a busy day ahead of us. I'm staying at the Holiday Inn about ten minutes from here. If you need me for anything, call."

There was a violent storm raging inside him that he couldn't control, a coldness so deep that he had no warmth to dissolve it. It had begun twelve years ago and had festered and burgeoned until now he found himself ready to erupt. The evil and the good in him had fought so furiously for dominance. Now the struggle was nearly over, and it seemed evil would win.

He'd been careless with Janice. It was important to keep his cool. Now he was nervous, certain there would be repercussions. John Falcone wasn't going to rest until he'd put all the pieces together. The nosy detective was getting warmer in his investigation every day. He had moxie, and for this Dimitri gave him credit. Not too many people would challenge Dimitri.

Dimitri sifted through the papers on his desk high above the city lights. He made two piles, one marked "Urgent," the other simply "Important." It was well after midnight, and he still needed to go over the day's receipts. *First things first,* he thought. Outside his office in the reception area, he could hear a tiny bell, then the rattle of a fax being transmitted. At last the machine's stutter ceased, and one of the receptionists working the night shift was at his door.

"This just came for you, sir. Maybe you should take a look at it."

Dimitri didn't glance up, only nodded and said, "Leave it. I'll take a look as soon as I get free."

"Sir," the woman persisted, "I think you should see this right away."

Now Dimitri looked up. She had his full attention.

"It's a copy of tonight's receipts. There's a note attached."

He took the papers from her and studied them. There was the usual list of credits, debits, and payments to winners of all games and slots. It took little time to realize that the numbers were doctored—someone had changed all the facts and figures. Dimitri knew that as far as the law was concerned it would come down to his numbers versus these, and the odds were that he probably would not come out the winner. Federal, state . . . all those "suits" were eager to put him away. And Joseph Braun apparently had the prosecution on his side, if not in his pocket. Evan's information about Braun demanding he throw the trial made his collusion with Kevin Allen all the more obvious. When Dimitri turned to the last page of numbers, he found a handwritten note: *"These figures will be submitted as evidence in court tomorrow."*

Dimitri slumped back in the chair and let out a disgusted sigh. Braun was not in a position to get his hands on any of Dimitri's figures. Someone in his inner circle was responsible for setting him up, and if he couldn't figure out who, the prosecution would be victorious. He turned back to the note and read on.

"Tomorrow we will also release to the press the transcript of a confession from a former member of the Laurel estate staff who observed the murder of Tom Calvetti and was ordered by James Miller to dispose of the weapon. He is now dying and wants the sin off his conscience."

The irony of the situation did not escape Dimitri. He put his head in his hands and thought about how he wanted to demolish the Millers. Here was the opportunity. The problem was that he wanted Evan as his attorney. Dimitri believed that no matter what, Evan would fight for him, which was part of his plan. If these revelations about Calvetti's murder were made known, Evan could be disbarred. And while he wanted Rose to get her due, he wanted it on his terms.

The man in the mask walked noiselessly through the palm trees, studiously avoiding the swath of lights created by the security lamps. Earlier he had plotted this path through one of the resort's splendid gardens to the swimming pool, where he knew Rose would be taking her nightly swim, alone.

He stood close enough to see her head bobbing up and down, then he moved to the deep end and crouched behind a lounge chair, out of sight. He watched as her body glided from one side of the pool to the other with grace and precision. Rose Miller possessed real beauty, not the kind that bleached hair and makeup bought. She was fresh yet elegant and sophisticated, the kind of woman who would be forever far from his grasp.

Too bad, my beauty. He slid the gym bag off his shoulder, unzipped it, and pulled out his latex gloves. By now Rose had reached the other side of the pool, flipped over, and begun to backstroke toward him. This time, instead of swimming gracefully underwater, she thrashed around a little, her arms pumping and crashing through the water, her head bobbing from side to side. Though she didn't know it, this was her final lap and he was ready for her.

He crawled from the chair to the edge of the pool. As she tagged the tile wall with her hand, he pulled himself stealthily past the edge, reached into the water, and pressed firmly down on her head with both hands. Her arms flailed, trying to pull down her attacker. Bubbles floated to the surface as she continued to fight for air.

He heard her as she swallowed a mouthful of chlorinated water. While she choked furiously, he pushed her beneath the surface again. Rose held her breath, her arms swinging wildly above her head, trying to free herself from his grasp. Then her movements slowed as she tired. He could almost feel her lungs bursting.

Rose felt herself fading into unconsciousness. Just when Rose felt herself slipping away, at the moment when she thought, *I'm going to die,* the pushing stopped. She thrust to the surface, gasping, and saw the shadowy figure disappear into the night.

As he lay in bed, Billy thought about how he hadn't meant to torture Janice, but she had misbehaved, forcing him to be bad, and he cursed her. He hated to be so brutal. Afterward he was so exhausted. Strangulation was a far less strenuous and much more personal way to make them die. He lived for the hands-on feel of stealing their last breath, being face-to-face with their terror just before the end, when their eyes bulged.

Gory murder scenes also attracted more attention, which was another reason he avoided them. He was convinced that this was partly why he'd managed to get this far without being caught. For a moment he could see his mother's disapproving look and feel her hand crashing across his face. Then her shrill voice: "You're a bad boy, a monster. Who would ever want you?"

But Billy knew she was wrong. Look how all these beautiful women wanted to play with him. He chuckled loudly, then whispered, "Billy is a bad boy . . . Bad boy, bad boy, bad boy . . ."

40

The glare of the overhead fluorescent light was the first thing Rose noticed. She was aware of voices.

"I think she's coming around, Doctor."

Rose was disoriented but able to put the pieces together: the ambulance's blaring siren, the ride to the hospital, the emergency room doctor trying to comfort her as they wheeled her through the corridors, rubber wheels bumping over cracked tiles. Suddenly there was a blue curtain enclosing her and the momentary fear that she was underwater again. Then a nurse appeared at her side and gave her a shot. Minutes later she had drifted off again.

Now she could see a clock hung between two small windows on the opposite wall. Ten o'clock. Through the windows, the bright yellow sun was up. Hours had lapsed, a new day had begun. She'd lost all track of time, safe in the comfort of drug-induced slumber. She was in an iron bed protected by rails on both sides, alone in the room. When she put up her hand to rub the sleep from her eyes, she felt a needle in her vein leading to an IV. Slowly the realization came. Someone had tried to kill her.

"Good morning," said an African American woman with close-cropped salt-and-pepper hair. "How are you feeling? Better, I hope!"

"Am I all right?"

The nurse smiled, then replied, "You're fine now. But you were in pretty bad shape last night. You'd swallowed a lot of water, and your pressure was low. It looked like you had nearly drowned."

Rose hoisted herself onto her elbows. The effort sent hammers of pain smashing into her temples.

"You're a lucky woman."

It was a man's voice. Dressed in a white coat, a stethoscope hanging around his neck, he was standing in the doorway, reading a chair she assumed was hers. "The manager of the Fontainebleau reported that a maintenance man pulled you out from the pool."

The doctor, whose pin read "Dr. Richard Sanderson," put his hand on her wrist, either checking her pulse or to calm her, she couldn't be sure. "Alexis is just fine. Detective Falcone has been here a number of times and told me to make sure to tell you the moment you were conscious."

"Can I go home?"

The doctor had a kind face topped by a shock of gray hair. The familiar shy smile he wore told her he was aware that she was famous, although infamous was probably closer to the truth these days.

"I don't see why not."

"Could we hurry and take out this IV?" she asked. Rose needed to get back to the resort. Whoever had tried to kill her hadn't succeeded—but neither had he been caught. She had to get Alexis out of harm's way.

Kevin Allen licked his lips, then let his eyes roam around the courtroom. He was more than a prosecutor today, he was a sniper with his target in his sight. His eyes rested on Dimitri, whose arrogant demeanor didn't get to him this morning—not when he was so close to the kill.

When he'd started this trial, he hadn't banked on it being easy. Even with his carefully calculated plan there was no way he could have predicted the people who would come into his corner and the evidence that would fall into his lap. He held the trump card in his briefcase, the one big break that guaranteed him a win. The DA tightened the knot on his red-and-blue-striped tie and straightened his cuffs. Next to him at the prosecution table sat his team of associates, each vying to please him. Inside Kevin smiled. A man could get used to having these sycophants fawning all over him.

Now he asked permission to approach the bench. The judge, a silver-haired woman in her fifties, looked down from her seat.

"Counselor, is there a problem?"

"Your Honor, the prosecution requests a sidebar."

The judge signaled for Evan to join them. Moments later, with Evan present, Kevin said, "Your Honor, I request a conference in your chambers."

Judge Knauer raised her eyebrows. "Is it that important?"

Kevin nodded. "Absolutely."

Evan gazed at the DA for a moment but kept silent.

"In my chambers," the judge said, then rapped her gavel on the bench.

Everyone in the courtroom rose as the judge walked through the side door. The jurors filed out of the room.

Inside the judge's chambers Kevin took a seat. Clutching his briefcase, he said, "Your Honor, I need a continuance. I request a postponement, due to newly acquired, critical evidence. I must interview a prospective witness, then take time to check the witness's credibility. I would really need two weeks, if the Court would allow."

The judge removed her robe, then pushed a strand of curly hair out of her eyes. "You will inform the Court of the full nature of this evidence on an ex parte basis?"

Kevin nodded. "Yes, Your Honor."

Ex parte basis! Evan thought. That meant only the prosecutor and the judge would know who the witness was and what was coming out during questioning. Evan was incredulous. "Your Honor, we are entitled to know who this 'surprise guest' is so we can prepare for our own questioning of the witness."

Kevin was prepared for Evan's request: "Your Honor, I must insist that the witness's identity be protected and all documentation about this matter be kept under seal for the time being." He paused for effect. "When one is dealing with a man like Dimitri Constantinos, it pays to be very cautious. The witness is very brave to come forward and deserves the Court's protection."

Evan, who had remained standing, was speechless. So the letter telling him there was an informant hadn't been a hoax. Someone was turning government's evidence, and there was nothing he could do to change the outcome. Then something clicked in his memory bank. Duke, the ex-FBI agent, had left a message earlier, but he hadn't gotten back to him. Now all Evan could think about was getting to a phone.

The judge responded to Kevin's request. "Granted. Trial will resume Monday February ninth. Let it be known the request will be inscribed on record, the witness's identity will be sealed from all inspection." She turned to Evan. "Have you anything to say, Counselor?"

"No, Your Honor."

She nodded and turned her attention to the pile of papers on her desk. "This conference is over."

As Evan and Kevin made their way out of the courtroom, they were engulfed by reporters. "Will either of you give us a statement?"

Evan studied Kevin, then turned to the cameras and murmured a polite, "No comment."

Ordinarily Kevin Allen would have been intolerant of reporters' intrusions, but he was beginning to appreciate how much he needed the press on his side. Speaking with a new silver-tongued style he was cultivating, Kevin, flanked by Chris Knowles and one other associate, led the reporters with their microphones and cameras outside the courtroom.

"There has been a new development in the Constantinos case. A very important one for the prosecution. I can't say any more at this time."

Dimitri pushed through the crowd and walked briskly down the corridor toward the exit. Evan clutched his briefcase, and they hurried to the waiting limousine.

As soon as they were in the car, Evan dialed Duke's number. "Have you got anything on that letter?"

"Yes. The report came back today. The prints match Jewel Braun—lucky she'd been hauled in five times for drunk driving out in Vegas. I'll send on the report."

Evan didn't want to say too much. "Thanks, Duke," he replied, and flipped the phone closed.

"What the fuck is going on?" Dimitri demanded.

"It's Jewel. She's the surprise witness." Evan's instinct was to look away and spare his half-brother the embarrassment, but he kept his eyes on Dimitri, curious to see how the news would affect him.

"And also the informer, obviously. Why am I not surprised?" Dimitri's expression changed only slightly. "So now what?"

41

John Falcone was looking right through her, making Rose feel like another piece of the resort's furniture, stiff and unfeeling. Brow furrowed, he was the picture of frustration. She didn't blame him. She'd acted like an errant child, going alone to the swimming pool.

It was warm in the suite, with only the cool ocean breeze blowing through the open windows. Yet she felt chilled, still in shock. Her head began to throb again.

"Why the hell did you go out alone?"

"I have trouble sleeping. The swimming helps." *Boy, that was lame,* she thought as she said it. She should have taken Malcolm with her.

"I was foolish. I took an unnecessary risk. What else can I say? It's hard to be tethered to security twenty-four hours a day."

But Falcone wasn't listening. Finally he reached inside the pocket of his worn suit jacket and pulled out some crumpled papers. "If you're going to be reckless, I suggest you look at these."

Last night he had told her about the girl in the motel room and the other women killed just as her victims had been murdered in her books. She hadn't wanted to know about the others.

He placed the article from *Newsday* on the table, and Rose quickly recognized the scene from *Thorns of a Rose*—complete with lace teddy and rose petals.

"These are the other police reports, take a look," Falcone insisted, showing her printouts from the central computer.

She sifted through each article and police report. Every horrific detail was familiar. She'd unknowingly written each girl's death scene. There was Peach from *The Devil's Daughter,* garroted in her lonely studio apartment on Long Island. Peach was dressed in satin and held one perfect pink rose. Danielle, the fabulously rich model's agent from *Last Rites,* thrown off the balcony of her penthouse apartment. And Leigh, from *Thorns of a Rose,* the girl found in the tiara and lace teddy. And now there was Amanda, the model for Marilyn's death, murdered in her apartment, surrounded by candles, stabbed, a gruesome scene. Who would mock her in such a diabolical manner?

Every day, it seemed, she changed her mind about whether or not Dimitri was the killer stalking her. The slightest sign could sway her opinion. His impenetrable eyes over the table at Match made him frightening; ambushing her at the awards ceremony revealed to her his dark side. Then there was his kiss, which was definitely evidence of a gentler Dimitri, one she'd bet her life on was innocent. She didn't know what to believe. Perhaps it was that her head saw something her heart ignored—or was it the other way around?

"Like I said to you before, John, I don't think Dimitri's the murderer."

Falcone raised his eyebrows. "Why?"

Rose looked absently out the open window, drinking in the sight and absorbing the sound of the waves crashing against the pier. "Believe it or not, Dimitri couldn't be that cold-hearted." She remembered the shadowy figure by the pool. "But whoever it is, I have to get out of here. He knows where we are."

Falcone sat beside her, nodding. "I agree. You have to get away from here, and until this guy is caught, you have to stay out of sight. So far, he's been cool, cunning, and calculating, always one step ahead of us. But maybe if he can't find you, he'll come out of hiding, blow his cover, and we'll get him."

"What are we talking about here? How long? Where?" The very thought of being away from everything and everyone she held dear made her head spin even faster.

"I'll find a place that's both remote and safe. As for how long, I don't know. However long it takes to draw him out.

"And there's one more thing, Rose," Falcone said.

She stared back at him, almost afraid to ask. "What now?"

"Alexis cannot go with you."

Outside, Alexis body-surfed as Myra and Malcolm looked on, close enough that Rose could see them as well. She was only kidding herself if she thought this psycho wouldn't hurt her daughter. The card delivered at the book signing had made his intentions clear. She knew John was right. Alexis would be safest at home; Evan would see to that.

"Tomorrow." She straightened her shoulders and looked John in the eye. "We'll leave first thing tomorrow. There's no reason to wait."

Malcolm found a pay phone in the main lobby, behind the concierge desk. The bodyguard glanced over his shoulder. There was no one in the lobby except the reservation clerk, and he wasn't interested in a guest's conversation. He searched around in his pockets for change, deposited a quarter, and punched in a number. On the third ring a man's voice said, "Hello."

Malcolm gripped the receiver, then said, "It's done. It was a success."

"Did you scare her?"

"Oh, she's scared all right. She'll be putty in your hands."

"Good. You'll have the balance in a day or two."

"Don't you want to hear the details?"

"No." Then click.

42

The next day, Rose, Myra, and Alexis, accompanied by Malcolm, took a late morning flight back to New York. John Falcone had taken an earlier flight; he needed to get back to arrange for Rose's "disappearance."

Rose tried not to worry about having to tear herself away from Alexis by tomorrow, but judging from her daughter's reaction, she wasn't doing too good a job of it.

"Are you tired, Mommy?" Alexis asked during the flight. John had managed to keep from Alexis what had happened at the pool, telling her only that Rose had "overdone her exercise" and succumbed to exhaustion.

"I'm fine, baby."

"You don't look fine." Alexis frowned beneath her Buddy Holly look-alike sunglasses.

"You mean I look ugly?" Rose faked a gasp, covering her mouth with one hand. Then she pushed Alexis's sunglasses up to rest on top of her black, wavy hair. "Look again. What do you see?" she smiled.

"You look sad." Alexis traced the bags under Rose's eyes.

Rose gently stopped her daughter's hand. "Have I ever lied to you?"

Alexis shook her head. The sunglasses fell back in place.

"Trust me, then, darling. You have no need to worry about me." Now Rose had told her the first lie between them.

Alexis seemed satisfied with this. Rose held her daughter close, and soon Alexis was asleep. To distract herself, Rose engaged Myra in small talk as her knitting needles click-clicked through the yarn she'd been fussing over. Malcolm sifted through some old militia magazines. Rose found it odd, but thought, *Whatever floats your boat.*

At JFK they gathered up the luggage and Larry loaded it into the Mercedes, then headed for the Belt Parkway. Rose would take Alexis and Myra back to the mansion, explain to Evan why she had to go away, and then spend the night at her Fifth Avenue apartment. Malcolm would stand guard outside the apartment while she waited for John to call her when all the arrangements were complete.

The Mercedes pulled past the wrought-iron gates and made its way down the long winding driveway up to the front entrance of the mansion. An acute wave of depression swept over her. Paradiso suddenly seemed like her personal hell.

Once inside, Rose checked quickly through the pile of messages and mail waiting for her on a marble-topped table in the entryway.

She could smell James's cigar smoke as she passed the library. But just as she headed for the stairs, he spoke.

"Rose," he said without glancing up at her. "I am very sorry for the problems you're having, but the fact is, you've brought them on yourself. And, in the process, endangered Evan's future. You've become a liability, as I always knew you would."

"I'm not interested in what you think, James."

Now he looked up at her. "Leave him. For God's sake, think about his future. He stands to lose everything he's worked so hard for."

Regardless of how she felt about James, Rose had to admit, he was right. She'd caused Evan enough pain. From the very beginning of their marriage Evan had sheltered her and afforded her entrance into a world that her own dear mother would have wanted for her. And how had she repaid him? By humiliating him publicly. James and Rose finally agreed on something—it was time to put an end to what she was doing to Evan.

"Where's Evan?" she asked simply.

James ignored her. "I'm willing to pay you a handsome sum if you'll agree to divorce him."

Rose couldn't help but laugh. She could hardly believe what she was hearing. The monster—even age hadn't mellowed him.

Once, long ago, Rose might have been stung by his words and the offer of money, which told her exactly what he thought of her. She would have crumbled. But that was before she had stared the devil in the face. She was a different Rose Miller now, harder and stronger, not about to be intimidated by this nasty old man.

"Keep your money, James. You can choke on it."

She ran from the room, up the stairs, and into the master suite. Evan was sitting in one of the cream-colored armchairs near the window. Fading daylight filtered through the open drapes, revealing the sadness in her husband's face. He was holding their wedding picture. She could read his mind. Where had it all gone wrong? Their union, their vows: *to love and to cherish from this day forward . . .*

She went to Evan's side and knelt beside him. He took her hand and squeezed it, but he did not look at her.

A weight, heavy as an andiron, settled in her heart.

"Tell me what you're thinking," she said, her voice shaky.

"I'm thinking how happy I was the day we got married. How much I loved you." His voice was low, barely above a whisper.

Tears began streaming down her cheeks as she stroked his face. Her world would never be the same, nor would his. For a moment they both looked at the framed photo in his hand, faded slightly from the passing of twelve years. It was taken at the second ceremony, the "official" wedding James had hosted. She was wearing a classic white satin wedding gown with simple lines. The gown was stored in the attic, put away for Alexis's wedding. Rose had been living with the photo for all these years, but this was the first time she noticed that her tummy looked just the slightest bit rounded from her blossoming pregnancy. Love for Evan, Alexis, and the world they had once shared struggled with the grief inside her.

Rose gained control over her emotions. "The bond between us will always be there," she told him softly. "No one can break that."

"Not even Dimitri?" His tone was now angry.

She squeezed his hand. "It's okay. You have every right."

When he did not respond, she put her hands on his face and brought his lips down to meet hers in a gentle kiss. "It really is over," she said.

She wrestled with her emotions. Part of her wanted to hold him, comfort him, tell him it would all work out—but the woman inside her knew that she'd allowed the dear man to settle for whatever place she would grant him on her list. Evan had the right to be first, and though she hadn't betrayed her vows to him, she hadn't given him all he deserved. And now she could cost him his future, too. It had to end.

With one hand she wiped away the tears from her cheek and said, "You'll make a fine governor one day, Evan Miller."

It was over, and Rose felt a sense of loss and loneliness. "I'll always love you," she said as she walked out the door. And she knew that in her own way she would.

Jewel was in their suite at the casino when he burst through the door.

"Get out," she screamed, "or I'll call Daddy! . . ."

Dimitri walked over to her, took her arm, and twisted it hard. "Listen, you spoiled little brat. Your father has no power over me. He's convinced he's going to ruin me, and he's using you as the bait. But it's not going to work. Did you think I wouldn't figure out that you were working together to set me up? You left a trail as long as the Alaskan pipeline." He twisted harder. "What do you Brauns take me for?"

"Stop it, you're hurting me!" she shrieked, mostly for effect.

He let go of her arm immediately and lowered his voice. "Jewel, did you send a letter to Evan?"

"I don't know what you're talking about, you bully." She rubbed her arm, exaggerating the pain.

"A letter that told him there was an inside informer who'd gone to the prosecutor?"

Jewel said, smirking, "You're not making sense. You accuse me of wanting to ruin you. So why would I tip off your lawyer and help you out. Fool!"

Though Jewel's logic was accurate, the thinking behind it had obviously been fed to her. Logic was not a word in Jewel's dictionary.

"Get out of here, Dimitri." Jewel was calm now, too calm. Her masquerade was frustrating him.

He moved in so close, his face was right next to hers. "You'll be beaten at this game, princess, whatever it is. You and your father can't outsmart anybody, least of all me."

"You're kidding yourself, *Mr. Robin Hood.* You don't have a clue. There's no one you can trust, except, of course, Mrs. Miller. And if I were you, I sure as hell wouldn't bet my platinum card on her."

Jewel's amber eyes glowed with hatred. Dimitri saw his reflection and was surprised at how evil he looked, with his eyes hooded and his lips formed into a menacing sneer. But he wasn't going to let up until he was sure she was panicked enough to make a mistake. He wanted to flush out everyone who was working with her to destroy him.

"I never had anyone to trust, Jewel, particularly you and your father. So, inside informers, star witnesses, whatever is thrown my way won't hurt me. I want you to know that I'm getting a divorce and you're going to agree to it. You'll sign the papers and I'll be out of your life."

"And if that isn't convenient for me? My daddy will—"

"Then he's going to have to kill me, because when I'm finished you're going to wish he had." Dimitri didn't know where the words were coming from. Rage had bubbled up and erupted inside of him. His pulse pounded in his head. It was as if someone else had taken over. He struggled to gain control of himself. "There's only one way to play the game, Jewel. My way." Knowing he was on a dangerous emotional precipice, he turned and walked out of the dressing room. Her nasty laughter followed him.

When she heard the door of the suite slam closed, the laughter stopped and her smug smile faded. Despite her brave front, Jewel was scared of him. After all, the police said he was a maniac, and maybe they were right. God knew Dimitri had hurt her enough to believe he could be cruel, even sadistic. *He's stripped me of all my dignity, humiliated me in front of the whole world.* The whispers behind her back, the jokes made within earshot about Rose and Dimitri, caused her intolerable pain. She wouldn't let him win. *I must stop him, but how?* And then it came to her. She knew what had to be done.

She reached for the phone and called her father. The housekeeper answered.

"Rina, I need to speak to Daddy. It's urgent."

Dimitri maneuvered the two-seater Mercedes in and out of traffic with precision. But then again, he had always performed best under pressure. The Lincoln Tunnel was backed up for three miles going toward the city. Traffic was almost at a standstill, and it was making him crazy. He had to get as far away from Jewel as he could. He had truly thought that he would lose control and hurt her. When he had looked in her face, all he could see was Joseph Braun. Just the thought of Braun and his machinations to bring him down made Dimitri sick to his stomach with fury.

It was clear she had betrayed him. She had found someone to doctor his books and then gone over to the prosecution's side. Whoever had doctored the books was obviously connected to the threats of exposure he'd received. Dimitri would have to consider carefully how to handle Jewel's betrayal. After all, she was working for the government now.

But he knew Jewel hadn't acted alone—she was tough, but certainly not bright enough to carry out this plan on her own. Her father was pulling the strings. Dimitri and Joseph were on a level playing field—each could be ruthless, but each knew the other's secrets.

The cell phone built into the dashboard rang, and on the second ring Dimitri answered.

"Yes?"

It was his secretary. "I'm sorry to bother you, Mr. Constantinos, but I received a call from Rose Miller. She said it was urgent. I told her you were out of the office. She insisted I page you, and she left a number. Do you want me to pass along a message?"

Dimitri grinned, loosened his grip on the steering wheel, eased up on the gas pedal, and exhaled slowly. "Give me the number."

43

I *don't have a choice,* Rose reminded herself as she packed her clothing into the Louis Vuitton suitcase. Falcone had warned her to bring only the essentials: clothes, her work, laptop, and just a few memories of home—some photographs and knickknacks that might make her comfortable. She moved swiftly, trying to outrun the memory of the conversation she'd had with Alexis before she'd left for the apartment.

"I don't want you to go." This was no child's selfish, plaintive plea; Alexis was speaking out of concern not for herself, but for her mother. What had she been doing while Alexis was changing into young womanhood? Rose wondered.

"It won't be long, sweetheart." They sat side by side on the bed in Alexis's room. Rose could see that Alexis was still not unpacked. Oversize blue jeans, T-shirts, and the two-piece bathing suit she'd fought so hard to be allowed to buy were all lying in neat piles on the floor, waiting to be put away. The sight made her wonder about all the little things she always made sure were taken care of for her daughter; who would be there tomorrow, to awaken Alexis when she was cranky and not wanting to go to school?

Evan could handle it, Rose reassured herself, and he could take care of all the essentials just as well as she could.

"Mom?"

Had Alexis been talking to her? "Yes, darling?"

"I said how long? And where are you going?"

Rose sighed. She'd gone through the same conversation herself with John—and then with Evan—but there were no answers.

"It won't be long," she repeated. "That's all I know. But I'll try to call you every day."

Alexis turned away, her shoulders heaving as she sobbed. Rose put her arms around her and bent her head against Alexis's soft hair. "Please, don't cry," she said as her own tears began to flow.

As she was about to leave Paradiso, Evan followed her to the car. "Isn't there a number where I can reach you in an emergency?"

Her only reply was, "Call John Falcone. He'll know where to reach me."

The less he knew, the better. Falcone had warned her not to confide in anyone, not Alexis, Dario, Myra, or Malcolm. Not even Evan. She would fly this mission solo.

A loud knock on the apartment door interrupted her thoughts. Surprised, Rose glanced at the clock. Eight-fifteen. She knew it wasn't John. He'd said he would call before he came. With Malcolm outside the door, she felt secure enough to look through the peephole. It was Dario.

When Rose opened the door, he wasted no time with pleasantries. She felt him assessing her pale skin, the dark circles under her eyes.

"What's wrong, Rose? You look terrible." Before she could respond, he continued, "What's with the guard outside the door?"

"I'm going away for a while," she said, thinking of exactly what to tell him. "The guard is just a little extra security while I'm alone in the apartment." She gave Dario a forced smile. "Evan insisted—you know how protective he is."

"Where are you going?" There was a look on his face she couldn't quite read. "To a secret hideaway with your 'friend'?" When Rose didn't respond to his jibe, Dario continued, "Rose, you haven't invited me in."

She cleared her throat and said, "It's not a good time, Dario. I have some more packing to do, and I'm in a rush."

Now the look in his eyes was one she recognized but was unfamiliar with: anger. "I have no intention of leaving until you tell me what this is all about. Why do you always put me in the position of having to chastise you? The tour picks up again next week—you know that. We've got the satellite radio interviews all confirmed. And don't forget, we arranged for them to be broadcast from your apartment instead of the studio just to make it easier for you."

Rose knew how headstrong and determined he was. She decided to jolly him along.

"I was just about to pour myself a glass of wine. Would you like to join me?"

Dario took off his coat and tossed it on a chair. His eyes rested on the open suitcase. "Why don't you let me get the wine. You can start unpacking. You're not going anywhere."

Rose ran her fingers through the tangle of hair she'd clipped in a haphazard pile on top of her head. She had to get Dario off her back. As he worked in the kitchen, she calmly continued packing. John had instructed her to bring warm clothing, which obviously meant she'd be going somewhere cold—clearly not the tropical location she had been hoping for.

Dario returned from the kitchen with an opened bottle of Armone and two Waterford wineglasses. She sat in a corner of the couch next to the open suitcase; he settled in the upholstered chair and lifted his glass to her in a toast.

"To you, Rose." His expression was melancholy. He drank deeply from the glass, never taking his eyes off her.

"You're going away with Dimitri, aren't you?" He didn't wait for a reply. "Are you in love with him?"

Though she considered herself impervious to shock at this point, his question caught her off-guard. Dario was a gossip—he loved to barter, using other people's secrets as wampum. In her gut she knew this wasn't where he was coming from now. She thought about the night she and Dimitri had arrived to find a crowd on top of the Ivory Palace. Dario's face came back to her, the look of anger and something else she couldn't decipher in his eyes. Now, suddenly, his presence made her edgy and uncomfortable.

"Dario, listen to me . . ." Rose put down her glass and used her hands for emphasis. "We both know there's plenty of time for the publicity people at Boardman to put together another satellite tour. I need to go away, but I can't get into the specifics." She stopped to let her words sink in, but his expression remained unchanged. She tried another tactic. "Look. Are you like the other vipers, making up gossip and pretending it's news? Is that why you're insisting this trip has something to do with Dimitri?"

Dario raised his eyebrows. "Are you questioning my loyalty?"

For a moment Rose faltered before his pointed question. "Do I have reason to?" she asked.

"Of course not," he shot back. "I'm worried about you. I only want what's best for you. And Dimitri Constantinos is not what's best."

"I'm not involved with Dimitri, despite what the world thinks." She brought the wineglass to her lips and sipped from it slowly. "If you want what's best for me, you'll let me take a vacation without hassling me. Anyway, why do you get that ugly look on your face whenever Dimitri is mentioned? You surprise me, Dario."

He leaned forward and put his wine down so hard that the clanging of glass against glass jolted her, causing her to jump.

"Given the circumstances? Come now, Rose, you've been caught with your hand in the till, and in front of the whole world, I might add."

Rose stood and wandered over to the window. The stillness of night had always enthralled her. She used to revel in the beauty of a full moon competing with the city's lights, the subdued night sounds that were distinct from the bustle of the business day. But now the darkness terrified her. She traced her finger along the windowpane, letting it slide through the moisture. Without realizing it, she wrote the word "help."

"I want you to leave," she said over her shoulder.

In one quick motion Dario came to her and, grabbing her by the waist, pulled her to him. It happened so suddenly that she gasped, and Malcolm called out to her, "Are you okay in there?"

Trying to push herself away from him, Rose answered, "We're fine." She didn't want to humiliate Dario by having her bodyguard throw him out. She tried again to wriggle free, but his grip was too tight. He pulled her even closer.

"Dario, let go of me or I'll call the guard!"

He ignored her as his lips roamed the crevice between her shoulder and her neck. He was mumbling something she couldn't make out. Pushing his hips close to hers, he rubbed his groin against her. Specks of white flashed before her eyes, and she wasn't Rose Miller anymore; she was Rose Calvetti lying on a bed in a barn, and he was Uncle Tom. She pushed him away as hard as she could and began to scream. His hand flew up to her mouth in an effort to silence her, and she managed to break free. The clip fell from her hair, and the neckline on her top was torn.

"Get out!" she yelled. Malcolm appeared in the doorway, but Rose motioned for him to stay out of the fracas.

Dario leaned his back against the wall. One hand covered his mouth, and he looked shocked at himself. Both were panting from exertion.

"This time you're fired, Dario. I want you out of here."

Rose saw that Dario realized she was serious. She was careful to keep her distance from him but stood in a position of power, arms crossed before her.

Dario caught his breath, then said, "You're nothing without me, Rose Calvetti. I keep you at the front of the public's mind." He grabbed his coat from the back of the chair, walked to the door, and opened it. "You need me to survive. Miami was just the tip of the iceberg. Next time you won't be so lucky," he said over his shoulder as the door slammed shut.

She didn't understand what he meant by his remark about Miami or how he knew her maiden name, and she was too tired to analyze it.

The shrill ring of the telephone jolted her back from near hysteria. Rose stared at the old-fashioned black rotary phone that she kept because it reminded her of the one in her parents' cottage. Stop ringing, she half demanded, half prayed. She couldn't speak to anyone now. Besides, it was probably John calling, and he would leave a message. But the steady ringing continued, and on the eleventh ring she remembered that she had turned off the answering machine. She grabbed the receiver.

Annoyed, she yelled into the handset, "What is it?"

Then she heard his voice. "Rose, it's Dimitri. I got a message that you called."

She didn't trust herself to answer at first, but she could hear her own rapid, nervous breathing. She tried to calm herself down, to match his casual tone. "Yes, I did call."

"About what?" he asked.

She wanted to say: *About why you did what you did for me. I need to hear you say it. I need to hear some answers.* Instead, she said: "Can we meet someplace? I'd rather not discuss it over the phone."

"Perhaps tomorrow morn—"

"No," Rose interrupted, "I'll be going away."

"Then in the Vanderbilt Suite at the Plaza. You'll have to come here."

The connection broke, the dial tone buzzed, but Rose still kept the receiver to her ear.

Was she doing the right thing by going to see Dimitri? Or was she just digging a deeper hole for herself, complicating matters even further? What did it matter? She'd have to bring Malcolm with her—John would kill her himself if she dared meet with Dimitri alone.

"We'll be going out," she said to the bodyguard. "Call Larry, will you? Tell him to meet us downstairs."

Malcolm nodded. He wondered how long it would take before she figured out that it was he who had tried to drown her in Miami. He felt kind of bad about going against Falcone like that, but the money had been too good to turn down. It was a good thing she was going away. Falcone had told him he wouldn't be going with her.

Rose changed quickly out of her sweats and into a deep purple Calvin Klein dress. She picked up her small purse and turned to leave. But near the apartment door something gleamed on the carpet, catching her eye. She must have seen Dario whip out this expensive accessory a thousand times over the years: the engraved "D" in the far right corner, the feel of the cold gold rectangle snuggled in her palm. The lighter at Marilyn's matched this card case. Without thinking, she crammed the case into her purse. Then she grabbed her camel's hair coat and flew from the apartment seeking shelter. Her instinct propelled her to Dimitri.

At the Atlantic City Police Station, Detective Barney Cole threw on his requisite homicide detective's rumpled sports jacket. "York," he yelled to his partner. "Get your ass in gear."

"Where are we going?" Dennis York took one more sip of coffee and cast a longing look at his uneaten sub. He hated to eat on the run. Too many crime scenes had cured him of that.

"We've got a black duffel bag found in a Dumpster two blocks from the Slocum murder scene. The forensics team is waiting for us to get there before they open it. They got the evidence van down there already. Come on, we're outta here."

Dimitri threw his Armani suit jacket over the arm of the sofa, walked straight to the bar, and poured himself some cognac. He'd waited for this moment for twelve years. Any time now Rose would walk through the door, and he would be ready for her.

The buzzing of the telephone interrupted his thoughts. He put the drink on the bar and answered it.

"Boss, it's Gino. I'm sorry to disturb you, but there's been an incident at the casino, something I know you'll want to be made aware of."

"What is it?" Dimitri was annoyed. They called him for every little mishap, every malfunction, and lately it was driving him crazy.

"Your wife, sir. There was a disagreement with someone from room service. I'm afraid an argument broke out. The girl is terribly upset and wants hotel security to call the police."

Damn you, Jewel. "What happened?"

The man continued, "It seems your wife placed an order shortly before eight for champagne and caviar. She requested it be brought up immediately. At eight-twenty, the girl knocked on the door of the suite, and when your wife answered, she spewed obscenities at her. When the girl wouldn't reply, your wife slapped her."

"That sounds like Jewel," Dimitri said as he unbuttoned the cuffs of his white shirt and rolled up the sleeves. "Get in touch with Bob Kogan in accounting. Have him write the girl a check for five thousand dollars. Make sure you get her name to my secretary and have flowers with a note of apology sent to her home. And see that personnel gets her a promotion."

Had he thought of everything? The girl would most likely run to the tabloids. "Listen, Gino, have my secretary set up a lunch appointment with her. I'll meet with her at the Verandah tomorrow." A little fatherly TLC at the casino's five-star restaurant couldn't hurt, Dimitri figured.

"As for Jewel," he continued, "I'll deal with her this weekend as well. Thanks for covering the bases for me, guy."

He was in the process of replacing the receiver when Gino said, "There's more, sir."

"What?"

"The young woman was convinced we were lying to her when we told her you weren't here. She is positive she saw a man your size in the bedroom of the suite. Part of the reason she's calmed down is we convinced her you couldn't have been there and that you wouldn't let your wife be disrespectful."

"So there was a man with her?"

"I'm sorry, boss, but you gotta know. The maid swore she heard your wife call the man 'honey.'"

Under different circumstances this news wouldn't have bothered him. He was sure Jewel had taken to fooling around, but he didn't care. However, right now anyone Jewel brought close to him was dangerous. He realized he better act quickly.

"Dimitri?" Gino said. "Anything I can do?"

"Set up a meeting with my business attorneys. Tell them I want all four partners to be available for a meeting. First thing in the morning. And I mean sunrise."

44

Rose had convinced Malcolm to stay with Larry in the car parked in front of the hotel, though truthfully the bodyguard needed less convincing than her driver. Now she entered the Plaza through the Fifth Avenue entrance. Just the name of the hotel conjured up images of opulence, grandeur, stateliness, and history. It was the hotel of choice for kings, presidents, stage, screen and sports stars—luminaries from every field. *How fitting,* Rose thought, *that Dimitri would use it as his home away from home during the trial.*

The lobby was filled with tourists from a dozen countries. She passed the Palm Court, one of the hotel's restaurants where people watching was honed to an art form. The melodious tinkling of the piano flowed into the lobby, with its exquisite marble floors. Rose made her way to one of the elevators and up to Dimitri's suite.

Once outside the door, she froze. She couldn't bring herself to knock. *Maybe I shouldn't have come,* she thought. *What will I say? What if he throws me out? This is a mistake.* She could still leave. Besides, she really should call John and tell him about Dario's behavior. Her strong side kicked in. She smoothed the lines of the silk dress, ran her fingers through her hair, then knocked loud and hard.

The hell with what he does. All I want to do is apologize. Then I'll leave. Five minutes tops.

The door opened and Dimitri appeared. His piercing blue eyes roamed her body. Neither of them spoke or moved. They stared at each other for what seemed like an eternity. Finally he stepped aside and gestured for her to enter.

Rose studied the magnificent room. It was enormous yet exuded a subtle warmth, with elaborate decorations dominated by graceful Chippendale chairs and Aubusson rugs. An inviting burgundy velvet love seat faced a sofa upholstered in burgundy silk with pale gray highlights. The drapes, now closed, were also heavy velvet. The room felt safe. The fireplace was lit, making the suite seem cozy and seductive.

He moved toward the sofa. "Have a seat," he said, taking her coat and pointing to the love seat.

Dimitri sat down opposite her. His eyes drank her in. "So, you wanted to see me?"

Rose cleared her throat. "I . . . I needed to speak to you about what you told me last Friday night." She caught herself mumbling, she couldn't get centered. As always, he threw off her equilibrium.

"What about it?"

His tone was nonchalant. Clearly he reveled in her discomfort. "You're not going to make this easy for me, are you?"

"Make what easy, Rose?" He leaned back, rested both arms along the back of the sofa, and grinned, confident, even a little teasing.

Rose saw all over again what drew women to him. He smoldered. It was effortless, a natural part of his makeup.

She stood and walked over to the fireplace. Facing the mantel, she said, "Maybe I'm too much of a coward to face you. Perhaps it's better with my back to you."

She stared into the fire. The dancing flames of bright orange, yellow, and blue temporarily put her in a trance. For a moment the image of the two of them making love filled her thoughts. She was eighteen, innocent and naive, yet despite her clumsiness it had all seemed so natural. The way his lips sought hers, his strong hands teaching her body to respond. Her face flushed, and she wasn't sure if it was from the heat of the fire or her own embarrassment.

"What's on your mind, Rose?"

The same blasé tone. She knew Dimitri too well. He wouldn't crack. It was up to her to topple his fortress. She sensed in his unconscious motions the young man she knew long ago, still hidden deep beneath layers of anger, distrust, and deception. How could she bring him back?

Rose traced one finger along the top of the wood mantel. "Do you remember the first time we met?" She waited for a simple yes or no. Instead all she got was silence.

"I came into the barn. You were currying Maxwell." She let out a small laugh, then said wistfully, "You asked me if I wanted to ride. You thought I was one of the rich girls." Now her eyes welled up and she turned, looking at him through her tears, a figure seen through a windowpane in a driving rain. She no longer felt intimidated by him, no longer cared what he thought. It was as though she were cleansing her soul, and it felt exhilarating and torturous all at once.

She stared deeply into his eyes and could swear she saw a glint of feeling. "I came back that night . . . I guess I was drawn to you."

Dimitri stood and walked over to the window. This time it was he who turned his back to her, opening the drapes as though this had been his purpose in coming near her. Outside, the lights looked like assorted gems sparkling brightly. He put both hands up to the glass, then said in the voice she once knew, "You brought me food."

Instantly some of the invisible wall came down. Even with their backs to each other, she could hear it in his tone. He sounded nostalgic, even wistful.

Rose plunged in. "I never meant to hurt you. You must believe that." Now the tears were streaming down her cheeks. But she didn't care. It was as though a part of her heart were breaking free. Feelings she'd kept buried for so long made their way to the surface and flowed outward.

"I'm sorry I married Evan. I was young and foolish. I had nowhere to turn. I thought it was my only way out. You must believe that I loved you, Dimitri. You were the one I wanted to spend the rest of my life with."

He turned to face her.

"If I'd realized at the time that it was I who had killed . . . I would never have let you take the blame. I've lived with the guilt all these years, trying desperately to put it all behind me. Pushing all of it out of my mind."

"You could have waited for me, Rose." Dimitri's voice was very low.

"There were other circumstances," she said, and for a moment she was tempted to tell him about Alexis. But she stopped herself. What good would it do, besides harm Alexis? It entered her mind that Dimitri might even try to take her away somehow. Her daughter's parentage remained her secret. And there seemed little point in trying to convince him she had tried to get him exonerated on the manslaughter charge, that in fact Evan had promised, but that James had aborted the plan. What purpose would it serve to tell him what might have been?

"What circumstances?" he demanded.

She walked toward him and stood just a few feet away. "I can't explain. Please don't ask me to. Just know that I felt the pain of losing you and, even worse, the virulence of your anger. I wanted to be there to comfort you, and you didn't want me. I was as confined as you were, except my prison was inside." She brought her hand up to her heart.

Her words seemed to jolt him. He made his way past her to pour himself another drink. He asked if she wanted one, but she declined.

"Do you know what *prison* is like, Rose? Do you have any idea what a young man is forced to endure?"

She couldn't look at him. "No," she replied softly. "I don't."

He gulped down his drink, then said with anger, "It's undiluted hell. You're thrown in with the big boys, stripped of your dignity, and forced to fend for yourself. I was in Nassau County Jail for two weeks before being transferred to prison, and in that two weeks I was in seven fights. Looking back, I think James was hoping I'd die there. I'm sure he paid guards to goad me into attacking them or fighting with other prisoners, and I fell for it every time. Hell, most of my six years was spent in solitary. Then the minute I was back in the general population, the provocation would start all over again."

Dimitri put down his glass and walked toward her. He looked menacing. "Then there's the mental prison. I thought about you every day, every waking moment. I hated you for what you did to me. The thought of Evan touching you made my skin crawl. Need I go on?"

She couldn't speak; she only found the strength to shake her head.

"I wanted you and the whole Miller family to feel my pain," Dimitri said. "I waited a long time to get my chance. All those years I might have exposed James's secrets to make money. I was approached several times about the Laurel estate murder. The public would have loved an exposé on the family; they still would."

"What do you want from me?" Rose asked. "What can I do to make things right? If only I had known then, what I did. I . . . I . . ."

"You would what? Would have gone to prison?" He let out a nasty laugh. "Dear old 'Dad' wouldn't have allowed it. Not while he had me as the sacrificial lamb."

Rose stared into his dark, somber eyes, hoping for a glint of understanding, but all she saw was rage and vengeance. The opening in the wall between them had closed. There was nothing else she could do.

"I have to go."

But before she could push past him, he grabbed her hand and pulled her back. They stood close together in front of the window.

He gripped her hand tightly. "I suppose I could hurt you, Rose. I could release all my frustrations, all my anger, out on you."

She didn't need to look at him to know he had no intention of hurting her— not here, not now. Emboldened by this intuition, she pulled hard enough to break his grasp.

"I want this payback to be personal."

She heard Dimitri's voice from far away. The room was spinning, and she felt sick. But she fought the feeling. "Is that why you staged those two episodes with the press present? Did you do that to humiliate me and Evan? Did you deliberately set out to destroy our marriage? Well, Dimitri, you succeeded."

A look of surprise crossed his face. "You can't believe that I would stoop to such tactics. Going to the press is not my style."

Rose pleaded with him one last time, "What do you want from me?"

He didn't speak anymore. They stood staring at each other, and the only sound in the room was the loud ticking of a clock.

Rose tried to read Dimitri's eyes, but they gave nothing away. She had to get out. She needed to run away as fast as she could, from this room, from Dimitri, from her past.

But in a sudden move he grabbed her again, effectively caging her between his arms. He brought his mouth down on hers with intense hunger. She should have pushed him away, struggled to break free, but she was too weak; she couldn't say no. The weight of him as he crushed her against the window was intoxicating, and excitement flowed through her, an incandescent liquid that made all her senses bloom.

Dimitri groaned, a sound from deep within. He leaned closer, his body hard, warm, protective.

Rose couldn't stop. It was beyond their control. She wrapped her arms around his neck, drawing him even closer. It felt right. All of her senses were drinking in the reality of his body pressed against hers. Still, she whispered, "Dimitri, I . . . I . . ."

But his mouth found hers again, and his hands moved across her back. He pulled her forward, and as he kissed her, all of the restless pieces inside her suddenly stilled. Her heart had found its resting place, and she stopped wanting to fight the feelings he had awakened, feelings she had been convinced were long dead. Rose gave in to his insistent caresses and her own driving need. They made their way across the room and into the bedroom, hands fumbling at each other's clothes, urgent, yet not rushed; insistent, yet not demanding.

They fell into the soft mattress of the four-poster bed. He was on top of her, stroking her hair, searching her eyes, whispering, "Rose . . . oh God . . . Rose . . ."

She stared back and wasn't surprised at what she saw: the softness, the innocence, the Dimitri of long ago. She melted into the experience. He no longer represented the mythical god the public and the press created. He was a young man, standing in the corner of a barn, hovering over an old cot and a crate filled with his belongings. The man who came to her each night in her dreams, the darkest corners of her fantasies.

She wanted him so badly, she ached. His hands explored her body, the same hands that had taught and compelled her that night long ago. But now they were practiced hands. He aroused her until the material world no longer existed. When she couldn't take it anymore, couldn't hold on, he entered her, finding his way inside her as though he'd always belonged there.

Her nails dug into his back, holding on to the flesh she had been denied too long.

After the ecstasy, she fell into a peaceful slumber, safe at last in Dimitri's arms.

Detectives Barney Cole and Dennis York were still at the Atlantic City Police Station, with the Janice Slocum murder file spread out before them.

The desk sergeant came into the cubicle the detectives shared and said, "The report came back from forensics."

Barney looked up. "Did you get anything?"

The desk sergeant smiled. "Not only did we get prints, we got a hair sample as well."

Cole let out a sigh of relief. Finally, a break. Maybe it would be a nice weekend at home with the wife and kids after all.

"Run the prints through," he ordered.

"We already have. Guess who they belong to. . . ."

45

Rose woke to find Dimitri curled up against her. His arm lay motionless across her waist; his right leg covered her thigh. A feeling of security and warmth enveloped her body and soul. She wasn't sure if what had happened last night was right or wrong, nor did she care. The only thing that mattered was they were together, here—now. Once again they were young lovers in an uncomplicated world. Rose remained still, though the feel of his warm breath on her neck and shoulders sent her into a frenzy and made her hunger for him again.

Now he began to stir, and suddenly she was nervous. He swung his body around to the other side of the bed, sat up, and rubbed his eyes. She dared not move. He picked up his clothes from the floor, stumbled into them, walked across the carpet to the desk, and picked up the telephone. Rose remained exactly as she was, listening to his conversation.

"Gino, push my appointment back with my attorneys. I'm running behind this morning. I'm afraid I won't be able to get to the office until"—he checked his watch—"until eleven-thirty. Make sure my lunch date with the girl from room service is set. And for God's sake, get me her name."

He slammed down the receiver and headed to the bathroom. The door stayed open, and she heard the sound of running water.

Dimitri hadn't bothered with pleasantries. He said nothing, and his silence infuriated her. Kicking off the blankets, Rose hastily got out of the bed. *How dared he?* She glanced at the porcelain clock on the night table and realized she had to call John. Barefoot, she hurried from the bedroom into the living room. She could still hear the shower running, so she dialed his number.

"John, it's Rose."

"Rose, I called you. Where the hell—"

"I'm okay. Have the plans been made?"

Falcone ignored her question. "Malcolm called and said you left him waiting outside the Plaza Hotel. He wanted to come up after you, but security wouldn't let him. They said they were protecting whoever was there with you, so he shouldn't worry. Constantinos, no doubt?"

His tone was angry. Rose sighed. She should have realized that the Plaza's security would be watching anyone who went up to the Vanderbilt Suite.

"I'll explain when I see you," she said, careful of the little time she had before Dimitri stepped out of the shower.

"Fine," Falcone replied shortly. "I'll meet you at your apartment at noon."

Rose heard the bathroom door open and quickly broke the connection. When she spun around, Dimitri was standing in the doorway with only a towel wrapped around him.

"Who were you talking to?" he asked, an accusing look in his eyes.

"Oh—my editor. I had to cancel a meeting."

There was a moment of silence. Both were at a loss for words. When the silence became unbearable, she finally said, "Would you like me to order up breakfast?"

"No," he said sharply, "I have an early meeting. . . . I really have to get ready. You can let yourself out."

His manner devastated her, but she understood. Watching him, the rational businessman, his sapphire eyes cold and deep as the Arctic Ocean in wintertime, she knew he couldn't stand the fact that she'd pierced the armor, rekindled the vulnerability he strove to mask.

Rose brushed past him and went into the bedroom to collect her clothing.

"You can use the shower," he said over his shoulder.

"No thanks," she mumbled. "I'll shower at my apartment."

Last night was only a memory, nothing more.

Fifteen minutes later, dressed and ready, she was headed for the door when he called out to her.

"Rose . . . I . . ."

She only nodded. He was partially dressed in a pair of black slacks, a silk tie draped around his neck.

"About last night . . ."

She was afraid for him to go on, knowing his words would be cruel.

"I needed to take back from my father and brother, if only temporarily, what they stole from me twelve years ago. Go tell your husband I've had you again. You owe me that much. If you don't, I'll make sure he finds out."

Rose knew she should have felt angry, but she realized instantly that despite his words and deliberate plan to humiliate her, their lovemaking had touched him as profoundly as it had her. Perhaps he needed to convince himself that last night was just a smooth calculation.

"It's okay," she replied. "I think we both understand."

This time he didn't reply.

"Anyway, it doesn't matter. I'll be going away . . . I'm not sure for how long, but—"

"Where?" he asked, and before he could cover it up, she detected his concern.

"I'm afraid I can't tell you."

He looked skeptical.

"Well, I've got to get some rest, you know, peace and quiet," she continued. "I have to finish writing my next book. There's too many buzzards flying around me right now, the media and so on. I've got to go away and not tell anyone where I'm going." She paused to assess his reaction, then added, "Not even Evan knows where I'll be."

"If I . . . if someone needed to reach you, where . . ."

"They would have to contact Detective John Falcone. I believe you've met him before."

"I know who he is."

There was a loud knock at the door, and they were both startled.

"Are you expecting someone, Rose?"

She shook her head.

He pushed past her, looked through the keyhole, then said, "Shit."

The knocking continued, now incessant and loud. He opened the door to two men.

"Dimitri Constantinos?" Dimitri nodded, and one of the men flashed a gold shield. "We'd like you to come down to Midtown North with us."

"What's this about?" Rose noticed that Dimitri didn't give an inch, no quavering in his voice, no sign of fear—no expression at all.

"An employee of yours—Janice Slocum."

Dimitri nodded. "But I've already spoken to Falcone—"

"We know that," the detective interrupted him. "The serial killer task force is involved. They think this case might be the latest in a string of murders. Are you coming, Mr. Constantinos, or do we need to read you your rights?"

Dimitri smiled at the officers, then said, "Sure, gentlemen. Just give me a few minutes to finish getting dressed."

All that had happened in this suite since last night was now blotted out by the detectives' appearance. Rose looked over at Dimitri, confused and concerned. *How was Janice Slocum connected to Dimitri?* But then again, Dimitri was always full of surprises. He seemed to be on a roller coaster, and it was impossible to tell from moment to moment how he really felt or what he might do. In a trance she left the suite, not caring about walking past the detectives, not even worrying if anyone recognized her. Nothing else could touch her at this point. Dazed and disoriented, she took the elevator to the lobby and walked out into the cold.

"Madame . . ." The Plaza's doorman touched his hat and opened the Mercedes's back door.

As Larry pulled the car away, Rose looked back over her shoulder to see Dimitri leaving with the two detectives. How could she ever pull her world together again? He had set out to ruin her, and he had succeeded. But it didn't look as though his life were going to be any easier because of it.

We're in the same boat, finally, Dimitri, she thought, then looked away.

46

Rose had just enough time to beep Alexis's pager and say goodbye during her daughter's lunch break before the doorman buzzed to say Detective Falcone was waiting downstairs in a cab to take her to the airport. They drove without speaking to the general aviation area at La Guardia.

Falcone broke the silence. "We'll be making the flight in that single-engine baby over there." He pointed. "It will take us an hour and a half, tops, depending on the weather."

"Why isn't Malcolm coming?" she asked, though truthfully she was not unhappy to be away from him. Solitude was a treasured byproduct of this journey to who knew where.

"I took him off the case," Falcone said. It was hard to read his tone. These words signaled something, Rose was sure of it. She wanted to ask why, but there were so many things to cover in so short a time. Soon she'd be a different woman, alone. She needed John to fill her in on the details of this other woman's life.

"I don't like that he allowed you to skip off," Falcone went on. "I don't trust him, so I fired him. You'll be less conspicuous if you're alone."

Rose considered this in silence. Then she asked, "Where are the other passengers?"

"Just us, Rose. I've chartered the plane. It's owned by an old army buddy of mine. He pilots it himself."

No tracks, no traces, Rose thought.

The cab pulled in front of the aviation building. The driver hauled the luggage from the trunk, and Rose followed Falcone into the hangar.

Sooner or later one of them would have to bring up her night with Dimitri. She saw the muscles of John's jaw tighten. Not a good sign. *Well, here goes.*

"I'm confused," she said. "This morning Dimitri was taken in for questioning on the Janice Slocum murder, which means if he's guilty, he's responsible for the other murders as well. So why am I still running?"

They stopped at the plane as it fueled up. Falcone introduced her to the pilot and put her things in the baggage compartment. Finally he answered, "I'm not positive he's guilty. We can't take any more chances, Rose. You seem to want to live dangerously," he said caustically, "so let's do this right. The only way to be sure is to have the killer come for you. When he makes his move, we'll be ready."

He had told her when they spoke in Miami that she'd be the lure. And she deserved to be. Hearing John say he wasn't convinced of Dimitri's guilt was like opening a window inside of her and allowing fresh air to rush in. She was almost certain he wasn't guilty of anything. But if she had to draw out the killer and put herself on the line for Dimitri, it was about time. She would help catch the psycho she had created.

From the air, Stowe, Vermont, had the charmed look of a small town in the Swiss Alps. The snow-capped mountains with their ski runs, open meadows, and forest shed of all its greenery created a wintry scene so ideal that it looked fabricated. The town was tucked in a broad, fertile valley between Mt. Mansfield and other peaks east and west of the large mountain. In warm weather, Rose knew, Stowe was also a famous summer resort. The gorgeous scenery, cool climate, and exceptional beauty of Mt. Mansfield, Smuggler's Notch, and neighboring hills and valleys drew tourists to the Stowe area in great numbers. This time of year, Stowe was the ski capital of the east. It was always bustling with people. *A great place to get lost in a crowd,* Rose imagined.

Her mind went back to last night, but she felt no guilt. She had feelings of insecurity, perhaps, and definitely confusion, but no regrets. Dimitri's body belied his words. His tenderness was what spoke to her. His assertions that all he wanted was revenge did not alter the compass inside her that pointed to the truth: he loved her, and she didn't care what he told himself.

Ironically, just as she was thinking about the previous night, John said, "Dimitri's prints were all over the bag found near Slocum's body. His defense team is going to have a tough time convincing a jury of his innocence."

Rose would not buy into this. "You just said you're not convinced he's guilty."

"I'm not. Someone could have set him up."

Rose straightened in her seat.

"Well, I'm convinced he didn't kill Janice Slocum or any of those other women, and he isn't going to kill me."

Falcone nodded but said nothing, leading her to continue, "I know instinct and intuition don't work as evidence in court. But here"—she pointed to her head—"and here"—her hand covered her heart—"I have dismissed Dimitri Constantinos of all charges."

"Maybe so, but right-brain evidence doesn't work for me. I need proof, data, and hard facts."

"What about the card holder that fell from Dario's pocket? And what about the fact that it matched the lighter I found in Marilyn's closet? Doesn't that constitute evidence? And of all the suspects I could conjure up now, he's the creepiest."

Falcone shrugged. "Yes and no. As I said, all the evidence points to Dimitri. What about Dimitri's fingerprints all over the duffel bag? And there's no hard evidence linking Dario to the murders. He could say he dropped his lighter at her place while visiting."

"In her closet?" Rose asked doubtfully. "Where her clothes had been ripped, her possessions destroyed?"

"Whatever, it doesn't prove anything," Falcone replied dismissively, "Besides, that's if it is his lighter. We don't know for sure."

"Well, consider this. Last night at my apartment, he asked if I was in love with Dimitri, then he all but attacked me. Malcolm can attest to that."

"Did anything provoke him? Did he have too much to drink?"

"No, just a few sips of wine. But that's not what troubles me. He said something about Miami . . . that next time I wouldn't be so lucky."

Falcone grew very quiet.

"Tell me what you're thinking," Rose said.

"I'm wondering why Dario would want to pay someone to scare you."

"Or kill me."

"No, it was obvious that the incident was a warning. Otherwise, believe me, you'd be dead. But what was the message he was sending you? Was Dario letting you know how close he's getting? Or does he have some other agenda?"

"Dario has a dark side to him."

"I thought you were close friends? Do you honestly believe he could have killed Marilyn and all these other women? He's got that much of a dark side?"

"I don't know what to think anymore. I don't know whom to trust," Rose snapped. "Ever since last night I've been wondering if he set things up to make it look like I was having an affair with Dimitri. He has always wanted to cause a rift between Evan and me, and lately he'd gotten pushier about it. But how would hiring someone to scare the bejesus out of me fit into his agenda?"

"But do you think he would go to such lengths to scare you?"

At this she felt her stomach knot. Dario had been close to her, an enormous force behind her success, but the cord of trust between them was permanently broken. "A week ago, I would have said no, now I'm convinced he could."

Falcone pulled a pad and pen from his shirt pocket and jotted down some notes. "Give me his address. I think I'll pay him a visit when I get back to New York."

The sound of the little plane's engine was all that filled the air for a few minutes.

Falcone's next question snuck up on her, as she was sure he'd intended it to. "How could you take a chance on spending a night with Constantinos? I'm beginning to feel jerked around, Rose."

What could she say except what she'd said before? "I don't believe Dimitri is the man you're looking for."

"Maybe, but that kind of thinking is dangerous," Falcone said. "If you get into trouble here, I won't be close enough to bail you out."

Just then the "Fasten Seat Belt" light came on, signaling the plane's descent to Burlington International Airport. Rose deflected the conversation. "Where will I be staying?" she asked.

"The Von Trapp Lodge. A friend of mine has a timeshare in one of the chalets. It's a hillside unit with a full kitchen, living room, two bedrooms, fireplaces, and a balcony. It's located on an outgrowth of the lodge itself. It's secluded, but not too far away from the general population. You'll have access to all the resort amenities. The library, sunroom, cocktail lounge, recreation room, anything you need will be right on the premises."

Great, Rose thought, *at least I won't go stir-crazy.*

After the plane landed, Falcone and Rose headed for the rental car agency outside the airport. The cold, biting wind slapped hard against her cheeks. They waited only ten minutes, but it was enough to make her hands and face numb. An attendant brought the black Lincoln Navigator around the corner.

"You'll need the four-wheel drive," Falcone said as he loaded her luggage into the back of the sport utility vehicle. "These roads can be treacherous, especially at night. Keep that in mind. Only drive when you have to." He looked up to catch her eye. "Then again, you should have no reason to go out at night, anyway."

He opened the passenger side door, and Rose hoisted herself up into the seat. Falcone climbed behind the steering wheel, fired the heat up high, and took off down Route 100.

Almost an hour later they came to Ten Acres Lodge, drove to the top of a steep hill, and turned left. From the distance, Rose could see what looked like a tiny village lit up with flickering clear lights. As they neared the lodge, she grew anxious. Falcone picked up on it right away.

"You'll be okay, Rose. Everything you need will be here." He had already told her that she was registered under the name of Linda Morgan, a recently divorced accountant. He reached into his duffel bag and handed her a large envelope.

"Inside you'll find a license, credit card, some bogus business cards, a black wig, and a pair of dark sunglasses. Here, Rose, slip into your new identity."

That won't be too hard, I don't know who I am anyway.

The Tyrolean architecture of the main lodge was accented by hand-carved balustrades, steeply pitched gables, and a cider shake roof. Falcone jumped out of the truck. "Wait here, I'll only be a minute. I need to pick up the keys from the reception desk."

Rose opened the passenger-side door and climbed out of the truck. "Don't worry," she said. John, she noted, was wearing his "Jewish mother look," the one she sometimes teased him about when he got overly protective. She put on her dark sunglasses and pulled the hood of the parka up around her face. "I just want to stretch and look around."

The air was bright and crisp, and the beauty of her surroundings had alleviated some of the dread she felt about the upcoming lonely nights. She wandered to an area close to the lodge where instructors were busy teaching beginners how to ski. A young woman of about twenty-one smiled adoringly at the handsome man who had his arms wrapped around her waist.

"You're doing fine," the man said. "Now pretend we're going down the slope, bend your knees, get your balance. There you go!"

The girl fell a few more times as Rose watched, and each time the young man helped her up with his strong arms, settled her on her skis, and encouraged her to try again. In the bright, body-hugging ski wear, the two made Rose think of healthy young animals at play. As she watched, the young woman sprawled yet again, her auburn hair coming undone from the braid that fell past her shoulders. After numerous attempts, the girl found her sense of balance and exclaimed, "Oh, I love skiing. Do you think we could continue this lesson over dinner?"

Rose made eye contact with the instructor, saw his embarrassment, then quickly looked away, hiding her smile. How she envied them.

Falcone returned with two sets of keys. "One for you, one for me." She looked at him quizzically. "It'll make me feel better if I keep a set. You don't mind? I'll fly back and check on you just to make sure you're staying out of trouble."

Rose shrugged. "Suit yourself."

47

Joseph Braun's signature dove gray limousine was waiting outside the hotel when Dimitri returned from the police station. Everything inside of Dimitri went tight as his cab rounded the circular entrance and he saw the car. But when he neared the limo he realized Braun was alone, and his tension eased. Braun never did his own dirty work.

"Get in," the old man said.

"Look," Dimitri answered, "you can't come here and order me around. I'm not one of your goons."

Braun shot him a menacing gaze. "You're gettin' a little too cocky, Dimitri. Jewel is right, you need to be put in your place."

Dimitri exhaled. It wasn't worth the hassle. He climbed in beside Braun, slammed the door, then said, "Take your best shot, Joseph." He leaned back against the seat and casually brushed a bit of lint off his jacket. "You don't intimidate me, you never have. Well, maybe when I was a kid. When you first took me on, you were my idol, my mentor, my father—all rolled up in one. No matter what's gone on between us since, I'll never forget you sitting in that bar downtown. Back in those days you were a real leader. Every answer or solution had thought and feeling behind it. But those scumbags you began to associate with made you change. Once that happened, I saw you differently. You're weak, Braun. So weak it's going to be a piece of cake bringing you down."

Braun glared at him. "Jewel called me yesterday. She was very upset. You've been slapping her around, she said. What's the matter, that Slocum dame wasn't enough?"

Dimitri's laugh was mirthless. "I grabbed your daughter's arm. Nothing more. Besides, it's none of your business." He wouldn't dignify Braun's crack about Janice Slocum with an answer.

"You can't lie worth a damn," Braun said.

Dimitri almost imagined he could see into the other man's soul. Braun's slightly graying hair was the same thin fringe it had been when Dimitri had first met him. His dark brown eyes didn't wrinkle much more at the corners than they had then. His body had become thick and flabby, but not to the point of looking fat. The passage of time didn't seem to have been that harsh on him. In a certain light he still looked as he had the first time Dimitri had sat with him in Big Tommy's bar all those years ago, while Braun counted hundred-dollar bills. Just a sprinkle of age marred his appearance. But inside, where his spirit resided, Dimitri knew Braun was washed up.

Years ago Dimitri had defended Joseph against a number of men who doubted his ability as a leader or dared to cross him. At one time they were two peas in a pod. Each understood where the other had been and what they'd both seen. They were products of the streets, doing what they had to do to survive. But over the years Dimitri began to see that Braun was a man without integrity.

Dimitri repeated, "Like I said, Jewel and I are none of your business."

Braun patted him on the shoulder, hard. Their eyes locked like two bulls going for the other's horns. Braun had once been the most feared man in the city. No one went up against him or dared question his judgment. But Dimitri had never known fear. It wasn't part of his emotional makeup. That was why Braun had grown to respect him so much. Perhaps that explained why they sat side by side now, adversaries rather than allies.

Braun broke into his reverie. "When it concerns my daughter, it concerns me."

Dimitri nodded. "I'm sure it does," he said, thinking about how they had both betrayed him.

"So what about what Jewel said?"

Jewel's claims didn't surprise him. It wasn't beneath her to make up some story to attract her father's sympathy and engage his dark side.

"Your daughter is a liar and a manipulator who's got you wrapped around her little finger," he said heatedly. For a moment he thought about telling Braun that he knew everything. He would love to see the look on the old man's face as he rattled off the chain of lies Jewel and her father had tried to snare him with. He wanted to ask him why they had gone to such lengths to break him yet at the same time had tipped off his attorney. What was the angle there? But that would be like the hunter warning the stag before he shot him: it didn't make for an exciting hunt. The Brauns were probably only part of the picture, and it was possible that father and daughter were working behind each other's backs as well. It would be delicious to watch them foul each other up. No, Dimitri would wait, and when the perfect time came, he would handle both of them.

Dimitri slipped out of the limousine, leaned on the door, and said, "Oh and, Joseph—about poor little Jewel's bruises. Why don't you ask her boyfriend? Maybe they had a fight."

Braun shot him a puzzled look. Obviously Jewel's father didn't know everything about his daughter.

Braun pulled the door shut, lowered the window a few inches, and said, "I want you to stay away from Jewel."

Dimitri shrugged. "No problem. In fact, I've asked her for a divorce."

Startled, Braun started to say something, but Dimitri had already walked away, his lips curled in a cynical smile. He was eliminating both Brauns from his future—on his timetable, instead of theirs.

Billy sifted through the scrapbook—magazine photos, newspaper interviews, his cherished collection of Rose Miller memorabilia. He came across a photo of Rose on the cover of *Redbook.* She was wearing a red knit sweater. It was an article about her life at home with Evan and Alexis—the "civilian" rather than the celebrity. *Lies,* he thought, *all of it lies.* Maybe Rose had never been the woman he thought she was. And this caused him pain.

But nothing could compare with the pain awaiting her. She would suffer as none of the others had. She deserved it. He would even force her to pretend she loved the torture he planned. They would enjoy her pain together . . . right up to the end.

Dimitri's four business attorneys sat through the emergency meeting, absorbing his every word.

"I want this divorce to look amicable in the press. I can't afford any more negative publicity. The important thing is to cut Jewel out of my life—today, so she has no access to any corporate information."

"And if she doesn't accept?" Lawrence, the senior partner, spoke first.

"Make her accept. Do whatever you have to. I want a clean break. I can't let this turn messy. Offer her the sun, moon, and stars. If she refuses, tell her you have pictures, recordings of her and her lover. Bluff it! If you have to, get some pictures, but get it done now."

He moved in closer to the table. "I'm really getting fed up with all this negativity and skepticism around me. I pay you gentlemen a handsome sum to keep me free of litigation."

The four men gathered up their belongings and, like soldiers, filed out of the room in lockstep.

Dimitri buzzed his secretary. "Get Evan Miller on the line. Tell him to meet me in my suite for dinner. Tell him it's urgent."

He sat in silence, thinking about last night with Rose. He had wanted to seduce her, to hear her beg for him and, at the same time, to hurt Evan and take another step toward satisfying his need for revenge. But it had backfired. He had fallen in love with her all over again. He'd slipped, and it had been gnawing at his gut all morning. When would he stop being vulnerable to her? How could he be so weak? It seemed the longer he was here in New York, near her, the more susceptible he became to forgiving her as well as to loving her more profoundly than ever. He made up his mind. From this moment forward, he was keeping his eye on the plan. Vengeance was important: it allowed a man to move on.

Dario sat at his desk and read the late edition of the *Post.* He stared at the headline and licked his lips. CONSTANTINOS QUESTIONED IN MURDER OF SHOWGIRL. Dimitri Constantinos was finished, which pleased Dario beyond his wildest fantasies. Between the racketeering trial and the suspicion of murder, Constantinos was going to be buried alive. *Kiss your ass good-bye,* Dario thought. *And while you're at it, kiss Rose bye-bye, too.* Now Rose would have to believe Constantinos was a monster. Dario sat back in his chair and rubbed his hands together. With Dimitri and Evan out of the picture, there would be no more obstacles in his way. Now he could turn his attention to getting Rose back to New York—if he could only find her.

48

From the living room window of the chalet, Rose had a picturesque view of the skiers swishing down the mountain. It was nearly seven o'clock, and evening was turning swiftly to night, except for the floodlights lining the trails. She loved night skiing. Evan had surprised her last Christmas with a trip to St. Moritz. They skied miles of downhill runs and taken long, romantic sleigh rides around the sparkling lake in the Engadine Valley, six thousand feet up the southern slope of the Alps.

Stowe brought back so many of those wonderful memories. As she sat and watched all the activity outside, she had to remind herself she wasn't Rose Miller, and her kind and loving husband and adorable daughter weren't waiting for her to join them on the slopes. That life no longer existed. To the dozens of tourists she met on her way from the main lodge to the chalet, she was Linda Morgan, an attractive brunette in her early thirties, on vacation alone.

I didn't have a choice, she reminded herself—hourly, it seemed—and wondered how she would sleep tonight. She thought about her new identity. It reminded her of Vicki Morgan, the pampered mistress of Alfred Bloomingdale, found murdered in her apartment. An ironic choice of name, Rose thought. Rose Miller, for the moment, was also dead.

Falcone had walked her through the steps. "Until this is over," he had told her, "everything you once were is gone. Forget all about Rose Miller. It's going to be tough, pretending you're someone else. But you'll get used to it. The key word is 'security.' You can mingle with the tourists, even make a few acquaintances, but never forget to wear your wig and glasses. And never forget your name is Linda Morgan."

Rose moved away from the window and eased her tired body onto the sofa. The partial manuscript of *Murderous Intentions* was arranged on the floor in stacks beside her. Her body longed for sleep as she lay embraced by the soft chenille cushions, but her mind fought the urge. There was work to be done, scenes that needed to be analyzed.

She picked up one of the piles, chapters 22 through 25, and sifted through each page. The deeper she tried to get into her work, the more she was soothed by the comfort of the sofa. Who was she kidding? She couldn't get any work done. Her mind was filled with what-ifs and what-fors. She couldn't focus, and under all the pressure, it was a wonder she was able to function at all.

It had been only two hours since Falcone said good-bye, and already she missed all he represented of familiarity, of home. And she missed the easy conversation that took place between friends. He'd promised he'd call as soon as he landed, but the call hadn't come. He was her only link, and without that contact she felt anxious, off kilter. She thought about donning her wig and glasses and taking a walk down to the main lodge, but she had so much work to do and was so tired already. Maybe she'd put off work until tomorrow.

Rose leaned her head back against the cushion and tried again to look over the manuscript, but finally she gave up, resting the pile on her stomach. She closed her eyes, and Alexis was there. Whom would her daughter tell her troubles to? The latest news about the boy in her class she thought was "cute" or the "neat" new shoes one of her friends just bought. Alexis was at the age where girl talk was not just the most enjoyable part of the mother/daughter relationship, but a necessity. Though Rose had promised to call as often as possible, it wouldn't be the same.

For all his wonderful qualities as a father, Evan was not a man who could understand the coiled-up emotions of a girl Alexis's age. She could picture her daughter in a thousand different places and situations: curled in the corner of her bed, reading her latest favorite book, *Are You There, God? It's Me, Margaret;* Alexis at seven in her white lace dress, ready to receive her first holy communion; Alexis at nine, opening the birthday gift Rose and Evan had spent so much time picking out—a one-of-a-kind Madame Alexander Doll. And there were the most recent memories of her daughter preening, attempting the mysteries of makeup, insisting that she be allowed to get a tattoo, "just a little rose, over here," she had implored, pointing to her ankle—how ironic, a rose. These thoughts of her daughter cascaded before her, and she rode them into a deep, dreamless sleep.

The driver headed east on the Long Island Expressway, and forty minutes later Dimitri reached an enormous estate, tucked neatly behind acres of manicured lawns. They drove through a tall wrought-iron gate, cruised down a long driveway, and stopped before a Tudor-style mansion set back against woods filled with trees stripped now of leaves. The chauffeur opened the door and Dimitri stepped out. Evan was waiting at the front entrance, but Dimitri took his time getting there. The mansion looked superficially different from Laurel, but the aura of prestige and privilege was the same. He was momentarily swept back to feelings of abandonment, loneliness, and the shame that came with being James's bastard son.

When he got close enough to see Evan, his instincts about his brother were confirmed. When Dimitri got the message from his secretary that Evan was a bit under the weather and couldn't meet him at the Plaza, Dimitri knew his lawyer was ducking him. Then Mohammad will go to the mountain, he had decided. Now he walked away from the car, pushing aside his annoyance.

Evan's shock at seeing Dimitri, who had not called ahead, was evident, though he covered it well. Dimitri knew then that Evan was more reluctant than ever to be involved with him. The racketeering business was bad enough. They had even defended the occasional murder suspect, like the toy czar, but those were extenuating circumstances. Miller, Miller, & Finch didn't handle serial killers.

The two men shook hands perfunctorily, and Evan led him through an enormous foyer, an unending strip of creamy Italian marble. When they reached the third door on the right, he gestured for Dimitri to enter first.

The fire was going strong in the library's enormous brick fireplace. The shelves lining the walls were filled with leather-bound books embossed in gold. A huge painting of Evan, Rose, and their little girl hung above the mantel.

"She's beautiful," Dimitri said, gesturing to Alexis's likeness in the portrait.

Evan didn't respond. "Please sit." He took a seat on one of the leather sofas and pointed to a seat opposite him.

The prince of the manor, Dimitri thought. He looks comfortable, so at ease in this magnificent castle. Born to it, bred to it, making it all seem so natural. A man in his own element. Then he wondered, *If all of this hadn't been handed to him on a silver platter, would he have acquired it on his own?* He knew the answer was no. Men like Evan needed a hand to feed them, nurture them, rock them back and forth when things got a little rough. In a way, he was glad James had thrown him to the wolves, sent him scurrying in the streets for a place to call home. The hidden terrors and unpredictable lifestyle had forced him to grow up at a very early age. From the time he was sixteen he knew what he wanted to do, who he wanted to be. Every time the pendulum swung away from him, he repeated the words he'd sworn to live by: *"Stay focused. You're a survivor. You'll make it."* That philosophy, coupled with his strong desire to prove himself to James and perhaps rub his father's nose in his success, was, like his anger at Rose, one of the things that drove him.

"I understand you're not feeling well. But this really couldn't wait."

Evan smiled, always the politician. "It's okay. I'm afraid I've come down with some sort of bug this morning, and I can't seem to shake my upset stomach."

Dimitri studied him. He did look rather pale, and when they'd greeted each other, his hand had been cold and clammy. Dimitri suspected, however, that Evan was suffering from a case of rattled nerves.

"I needed to talk to you about the police's suspicions. Two of them questioned me for a couple of hours. What do you think of this Slocum thing?"

Evan crossed his arms over his chest. "Dimitri, if you wanted my advice, why didn't you insist on my being there?"

The brothers stared each other down. *I was humiliated,* Dimitri thought. *I couldn't let you see me that way.*

Out loud he said, "I thought it was no big deal. I know I'm innocent. But once the DA's damn continuance is over, I'm thrown back in that courtroom again. How badly will it affect my ongoing trial?"

"I can tell you, it won't look good. Whatever sympathy vote you might have gotten is certainly going to go up in smoke now that you're a suspected serial killer. They will no longer view you as the modern-day Robin Hood. Tell me about the interrogation."

Dimitri tried to get his thoughts straight, but for some reason, being questioned for Janice's murder had gotten to him. "They asked where I was that night, how well I knew her. I suppose it was routine."

Dimitri's eyes told Evan that his brother was frightened and hurting. *Good. Now he was hurting, too.*

"So, how well did you know Janice Slocum?"

Dimitri thought of his night with Janice in his suite—how he had called out Rose's name and then how empty he'd felt.

"Dimitri? You can't lie to your attorney." Evan was all lawyer now, and Dimitri respected that.

"I slept with her—once, maybe twice. Actually, the second time wasn't really my idea. She was . . . clingy. But you don't think a man would murder a woman because she clings, do you?"

Silence. The Seth Thomas grandfather clock chimed ten times.

"Men kill women for lots of reasons," Evan replied.

"In other words, I'm tainted," Dimitri said. "No juror could ever stay totally away from this news. I'll be seen as guilty of murder before the other trial concludes, and then when they convict me I'll sit in prison and wait for a murder trial?"

Evan nodded. "That's the sum of it."

"I didn't kill Janice or those other women." In a desperate plea, Dimitri asked, "Do I have a chance here?"

"What I've been told by one of the detectives on the case is that if—"

"John Falcone?" Dimitri interrupted. "I've already spoken to him."

Evan made a mental note to question Falcone about any conversations that had taken place between him and Dimitri. Then he continued, "Your fingerprints are all over the duffel bag they've found. The woman wasn't raped, she had no skin beneath her nails, so there seems to be no way to obtain substance from the killer to test for DNA. Nothing substantial—yet. But you'll need an alibi. Did you leave the party at all?"

Dimitri thought for a second, then answered, "Only for a short time. I was up in my suite at the casino."

"Can anyone attest to that?"

Rose had met him in the suite at least an hour after he left the party. She could be his out, his alibi. But not one person had seen them leave together, and there was an enormous period of time left unaccounted for.

"The police will be investigating this case with intense scrutiny. They'll leave no stone unturned. Right now, you are their prime suspect. They are moving for an indictment."

"I'm innocent. I didn't kill her."

Evan met his gaze and said, "I don't believe you did. There's a lot I think you're capable of doing, but murdering that young woman . . . no. I believe you are innocent."

Dimitri could tell by the sincere look in Evan's eyes that he did believe him.

"But you will need an alibi. An account of every minute you were away from the party. Who . . ."

Evan stopped, then looked away. Dimitri felt a sudden frisson of alarm. Evan knew he was with Rose. He had left the party before Dimitri. He had returned to find them getting out of the helicopter. Everyone had seen them.

In a sudden burst of anxiety, Dimitri changed direction: "This is quite a place. Is . . . ?"

Evan shook his head. He knew what Dimitri was thinking. "No, Father is not here."

Then a voice echoing through the foyer called out, "As a matter of fact, I am."

Dimitri turned his attention to the doorway of the library. James Miller stood there, his face beet red, his eyes full of rage.

"How dare you come here!" he yelled. "How dare you come into my home!"

"Funny," Dimitri said caustically, "I thought this was Evan's home—Evan and Rose's."

"I don't want you under my roof. I thought I made that clear years ago!" James shot back.

Dimitri paused for a moment, scanning his father's face with his eyes, searching for any hint of remorse. Instead all he saw was disgust. The old man didn't have any regrets about alienating him; in fact, Dimitri could tell James still believed he'd made the right choice. A part of him, the wistful boy he was so many years ago, had always clung to some faint hope of acceptance and reunion. But his realistic side convinced him it simply wasn't possible—not now, not ever.

"The best thing you ever did, Pops, was throw me in the gutter," he said, sneering. He turned to Evan and said, "I was just leaving."

He stood, gave Evan a polite nod, then pushed past James.

"Don't ever come back," James yelled as Dimitri grabbed the handle of the front door. "You're not welcome here."

And I don't belong here, Dimitri decided as he slammed the door.

"How could you allow him into our home?" James stared intently at Evan. "Hasn't he done enough to ruin us? He ran off with your wife and made a mockery of you. Do you know what it's going to take to clean up the mess he's made, the mess he and Rose made?"

Evan said nothing. He stared into the roaring fire and thought about the look on Dimitri's face when he confronted James Miller. He felt for him. Despite their differences, they were brothers, linked not by name, but by blood. Few people knew their secret. Now, as he heard his father's cruel words, witnessed the loathing in his eyes, he wondered how James could completely ignore the fact that Dimitri was his son—no matter what the circumstances. A terrifying thought that he'd always repressed crept to the surface. *Rose was right, he truly is a monster.*

49

She was awakened by an unearthly noise. Rose fought to stay asleep, but the ringing forced her to consciousness. Where was she?

She scanned the living room where she'd fallen asleep; the phone kept ringing. Then she spotted it on the desk next to the entertainment center. As she bolted from the sofa, the papers resting on her chest scattered about the floor.

"Damn," she cried out before picking up the receiver. "Hello?"

"Rose?"

"Yes." Her voice was a hoarse mumble.

"You failed the test. Linda, remember? Are you okay?"

She looked at the digital clock on the television. She couldn't believe it was 7:00 A.M. It still felt like the middle of the night. The last thing she remembered was reading pages of her manuscript.

"You're right, I'll have it down the next time you call. Anyway, I'm fine, John. Is everything okay on that end?"

"I got back and checked my service. There were three messages from Dimitri."

Sound stilled; time stopped.

"I called him back a few minutes ago. He wants to see you, Rose. He insists it's urgent. I told him there was no way—"

"Get me a number where I can reach him."

There was a long pause, then: "Rose, I can't let you . . . it's not safe."

"I'll call from an outside line, somewhere in town."

Another long pause. "I can't allow it. What I can do is have Dimitri come to the station at an arranged time. You can call him there, from an outside phone."

That would have to do.

"The key word is 'security,'" Falcone reminded her again. "No contact with anyone until this is over. No letters, cards, or phone calls unless they go through me. I'll be up in a few days. I'll call you in the morning and let you know when."

"What about Dimitri's call?" she asked, trying not to sound too anxious. "Shouldn't we find out what he wants? It could be important."

"I'll arrange it for tomorrow. Go into the village. Find a pay phone and call me at exactly 1:00. I'll arrange for him to be here."

Rose felt relieved. "Thanks, John."

"No problem," he said, though his voice was laden with concern. "Tomorrow, then."

After they hung up Rose walked over to the sofa, crouched down, and gathered up the papers of her manuscript. She had held back her tears while talking to John, but now she felt her eyes fill as she thought about Alexis.

"Mommy's okay," she whispered, as though by assuring herself, she might also send words of comfort to her beloved child.

The realtor walked Dimitri through the old house with brisk efficiency, showing the best features, rushing him past those places that might require work. It was obvious the young woman had shown the place to many a prospective buyer. Odd how little he felt coming here. He had thought he'd be barraged by ghosts and memories. But his mind stayed focused on the present and his plans.

"Who were the previous owners?" he asked.

"A rich family from Iran. They bought it from the Millers, as in James Miller. You are familiar with the name, Mr. Constantinos?"

Dimitri smiled politely and said, "Maybe, I can't be sure."

"The couple had two sons, and once the children went off to college, there was no reason to keep such a big house. I think they bought a condo in Palm Beach."

She stopped at the top of the stairs and said, "Would you like to see the guest bedrooms first or go right to the master suite?"

"Whatever is convenient," he answered, his eyes searching each room. *Did Evan and Rose make love in here? In the den? Perhaps the floor of the sunroom?*

He followed her into one of the larger bedrooms, whose windows overlooked the stable area. This had to have been where Evan and Rose had slept. He knew because of the bitter taste that began in his stomach and rushed to his throat.

The agent went on with her sales pitch. "It certainly has a lot of charm, and with the right touch, I'm sure it can be—"

He turned to her and said, "I'll take it."

Dario used the spare key Rose had given him long ago to get inside her Fifth Avenue apartment. A hint of her perfume struck him immediately. Faint as it was, it brought her back to him in living color.

He went to her writing desk, which was placed flush against the creamy white wall of the living room. The Tiffany-framed black-and-white photo of Rose and Alexis had collected a patina of dust in her absence, and he rubbed his thumb over the images to clean them. The resemblance between the two was most apparent in their smiles. They were dressed in summer clothing, and Dario guessed it had been taken in Tuscany, on a vacation the family had taken earlier in the year. Rose was hugging Alexis. The girl was the most important person in her life, Dario knew—and possibly his only way to find her.

He opened the top drawer of the desk and rummaged through its contents in an effort to find any bit of information telling him where she was. He sifted through some old mail, a daily planner. Nothing.

Dario slammed the drawer shut and went to the bedroom, where he noted only the bed: the very heart of her. It contained secrets, whom she had invited there. He sat on the soft mound of quilted comforters and blankets, running his fingers over her pillows. Her presence seemed most powerful here. He pushed back the comforter and climbed into the bed. His outstretched arms roamed the mattress, reveling in the feel of it, so feminine, so frilly, so Rose.

Images of her struggling to free herself from his grasp chased away his momentary peace of mind. Yet he did not regret what had happened because all that was left for him was that brief taste of her. He had held on to that memory, brought it with him last night to his dreams: it was there this morning when he woke and consumed his thoughts throughout the day.

Dario climbed out of bed and walked over to the chest of drawers. Just a quick look, he thought. He didn't want to stay too long, he couldn't risk being seen leaving the apartment by a neighbor. Just a quick hit of Rose Miller's essence was all he could hope for right now.

He opened the top drawer and thrust his hands into the hill of lingerie. Panties, bras, silk nightgowns, and camisoles slipped through his fingers. Each piece of clothing was sweetened with Rose's scent. He buried his face in the silky fabrics. He had memories of Rose that went back over years. He was besieged by them now. Held hostage, his heart suddenly raged.

Wherever you are, Rose, I'll find you.

Kevin Allen maneuvered his way past the crowded bar at Rao's to the corner booth in the back. Joseph Braun was talking with a middle-aged man wearing a distinctive vest.

"Hey, get a good look at his vest, Kevin," Braun said, so loud that half the patrons in the restaurant turned to look. Kevin wondered briefly how familiar the restaurant was. How many of the patrons here recognized Braun? Would he read about this dinner in tomorrow's paper? "It's hand painted," Braun continued. "He collects the vests. No one knows where he gets them. That's why he's nicknamed 'Nicky Vests.'"

Braun and Nicky shared a laugh. Then Nicky Vests rose and said, "Enjoy your drink, Joseph, it's on me."

When he disappeared, Kevin slid into the booth across from him. "I don't think it's such a good idea that we meet in public, Mr. Braun."

Braun puffed heavily on his Cohiba, swigged back half of his Dewar's, straight up, then said, "What's this 'Mr. Braun' shit? When did we become so formal?"

"We got formal when you traded me information on Constantinos in exchange for immunity. I don't like friendly business relationships."

"Oh, stop, Kevin. Just relax. You can't lose this trial."

Kevin instinctively looked around him to make sure no one had overheard.

"Stop watching your tail, kid. I've got lots of guys like you around me—in my pocket, up my ass. I'm not like the scum element you associate me with."

His revelation didn't shock Kevin. Corruption was everywhere, in the streets, in the courtroom, even in the White House. He wanted to say, *"Spare me the histrionics. I know all about your dirty money and dirty businesses. I know that all the rumors about you are accurate, and one day, you piece of shit, I'm going to put your ass in jail. After I win this trial and then the governorship. Fuck immunity."* Instead he said nothing. He only sat and listened. At the moment, he needed Braun a hell of a lot more than Braun needed him. The man was his main source of information. Braun and his bimbo daughter. Together, father and daughter held the key to the box of secrets that would bring down first Constantinos, then Evan, and finally James. Right now the Millers had goods on Kevin that went back to that cover-up twelve years ago. Which was why it was essential he get all the goods he needed to keep them at bay.

Kevin Allen knew there was something at the very heart of that long-ago cover-up, and once he found it, the balance of power would shift enough for him to push Evan out of the primary and maybe even enough to force the Miller men, with all their money, to back him. So he'd be real quiet now until he had all his ducks in a row. And then all those naysayers and doubting Thomases could go to hell.

Nicky Vests returned with another round of drinks as Sinatra began to sing from the antique jukebox against the wall. As if on cue, one of the restaurant's owners, Frank Pellegrino, sang along to "My Way."

This seemed to please Braun, even more so when Pellegrino approached their table and sat down next to him and the two sang together.

As if neither one had a care in the world, Kevin thought, as he smiled inside.

50

By early the next morning, the face lift on the Laurel estate was already under way. Landscapers manicured the neglected area immediately surrounding the house; wallpaper hangers and painters tripped over electricians. Dimitri, a man possessed with one mission, had put aside all thoughts except those that expedited his plan. The continuance was at the end of its first week. Today's front page of *The New York Times* "Metro" section had his photo with an inset of Janice Slocum. The caption read *"Robin Hood? Tax evader? Extortionist? or serial killer? It's anyone's guess right now."* Dimitri hadn't bothered to read the article, nor did he call Evan to see what information they might have gained on Kevin Allen's surprise witness. Those troubles belonged to another man. Since he'd purchased Laurel, he had only one thought on his mind. Soon all the pieces would be in place.

He had paid for the property and, with the help of his business attorneys, hastened the closing. The sellers weren't about to let a cash deal slip through their hands.

The enormous construction crew made it possible to proceed rapidly. By late morning the new Andersen windows were in place, the interior floors were carpeted, and the walls were given a fresh coat of paint. The truckload of furniture ordered from an exclusive interior decorator was arriving today.

Susan Fields had worked as the director of the Saks Fifth Avenue Personal Shoppers Club for ten years. Her client list boasted dozens of New York society women, many of whom were often traveling when the new fashions came in and wanted the collections shipped to wherever they were; actresses from Los Angeles who did not want always to wear the same designer's clothing; debutantes who were clueless about what to wear after their coming out ceremony; executives, particularly in the more conservative fields such as banking, who didn't want to dress in suits like men. Susan was a tall woman with short dark hair, intense blue eyes, and a lanky body any shopper would envy. Today she had only one thing on her mind.

Dimitri Constantinos had called her the night before and requested she put together a wardrobe for a "friend." He was very specific about what he wanted: Black evening gowns by Ungaro, Armani, and Valentino; afternoon business suits from Yves Saint Laurent, Oscar De La Renta, and Richard Tyler; and cocktail dresses by Victor Costa, Vera Wang, and Versace. Six gowns, five suits, and ten dresses and accessories for all.

She sailed through the aisles of the store. The designer shoes salon on four. Two pairs of Manolo Blahnik evening pumps, three pairs of Ferragamo slingbacks, two pairs of Anne Klein leather boots, and four pairs of assorted Gucci pumps.

"Send all of this up to Salon B. Tell Gloria I need it all packed and ready to go immediately," she instructed a young salesgirl, who obeyed diligently.

In the fur salon she pulled two sable coats, one a brown Revillion and the other a black Louis-Feraude. To another salesperson she said, "Take these up to the Club, Salon B. Have them wrapped immediately."

Last was a visit to the eighth floor for lingerie. Susan picked out three black Valentino nightgowns with matching robes, two La Perla chemises with matching bed jackets, six pairs of silk pajamas, and three pairs of Natori velvet slippers.

When she returned to the Club, all of the packages were beautifully wrapped in gold foil paper with large white ribbon tied into bows.

Not bad for two hours, she thought, proud of her expertise. When everything was ready to go, she called the number Dimitri Constantinos had given her earlier and said, "Everything's ready, sir."

"Here's the address I want everything delivered to today," he said abruptly.

Mick Jones thoughtfully stroked the clipped silk of Romeo's neck, then led the black Arabian horse over to the waiting trailers. Mick was the number one horse breeder on Long Island. His Timber Bay Stables was the most exclusive place to board or purchase a horse. Its "Members Only Club" boasted some of the North Shore's finest equestrians, confident that their priceless animals received only the best care. Marty, a young though experienced groom, followed behind Mick, leading Juliet, a chestnut mare with a feisty temper. As the horses approached the trailers, Juliet pulled back.

"Come on, Juliet," Marty growled. The young woman tugged on the horse's lead line. "You were sold for a fabulous price, there's nothing I can do."

Mick turned and offered an apologetic smile. Marty had grown quite fond of Juliet; in fact, the young woman had ridden her every day for the past six months. He realized how hard saying good-bye was. Romeo and Juliet were the most valuable horses among the dozens in his stable.

Juliet flared her nostrils, refusing to enter the trailer. Marty dug into her pocket and produced a cube of sugar, dangling it in front of her, coaxing her up the ramp and into the trailer. Then the groom held out the cube toward the horse and, wiping away her tears, turned to Mick and said, "Why did he have to choose Juliet?"

Mick just sighed and said, "What Mr. Constantinos wants, Mr. Constantinos gets. You'll get over it, Marty."

As the trailer pulled away, Mick thought about his conversation with Dimitri Constantinos that morning. The fact was, he hadn't wanted to part with these particular horses, either, but the man had been adamant that it had to be a black Arabian and a mare, a chestnut Thoroughbred, and no other horse Mick offered at any price would do. Mick wondered why.

No boutique for adolescent girls had taken over where Ferucci left off in the late 1980s. But Christine Mullen was the next best thing—a personal shopper with a knack for satisfying the slick taste of rich Manhattan kids. The instructions had been clear. It wasn't only "cool" clothes Mr. Constantinos wanted. He needed also a complete bedroom set suitable for an eleven-year-old and an entertainment center with the latest in

CD-ROM technology and a mammoth digital television that could accommodate, via Web-TV, a full-range, high-end computer setup. It was a Bill Gates fantasy, and she had forty-eight hours to have it all shipped and installed. There was no way in hell she was going to screw up any detail, no matter how trivial.

51

The two-hundred-year-old village of Stowe offered shopping, art galleries, a small museum, romantic bistros, and many outdoor activities and events. Tourists crowded Main Street, geared up in warm winter wear, their faces barely visible beneath heavy scarves. As Rose killed time before making her phone call, she walked around town. On one side of main street sat the imposing community church, on the other were Shaw's Store, Val's Market, Clark Newton's house, the home of the late Mrs. Gale Shaw, and the Carriage House Shops and Apartments. All of these structures sat on land formerly occupied by the Mt. Mansfield Hotel, known as the "Big Hotel." Now only the hotel's huge stable remained. For many years the barn had been used by the officers of a logging group. In 1953 the structure was demolished and the quaint shops erected in its place.

Rose still had a half hour before she was to call John's office.

Inside Shaw's general store the scent of vanilla filled the air. Rose browsed through the aisles of paraphernalia appropriate to a small-town general store: groceries, hardware necessities, simple items of clothing, handmade soaps, rich herbal oils, local crafts, and neatly packaged gift baskets. She chose a hand-blown glass horse and small, sterling-silver earrings. *Alexis will love these,* she decided. She paid for the gifts, had them wrapped in a pretty pink-and-white paper, then stuffed the card under the ribbon:

My Dear Alexis,
With love and kisses,
Mommy

Before leaving the store, she asked the elderly woman behind the register, "Where is the nearest pay phone?"

The woman looked up over wire-rimmed glasses and said, "The Green Mountain Inn. It's about fifty feet down the street."

"Thanks," Rose said.

Outside, light snow blanketed the sides of the road. Rose clutched the presents securely against her chest. Their touch soothed her; they were a connection to Alexis. There was an empty hole, a sullen sense of loneliness in her heart, and nothing she did could ease the pain.

On her way to the phone, Rose passed a bistro where she noticed the young couple from the slopes huddled in the doorway, embracing, wrapped up in each other as though they were the only two people in the world. In a sense, Rose realized, they were. As she remembered those feelings, pangs of loss stabbed at her. The mere thought of being so consumed by another individual brought her back to Dimitri. Her hand was shaking as she rang John's number. Three rings, then she heard his voice. He answered with a simple "Hello" as opposed to his usual "Detective Falcone."

She gripped the receiver. "Is he there?"

A small pause, then, "Yes, Rose. Hold on."

He sounded unsettled, and she didn't blame him. She was making him choose between his empathy and his profession. But no amount of evidence would convince her that Dimitri was a murderer. She loved him, needed to renew their connection. Perhaps some would see it as desperation, clinging to the past, or a need to hold on to someone as she and Evan parted.

"Rose, are you there?"

It took her a moment to catch her breath, then she said, "I'm here, Dimitri."

"We need to talk."

His tone was urgent, and Rose panicked. "What's wrong?"

She heard a vacuum between them, then realized he'd put his hand over the receiver—to ask for privacy. She heard a door close and assumed Falcone had left the room. "I need to see you, Rose, it's an emergency."

"Security" is the key word. John's voice resounded through her system, while a separate, primal force pulled her in a different direction. Dimitri must have sensed her ambivalence.

"Please—I've never asked you for anything. Just this once could mean everything: my life, my freedom. Detective Falcone can take me to you. You have no reason to fear me."

Rose did believe him, but she couldn't let John down. And what if she were wrong about Dimitri, blinded by her feelings, and this was a ploy? But would he volunteer to bring John if he meant her any harm? He might, if he knew she wouldn't ask that of him. Her mind whirled in confusion. "I . . . I don't know, Dimitri. It could be risky—"

"Rose," he interrupted, "not you, too. You can't believe I'm the monster the papers say I am."

His sense of her betrayal did not escape her. She couldn't do that to him again. "I'm at the Von Trapp Lodge in Stowe, Vermont. I'm staying in a chalet registered under Linda Morgan."

"I'll be there in a day or two." Dimitri's voice was calmer now, and she could picture his mouth relaxing from a frown into the half smile she knew so well. "I think it's better if we don't arrange a specific day or time."

"I . . . I understand," she said tentatively, and then broke the connection. She stayed at the phone booth, thinking, *What did he mean by not arranging a specific date and time? Was it a threat?*

Still, she refused to fill her head with more suspicions. She owed Dimitri, plain and simple. *How mad would John be? Did it matter?* It was her life and, right or wrong, she had to live out this scene with Dimitri.

52

The snowfall was turning heavy. The windshield of the Navigator was covered with snow. Rose put on the defroster and the wipers, then watched as they swung back and forth, making a swishing sound, almost mesmerizing her.

She turned right off Main Street, made her way back to Route 100, and headed up to the lodge from town, all the while holding Alexis's beautifully wrapped presents in her lap. An old memory suddenly came back to her. When she was a little girl, her father had made her a doll carriage. He'd constructed it meticulously, with corners fastened together without nails and her initials engraved on the sides. Her mother filled it with three handmade dolls she had purchased at a church rummage sale. Every piece of the carriage was perfect, each doll special and beautiful. After her uncle Tom came, everything was different. He got rid of the dolls and the carriage. Though Rose had blocked out the details, she suspected he had sold them all.

Rose pulled into a parking space in front of the main lodge. She didn't want to go back to her chalet yet. She hated how quiet it was there.

The lobby was bustling with activity. Dozens of strangers smiled at her as she made her way to the front desk. She was greeted by a pleasant young man with a perfect smile and wavy black hair. "Oh, Ms. Morgan, you have several messages." He returned with three slips of paper, all of which read, "Call me. I want details on your conversation. Urgent. Falcone."

She bit her lip, feeling terrible for holding out on him. But her heart was leading her without trepidation.

She turned back to the clerk at the desk. "Can you please tell me where the Austrian Tea Room is?"

The young man nodded. "Of course, Ms. Morgan. It's just down the corridor on the left-hand side." He pointed to the east end of the lodge and said, "Follow the roaring fire."

Rose chose a small table with two oversize club chairs in the back. She got comfortable as she prepared to read the partial manuscript of *Murderous Intentions* that she'd had copied in town. She ordered a cup of English breakfast tea.

"Would you like a scone?" asked the waitress.

"No," Rose said. "I'm fine, thank you."

When the young woman disappeared, Rose dug her hands into the manuscript box and pulled out the papers, separating them into part I and part II. She stared down at the last words of the last sentence: *"Not too far from the apartment window, sitting on an old rickety park bench, he sat watching, and waiting. . . ."*

She had written this material right before she'd met Marilyn at Bergdorf's. She'd been excited by the pages, happy to fit them into a busy morning's schedule. It had been the last time she'd written a word. Each time she sat down to write she wondered who might be watching, who might get his hands on her pages and use them to find ways to kill people. If she didn't write soon, the ulcers she always suffered when she kept her words and feelings bottled up would erupt. How could she write? How could she not? The spot inside that needed to be nourished screamed, *Not now! Not until he's caught,* if *he's caught.*

Rose combed through the pages of the last chapter she'd written searching for anything: a clue, a sign. The last piece she had written involved the stalker burning the victim alive in a secluded cabin. *Scene One: The Stalker:* He takes his victim, an aspiring actress, to a romantic cabin tucked away in the woods, where he wines and dines her.

Scene Two: The Seduction: He makes romantic overtures, strokes her hair and her face lovingly, then lures her into the bedroom.

Scene Three: The Terror: He pours her a glass of her favorite red wine, which he's laced with Valium; strokes her, tells her stories about their made-up past. Just before she passes out he sets the wooden structure on fire. The heroine, only partly conscious and half-dressed, finds she's tied to a wooden beam. Smoke fills her eyes, nose, lungs. She coughs. Her chest aches, an excruciating pain, and she knows at the last second that he has murdered her, though she doesn't know why.

Rose shuddered. Yes, she wrote it, but for the intention of entertaining those readers who liked to be a little scared. She'd never dreamed what a psychopath might do with this information.

She reached inside her purse and pulled out a five-dollar bill, then tucked it neatly under the saucer. She checked her watch—four o'clock. Still too early to go back to the chalet. She gathered up the manuscript pages and placed them neatly in the box. She pulled a pad and pencil from her briefcase and wrote:

Darling Alexis:
I miss you more than you can imagine.
I love you. I hope you enjoy the gifts.
XOXO
Mom

She wished that she could spill her love across the pages. What else could she write? Certainly not about the mounds of fresh, untouched snow—a giveaway that she was somewhere cold. She couldn't mention the cozy, quaint town. That was the kind of information John had warned her about. *Keep it brief, stick to the basics.* The short note would do for now.

Rose folded the letter and put it in an envelope. She'd send it to John, and he would forward it. Even though the letter would be delivered to Alexis secondhand, the knowledge that it would touch her daughter relieved a little bit of the ache in her heart and gave her a tenuous link to home.

A busboy came up behind her, clanging together some cups and saucers, and she jolted forward with such force, she nearly knocked over the table.

Stop it! she admonished herself as she gathered her things and stuffed them back inside her briefcase. Hoping the gusty winds and falling snow would be cleansing and change her mood, she donned her lavender down parka and entered winter's late afternoon air.

53

Dimitri headed down a gloomy passageway lined with ancient walnut bookcases. Along one side ran endless rows of leather-bound copies of New York statutes dating back to the eighteenth century. Along the other side were paper-bound volumes from more recent years.

He greeted Karen, Corbin Tyre's secretary, who had been with the firm for as long as Dimitri had been a client. Tyre was the best corporate attorney in the country and no doubt the most dedicated, working even on Sundays. He was also the most expensive, but when it came to securing his assets, trusting someone to oversee an empire and keep it free from litigation, Dimitri spared no expense.

Dimitri had given Tyre a glimpse into his philosophy at their first meeting. "If the IRS wants three million, give them four," Dimitri had said. "Tell them to hang on to it just in case. I don't want any room for error. There will never be any reason for them to come knocking on my door demanding to see my books." Had he ever been wrong! This bogus case certainly had taught him that.

Tyre met him at the door. A man in his early fifties with a full head of gray hair, brown eyes, and a slight build, he certainly didn't look intimidating, but anyone who went up against him in litigation learned the hard way how ruthless he could be. His claim to fame was a case he'd won against the Internal Revenue Service. Claiming his income had been underreported and his accounts "suspicious," the IRS tried to attack the property, including book royalties, of a well-known author/businessman. Tyre had taken the position that his client was being harassed by the IRS, which had used illegal search and seizure to gain their evidence. A few years later the entire IRS was scrutinized and, because of the investigation kicked off by Tyre's case, forced to undergo a series of revisions.

The two men exchanged handshakes, and Tyre ushered Dimitri into his office.

"Make yourself comfortable," Tyre said.

Dimitri claimed one of the chairs in front of Tyre's desk. "You look well, Corbin. Working hard, I hope?"

Tyre's soft, rolling chuckle echoed briefly in the air. "Your troubles alone are enough to keep me busy and wealthy."

Dimitri assumed the lawyer was referring to his divorce from Jewel, which Tyre had begun by splitting their net worth. "I need to liquidate some of my assets and change my corporation's structure."

"Why, is the trial going badly?"

Dimitri raised his eyebrows. He knew that Tyre would not refer to his problems concerning the Slocum murder, even though they both knew the impact this had on the racketeering trial. Tyre would never be that unsubtle.

"I don't know, but I want to be careful." Dimitri reached inside his briefcase, pulled out a file, and sifted through the papers. "Here's what I want done." He handed one of the papers to Tyre.

As his eyes roamed the sheet, Dimitri said, "We've gotten everything out of Jewel's name. Now I want my corporation liquidated and dissolved and a new one formed."

"What's this about, Dimitri?" It was apparent Tyre was asking as a friend.

"I believe Jewel has become the prosecution's star witness. Her father has got something going on with the prosecutor—I know that from my attorney. But there's something else. Someone else close to me is trying to use corporate information to incriminate me. Move all of my assets, change the officers, do what you do best. I want a fresh start."

"The corporate stuff is no problem. Now, we've started the divorce, but we're having a problem with your wife. . . ."

"I'll handle my wife," Dimitri replied sharply.

Evan's eyes roamed the grand salon of the mansion. The room was nearly bare except for a few antiques, one or two paintings, and a large Steuben chandelier hanging from the ceiling in the center of the room. There was a heavy draft coming from an open flue in the fireplace, dispatching a chill throughout the room.

Until a few weeks ago—in fact, until Dimitri turned up—this room held nothing but sweet memories. All of Rose and Evan's most important celebrations had taken place here, since they had moved from Laurel: Alexis's christening party, the celebration of Evan's first big legal victory, James's sixtieth birthday—and twelve years of Christmas, birthdays, and, most important, anniversaries. Evan fingered a crystal heart ornament kept on the mantelpiece as a memento of their tenth anniversary—could it have been only two years ago? Rose had surprised him with a special dinner, their own private celebration. It was early February and already she was ready for Valentine's Day. She loved decorating the house. Each holiday she bedecked the grand salon with fresh flowers and special ornaments and her favorite music boxes. On that night, long-stemmed red roses surrounded by bunches of baby's breath were scattered about the room, a traditional romantic theme. There were flower centerpieces low enough so the guests—in this case just the two of them—could see each other, red and white burning candles, and an exquisitely set table arranged with fine china, silver, crystal, and linen. A ten-foot fresh topiary decorated with Victorian ornaments and framed photos of family and friends stood in the center of the dance floor. The finishing touch was the crystal hearts from Tiffany's that dangled from the ceiling.

One hundred and twenty hearts. *One for each month we've been together.*

So tonight, with the delicate piece of crystal reminding him of that happy time, Evan stood in the center of the stately, gaping room on the eve of their twelfth anniversary, and he relived that night. The music played by the string quartet echoed melodiously through his mind. And the image of Rose, dressed elegantly in a beautiful red ball gown, the sweet smell of her perfume—this, too, lingered . . . a haunting memory.

Though everything in the room looked as it had that night, the most important element was missing—Rose.

Jewel Constantinos writhed beneath James Miller. For an old man he was an ardent lover, and always he brought her to ecstasy many times during their special rendezvous. She was almost there now, and as his body moved with practiced rhythm she felt the flush begin, starting at her breasts and spreading to her cheekbones.

Suddenly she sat up, pulled the transparent white peignoir over her body, and said, "It's over, James." So there would be no misunderstanding, she added, "I mean us and this. We're through."

He was silent, obviously speechless. The late afternoon sun, bright for February, spilled through the curtained windows in James's suite at the Pierre Hotel. After lunch they had come upstairs for what James referred to as "a little afternoon delight." He'd poured Cristal into Baccarat flutes, and she'd changed out of the perfect little black Helmut Lang dress into the robe James kept for her here. They'd been lovers just long enough for Jewel to get what she wanted.

"James? You did hear me?"

He only nodded. Suddenly she became aware of the more than forty-year difference in their ages. She could see him sag before her eyes, and the titan was suddenly just a naked old man.

"I can't risk Dimitri figuring out the link between us until he's behind bars. Besides, I'm in the midst of a divorce. I need to uphold my reputation. And believe me, I know my husband. It won't take too long for him to piece you, me, and Daddy together. He'll know all three of us screwed him." She paused. When he didn't speak, she needled him. "But you know all about screwing Dimitri, don't you?"

Early in their marriage, Dimitri had alluded to the shabby treatment he'd received at James's hands, though the specifics weren't ever made clear. In the days when she was in love with him, it made her feel sorry for him. Now her only thought was to screw him again.

"What about us?"

James stayed on the soft velvet couch with its angora throw. His vulnerability was annoying to her. He sat there exposed, not bothering to cover himself. Perhaps he was too stunned to think about it. *Serves him right. Men think they're the only ones who can do the dumping.*

Jewel rolled her eyes. "There is no *us.* We all got what we wanted, and now our business is concluded."

"I care for you," James said in a small, sad voice that made Jewel want to hurt him even more.

Wimp, she thought.

"Look, we used each other to get Dimitri. That's it. Over. *Fait accompli!* Kevin Allen has everything he needs to put Dimitri away. It's been perfect. You've got what you need to make your precious Evan look good. And Daddy, your other biggest client, also has everything he needs to cover his ass." She wanted to add that there was also the backup insurance that Evan would throw the trial, but this was a piece of the puzzle that had been kept from James, at least by Jewel and her father. Instinct told her Evan hadn't told his father, either, or James would have mentioned it.

She continued, "You see, James"—she came to him now, put her hand beneath his chin, and forced his eyes up to hers—"we've diddled them all." She tried to coax a smile out of him. "Come on, hot stuff, we were one great team!"

She dressed quickly as she spoke. "I've got photos, tapes, more than enough to not only make me a very wealthy woman, but to ensure that Rose Miller is publicly humiliated as well. You wanted that, too. That's what you said."

It was amazing to her that he was shocked by this. What kind of businessman wouldn't have planned the endgame? "Come, let's get out of here, it's stuffy." She tried to cajole him into getting up, even walking toward the bathroom to turn on the shower.

"Stop right there!" he suddenly shouted.

She turned to face him as he stood, now belting his white terry robe. He was growing angry; she could tell by the flush of his face and his ugly scowl.

"You can't just cut and run when you decide the game is up," he said defiantly. "You toyed with me. Dimitri will figure out the link, and I'm left hanging while you're just the poor scorned divorcée. You won't get away with this."

Picking up her white cashmere coat from where she'd left it on the floor, Jewel smirked and said, "Oh yeah? Sit back and watch me."

James tried to stop her, but she was already out the door.

She won't get away with it, he swore to himself. *No bitch is going to make me look stupid.*

Outside his father's supposedly secret suite, Evan sat in his Lexus and listened to the bugged conversation. This time his father had crossed the line, and this time there would be consequences.

The trial had five more days of hiatus, and Dimitri had plans to fill it. When he arrived at the Plaza to pick up some things, Jewel was waiting for him. He nodded to her, then walked silently into the room he now used as his bedroom. She followed him. Jewel, he noticed, was looking slightly ragged, as though she'd clocked too many miles in her twenty-three years. Viewed dispassionately, she looked mean and hardened.

Dimitri glanced at his Breitling watch and threw his garment bag across the bed.

"Going on a trip?" she asked.

"As a matter of fact, yes. I have some out-of-town business."

"Are you going to meet *Rose?*"

"Why? Are you plotting to set me up for anything else?" He kept his back to her, throwing things into the bag.

"Yes, you're right. I am plotting. And I'm not alone."

Now he turned. "What are you talking about?"

"You think you're going to get away with murder, Dimitri?"

With enormous effort he tuned her out, but she kept talking, her harsh voice polluting the air.

He grabbed some files off the desk and picked up his garment bag, and as he headed for the door he said, "My attorneys assured me that our divorce won't take long. You're out of my life—you and your father. I know everything you've done, every cheap, fraudulent trick you've pulled to get me. But I'll get you first. As for your father, I'm confident he'll do himself in."

"You're missing an important player here, Dimitri," she said, smirking. They were standing at the threshold between the bedroom and the living room of the suite. He noticed her lips were bruised, as though she'd been kissing someone violently. But he didn't care.

"James Miller and I have struck up a . . . well . . . a friendship. He told me about the murder of Rose Miller's uncle. Of course, his story was a lot different from the one you told Daddy."

Obviously she wanted him to know that she and James were lovers.

"And?"

"James is determined to get rid of you. He doesn't care how. At the moment, he's hoping the law will take care of you, even if it means Evan loses the trial. Well, this trial or the next, no matter."

"Why are you telling me this, Jewel?"

"Because I know how cruel you are, and I want you to know that we're all going to get you. And if you think you and Rose Miller are going to end up happily ever after in lovey-dovey land. You don't stand a chance. Don't you think it's time you stopped covering for that low-class servant girl?"

Dimitri dropped his luggage, grabbed Jewel by her shoulders, and shook her. "I could kill you right now with my bare hands." He was seething. He stared at her for a moment, saying nothing. Then he released his grip, retrieved his garment bag and suitcase, and said, "I feel sorry for you, Jewel."

As the door slammed, she let out a huge smile, then reached inside her purse and pressed the off button on the tiny tape recorder.

I could kill you with my bare hands.

She had the last piece of evidence she needed. Now it was time to go shopping for some new shoes.

Dario left the office before nine, later than usual. Nightfall crept like a thief into Manhattan. Above, the sky exploded into a carnival of white confetti. He was walking rapidly, wanting nothing more than to reach the warmth and comfort of his apartment. *My warm, comfortable, lonely apartment.* Well, he'd only have to live with the "lonely" a bit longer. Now, before he could go home, there was business to attend to.

Rose had just picked up and fled, with no explanation and no valid reason. He was left to hold down the fort. Her career was suffering, her popularity lapsing. People were no longer sympathetic to the socialite author who wove tales of betrayal when they perceived her as a betrayer.

She was no longer enigmatic. Her whole life, past and present, was public knowledge. Did she expect him to pick up the pieces? To clean up the mess she created even after she'd fired him?

I need you, Dario, you're one of my dearest friends. Then, *You're fired! Our relationship is over.*

Make up your mind, Rose. Which one is it? Of course, it didn't matter because in the end the result would be the same no matter what she felt.

He hoped the information Malcolm was uncovering on Rose's whereabouts would send him to a warm tropical island in pursuit of her. Malcolm, as it turned out, had great inside information and had been happy to share it with Dario—for the right price, of course. He'd find her, and then he'd make sure Rose understood that it was in her best interests to be very, very good to him.

Leaving his luggage at the front desk, Dimitri ignored the doorman's offer to get him a cab and began walking east, toward Madison Avenue. His private plane was waiting for him at JFK. They should leave soon if he was going to get to Vermont before midnight. He turned into the Carlyle Hotel and sat at the bar. He needed to think. At his request, the bartender brought him a Sam Adams, but he didn't touch it. What should he do? Call Evan. Call his lawyer.

From a pay phone he dialed Evan's private line. "Hello," Evan said.

Dimitri clutched the receiver to his ear, grabbing at his brother's voice. There was no one else left to trust. He told Evan the whole sordid story—Jewel, Joseph, and their father.

"Why did she tell you this?"

Dimitri could tell Evan was dubious. "I have no idea. Jewel doesn't always need a reason for things. Maybe she wanted to provoke me so that she can convince people that I'm a wife beater. I wouldn't put it past her."

Dimitri heard Evan's other line ring. It kept on ringing. No one answered it, and Evan wasn't talking. "So, what do you think?" Dimitri had a sudden image of the two of them as boys, with Rose. How young and stupid they had been. Still, bad as it had been, it had been Eden compared with the rest of his life.

"I need some time. Look, Dimitri, if they're setting you up, the DA has no case. I need a few days to think about this. Where can I reach you?"

"I'm not sure. I'll find you. You'll be at home?"

"Yes. Have you told me everything I need to know?" Evan's voice was still foggy with doubt.

"Evan, I'm telling you the truth."

"That's the problem. I know you are. And it isn't a pretty picture."

Dimitri unconsciously checked his watch. He had one more piece of business to take care of before he could go. "I've got to run. I'll talk to you in a few days."

"Right," Evan said, and they both hung up.

Evan thought about the call for a long time, putting it together with the conversation he'd bugged between Jewel and James. Then he dialed Kevin Allen's number. He knew that at nine P.M. the DA would still be in his office. One thing all lawyers shared—they worked insane hours.

The DA answered his own phone on the first ring. "Kevin Allen."

"Kevin, it's Evan . . . Evan Miller."

"I know which Evan you mean."

Evan couldn't tell if that was lighthearted or not. "I have something to tell you."

The two men met at the Monkey Bar in the Hotel Elysee in midtown. The piano player was into blues, and the crowd seemed mellowed by the music. Cigars were not permitted, but cigarette smoke cast a noxious haze over the dark room.

Without preamble, Evan launched into the story that Dimitri had told him. When he was finished, Kevin had his eyes down, gazing into his beer, but Evan was sure he was listening to every word.

"You have no proof, Miller." *And this is the trial that's going to make my career.*

"I think I do. There's been something bothering me about the material you gave me early on, when you released evidence to us for discovery, and it fits."

"What's that?"

"The numbers on the Las Vegas casino, for one. Dimitri never operated anything at a loss, and he wouldn't pretend to. It's not his style. He's a guy who overpays the IRS just in case."

"He's a crook, Miller, don't lose sight of that."

"Maybe."

Kevin studied Evan with great intent, as though looking for something. "Look, I'm not the most diplomatic guy around, so pardon my being so blunt. He's screwing your wife. Why are you so determined to help him out?"

Evan had no answer except the knowledge that he had always had everything while Dimitri had nothing, and in his heart, it was time to even the score. But he couldn't explain this to the DA. So he said, "Because he's innocent. And because my father tried to destroy him, and he didn't care what it would do to me. That's ugly." Evan paused. "Are your parents alive?"

Kevin shook his head no.

"Were you close?"

Kevin frowned and took a sip of his drink. He didn't want to answer these questions or let Evan move in too close. "Let's talk about that another time. What about the murders?"

"You know damn well Dimitri isn't the guy you're looking for. You know it in your gut, just like I do." Evan leaned toward Kevin, getting right into his space. "Listen, if none of this convinces you, let's make a deal. I'll find enough to give you cause to drop the case. Now let's talk quid pro quo. If you drop the case, I can make it worth your while."

All the time that Evan was talking, Kevin was thinking about how he wouldn't have to play along with Braun anymore if he and Evan came to terms. And how his record would be good. *"I want what you have—money, influence, power—and I don't stand a chance," was what he wanted to say.*

Evan hadn't taken his eyes off Kevin. "I know exactly what you're after, and I can make it happen." His eyes shone with an intensity that was scary, and drops of sweat formed on his forehead. Kevin wondered for a second if Evan hadn't flipped a switch over this business with his father.

"Let's talk about politics. Let's talk about you coming on board as my candidate for lieutenant governor."

Now Kevin knew he was crazy. "Why would you do that?"

"Because I don't give a shit about being governor. My father's the only one who cares. And I don't feel like being his whipping boy anymore. If we join forces, there's no one to run against us. We can make this happen, and both you and I will get everything we want. I'll do one term, that's it. Then, when it's over, believe me, you'll have enough money and support to be a shoo-in for governor."

"And what do you get?" Kevin didn't expect good things to fall in his lap without strings attached.

"I've had everything I could ever want—except it hasn't worked. Deep down there's a hunger, you know what I mean? It's like there's no thrill."

After a long pause, Kevin said, "I'm in."

54

The word "Paradiso" in the estate's wrought-iron gate mocked him. There was no more paradise here. He wanted to live the last few months all over again. He wanted his old life back.

Evan wasted no time. He found James in his usual spot in the library, reading the financial papers he hadn't gotten to this morning: *Bloomberg* at the moment. His father didn't bother to lower the paper or say hello.

"Dad, I quit." He said the words very quietly and handed James a memo he had hastily composed before leaving the city. It documented everything that he had learned, including that the evidence handed over to them to study during the continuance was tainted. "You conjured this up, this whole ugly scheme. You and Joseph Braun. Jewel never could have accomplished this on her own."

"Son . . ." James put down his paper, his face calm. "Whatever would I be doing with Jewel Constantinos?"

"Fucking her in that suite you keep at the Pierre." If James was shaken, he didn't show it. "Look, don't bother denying any of this; Jewel told Dimitri everything."

That got a rise out of James. Before he could even open his mouth to speak, Evan continued. "I don't care about any of this." He gestured around the room. "You know, Father, I actually wish I had been Dimitri and he'd been the legitimate son. He had the chance to become his own man. Kevin Allen now knows he has no case. He and I are making plans. You'll use everything you have to get me on the ticket, and I'm taking Kevin with me."

"Aren't you forgetting something?" James looked a little like the Cheshire cat. "There's the little matter of a few murders and only one suspect."

"I'm not going to dignify that with an answer. I don't have to. The facts will come out. Dimitri, your son, is cleaner than you are. He's not a murderer. Are you, Father?"

Evan excused himself, but as he walked out the door, James yelled after him, "You're as bad as he is. And you won't get away with this. Remember who I am."

Evan turned. "No, Father, now you will begin to learn who I am."

The ringing telephone startled Jewel. She ran to answer it.

"Jewel, it's Nancy Silton from the Children's Diabetes Foundation. I was wondering if I could count you in as an honorary chairwoman for our upcoming gala?"

"I can't," Jewel shot back. "But thanks for thinking about me. I'm just swamped with far too many social dos."

"He really keeps you busy, that wonderful husband?"

Wonderful? Yeah, right. All of you were always so phony when you tried to get my name on a committee.

"Well, thanks anyway," the other woman said. "Maybe next year?"

Jewel finished packing her bag, checking to make sure that the little recorder was packed safely away. She looked around the room once more. Catching her reflection in the mirror over the bedroom bureau, she was satisfied with what she saw. She had outsmarted all of them. *The dimwits.* She straightened the skirt of the pink mohair Chanel suit. There was one more call to make.

The message machine picked up and she said, "James, I'm calling to warn you. Dimitri knows everything we did. I don't know how he found out, but he threatened to kill me. Be careful."

That was that. Now she was going home to her daddy until Dimitri was safe behind bars for murder. She knew Dimitri would be back in town soon because James had told her the police wanted him for more questioning in the Slocum investigation. Jewel stuffed the papers in her attaché case, put on her coat, picked up her purse, and started for the corridor. She had almost reached the front door when she heard the click of the electric lock.

Jewel stepped back. The door flew open, and she gasped as she stared at the dull glint of the gun barrel aimed at her forehead.

"You bastard!" she yelled just before the fatal shot rang out.

Rose got undressed in front of the mirror. She supposed her long, thin body, with surprisingly full breasts, was attractive—some might say beautiful, especially for a woman who'd had a child. Rose reached for the flannel nightgown hanging on the door and slipped into it, then into her warm terrycloth robe, and found a comfortable spot on the sofa. It was time to get to work. Time to figure out her fictional killer's next move.

Determined to locate the remaining pieces of the puzzle, she laid out the last three chapters page by page, side by side, on the carpeted floor. She read and reread each one four times. When it came time for the character to be understood, Rose would dig deep into her own soul and find the compassion she had for these murderers, who were also tormented souls.

Now she sorted out the facts in this case, the chain of events, sifting through each scene in an effort to build a psychological profile of the serial killer. All the psychopaths she had written about had been schizophrenics, men who heard voices ordering them to kill. For the new book she had gravitated toward a multiple personality, a man who had splintered because of a loss or trauma. Her killer had a very functional side. He lived a double life as an extremely successful executive. Then, as Rose began to think like her character, she was aware of a relentless struggle inside him, and at certain points in the book the damaged, violent personality forced the other aside.

Rereading these chapters, she returned to the place in her gut that had created her latest killer. This one took no risks in life or in the act of murder. He was cold and calculating. He thrived on power and control. There were certainly pieces from her real life that fit into this puzzle: a monogrammed lighter and card case . . . Dario's need to control . . . Dimitri's nurturing side that could suddenly fracture into an ice storm . . . The characteristics of every male in her life blocked her vision of her own creation's next move.

Mentally exhausted and despairing of finding an answer, she stopped examining the manuscript. She had used all of her knowledge drawing up psychological profiles, all the empathy every writer needs to understand each character; and still she had failed to decipher the madman's plot.

On an impulse, Rose gathered all the pages and threw them and her disk into the fireplace. Back at the computer, she double-clicked on her screen and trashed the backup file. Nothing survived. It felt surprisingly good, watching the work into which she'd poured her heart and soul turn to embers. In less than a few minutes each page, filled with the pain, frustration, and joy, was gone.

Her tormentor, whoever he was, had won. *You've already killed me. Because you've taken the joy from my work—why should I write again? Rose Miller is dead.*

That night she dreamed she and Dimitri sat in front of a crackling fire in the cozy living room of the Stowe chalet. Everything was perfect, the way she'd always imagined life would be with Dimitri.

He stroked her hair and stared into her eyes. They sipped cognac from small crystal glasses. Bach played from unseen speakers, the music drifting softly in the air. Everything moved in slow motion. Her limbs felt heavy, weighted.

She heard a noise somewhere behind her and turned to look. The flickering light from the fire cast dark, dense shadows against the walls and windows, but she could make out Dario's face glowing in the moonlight, outside the window. He grinned as he raised his gun.

Rose bolted out of the dream, a scream clawing its way up her throat. Her eyes snapped open, and the memory of Dario's face was there, as if burned into her retina. The sheets had wrapped around her legs, trapping her like a fly in a Venus's-flytrap. Her heart hammered and perspiration dampened her nightgown. She kicked off the covers, sat up, and glanced at the clock. It was almost midnight. The fuzziness of the dream dissolved, and she returned to reality. Was her subconscious trying to tell her something? Did Dario's face in the window mean he was the killer? Or was Dario simply trying to warn her that Dimitri was?

Her mouth was dry. Clumsily she got out of bed, her hand searching for the handle in the blackness that enveloped the room. She heard a noise—something crashed to the floor and shattered. She snapped into full awareness.

Rose opened the door, cautiously poked her head into the dark hall, and listened, straining to hear something, anything. There was nothing, only the relentless moaning of the wind. Then silence.

She moved quietly through the hall of the chalet, spooked by something she couldn't explain, and turned on the light.

"Who's there?" she called.

Her voice echoed in the silence. Then, a shutter on one of the partially opened windows creaked. She walked toward it slowly, the skin tightening at the back of her neck. As she got closer to the window, she felt a draft of cold air rush toward her, licking her face.

A floorboard creaked behind her, and she spun around to face Dimitri.

Her shock paralyzed her and rendered her mute. She simply stared at him, her thoughts racing, her eyes scanning his face. He looked tired, disheveled. There was the icy stare she had learned to recognize, and yet, looking deeper into his eyes, the other Dimitri was also there.

"I came in through the window. I knocked on the door, but you didn't answer."

Through the window? He must be crazy.

"I . . ." She started to tell him about the dream, but nothing came out. He touched her arm, and electricity leaped between them, a burning current that shot right through her. The feeling came from the past, familiar for all the wrong reasons.

She jerked her arm free of his grasp and said, "Why the intrigue? For God's sake, Dimitri, pounding on the front door would have startled me a lot less than waking to find someone's broken in through the living room window."

She expected him to come back at her with one of his sarcastic remarks; instead he stood silent, making her more nervous.

"When we spoke earlier, you said you would come in a day or two. Why are you here now? What is so urgent that you had to see me?"

He didn't answer her right away. Rose watched as he went to the fireplace and threw two logs into the grate, reaching up for the antique match holder next to the mantel. Seconds later a fire roared. Twigs crackled, hissing, sending up plumes of smoke.

Sensing he needed time to get around to the reason for his visit, Rose forced herself to slow the pace. She pulled two chairs over in front of the fireplace.

"Sit," she said. "I'll make us some tea."

She started for the kitchen when he said, "A bottle of wine would be better."

The flames leaped and crackled, and the fire's warmth finally penetrated the chill lodged in her center. Dimitri took the open bottle of red wine and poured two glasses, then handed one to Rose. Holding up his glass, he said, "To happy endings."

His toast seemed so inappropriate she didn't know how to respond. She thought she knew him well, but she couldn't read him tonight. He looked troubled and angry but, at the same time, desperate and pathetic, his eyes mysterious.

Rose took a gulp of her wine and nearly gagged. She began to feel the effect immediately. She set the glass on the floor and focused back on Dimitri. Leaning, tensed, toward the fire, eyes blazing blue, he said, "You know, Rose, I never thought I would need to ask you for a favor."

She said nothing, waiting, listening to his silence. "When I went to prison, as angry as I was, I never thought I'd need your help in kind. But I need to ask you to return the sacrifice I made for you."

He grimaced, and she knew how difficult this was for him—what a devastating blow to his pride. "You do believe me, I hope, when I say I didn't kill Janice, or any of those girls, for that matter?"

She gave no reaction, showed no emotion. Her insides were churning as fear crept over her entire body. What did he want from her?

"The police think I did."

"I've heard your fingerprints were all over that duffel bag," she blurted without thinking.

"It's true, the duffel bag belongs to me." He hadn't taken those sapphire eyes—their daughter's eyes—from hers. "But someone took it, used it, and framed me while he killed Janice."

He continued, "There will be an indictment. I'll need an alibi. I need you to attest to the fact that we were together in the barn the night of Janice's murder."

Dimitri turned his attention back to the fire.

She believed him, but the side of her that knew people could change warned her to proceed with caution. "You weren't in your suite when I got there."

"You will attest to it, Rose, won't you?"

Rose realized he wasn't asking her, he was telling her.

The years he'd lost, the stripping away of his innocence: she owed him an alibi; she owed him much more. She did not need to say a word. He read her.

Dimitri reached across the small distance that separated them and took her hand. "Thank you," he said softly.

Now there was yearning in his eyes. He drew her close to him. The small gap that separated their lips closed as he brought his mouth down on hers and the heat of him against her was nearly overwhelming. But this time she fought the familiar feeling of desire and pulled back.

"Dimitri . . . I . . . can't."

"I know, Rose. I know. I behaved badly the other night—"

"No." She put her fingers to his lips. "Don't think that. . . ."

It's because I'll never want to stop kissing you, loving you, making love with you.

Abruptly he changed the subject. "I bought the old Laurel estate." He put down the wineglass and walked to the window. It was nearly covered with snow.

Confused by his quick switch, she said, "What?" Everything inside of her suddenly began to rumble and shake; memories broke loose from her brain, rushed toward her heart, and slammed into it.

With his back still to her, he said, "If something happens—if I lose the murder case, I want you and Alexis to have it."

Was he trying to torment her? Buying Laurel seemed an abomination.

He turned around and walked back to her, hovering, staring down at her. "And if nothing happens to me, then I want a constant reminder of what we could have had."

Rose searched his face. All the reasons he might have for buying Laurel ran through her mind: to prove something to James or to Evan; to satisfy some unresolved business she couldn't define. No, every bit of her believed him—he had no nasty, ulterior motive.

He reached down, took her hand, and drew her up against him. "I love you, Rose. You must know that. You must never forget what I did for you." Then he kissed her again. This time she didn't resist.

Afterward she would not remember how they moved to the bedroom of the chalet, back under her already warm sheets, and were naked together, Dimitri's body so hungry on hers. His taste, the feel of his mouth, smells, each body's essence mixing with the other . . . Soon they would satiate each other's hunger. When she could hold out no longer and her need for release was unbearable, their bodies fused magically as they rocked in unison back and forth, arms and legs intertwined, and they were one person for what seemed a long time. Rose found herself clinging to Dimitri for dear life.

Slowly she released him from her cradling arms. She shifted slightly to adjust to the weight of him on top of her, but he kept her hips in place and began to rub his chest against hers. Their heat and sweat mingled and they made love again, this time pretending they had all the time in the world.

Afterward they talked quietly, propped up against pillows before the chalet's bedroom fireplace. He kept stroking her body and hair, luring her into his arms again and again.

It was time for total honesty. She regretted terribly that he didn't know Alexis was their child and hated living with the secret.

How should she begin?

She pushed herself up on one elbow and said, "What is it you regret most about your life, Dimitri?"

He stroked her face, brushing a few stray hairs from her eyes. "I don't regret what I did for you. I will admit, I've lived with a lot of hate and thoughts of revenge. But I'm past that now."

In the distance, the stereo in the living room played Streisand's rendition of Andrew Lloyd Webber's "As If We Never Said Good-Bye."

As though picking up her thoughts, Dimitri said, "We could have been so happy. I would have made you proud. I would have given you a home, children, anything you asked."

"Yes," she whispered. Without censoring her thoughts, she said, "Tonight, Evan and I would have celebrated our twelfth anniversary. . . ."

"I know," Dimitri said.

It struck her as odd that he would remember. Then she realized there was no way Dimitri would have forgotten the day she betrayed him.

"I've lived a lie for twelve years. Though I care for Evan, in a way, it was unforgivable of me to take all his devotion and give so little back. He deserves so much, and I've made him suffer unnecessarily"—she paused, thinking how to phrase it—"since you've returned."

Dimitri moved his head, and his eyes retreated into the shadows. "I don't understand. Why do you live the lie of loving him? Why did you marry him?" He spoke in a whisper, and she could tell he was not angry, simply bewildered. "I know you could never have married him for money. I tried for a long time to convince myself that you were that shallow, that you had fooled me into loving you. For a while I believed you played up to me so I would marry you and release you from Tom's guardianship. And then, once he was dead . . . well, anyway, I can't believe that anymore."

Rose took both his hands in hers, toyed with each of his fingers. *What will I say next? Where will the words come from?*

"Alexis—" She stopped after speaking her child's name. "I . . . I was scared."

Dimitri put his hand over her mouth. He was making sense of her disjointed words. He remained silent and still. She knew the moment he figured it all out because his face changed. His shifting expressions told the tale of how this information affected him: first, there was rage, then a terrible sadness that turned his sapphire eyes nearly the color of onyx. Rose gasped when she saw this, as though she'd been slapped. It took her a moment to realize Dimitri was speaking to her.

"How could you keep that from me all these years?"

There was nothing she could say. He sat up, his head cradled in his hands.

She clutched the blanket they'd brought over to the fireplace and moved toward him. "Dimitri, please try to understand. I had no other choice." She placed her hand on his shoulder, but he pulled away. *Yet another betrayal,* she could almost hear him thinking. But he kept his thoughts to himself.

Tears spilled down her cheeks, and she whispered, "I'm sorry . . . I'm sorry. Oh, God, I'm sorry."

Dimitri dragged himself away from her. She couldn't see him as he stood in the dark corner of the bedroom, but she heard him dressing. His sadness was palpable, almost an active energy, pulling her in. Eventually he stepped out of the corner and became visible. He seemed to be getting himself under some semblance of control. When he spoke, he sounded subdued, almost as though he were on automatic.

"Look, I have to go back for questioning in the Slocum case. I'm not sure I can take much more of this legal garbage. I can count on you for an alibi?"

She nodded.

"That's decent of you."

His sneering tone felt like a body blow after they'd been so close. She could see his eyes were glassy.

"Why should I be surprised that you'd keep my child away from me? You are one of them, after all."

He headed for the door. Rose ran after him, begging him to let her explain, but he couldn't hear her. He was caught up in his fury and pain, once again a man who would have to piece together a shattered lie—*if* he could exonerate himself. He couldn't afford to think of what Rose had done to him, not yet.

55

Dario entered the old brownstone where he lived, in a third-floor apartment that overlooked Gramercy Park. The building, a charming three-story red-brick, was home to four separate floor-through apartments. Considering the square footage available in Manhattan, Dario's apartment was huge, with a master bedroom, two guest bedrooms, a huge old kitchen, a paneled dining room, and an elegant living room and library. He put the key in the lock, opened the door, flicked on the light switch, and threw his coat over the sofa. He wandered into the kitchen and grabbed a stale doughnut from the Krispy Kreme box he'd bought two days earlier. He had seen Rose's beautiful face staring up at him when he grabbed the *National Enquirer* from the newsstand; the story was pure gossip. Of course, he knew more than he could ever learn from the *Enquirer,* but it was great to see Rose's peccadilloes laid out in color. He read the caption: NOTED AUTHOR, ROSE MILLER, MISSING!: "No Foul Play Considered."

The story beneath reported Miller's abrupt cancellation of her satellite interviews and two book signings: "Without even the courtesy of a phone call," the tabloid reported. "Is she getting too big for those gorgeous designer britches?" Dario knew that hundreds of people had been left standing in line for hours. His office was flooded with calls from her publisher, her editor, the bookstore owners, and, of course, the press. He should have said, "I'm no longer employed by Mrs. Miller," but why do that when he'd set up the plan to flush her out?

He opened the silverware drawer and pulled out a pair of kitchen shears. Then, carefully, he cut out Rose's picture and, with each cut, pretended that she felt pain.

He left the shears on the counter next to the cut-up newspaper and carried her picture into one of the guest bedrooms he'd converted into a den. The room was sparse, just an old sofa, a wooden desk, and a floor lamp. Only the walls gave him the satisfaction he craved. He stood in the doorway for a moment, admiring the clippings, pictures, articles, and posters of Rose pasted all over the room searching for an empty spot. Then his gaze fell on a speck of white paint on the back wall, almost at the ceiling. He pulled the glue stick from his desk drawer, dabbed some onto the back of the clipping, and slapped it against the wall.

Charlie Dawkins's call came at twelve-fifteen. Dimitri Constantinos's wife had been found murdered in her suite at the Plaza. The task force was once again on call to investigate a murder case that swirled around Dimitri Constantinos and Rose Miller. As soon as he was notified, Charlie alerted Falcone.

Falcone was groggy from sleep. He thought back over his evening. That night, Evan Miller had called to say there were things Falcone should know; he'd asked if he could speak with Falcone in person, at his house. The thought of Evan Miller in his dive was too much to imagine, so they'd agreed to meet at TR's Pub in Williston Park. Miller, casual in jeans, a long-sleeved pinstripe shirt, and blue crew-neck sweater, seemed a different man. Falcone knew immediately something was up.

Over the course of an hour and three drinks each, Evan explained the collusion among both Brauns, James Miller, and Kevin Allen. The fact that his father was involved didn't seem to shock Evan at all. Nor did it shock Falcone. He told Evan that when the dust settled, they'd get back to James Miller's involvement. "Your father should be charged with the same crimes that Constantinos is."

"And the prosecutor?" Evan asked. Falcone was cynical in general about those with political ambitions, so he kept his mouth shut.

Neither of them bothered discussing Braun. It was a given he'd do anything that served his purposes, including using his daughter.

"I like you, Falcone," Evan had said, "and I'm going to say this to you first and then I'll probably have to tell a lot of investigators, lawyers, and judges down the line: My father protected Joseph Braun. I thought it was because of a rather unimportant business partnership. . . ."

"The escorts," Falcone remembered saying. "We know about that. Everyone in law enforcement in the tristate area knows that."

Falcone distinctly remembered Evan saying, "Well, something tells me I'm going to discover a lot more dirt, now that I'm not in denial."

"Thanks, Evan. We both know you're taking a risk. I have no idea what the implications are for you."

"I do," Evan had said. "I'm an attorney, remember?" He smiled sadly. "I could get charged along with my father on some of the Braun business, but that's minor." He waved his hand in a dismissive way. "The important thing is to expose this conspiracy."

Wide awake now, Falcone dressed hurriedly and got into his car. The sky was black. He raced on the Long Island Expressway doing seventy-five, tore through the Midtown Tunnel, and headed up to 59th Street and Fifth Avenue. He pulled up to the Plaza's front entrance, flashed his badge, threw the keys to the doorman, and headed up to the Vanderbilt Suite.

Charlie met him in the hall and led the way into the living room, brushing past the boys from the coroner's office and the forensic technicians. Jewel Constantinos's body was sprawled out on the carpet, next to the sofa. A bright red puddle of blood covered a two-by-three-foot section of carpet. Huddled in the corner were police officers and detectives questioning a maid and two security men.

"Who found the body?" Falcone asked, taking in the entire crime scene. Charlie pointed a finger at the young Mexican woman crying in the corner. "The maid. She says Constantinos requests turndown service precisely at midnight."

The ever-put-together Mrs. Constantinos was dressed in something expensive, Falcone noted. Her body was clothed, she was wearing her coat, so sexual assault was probably not the motive. She had been shot once in her right temple.

"Anything I should know about?" Falcone asked as he took his pad and pen from his pocket and began taking notes.

"A tape recorder was found in Mrs. Constantinos's suitcase. I think you should hear this conversation between her and her husband." Charlie called out to one of the detectives, "Can I have the recorder?"

A cop rushed over with the tape.

"Here, listen to this." He pushed down on the play button, and Falcone listened to the recorded dialogue.

"I could kill you right now with my bare hands. . . ."

Charlie hit the stop button. "Impressed?"

Falcone scratched his head. "It's enough for an arrest warrant."

"Done. APB. Now all we have to do is find him."

"Have they tried the casino in Atlantic City?" Falcone asked.

"Everywhere. No one's in his office, his service hasn't heard from him. The only information his personal assistant could give us was he left for an undisclosed location hours ago in his private jet. We haven't been able to reach the pilot, so it looks like Dimitri is on the run."

Suddenly a wave of panic swept over Falcone. Rose, the lodge . . . could he possibly have figured out where she was? Had she told him over the phone?

Charlie pushed an envelope in Falcone's direction. "This was found in her purse."

Falcone pulled some paper from the already opened envelope and studied it. It was a receipt of a check made out to Dario Roselli for five thousand dollars.

What connection did Roselli have with Jewel Constantinos?

Myra's piercing screams echoed through the cavernous hallway, sounding like those of a wounded animal. Evan stumbled from his bed, through the door of the master suite, and found her crouched over the top landing, barely able to breathe.

Evan ran to her, yelling, "What's wrong?"

She didn't speak. She was clutching her chest and pointing to Alexis's room.

Evan raced to his daughter's room. Her bed was empty, the blankets thrown to the floor. A huge gust of wind blew the curtains back through the open window, and the sudden rush of air on his face threw him into action.

He went to the window and searched below: nothing but blackness.

He shut the window, and that was when he heard a faint scrambling sound coming from the closet. The man they'd hired after Falcone fired Malcolm was handcuffed and shackled, his mouth duct-taped. Evan ripped the tape from the man's mouth and learned that the guard had gone to relieve himself and returned to find a man with a stocking over his face and a watch cap pulled low over his eyes—with two semiautomatic pistols drawn. In a high-pitched disguised voice, he'd threatened to shoot the girl if the guard made a move. Alexis remained quiet while the man handcuffed the guard, shackled his feet, and made him crawl to the closet.

Evan ran to the phone and dialed 911. His hands trembled so badly, he nearly dropped the receiver. When a man answered, he shouted, "This is Evan Miller, someone's kidnapped my daughter! . . ."

Falcone got the call from the Twentieth Precinct, Charlie's division, just as he was leaving the Plaza to call Rose. "The Miller kid's been kidnapped," the desk sergeant blurted. It was a poor connection, and Falcone wondered whether or not he'd heard correctly.

"Alexis Miller?"

"Yes," the sergeant replied. "The call just came in from Evan Miller. Maybe you should get over there right away."

Falcone's heart was racing. He checked his watch. "I can be there in an hour. Tell Mr. Miller to sit tight. I have one stop to make, an important one."

He broke the connection, shoved the cell phone inside his coat pocket and thought, *How am I going to tell Rose?*

Rose lay awake in bed, thinking about what had happened. Making love with Dimitri had only solidified her feelings for him. The satiating comfort she felt in his arms was out of love for Dimitri Constantinos—who he was, who he had been.

She was not a woman who wallowed in what might have been. She had told Dimitri the truth, and it had made him angry, but it wasn't something she could help him resolve. Still, the solitary hours she spent thinking about their two nights together made her frustrated and lonely, wounded and troubled.

He had accused her of hiding behind the Millers' wealth and power. He'd told her that she was a fake and that keeping the fact that he was Alexis's father from him made her a liar. The truth hurt. She'd lied the entire time she was married to Evan, each time she told him how much she loved him when all the while she was thinking about Dimitri. What she had to do was come clean with everyone. The more she thought about it, the deeper her pain went. She thought she had been protecting Alexis, but at the same time she had been hurting Dimitri and Evan, the two men who loved her.

Dimitri's traumatic exit had left much unresolved between them. The whole scenario played out in her mind. *I bought the Laurel estate. . . .* She realized in his own way, Dimitri too was holding on to their past. What was his motivation?

The room was chilly. By two A.M. the fire that had been burning wildly earlier had died. At two-fifteen the phone rang.

"Rose, it's John."

Why would he call now? she wondered, her heart beginning to race. Did he know Dimitri had been to the chalet? Or was it something else?

"What's wrong?"

"Is Dimitri Constantinos there?"

"No . . . but . . . he—"

Before she could finish, he said, "His wife was found murdered in his suite at the Plaza. He's nowhere to be found. I want you to come back, Rose. The police have him on tape threatening to kill her." A pause, then: "Alexis is missing. She was taken from her bed about a half hour ago. I'll arrange for a pilot to meet you at the airport in one hour." He stayed on the line, not saying anything. "Rose? Are you going to be able to get yourself together?"

"I'll have to," she said. Her mind was running on two different tracks.

Alexis was missing.

I need an alibi, Rose. . . .

A light rain fell as Falcone drove the ten blocks to Dario's apartment. The dark, sagging clouds were nearly swallowed up by the blackness that fell over New York City. His brain was still trying to piece together the puzzle. Jewel and Dario . . . what was the connection? Was there any way that it might lead him to Dimitri?

He turned off the headlights, slipped on his raincoat. Wet rain slapped against his face. His worn loafers squished through the standing pools of water on the sidewalk.

By some stroke of luck the door leading to the interior lobby was unlocked. Inside the brownstone, he took the stairs two at a time. At the top landing, he turned left and headed for apartment 3B. He knocked lightly at first, then realized it was two-thirty A.M. Dario was most likely asleep. He pounded harder with his fists—still no response, except from the elderly woman in 3A, who peeked out into the hall and yelled, "He's not home, stop making all that racket."

Falcone waited until he heard the door slam, then reached inside his raincoat for a leather pouch and brought out a long, slender tool that could pick almost any lock. He inserted the tool, and moments later the door opened. He stepped into the dark hall, shut the door, and listened. Silence. He crept forward.

Outside, a distant roll of thunder cracked, followed by a lightning flash. He made his way into the kitchen. In the moonlight gently spilling through fine, prewar casement windows, Falcone could see the room to his left was a long living room, dining room area. It wasn't hoity-toity by any means, but it worked . . . and the apartment was neat, something he always envied. *So this guy's Felix Ungar and I'm Oscar Madison. Makes no difference; we all eat, breathe, and shit the same way.* His hands roamed the walls until he found a light switch.

He sifted through some old mail on the counter—bills, advertisements, brochures. On the bottom of the pile was a check from Jewel Constantinos in the amount of five thousand dollars. The memo at the bottom of the check read "Braun—fee for PR services rendered/Ivory Palace." Interesting, but it seemed totally unrelated to Jewel's murder.

Falcone quickly searched through the apartment, hunting for any other clues. He made his way down a moonlit hallway past the living room. There were three doors; one near the left was a bathroom. He opened the door to another room farther on, which held nothing but a bed, a comforter, and some pillows: a guest room that looked as if it had never been used.

He closed the door and moved on to the next one. Nothing in his wildest dreams could have prepared him for what he saw. Lightning flashed in the windows again, illuminating the shrine of obsession.

He'd heard about such obsessions, but he'd never run across one. While his work brought him in contact with parents who kept missing children's rooms untouched, toys still scattered on the floor, witnessing a veritable shrine to a woman was jolting. The entire wall was covered with Rose's photos, book jackets, and magazine articles. On the rose-colored carpet, in the center of the room, was a large jar of lifeless petals that made a mulch—maybe what some would call a potpourri. Falcone knew he was looking at craziness.

"Holy shit," he uttered, as he absorbed the full force of shock that swept over him.

There was a hard bump as the small twin-engine, four-passenger plane landed on the runway and began taxiing. The ride from Vermont was rocky, the plane shaking wildly from the turbulence as the treacherous storm showed its rage. It had taken the pilot nearly two hours to negotiate the bad weather.

Rose pulled a bag from under the seat in front of her, her hands checking through its contents for her phone book with Falcone's cell phone number while her mind kept going in and out of focus. Twice she forgot what she was searching for and stopped fiddling, but without a distraction her overwhelming terror returned. The image of Alexis was unimaginable; was she frightened, cold, hungry? Was she hurt? Oh God, had someone violated her beautiful baby? The thought of that made Rose want to give up, and she went back to rummaging through her carry-on.

Every minute of the ride from Vermont to JFK seemed interminable. She imagined Alexis crying, terrorized. She blamed herself. She shouldn't have left her, shouldn't have told Dimitri that she was at Stowe, shouldn't have told him about Alexis. What was she thinking? She had allowed her judgment to be clouded. Now his wife was dead and her daughter was missing. She had been sleeping with the enemy.

She thought about her impulsive admission to Dimitri that Alexis was his daughter. She winced, wishing she could offer herself instead of Alexis, for torture or death, whatever would free her baby. How could she have been so reckless? Obviously her confession had once again released the beast in him.

Recalling the condition Dimitri had been in when he'd left Vermont, she knew he could easily have snapped and rationalized kidnapping Alexis. She remembered the conversations they had so long ago, at Laurel, as they shared their similar yearning for family. Alexis could easily be Dimitri's Achilles' heel. Then the words came back to her: *I've bought the Laurel estate, in case something happens to me. . . .* That was it. In one rapid moment the pieces of the puzzle fell into place. That was where he'd taken Alexis. And he knew Rose would come for her.

"Don't let me be too late," she whispered. "Please, God, don't let him harm her."

Rose saw the unmarked car with its single flashing light waiting below. Thinking quickly, she dashed for the terminal exit. There was no time for questions from the police. She needed to get to Laurel—to Alexis. Outside, only one cab sat parked at the curb. The driver was asleep. She tapped loudly on the window. The man jumped. "I need to go to Brookville. I'm in a terrible hurry."

He stared back at her, his eyes still full of sleep. "No," he said, shaking his head. "I can't go to Long Island. New rules, new jurisdictions. I could lose my license if—"

She took out her wallet and shoved a hundred-dollar bill at him.

"Get in."

56

The girl was beginning to stir again. She couldn't speak because Billy had shoved a handkerchief into her mouth and slapped a piece of duct tape across it. The child peered down at her taped wrists and ankles; a look of confusion entered her enormous blue eyes.

This child, who had been sheltered, pampered, and protected since the day she was born, saw her wrists taped, knew the trauma of being in a madman's grasp. She was vaguely aware that her head was caked with blood and remembered scraping it against a concrete floor. Her white flannel nightgown, brand new when she and Myra had unwrapped it tonight, was now covered with mud, torn, nearly shredded. Behind her, she heard the man move and pretended to be unconscious.

Billy went to the far corner of the barn, passing the horses watching him lazily from their stalls, and moved some old crates, locating a three-gallon gasoline can, which he carried to the barn door. A mountain of hay was piled up in an empty stall. The man scattered the bales, distributing them evenly around the barn. Then he picked up the gallon of gasoline and walked slowly around the room, spilling the liquid, keeping a steady stream behind him, dousing not only the bales of hay, but everything in sight. Then he walked over to Alexis and soaked her nightgown, the soft delicate skin of her arms and legs, and the ringlets of black curls matted with dried blood.

"It will all be over shortly, you'll see." Billy spoke softly. "Your mommy will come and then there'll be just the three of us."

As Rose and the cabdriver made their way, she had the sensation of time slowing down. The stoplights were red forever, and the driver was in slow motion. She wished he could drive faster. They were running out of time. Desperately she tried to reach John from her cell phone, but with the severe weather conditions, the connections were down.

The driver was entering Old Brookville: only a few minutes more now. Her heart beat rapidly. Rose hugged herself to stop from shaking and thought about the gifts she'd sent Alexis from Stowe. Her daughter's face appeared to her as a hallucination. *Oh, sweetheart, hold on.* Rose was besieged with guilt. *I shouldn't have run away, I shouldn't have left Alexis,* she thought. *Please, God, let her be safe.*

The driver turned the corner just before the estate, and she felt her stomach churn. He drove past the open gates and followed an unpaved, barely lit path past the guest cottage, the barn, and the servants' apartments above the garage, making his way to the main house.

She jumped from the cab literally before it stopped moving. Her senses flashed back to all the traumatic times through which she had lived. Her mouth had the metallic taste of despair she'd had when her parents were buried; her insides went numb the way they had the day Dimitri was put away—on and on, the memories filled her mind as her body propelled her forward.

The unmarked car was coming down the winding driveway of Paradiso. Falcone ran outside past the battalion of squad cars and pounded on the driver's-side window.

"Where is she?" he yelled. "Where's Rose?"

The officer stumbled from the car and nearly slipped in a puddle. He looked aghast and bewildered all at once. "I . . . I lost her." He took a deep breath, exhaled, then continued, "I never saw her get off the plane. I think she slipped past me."

Pieces fell together. Ingrid, the private investigator, had reported on Dimitri's meeting with a woman who Falcone learned was a real estate agent. Ingrid had been unable to identify the property Dimitri had looked at. Now Falcone knew in an instant: the Laurel estate.

Rose wasn't surprised to find the door ajar. *It's part of his plan. He knows I'm coming.*

Inside, the house was dark and gloomy. She reached for the light switch she remembered was right to the left of the entrance. Bright light flooded every corner of the room. Rose quietly made her way around Laurel. The marble floor chilled her; a sudden inexplicable creak on the step down to the sunken living room made her jump. She listened carefully for any sound as she walked through the dining room and the kitchen. The house looked different. Once cold and baroque, it was now warm and the light was cheery, making it hard to believe anything dark could happen here.

As she went from room to room the years faded and she was a housekeeper again. Here was James Miller's room, which, though decorated now in modern minimalist shades of gray, she remembered it as it was, fussy, dark, musty with the smell of him. And the room she remembered as Evan's before he left for school now had a bleached wood floor, an entertainment center, and a large brand-new television.

Still she moved about, searching, but there was no movement, no sound. She felt as though she were living on two planes: the present, with the palatial mansion redone to perfection, and the old memories of a place that had held her hostage.

Rose made her way up the peach carpeted stairs, down the hall. Something drew her into one of the guest bedrooms. The room had been lavishly decorated. A leafy green pattern had been used for the upholstered love seat, and it was picked up in the bedding and ballooning curtains that covered the wall of windows. The freshly painted walls were the same peach color as the carpet. In the corner were bags from clothing stores. It was an ideal room for an eleven-year-old girl.

Rose made her way to the room she had shared with Evan at Laurel. Her mind swirled. It wasn't Evan and Rose Miller's room now. Dimitri was everywhere she looked. Or, more specifically, Dimitri's interpretation of Rose's fantasy bedroom. Wallpaper of muted pastels brightened the once mundane atmosphere of the room. A canopied brass bed with gauze curtains faced the window where Rose used to daydream. A lump filled her throat. High-velocity feelings struggled within her, drowning out everything else. *He could creep up behind me and I wouldn't hear him.* She then whirled around.

At the foot of the bed was a silk Dior nightgown with matching velvet slippers. The sitting area was perfect, with curved back ivory moiré chairs and a matching rounded armchair situated on a highly colored Bessarabian rug. Sheer panels took the place of traditional heavy drapery.

When she'd shared this room with Evan, it always gave her a cold feeling. The heavy wood furniture, the burgundy upholstery, all of it had depressed her. Now it seemed restful, nurturing. Yet how could that be when the man who created it was a monster who had taken her daughter?

She snapped out of the past and focused again on finding Alexis, listening closely for any noise, even a whimper. *Check the closets,* a voice in her head told her. She opened the doors slowly and let out a stifled sob. It was full of clothes, all brand new, still tagged from Saks Fifth Avenue. She sifted through the hangers. There were gowns, dresses, and suits from all the top designers. She checked the tags: size four. Jewel was at least an eight. On the floor were nearly a dozen pairs of expensive shoes, all set up neatly in a row.

"Do you like them?"

She was so concentrated on her own swirling thoughts, she hadn't heard him until he was upon her. She spun around and came face-to-face with Dimitri. He stood inches from her. He looked disheveled, his eyes bloodshot, the pungent smell of booze on his breath.

Rose didn't know whether to draw back. This might infuriate him. How would her heroine act in this situation? That gave her direction. She smiled, forcing any sign of fear from her body or eyes.

"I did it all for you, Rose . . . and your—our daughter."

His words shattered her heart; her feet took root in the carpeted floor and her body seemed so heavy, she couldn't even lift her arms. Her eyes welled with tears, and Dimitri's face began to blur.

He leaned in close to her, his warm breath on her face. "You always wanted simplicity and elegance, Rose. I hope you like it . . . I tried my best."

"Dimitri, please don't do this." Outside, the distant sound of thunder unnerved her.

A hint of something unreadable had crept into his voice. She thanked God he hadn't made a move to touch her.

"Dimitri . . ." She held up her palms to disarm him.

"I just wanted to make you into a real-life Cinderella. You own this house and everything in it. I bought it in your name."

Now he took a step toward her.

"I promised you I would give you the world one day. Here's a good start, don't you agree?"

He grabbed her, put his arm around her, and pulled her against him. Her body felt like wood, heavy, rigid, and paralyzed.

"It's true. I was angry when I left Stowe, but then I realized, my precious Rose, you've given me the most incredible gift in the world, a daughter, a legacy for me to leave behind." He smiled, and this time there was no masking his emotions.

What does he mean, leave behind? Dimitri put his lips close to her ear and spoke softly. "For so many years I was nothing better than a mongrel, the bastard child, while my brother, the golden son, enjoyed all the accoutrements of our father's success. Me, I struggled, clawed my way to the top. When I was at my lowest point, the only thing that kept me focused was revenge."

Rose tried to speak, but he put his fingers to her lips. "Shh, let me say what I have to. I'm not the same man who arrived in New York a few weeks ago. I thought I was hardened against you, but I was wrong. You've gotten to me; softened me. And you've changed my mind about a lot of things. I understand now why you couldn't tell the truth about Alexis. She's so precious. And now I know she's mine."

Rose would hear no more. "Where is she? Where is my baby?"

"I'm not finished." At this he took her hands from her sides and clasped them behind her, leaning his body into hers. She could smell the alcohol on his breath, and for a moment she was back with Uncle Tom. She recoiled.

"Don't," he said softly yet forcefully. "Don't treat me that way. I'm not going to be here much longer, Rose. Jewel is dead, and Joseph's going to come after me. I have this strong feeling something is going to happen. One way or the other, I'm going to die. So I want you to look around and know that all of this is for you and our daughter."

"What do you want from me?" She yanked her hands away, her heart moving from her chest to her mouth.

He became very still, and she took the opportunity to observe him in the comforting pale pink light of the master bedroom. His eyes burned beyond bright, and they were frightening. When he spoke it was still in the quiet, forceful tone.

"I want only for you to remember me forever. And I want you to tell Alexis about me."

He's mad, she decided.

He cupped her chin with his hand and brought her eyes up to meet his.

"Let go of me," she begged, fighting his grip.

"Have you seen the beautiful horses I bought for us? Romeo and Juliet. How appropriate, don't you think?" He'd changed the subject so quickly, she couldn't catch up right away.

The halogen sconces on the bedroom walls softened the evil glint of the pistol that had materialized from Dimitri's pocket.

"Where's Alexis? What have you done?"

Dimitri disentangled himself from Rose and gazed past her, out the window to the barn. "I don't know what you mean."

Then it all tumbled around in her head and struck her like a bolt of lightning—the barn, of course! All it had taken was following his gaze; memories of that night surfaced, as fresh in her mind as the terrible phone call. All of her villains returned to the scene of the crime. It was part of the thrill. Dimitri had put together this entire masquerade just to get back to the barn and create mayhem. It was a repeat performance of the night he'd absconded with her back to Laurel—to the barn. But this time his scenario was going to be played out with Alexis. And she was certain the scene would not stop until her daughter was killed.

He pulled her against him tighter now. "It made me sick, thinking about you and Evan, his hands all over you. But that's over now. It's all in the past."

Her sobs turned to shrieks, and in an instant she brought her knee up and jabbed it full force into his groin.

Dimitri fell back, groaning, and Rose pushed past him, nearly stumbling down the stairs, out the front door. She ran wildly, blindly. It was raining even harder now, and she had to fight the dense fog and heavy wind. About a hundred yards away she could make out the barn. She didn't look back; she knew Dimitri was behind her.

Falcone sped through the blinding rain to the Laurel estate. Charlie Dawkins sat beside him in the passenger's seat. Falcone glanced into the rearview mirror at the battalion of squad cars behind him.

"This guy Dimitri is one sick pup," Dawkins said. Falcone had briefed him on the whole story.

Falcone let out a barely audible, "Yeah," but his mind was elsewhere.

The dispatcher on the radio was asking for him. When he announced himself the woman gave him a code. She was reporting a suicide—Dario Roselli. "Details to follow on screen." Before the woman logged off, she announced that helicopters and ground search parties had been sent out, but gale warnings for Long Island were in effect and the air search was difficult.

Beyond shock, Falcone thought back to his collision with Dario in the hallway of his apartment building. Since they were there and he would have to interrogate the man anyway, he decided to use the element of surprise to see what he could get out of Dario.

Without preamble he confronted Dario about the "shrine" in his apartment.

"You know what that says to me, Mr. Roselli? It's not normal. You were a little nuts for her, am I right?"

"Why don't you come back inside, Detective, and have a drink with me?"

Falcone and Dario walked into the apartment, but Falcone was quick to say, "This is no social call."

"Of course." The slender man sat at a desk in the living room while Falcone remained standing.

"About the shrine, Mr. Roselli?"

"I've always been in love with her; it was no secret."

The man was clearly humiliated, and Falcone struggled not to feel sorry for him. Dario stood and walked to the bar in the living room, poured himself a glass of port; then, lifting his glass, he said, "Here's to unrequited love, Detective." And at that moment Falcone knew in his gut that this pathetic, lovesick man was not the one they were looking for. Still, there were questions that had to be answered.

"You left a lighter at Marilyn Grimes's apartment, didn't you."

The other man looked surprised. "Yes, it's mine. I was wondering where it went."

"That's not an explanation, Mr. Roselli," Falcone's interrogation was half-hearted.

"I don't have an explanation. I lost a lighter and matching business card case, and it is very possible that since Marilyn and I had a brief fling, I left the objects at her apartment."

Falcone said nothing and didn't take his eyes off Dario, waiting to see if anything else would emerge.

"Have you ever been nuts for someone, Detective?"

Without waiting for a reply, Dario continued. "I loved Rose, obviously too much, and was willing to use Marilyn if I thought it could get me closer, gain me access. Sometimes the three of us would go out together. And it was better than not having the time with her at all. I'm a sucker, sure. And probably somewhat of a creep, but I'm not a killer."

"She believes you tried to have her killed in Miami." Falcone was determined to get an answer to all the questions in this case. "Is it true?"

"How about that drink, Detective Falcone?"

"Not for me."

Dario excused himself to refill his glass. When he returned, he sat at an old-fashioned roll-top desk in his living room. "About Miami. I didn't want to hurt her. I just wanted to scare her back to me," he said, not risking a look at Falcone.

"I did have a plan," he continued.

Perhaps he was loosening up after the two glasses of port he'd gulped down, Falcone thought, or maybe he was intimidated. "Don't hold anything back. You're not under arrest, so I'm not going to read your rights, but if you want an attorney, we'll stop right here." Falcone wasn't a detective who believed in hustling up confessions.

Dario dismissed the need to call an attorney. "It's all too humiliating. Seeing all of this"—he pointed toward the guest room—"makes me take a look at how disgusting I am."

Then Dario confided in halting words his first move, revealing Rose's background to the media so she'd need him to bail her out.

"I was so certain it would bind her to me, but it didn't. Rose actually seemed more aloof than ever after that." He paused to sip his drink.

"Now that I think of it, I was pressing her. I even convinced her to leave her husband home the night of the awards ceremony."

"The night the photo of Rose and Dimitri was taken?" Falcone clarified. Dario nodded.

"And then?" Falcone prodded. He wasn't taking notes and as a result felt more like a priest hearing a confession than a homicide detective.

Dario described the scheme that had actually gone into motion with the photo taken at the Mystery Writers Guild dinner and the Enquirer *article.*

"But we couldn't find out where you hid her." Dario's smile was actually sweet. "You did a great job of keeping the killer from her—whoever he is—but he's not me."

"What you did is against the law, you realize that?" The detective's admonition was somewhat lame. This man wasn't dangerous. He was certain Dario Roselli was no killer. More than likely he would leave Rose alone now, disappear somewhere into the woodwork. But the cop in him knew he had to play by the rules.

"I'm calling for backup. I'm afraid you'll have to accompany the officers to the station house."

"Falcone—" Dawkins pointed to the car's computer, interrupting Falcone's thoughts. There was a message giving the details of Dario's death by a self-inflicted gunshot wound. Apparently one of the officers had allowed Dario to go back into the guest bedroom to collect some "belongings." Moments later the fatal shot had rung out.

Falcone had seen enough obsessive love affairs gone wrong to understand that often these things ended up in violence or death.

He slowed down the car.

"What's wrong?" Dawkins asked.

"It's almost impossible to see the road."

The windshield wipers whipped back and forth across the glass, and the defroster was fired up high.

Falcone glanced again at the squad cars behind him, their sirens shrieking, their lights flashing. He thought to himself, *Goddammit, hang on, Rose!*

Arms pumping hard at her sides, her waterlogged shoes discarded, Rose charged down the graveled path to the barn. Despite the sounds of the rain slamming on the ground and the incessant moaning of the wind, she could hear his footsteps behind her in the gravel. She would never outrun him.

Rose continued through the impossible fog, tore through the branches . . . she was getting closer. Panting, hardly able to catch her breath, she thought, *Just a few more feet.* She heard a groan over her shoulder, then a shriek and a loud thump. She whirled around to see Dimitri's body lying motionless on the ground. He'd collided head on with a huge low-swinging branch and knocked himself unconscious.

Slowing to a fast walk, glancing over her shoulder to make sure he still lay there, Rose made her way to the barn. One lantern light at the back of the barn drew her there.

"Alexis," she dared only whisper. "Honey, where are you?"

Two horses came to the front of their box stalls and made nervous sounds. The smell of gasoline filled the area. It was obvious he had planned to burn them alive. She called to her, over and over, "Alexis . . . Alexis . . . it's Mommy, where are you?"

The gasoline fumes made it difficult to breathe, and soon she was having trouble speaking. She placed a sleeve over her nose and mouth and kept on going while her heart pounded in her chest. Her mind was numb. She couldn't think clearly. The barn was icy and damp. Was Alexis dressed warmly enough? Rose was chilled and shivering, her clothes soaked through; she pushed on, silently following the light in the barn.

Her progress was stopped by a pile of something blocking her way. Stabbing at the shadow, she realized it was a mountain of hay. Now what? Suddenly the barn doors flew open and the wind rushed in. With the wind's help she practically flew behind the hay and huddled down to the ground. Dimitri must have come in, and now he was coming to light the fire that would kill her and Alexis, his own child. Where was he? She crept around the edge of the hay pile. Headlights impaled her, and a figure seemed to glide through the light like an angel or an apparition.

"Rose!"

A wave of relief came crashing over her as she recognized Evan's voice.

Rose couldn't fully see him. The moonlight trickling in the background was directly in her eyes, and the dark of the barn blinded her. All she could make out was the silhouette of him standing in the doorway.

"Rose . . . where are you?"

She jumped out from behind the mountain of hay and charged into him, throwing her arms around his neck.

"Evan! Thank God, you're here . . . Dimitri's the one who kidnapped Alexis. She's here, I know it, and we've got to find her . . . before . . ."

Evan disentangled himself from her. He looked toward the lantern light in the back. With his eyes averted, he suddenly seemed far away.

"He bought the estate . . . he's gone mad . . . he . . ."

Rose grabbed his arm, trying to pull him back to her. She thought he must be in shock. She tugged at his sleeve; when she couldn't snap him back, she slapped him. She had to. Otherwise all their lives would end in this barn.

"Evan, did you hear what I said?"

No answer. She leaned against him now, sobbing into his shoulder. She couldn't penetrate the fog he was in.

"Rose, this isn't Dimitri's house," he whispered. "It's Billy's house."

"Billy?"

"That's right, Rose. Billy lives here."

Suddenly Evan let out a soft chuckle. "That's my real name. My mother used to call me Billy whenever I was a bad boy. She said I had a good side and a bad side. Evan was good, Billy was bad. I like the name Billy so much better than Evan, don't you?"

He was staring down at her.

Rose could not bear to look in his eyes. "No . . . I . . ." Confused and horrified, she began to back away, both hands covering her mouth. She lost her footing and stumbled. She tripped over a bale of hay that had fallen from the pile and landed, hard, on the concrete floor, with her arm twisted under her. The pain was agonizing, the smell of gasoline a terrifying preview. Instinctively Rose knew to stay quiet and calm. Slowly, so as not to startle him, she pulled herself up. His voice was muffled, maybe because of the wind moaning behind them. Or else Billy had a voice of his own, different from Evan's.

"You can't run away from me, Rose. I know you're here." He let out a wholehearted chuckle. His tone was high-pitched, as if he were trying deliberately to sound like a child.

Then she saw the beam of his flashlight, poking here and there into the shadowed recesses of the barn. The beam combed over the two stalls, the floor, struck the ceiling, and fell again.

All he has to do is strike a match, and this place will go up in seconds. She heard his footfalls. He was getting closer.

"Come out and play, Rose. It's no fun without you." He let out another menacing, maniacal chuckle, then chanted, "Bad boy, bad boy, bad boy . . ."

In the moonlight Rose got a glimpse of his face. No, this wasn't Evan; yet it was. The scant light revealed mean, sneering lips, and his eyes, covered by shadow, made him look like a monster.

"Get up." He spoke calmly, quietly. "It's time to play."

Helpless, she stared on with horror as he reached down and pulled her up. He was holding her tightly against his chest, crushing her. She couldn't breathe.

"Look what I've done for us." He aimed the flashlight at the back of the barn, where there was a table and three chairs. The arm holding the flashlight moved. With his free arm he took her from behind, grabbing her throat in a tight hold. "Look . . . see, we have company." He placed the beam of light on one of the chairs. Alexis was tied up in one of them, her mouth bound with electric tape. Rose looked closer, squinting through tears. Alexis was wearing a white nightgown. Rose sobbed. Alexis's head was dangling, just inches from the table, her eyes closed. She opened her mouth, frantic to gulp in air, and could find none. His grip tightened, and she started to gag. Rose silently thanked God that Alexis wouldn't see Evan as a madman.

"'*I'll be watching you*'—sing it with me, Rose. You know the words. You wrote them. God knows I've sent you enough cards. Remember how the antagonist from *Thorns of a Rose* hummed them ever so gently just before he committed each murder? I must admit it's my favorite song." He loosened his grip, eased off just enough for her to get a full gulp of air. Then he jerked her neck forward and back the way a child would shake a rag doll.

"I said, sing it!"

Through stifled sobs, she began to chant along, "From the moment . . . you wake . . ." More sobs—another jerk of her neck, then: "Let . . . there be no mistake . . . I'll . . . be watching you."

He dropped his calm tone and moaned with pleasure. It was obvious Evan was going to drag this out before he killed them. Trying her hardest to keep her eyes away from Alexis so she wouldn't go crazy, Rose took a quick look. She couldn't tell if Alexis was unconscious or dead.

On the table were three place settings in white Lenox china. Rose gasped when she recognized the sterling silver they'd picked out when they married, two brass candelabras also from their early marriage, and a spray of fresh roses to complete the macabre tableaux.

"Look, see all the trouble I've gone to for us?" Rose realized this was his way of "celebrating" their anniversary.

He pushed her into an empty chair, reached in his pants pocket, and pulled out a roll of electrical tape.

"Put your hands behind your back," he said, ripping long strips of tape from the roll.

"Please, Evan . . . don't—"

"Shut up!" he yelled. "Don't talk, you'll ruin it. Everything I've worked so hard to do." His outstretched arms circled the barn. "I've done all of this for you."

"How did you know I'd come?"

He smirked. "I followed Dimitri yesterday morning. I was amazed at what he'd done with the place. All of it for you. I knew sooner or later you would return to your little love nest. To find Alexis, I mean."

They both glanced at the inert figure dangling lifeless. *My child,* Rose thought, *Oh, Alexis, I'm so sorry.* Evan focused his eyes on hers, and now she could see they were full of madness, the pupils dilated, his eyes wide and staring.

"No . . . no . . . she's not dead, not yet. I gave her some tranquilizers. I thought it best if we spent some quality time alone, together first, before the final act. I mean the final page." He tugged hard on her arms, pulling them behind her back and around the chair, taping them tightly together. "You always played with me after we were married; then Dimitri came back. I knew it was only a matter of time before you stopped playing with me. You were a bad girl, Rose. You always chose Dimitri . . . never me. You made me so mad."

She knew he was insane, but she realized she had to keep talking to him rationally. It was her only chance of buying time.

"Why, Evan, did you do this for me?"

"I told you, my name is Billy. Don't call me Evan." He sat in the only empty chair, stared at her with a distant look, and said, "Dimitri's gone, you won't have to worry about him coming back. I killed him back at the house while you were running. Aren't you ecstatic? I know I am."

Another maniacal chuckle, then: "My mother always called me such a 'bad boy.' She made me so mad that day, I had no other choice but to push her. I loved watching her squirm at the bottom of the stairs." His eyes rolled. "Her whole body twitched for a few seconds, then stopped. She never took her eyes off me, not for one second. She stared up at me the whole time she lay there dead, until they took her away. Poor Evan, he cried for days, he really loved her. But I didn't, and I'm glad I killed her. Of course, my father took care of everything, just like always. He's so good at covering up things. I always admired him. Evan was afraid of him, so intimidated. But Billy wasn't. Anyway, no one ever knew the truth. Father told the police she lost her footing and stumbled. Actually, looking back, I realize I did him a favor as well. He had much more time to spend with all his lady friends. No more nagging and whining. I must tell you, killing Mother was a fantastic feeling—almost as thrilling as killing the other girls. Watching their eyes roll back into their heads, sometimes bulging. Every time I took the last breath from them, I imagined it was you, Rose. Shooting Jewel in the head was so unlike my style, but it really was exciting. I knew you didn't like Jewel, so I did that one for you."

He was rambling, and Rose couldn't hear some of the words. Her eyes were now glued on Alexis. Please don't let her come to, spare her the horror, she prayed.

"I know what you did, Rose." He had her full attention now. "You killed your uncle Tom. I saw you." As he said this, Evan's sneer returned and his voice grew louder. The more he talked, the more aggressive he became.

I can't let him see how scared I am. I have to keep him talking.

"How do you know that?" Rose fought for time, praying for someone to rescue them. She had to stay focused.

"I followed you to the barn that night. I was hiding behind the door. I saw you naked. Dimitri's hands were all over you. I couldn't stand to watch, but I couldn't stop watching. I cried while Dimitri touched you. As soon as Dimitri went for blankets, I snuck inside and hid in one of the stalls. I knew I should have helped you, but I was so angry."

"Angry?" She said, hoping to drag him out.

"Yes, because you wanted Dimitri and not me. I could have killed you, but I loved you, so I just stayed there while Tom hurt you."

The timbre of his voice changed and became high-pitched. "I saw you shoot him, Rose, I saw what you did. I loved you even more. Don't you see? We are both murderers . . . the nineties version of Bonnie and Clyde. Screen idols! Don't you think that's exciting?"

Rose forced her eyes to stay on his, hoping that would reach him. "Why do you want to hurt me? Why do you want to hurt Alexis, Evan?" she began.

He jumped up from the chair and slapped her. Rose's head snapped back, and she gasped in surprise and pain.

"I told you, my name is Billy—Evan's not here. I hope he never comes back."

Evan suddenly became silent, a child's sullen look on his face. She had never seen anything like this before, and she couldn't believe it. In the silence she tried to focus, to come up with a plan. She'd have to get her hands free first. . . .

He came out of his funk, dropping his arms to his sides and letting out a relaxed sigh close to a yawn. In a friendly voice he said, "It's time. We've played long enough, and now I have to go."

Rose looked at him; instantly his eyes turned empty and blank. Gone was any hint of the husband she knew.

He stood up, and a wave of terror swept over her as the realization sank in. It was the last scene she'd completed for *Murderous Intentions*—the fire, the agonizing screams. She saw Cassidy Rimes, her heroine, taped to a chair much like this one; she smelled the flames licking the curtains of Cassidy's room—or were those flames here?

"Please, Billy," she begged, this time staring at Alexis. "Don't do this."

He only shrugged and smiled. "No—you wrote it that way, Rose. It's the way you want it. It's from your next book. Actually, it's too bad you won't be able to finish it. From what I've read so far, it's my favorite. You created your own death scene—are you proud of yourself? I am. I loved every creepy chapter in your book. I especially loved the props. Everything was so carefully planned out, so electrifying."

Rose watched in sheer terror as he pulled the book of matches from his shirt pocket.

"It's over, Rose. Now you truly belong to me. . . ."

Ahead of them two telephone poles were down, leaving live electric wires to swim in the flooded highway. Dawkins swore under his breath. "The main road's flooded."

"No shit, Sherlock," said Falcone, trying to keep the sarcasm out of his voice. It wouldn't help to keep those around him on edge.

"What are we going to do?"

Falcone could feel defeat creeping up inside him. His gut told him this had changed from a race against time to save Rose and Alexis. Now it seemed like an exercise in futility.

There was probably a back road through the woods, but none of the vehicles were equipped for off-road driving. He had no other idea. "We're going to find the back roads." The wheels screeched as they made a U-turn. All the squad cars followed suit. Falcone directed Dawkins to ride over an adjoining estate into the woods.

"Hang on, Rose," he whispered. "Please hang on. . . ."

She lowered her voice, fought back the tears, and tried to seem composed in an effort to calm him. "You don't have to do this, Billy. . . . I . . . I can help you . . . we can play now. I promise I won't leave you again . . . please."

But he couldn't hear her. He was chanting loudly, the lyrics: *"From the moment you wake . . . I'll be watching you . . ."*

He tore at one of the matches and put it to the strike.

"Billy, wait . . . don't . . . please let Alexis go, she would never hurt you. She loves you. Alexis always played with you."

His eyes darted to Alexis, still slumped in the chair, and for a second Rose thought she had reached some sympathetic part of him. Then he let out another maniacal chuckle.

"She's bound to grow up like her bastard father." Rose's shock must have reached her face. "Did you think Evan didn't know who fathered that child with those sapphire eyes? No, Alexis is Dimitri's, and she has to die before she turns into another betrayer."

He lit the match with determination, as though he'd finally, irrevocably, made the decision to go ahead with his plan.

The flame danced wildly in front of her eyes. She watched as the lit match found its way to the floor, floating before her eyes in slow motion, as though to prolong her agony. She opened her mouth and tried to scream, but no sound came out. Her body twitched wildly in an effort to free herself.

Then the explosion echoed through the fire and rain. She thought she saw Evan stumble back, grabbing his shoulder. Were those moans coming from him? Through watery eyes she saw Evan running to the door. She gagged and her head fell forward.

The stench of gasoline was replaced with suffocating smoke as flames turned to sheets of fire, a wall of fiery hell. She prayed Alexis remained unconscious before the end.

"Rose . . . Rose . . . where are you?"

She snapped to and fought to focus. Was it Dimitri's voice, or was she dreaming and being lifted away? Her nostrils burned, and the heat below her feet was so intense, smoke filled the air, making her cough. "Rose . . . hold on."

Vaguely she heard loud staccato sounds. Was someone trying to help her? It's too late, she thought. Just as she drifted into unconsciousness, she heard another explosion.

Dimitri threw the gun to the floor, ran to Rose, and in a final burst of strength tore at the tape that bound her hands. When she was free, he carried her limp body out of the barn into the pouring rain and gently laid her on the ground. She started to gag; groaning sounds made their way up from her lungs. "Alexis . . . Alexis," she said in a hoarse whisper. "Save her."

Dimitri saw Evan's shadowy figure running toward him. Soon Evan was close enough for Dimitri to see the blood pumping from his left shoulder. Before Dimitri could move, Evan tackled him, pinning Dimitri to the wet ground. Evan fought like a man possessed, but for Dimitri the stakes were higher. He fought ferociously, clawing at Evan's face, his neck. Tightening his grip with savage strength, he choked Evan until he could no longer fight, and his body jerked wildly, until he lost consciousness. Dimitri rolled out from under him and ran back inside the barn. There was no way to get around the fire, but somehow he fought his way through. It was impossible to see, to make out her tiny figure. He followed her screams.

She was awake, eyes filled with terror, screaming, "Mommy! . . . Mommy!" He ripped through the electrical tape, first her hands and then her feet. His daughter was alive but woozy. He tried to pick her up in his arms, but she threw him off balance and his body hit the concrete. "Run!" he shouted, pointing to the door. Through burning eyes he watched her clumsily make her way to the entrance. She staggered for a second in the doorway. He heard her shout, "Mommy!" once more then disappear.

He fought to pull himself up. His body seemed so massive, like a chunk of rock. The flames licked his clothing. The smoke clogged his throat, and he couldn't breathe, couldn't get one breath of clean air. Above, he heard the crackling of the massive beam breaking free. In the distance, Rose's agonizing screams: "Dimitri! . . . Dimitri! . . . Oh, God . . ."

Then darkness.

Falcone descended on the Laurel estate with the battalion of squad cars covered with mud, their sirens and flashing lights creating chaos. There were flames everywhere. The smoke obscured the night sky, and every man held a handkerchief to his mouth. Any moment the smoke would reach them here, and it would be too dangerous for his men to stay close. Through eyes spilling water from the smoke and fire, he saw two figures huddled together and a third about ten yards away on the ground. He leaped from the car and ran toward the figures in the shadow, fearing the worst, praying for a miracle.

Then he saw them: Rose clutching Alexis. He ran to check how badly hurt they were.

Rose raised her face to him, and he could see right away that she had suffered minimal damage. Her clothes were nothing but burned rags, and a quick check revealed that she was miraculously intact. Alexis, too, was breathing.

Rocking back and forth, Rose clutched Alexis to her as though she would never let go. The two of them clung to each other, Rose sobbing and repeating, "Alexis, Alexis," over and over. Alexis, traumatized, was mute. Falcone dropped to his knees in front of her.

"Everything's all right, Rose. . . ."

But she couldn't hear him. Dimitri's voice inside her head took over. *I love you, Rose. . . . I'll always protect you.*

She lifted her trembling hand and pointed to Evan. "It's him," she whispered. "It was Evan."

Billy fought the two officers as they snapped the cuffs on his wrists. When he was subdued, trapped, he began to recite in a singsong voice, "Bad boy . . . bad boy . . . Billy is a bad boy!"

EPILOGUE

The last expected snowfall of the season fell on the last Sunday of March, covering the landscape like a chiffon veil. The tangerine sun came up, gleaming off the ponderous mounds of white. The orange haze haloed the bare trees, whose skeletal forms reminded her of death.

From the window of her recently furnished office, she looked out at the lingering signs of winter. The Laurel estate looked fresh, cheerful, as though nothing bad could ever have emanated from such a place. For a moment she imagined Dimitri outside in the snow, smiling up at her. She heard his voice—"I love you, Rose." Then, as rapidly as it had come, the apparition vanished, leaving her alone once again in the solitary sadness that had burgeoned inside of her since his death.

The sights, smells, and feelings of the day they had buried him would never leave her. She was haunted by the memory of Dimitri's coffin being lowered into the ground; James's look of remorse over the embarrassment of never acknowledging his true prodigal son; the memory of Alexis beside her, staring, a confused look on her face, mourning the man she'd never come to know as her father. Tears obstructed her vision as she examined the grounds below, each piece of which held a memory. Rose's gaze focused on the plot of land where the barn once stood, now just a small mountain of snow.

The estate held nothing but recollections, mostly sad. Why was she here, living in the very core of her wretchedness? Her heart knew why, even though sometimes her head protested. She was here because Dimitri wanted her here. After the funeral she thought about leaving Long Island entirely and living in the Fifth Avenue apartment. Falcone warned her not to.

"Alexis has suffered enough," he said. "The Laurel estate is a perfect place for her to grow up. Push the past aside. You've faced all those demons, now put them behind you and move on."

Falcone's answer struck a chord. The past was gone. She realized that if she left Laurel, she would leave behind all of her memories of Dimitri. She needed to be close to his presence, to feel it, to remember his voice as it sounded when they were young lovers. He had purchased the estate to create a paradise for her. Rose had given it much thought, and it was obvious that he had taken such great pains to refurbish the estate in hopes of moving them toward a reunion, uniting them, not as two, but now as three, a family. She felt strongly that Dimitri had seen a chance to recover the life that had been stolen from him. That was his dream, and ultimately it was where his twelve years of envisioning "getting back" at the Millers had led him—to reunion instead of revenge. Yet he'd had the foresight to leave instructions with Tyre Corbin and his attorneys that if something should happen to him, everything he owned would go to Alexis. Rose believed part of the reason he had moved so quickly to eliminate Jewel from his estate was his suspicion that Alexis was his daughter—and he would want to take care of her, just as he'd wanted to take care of Rose. She would stay at Laurel. She owed it to him to keep his dream alive.

Rose brought her hand to her swollen abdomen, rubbing it in a gentle circular motion. A smile embraced her lips. The tiny life growing inside her would never know all the pain this family had endured. Dimitri had been and always would be her only true love. But she had known all along that theirs would not be a happy ending; they were not destined to end up as a content, "normal" couple—too much madness had surrounded them. The history that had made their union impossible could now be put behind them, and she could savor the good memories, pass them on to her new baby. She had decided at Dimitri's funeral that she would remember only the loving moments from now on. Dimitri's baby would grow to be healthy and strong. She would teach him about his father's courage, the respect he commanded from others, the powerful love he carried within.

Outside came the screech of a car halting abruptly, and the sound startled her. It had to be John. And it was, carrying a large shopping bag, obviously filled with presents for her and Alexis. After the funeral he had held her close, their tears mingling. "It will be all right," he had said in a comforting, paternal manner. "I'll always be there for you and Alexis. Consider me part of the family—perhaps a stand-in for her father."

She had been grateful then for his words, and ever since, he had showered them with kindness.

She closed her eyes against the memory of the night Dimitri died. When she opened them she was staring at the computer screen in front of her. Rose Miller, author, was no longer dead. She was bursting with creativity and longing to have her voice out there again. There was such joy in knowing that her artistry, just like the life inside her, was ready for a new beginning. Her fingers tapped the keyboard as if of their own volition. The story of Dimitri's life would finally be told.

I NEVER KNEW WHAT I HAD DONE WRONG EXCEPT TO LOVE MY SPECIAL MOURNER TOO MUCH, ENOUGH TO SACRIFICE MY OWN LIFE FOR HER. I CALL OUT TO HER, BUT SHE CANNOT HEAR ME, FOR I AM ONLY AN APPARITION. GO ON, SWEET LOVE, BE STRONG FOR BOTH OF US, SO THAT YOU MAY NURTURE OUR CHILDREN AND FILL THEIR HEARTS WITH LOVE, GUIDANCE, AND MEMORIES OF ME. . . .